Thrill Chase

John Spietz

Black Rose Writing | Texas

The author grants the final approval for this literary material.

Chart images reproduced from Admiralty charts 142 and 2717 with permission from the UK Hydrographic Office. Other illustrations are by the author.

First printing

ISBN: 978-1-68433-639-5
PUBLISHED BY BLACK ROSE WRITING
www.blackrosewriting.com

Printed in the United States of America
Suggested Retail Price (SRP) $19.95

Thrill Chase is printed in Baskerville

I dedicate this book to my wife, Karen. I could not have completed this work without her support. Her willingness to read my drafts, ability to come up with the right word when I could not, and patience when I could talk about almost nothing else for four years, deserves my everlasting gratitude.

ACKNOWLEDGMENTS

For lack of local employment, I retired in 2016. Like many retirees, I considered what I could do to remain relevant. After much consternation, I wrote a book I would like to read. I lived in Alaska for many years and learned to hold commercial fishermen in high regard. I have to admit to being a commercial fishing groupie. I have been a student of history, particularly maritime history, and a political liberal all my life. My book combines these interests.

Thanks to my dear friends Charlie and Jan Clark, for their undying support. Their patience in putting up with me during my visits to their island is remarkable. Thanks to Tom Anglin for inspiration. His exploits fall somewhere between Han Solo and John Paul Jones. He befriended me and provided a cherished window into Alaska's commercial fishing culture. The men and women of the fishing fleet are way underrated. And a shout out to Cheston Clark, Danny Rear, Chris Burchard, and Chris Christensen, for details and a slice of the trolling life.

I want to acknowledge technical support from Doctors Raul Gaona, Jr., and Mo Saidi for their broad knowledge of medical issues. Thanks to Gus Glasier and Arch Ratliff for extensive information about weapons technology. Also, James at Dock Street Brokers for details on boats and permits.

I could not have gotten this book underway without original input from Michelle De La Garza and her course on how to write a novel. And special thanks to Jean Jackson and Jerry Winkler for reading early drafts and the whole ALIR Writers Workshop for their insightful criticism and support.

And a special thanks to Black Rose Writing for believing in me and help with the final manuscript.

Finally, thanks to Local Coffee at The Pearl, CommonWealth Coffeehouse & Bakery, and the Coates Library at Trinity University for providing me with excellent writing conditions and interminable cups of coffee.

Thrill Chase

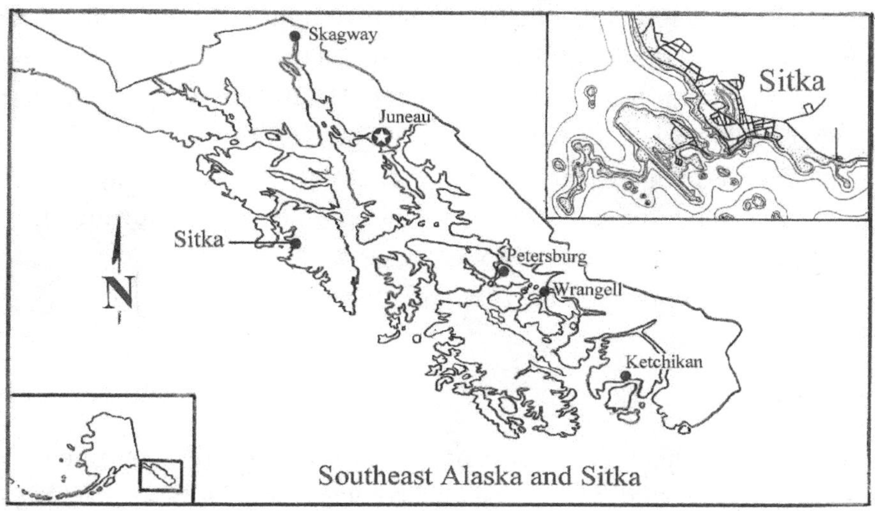

Southeast Alaska and Sitka

1
SITKA

February

Alaska's Flight 70 hit the runway. Jason grabbed his armrests while the engine exhausts reversed. “Welcome to Sitka. The local time is 6:32 P.M.” He clicked his phone on and tried Loren again—no answer. He called Al.

“Hey Jason, you back?”

“Just got in from Dutch Harbor. I haven't been able to reach Loren for several days. She's not picking up my calls. What's going on?”

“I'm sorry, but I have sad news. You remember the civil engineer on the Airport Project? Well, she ran off with him to Anchorage.”

“Ran off? Shit! I was afraid of something like that—my stomach's been churning for the last couple o' days.”

There was a lengthy pause. “You gonna be okay, Jason?”

“Yeah, I suppose. What did she do with Eluk?”

“She took your dog with her.”

“Man, I sure am coming back to a cold homecoming, aren't I?”

“How was your trip?”

“The trip was decent—we found king crab, but the Bering Sea in winter isn't my favorite spot.”

"Oh, hey? Maybe I can lighten your load a bit. I have a proposition. What would you think of thirty-thousand dollars for a five-day cruise on someone's custom-built Seattle rag-hanger? I don't know where you'll go, or what you'll do, but it's not supposed to be illegal."

"A Seattle sailing yacht? What's worth thirty G's for five days?"

"I can't tell you over the phone. Meet me tomorrow morning at the Backdoor Café? I'll lay it out for you."

"Sounds interesting. Okay, see you there."

▪ ▪ ▪ ▪ ▪

Jason sank into his favorite seat behind the corner table. Here he could watch everyone and hold a private conversation. Outside, the storm howled between sleet and snow. *A chance to make a quick legal score, huh? Gotta hear this.*

Everyone ignored the weather. They overlooked the smell of moisture wafting from their coats, somewhere between damp dog and locker room socks. The aroma of fresh pastries and quinoa vegetable soup captured their attention. Rubber boots squeaking on the wet wooden floor, rustling jackets, cheerful chatter, and kitchen clanks buzzed in the background. A morose morning light slanted through the dirty window, and the wind wailed against it.

So,... Loren's gone. Damn—miss that woman—hollow without her. Didn't even leave a note—and took Eluk! Jason laid his jacket on the bench. *A decent trip, though not enough money to buy a boat or fun like dealing. Gotta call lawyer—see how my case is going.*

Bushy blond hair framed his clean-shaven face. At twenty-eight, he had not acquired that grizzled Alaskan look. A good night's rest had erased his Aleutian Stare—that thousand-yard unfocused glare familiar to those working thirty hours straight on a heaving crab boat. He smiled when the door opened. Catching the waitress's eye, he signaled for two cups of coffee.

Al Paxton came down the stairs breathing hard. His withered halibut jacket hung open. Such a coat in a Sitka winter means a chugging metabolism, machismo run amok, or somebody cold. The old Greek Fisherman's Cap, long since shrunk, barely covered his head. A trimmed white beard did not overcome his frumpled appearance, but twinkling blue eyes and a toothy smile were disarming as ever.

As a highliner, his opinion carried a lot of weight in the commercial fishing community. His upright posture and piercing eyes exuded authority. With an athletic twist of his massive frame, he lowered himself next to Jason. The butt-polished wood seat creaked.

Jason turned toward Al and muttered, "Okay, you sure have aroused my interest."

Al glanced sideways to verify no one might hear. "Well, Jason, here's the story. If the captain accepts the guy I recommend, he gets $30,000, and I get a finder's fee of $12,500 besides the 2,500 I already got. I ain't in no position to turn down five digits, provided it isn't dishonest, even if the first number's a one. I've considered everyone I know. What's needed is an accomplished seaman with a cool head who can fix broken boat stuff and knows how to sail. A vigorous sense of adventure wouldn't hurt, either."

The young waitress glowed, bringing two fresh brewed coffees in thick white mugs to the table. Faded jeans appeared painted on her lithe figure. Large, shiny earrings gleamed against her long, black hair.

Jason noticed her sparkle. *Bling to attract salmon and men… timing and flash, timing and flash. Present the bait just right…. She'd look great in heels—Loren's sexier, though.*

The waitress lingered, gazing at Jason. He declined eye contact.

A gust of wind and a burst of sleet battered the café's window. Jason warmed his hands around his cup and grinned. *Fun—like doing a dope deal.*

Al patted his pocket, pulled out a crinkled list of notes, smoothed it on the table, and smiled. "Jason, sometimes you remind me of my younger self when everything was an adventure."

Jason leaned in and murmured, "So, run this by me again. I get $30,000 for a five-day cruise, but I won't know in advance where we'll go or what we'll do?"

"Well, sorta. First, you gotta answer a few questions. Then you'll get 2,500 upfront to attend a meet in Seattle plus your travel expenses. There you'll get another 2,500 even if you don't go on the trip. It's show-up money. You'll see the boat and meet the other crew members. The captain—I'm told to call him 'captain'—has to approve you for the trip. If you two agree, you'll get another 25k before you leave the dock."

"Let me get this straight. Someone's paid you 2,500 to look for a suitable crew member, and you get another 12-5 if the person you recommend agrees to go on the trip?"

"Right."

"And I'll get 2,500 for agreeing to go to the meet?"

"Yeah."

"And when I show up, I'll get another 2,500 whether I go on the voyage or not?"

"Yeah, right, plus your expenses there and back."

"And if the captain accepts me, and I agree to go, I get another twenty-five Gs?"

"Yep."

"... When do I get the first 2,500?"

"Now, if we make a deal. Got a cashier's check in my pocket. The captain will explain this trip at the meeting. Here's pretty much all I know: You'll be on a custom-built rag-hanger for five days. The boat will leave from Seattle somewhere and return to where it started. Whatever's goin' on won't have anything to do with Canada or any other North Pacific country. I've no idea why that point's important, but I'm supposed to mention it. Also, there's nothing illegal involved. You'll inspect the vessel before making your decision."

"So, I get to weigh this thing and meet the rest of the company before I commit?"

"Yeah."

"How big's the yacht and crew?"

"Dunno. Guy told me it has an engine, generator, hydraulics, and," Al made finger quotes in the air, 'innovative sailing technology.' From the little I know, I 'spect it'll be a larger vessel than what you've sailed, but I figure sailing is sailing. You've sailed thirty to forty-foot yachts, right?"

"Yeah, that's right, in the Around Admiralty Island Races."

"The forces are greater on a larger vessel, but sailing is the same on any fore and aft rigged sailboat. I expect you can handle it. If you agree, you'll receive an electronic transfer to your bank account. You'll be able to use your cell-phone to verify the deposit. Then you'll board for the duration of the cruise."

"Hmm. Sounds dubious. There's something wrong here."

"Could be. But if you don't accept, I don't get the 12-5. The boat's s'posedly well provisioned and sea-kindly, and a hell of a lot more agreeable than winter crab fishing in the Bering Sea, I'll bet. My contact assured me the crew would eat well, have good accommodations, and enjoy a vessel well-prepared for exigent circumstances."

"Exigent circumstances? What the hell does that mean?"

"I dunno, let me finish. Remember, acceptance is a two-way door. If you agree, you'll sign a non-disclosure agreement. The front money is yours either way. You'll spend the rest of the day becoming familiar with the vessel. On day two, you'll leave. On the fifth sea day, you'll return."

"Yeah, maybe.... This whole secrecy thing stinks. The situation might change once we're at sea." He wrinkled his brow. "Would you take this offer if you were in my shoes?"

"Yeah, I would." Al stiffened in his seat. "Although I'm at a later point in my life, I must admit to longing for the adventure of my youth, but the money's a red flag. Some danger involved, I suppose, to justify 30k. However, I doubt this excursion is in any way illegal. The person who found me was quite inspiring. He told me a high-tech Seattle billionaire dreamed up this entire thing—whatever it is—as fun.

"After the Seattle meeting, if either you or the captain decline goin' forward, you get to keep the second 2,500 and your Sitka ticket. But then I won't get paid. And I want to get paid. My Twin Disc is 'bout to go gunnysack and needs a rebuild—prob'ly eat my whole fee. So, I've mulled over who is qualified and might accept." Al leaned closer and looked him in the eye. "I can offer it to only one person."

Jason chuckled, sat back, and took a sip of coffee. "I gotta know more, Al. This thing's just too far out."

"Well, you must answer some questions. Your responses determine if we go forward from here. Okay?"

"Okay."

Al pressed his notes against the table with both hands and gave them a scan. "If attacked at sea, how do you feel about defending yourself and your ship?"

"Aw come on, Al, what-the-fuck? Is that the 'some danger involved?'"

"Maybe, but you must respond to go forward."

"Well, shit. Attacked at sea after a short cruise out of Seattle? The question's ludicrous. Attacked by whom? Pirates don't raid too often in Puget Sound. Know what I mean?" Jason's face widened into a wry grin. "I doubt there's been an Al-Qaeda attack in those waters for days, maybe even weeks."

"Beats me, but you gotta answer the question for us to go forward."

"This is bullshit."

Al did not blink.

"All right, I'll play. I suppose it'd depend on the circumstances. You're aware I'm not above an unlawful act now and then, but I've never hurt anyone who wasn't aiming to hurt me. And I try not to do anything I'd consider dishonorable. I never seek a fight, but if a fight comes looking for me, you can bet your sweet ass, I'll uphold my end." He pointed his finger at Al. "And I know you know what I mean. How much danger do you think there is?"

"I dunno, but the ship's supposedly well-prepared for potential threats. I've no idea what 'well-prepared' or 'potential threats' means. If whatever's goin' on ain't illegal, I don't see how there can be much danger in a five-day trip out o' Seattle. Anything blatant would be foolish considering the boat traffic, Coast Guard, military bases, and planes overhead. I doubt you'll ever be out of sight of someone."

"Fine. What's the next question?"

Al's face broadened into an embarrassed grin. "The next question is strange." He picked up his notes with both hands. "What's your opinion of ISIS?"

"ISIS? What's ISIS got to do with this?"

"I do not know."

"Holy shit, Al! What-the-fuck IS going on here?"

"Honestly, I don't know." Al's face fell. "It's way out there."

Jason studied his friend.

Al continued, "If I was younger, and the opportunity was mine, I'd at least go to the crew meeting. The decision's yours. Really. But you gotta respond to the question for us to move forward. Maybe it's a religious bias test."

"Hmm, okay. ISIS is intolerant of other religions. They disdain other points of view, even those of non-Sunni Muslims. The sooner ISIS drops off the earth, the better. But I feel the same about religious extremism in any form. The only difference between ISIS and your basic Jesus Nazi is the degree. Faith-based terrorism has infected humanity for centuries. Come to think of it, 'Allah Akbar!' yelled by a guy ready to blow himself up isn't much different from 'God wills it!' yelled by your basic eleventh century Christian Crusader before killing some poor Islamic shmuck."

Al squirmed, and his seat creaked. Someone looked in their direction.

Jason lowered his voice. "ISIS and the crusades are equally offensive. History is full of whacked-out holy men pushing religious war against anyone who doesn't believe what they do. What a pile of crap. Once you suspend reason and make the jump to the spiritual realm, you can envision anything. There isn't an ounce of difference between Muslims and Christians petitioning a theoretical omnipotent being to interfere with the laws of physics on their behalf.

"We'll never solve the world's problems if we persist in passing them off onto an all-powerful fantasy. Without action based on evidence and logic, the long-term prospect for civilization ain't good. Our fact-averse world is a dangerous place."

Al suppressed a playful grin. Most of the Sitka fishing community had heard some version of Jason's deity lecture. It was better not to feed it by replying.

Jason diddled the handle of his coffee cup, weighing the consequences. *Thirty-grand—nice chunk toward a boat. Free trip to Seattle—get outta winter. Hmm… bail bond might be a problem.*

"I admit it piques my interest." Jason took a sip. "The exposure on my part appears minimal, and it's better than another night at the P-Bar. And, yeah, it has to be easier money than crab fishing. So, to answer the question, if someone buys into this 'die for Allah' ISIS shit and attacks me or my ship, I'll kick his ass."

"Good! Marvelous answer." Al reviewed his list. "You're right-handed? It's a box I have to check."

"Yeah, but I don't see the relevance."

"I don't get the relevance either, but I have to verify anyone I recommend is right-handed." Al shifted in his seat. "I want to discuss one more issue. Any vessel has a command structure. I'm uncomfortable with your following orders from someone we don't know, going we don't know where, and doing we don't know what. What's your opinion of that?"

Jason took a deep breath, trying to imagine the possibilities. "Every boat has a boss. You think this might be a violent intervention of some sort? I'm not into being a mercenary or any more legal complications."

"I really don't know. While this cruise has adventurous aspects, it's allegedly not doing anything illegal."

"Adventurous aspects? We're back to the 'some danger involved.' Okay, I get it. But, assuming Cap'm Bligh ain't runnin' the boat, and we're not doing anything illegal, I suppose I could handle it for five days, and well, thirty-grand. What's my position?"

"Other than crew member, I dunno. There'll be a professional chef, so I'll bet there'll be great food. Otherwise, you'll get the story at the Seattle briefing."

"Look, Al, there's some hidden aspect. Let's see—meeting day, five sea days, a day back—a seven-day commitment." He stared out the window at the weather. "Okay, I'll go to the meeting. I mean, short of piracy, there can't be too much trouble on a five-day sail. So, I understand why you picked me, but how'd this guy pick you?"

"I've no idea. Guess someone believed me capable of finding a qualified guy. I was workin' on the boat last week and noticed the gearbox was gettin' hot. Found metal in the oil and bearing shells loose in the casings. I was contemplating the cost of a rebuild when there's a knock on my hull. I peeked out. A man who looked like a lawyer hollered, 'You Al Paxton?'

"He asked permission to board to discuss a proposition. His suit, polished leather shoes, and a London Fog coat—wasn't from around here. I invited him aboard. The smell of diesel fuel and rank clothing lying around the cabin may have put him off a bit. Anyway, I cleared the galley seats, offered a cup of coffee, and asked his name. Said he wouldn't tell me who he was or his client. Claimed a wealthy person hired him to make an offer to a list of various guys with the kinds of contacts who might recommend crew for a sailing adventure—men who will accept a slight risk for a large reward. Then he told me pretty much what I've told you.

"He gave me this list of questions and stuck out his hand. He said, 'If you agree, on your honor, to make a serious effort and keep it confidential, I'll give you the money.' We shook hands, and I got the check and this here packet."

Al took a small manila envelope out of his inside pocket and laid it on the table.

"There's a cashier's check for 2,500 inside made out to cash with instructions. If you accept, call the phone number inside for travel arrangements. Somebody will pick you up at the airport and drive straight to the meeting place.

"Two more things." Al furrowed his brow. "First, you can't share this with anyone until you return from the trip—it's part of the deal. Second, whatever this thing is, it's strange beyond anything I've encountered. I expect you to keep your sense of ethics. If you go through with the deal, don't do anything you'd be embarrassed to tell me, okay?"

Jason tilted his head and studied Al. "Okay."

Al returned his notes to his pocket, took a sip of coffee, and paused. "What happened to you and Loren?"

"I don't know. Didn't even leave a note. I wasn't there for her, I guess. She sure left me aground." He twisted his cup. "How d'you find out?"

"Rita at the P-Bar told me. She thought it was a sudden decision."

"Shit. I presume Loren wanted more stability. Tell ya the truth, I feel lost. And she took Eluk? He was MY dog. God, I miss her, and I still owe her a chunk of money."

Al was silent for a moment. "When does your case come down?"

"Soon, I hope. I beat the assault charge. Dude returned to California. The court's decision is due. What remains is a constitutional question: If a cop busts you on your porch in the bush, and he believes he sees something illegal inside, can he enter and seize evidence without first getting a search warrant? But, I'm allowed to leave town, with permission to work."

"So, you're outta the whole dealing scene?"

"Yeah, I'm out. But I gotta tell ya, I miss it." He aimed his unfocused stare at the table. "I miss the thrill. I miss organizing purchases and distribution. I miss having people dance to my tune. I miss the personal interactions and loyalties, and the danger and freedom of living outside the control of Big Brother. Unless you've done it, you can't imagine the vitality of being beyond the system… looking in on so much meaningless existence."

"Jason, everyone must decide for themselves what makes life meaningful. Dealing sucks for making a meaningful living."

"You're talking about making a living. I'm talking about being alive."

"Hmm. Well, I admire your passion, but it gets you into trouble. Politics, religion, draggers—whatever—you love jumping in someone's face. What do you get out of it?"

"I don't know, Al." Jason stared at his cup for a moment. "I suppose there must be a payoff—an enzyme rush feedback loop, maybe. Anyway, I recognize the risks of seeking ever-higher levels of excitement. Hope I don't reach the point where I go over the edge."

"You're just gonna have to find another way to get your kicks. The Woodstock Nation is long gone—if it ever existed. Big Brother bites back."

"Yeah, I get it. I must change. I need a boat of my own. It'd give me stability, and I'd be the boss. But it'll take more money than I can make as a deckhand. I can't finance anything with my case pending."

"Look, Jason," Al put his hand on Jason's shoulder, "you've done well gettin' your life back on track. Don't slip your mooring for this little adventure. Money is not an end-all. It may play a part, but being content with your life is the ultimate aim. You get my point?"

They exchanged a glance.

Jason lifted a corner of the packet. He spotted a check inside on top of a folded sheet. "Yeah, I do."

"I have to tell ya, Jason, don't take that unless you're at least gonna go to the crew meeting in Seattle and not tell anyone."

Jason deliberated. *Good score—5,000 and an all-expense Seattle trip. No near-term legal proceeding. Loren's gone—loose ends—no other commitments.*

"Okay." Jason picked up the packet.

2
TURN

February - Sitka

Thump! Jason slammed the door of his '49 Chevy pickup—instant quiet against the howl of the storm. The old truck's smaller cab and little back window made it more intimate than a modern truck.

Jason reflected on the packet in his hand. *Al's reduction gear can't be the deciding factor. His 12k or not—doesn't feel right in Seattle—gonna pass.* He opened the envelope, scanned the check, and unfolded the instructions.

Instructions

Thank you for accepting our offer to consider joining this adventure.

Please call 888-794-2870. My name is Doris. I answer the phone during regular Seattle working hours and make the travel arrangements. First-class seats are not always available, so please call soon. I will provide a round-trip ticket with an open return date so you may depart at your discretion.

Thank you for your interest. We look forward to meeting you.

Doris

Executive Assistant

Ullage Enterprises

He put on his cell-phone headset and placed a call.

"Shackleton and Bayer. May I help you?"

"Yeah. Hi, Shannon, Jason Oliver here. How's the weather in Juneau?"

"Hello, Mister Oliver. Cold and snow here."

"Figures. Is my beloved attorney available?"

"Just a moment, I'll check."

Frank Atherton was a Cheechako—new to Alaska. Fortunate to land a position at the prestigious law firm of Shackleton and Bayer, the opportunity to argue in front of the Alaska Supreme Court would be a feather in his cap.

"Hello, Jason. I was just going to call you. I have good news and bad. The good news is the Superior Court ruled in your favor and suppressed the evidence. The bad news is the State has appealed to the Supreme Court."

"An appeal? Shit. Hell, it was only pot and will become legal soon, anyway."

"Yeah, well, you had two hundred pounds. The D.A. can't ignore that quantity. From the State's point of view, this case challenges the police's authority in the bush. They had an arrest warrant for the assault charge, but nothing else. Arrested outside your dwelling—on your porch—the officer had no excuse to enter."

"That's true. The dope wasn't visible from the porch. The cops are lying. They had to cross the threshold to spot anything illegal."

"Well, the State wants to argue remote locations are a special circumstance. I am confident we will prevail. Continue doing what you're doing and keep your head down."

"When's this going transpire?"

"It'll take time. The D.A. has to write the appeal, and I'll write a response. Then we'll argue before the court. It meets in Juneau at least quarterly, but the date depends on their calendar."

"Damn. Well, some rich guy's offered me a decent chunk of money to crew on his sailboat for two weeks out of Seattle. Would it be okay to travel to Washington for a brief stint on a fancy sailing yacht?"

"Sorry, dude. The court supports working on fish boats in Alaska for pending cases, but going out of state is a tough sell. Don't violate the terms of your bond. Stay in Alaska until your case clears. We have a decent chance to get an April date."

"Okay, thought I'd ask." *A shot of extra cash....*

"No problem. I'll be in touch as the legal proceedings unfold."

“Thanks, Frank. I guess I’ll talk to you later.” Jason clicked the off button on his headset.

Alone in his truck, he inserted the key in the ignition and let it dangle. *I need to make a turn. The money would be a kick, and Seattle sounds good.* He starred out the window and sighed. *Loren sure cut my anchor rode.*

He adjusted his coat, inhaled, and looked around, hoping someone might help him decide. The windows began to fog. He started the engine.

Hope I'm not adrift with a lee shore. Out of my league? A shit sandwich... but what kind? Hmm. Hell of an adventure. Too weird, still pull out in Seattle—keep show-up money. Back in Sitka before anyone notices I'm gone. Doubt Frank'll hear.... Oh, what-the-fuck.

He called the number on the instruction sheet.

“Ullage Enterprises, I'm Doris. May I help you?”

“Hi, Doris, I'm Jason Oliver in Sitka. I'm calling to accept your offer.”

3
ADRENALINE

February 24 - Seattle

Mildred Rosen's diamond earrings set off her short silver hair, high-collard blouse, and flawless skin. She sat with her legs crossed in her warmly lit therapy office. Drizzle trickled down the window, obscuring her view of Seattle's Elliott Bay. Joe Cochrane's file rested on her lap, and she took notes with a fountain pen on a sheet over its outside cover. It was Joe's third session.

He sat in a linen wing chair facing her, elbows on its arms, making a steeple with his fingertips. An imposing man, tall and lean with black wavy hair, his turtleneck, tailored jeans, and ostrich skin boots gave him a rakish air. His eyes were penetrating.

She extended her pen hand and spoke with the assurance that comes from experience. "A constant need for an adrenaline rush does not rise to the level of dependence unless it interferes with your ability to manage life. You have an adrenaline habit. It is not clear whether this tendency has risen to the stage of dependence. However, there is a risk of you becoming a thrill junkie."

Joe crossed his legs and grasped the chair's arms. *Thrill junkie? Hmm. Don't want to be a junkie.*

She continued, "You create stress to get an adrenaline rush. It makes you feel invigorated, powerful, invincible—a huge high. You pursue unique and intense encounters without regard to personal, legal, or economic consequences. Sex with the wives of your associates, back-room intrigue—there's no upside gain compared to the danger these episodes entail." She transferred her pen to her left hand, bent forward, and held out her arm. "Let me see your hand."

He blinked. *My hand?* He hesitated, then leaned forward and extended it.

She turned it palm up and compared the length of his index and ring fingers. His ring finger was longer than his index finger. She released his hand and sat back. "There's research to suggest having a ring finger lengthier than an index finger in men correlates to certain traits, including risk-taking, aggression, decreased empathy, and womanizing. Do you recognize any of these traits in yourself?"

Her observations struck a chord. *Few people talk that way to me.* He twisted his mouth and crossed his arms. His position, confident demeanor, and resonant baritone intimidated most into more deference.

Mildred went on, "Under the circumstances, your success is remarkable. You're a gambler who has to play for higher and higher stakes to get the same thrill. You keep raising your danger level to get the release of the same adrenaline—the same stimulation."

Joe shifted in his chair. He checked the clock with his peripheral vision, uncomfortable with not being in control. *She can't imagine. Meet my crew after this session for a thrill beyond any other... A bridge too far?*

"You make an excellent point," Joe responded. "My gambles have held up so far... and I understand how higher risk increases my exposure to the possibility of failure. Even so... the adventure, the fun—I can't imagine living without it." He leaned forward. "There's nothing to gain if there's nothing to lose. I relate achievement to the danger or challenge conquered." He shook his head, then peered straight at her. "I get what you're saying, but it's what makes life worth living."

"So, it may be useful to examine whether the adrenaline rush you crave impedes, or will impede, your capacity to function in life." She put the cap on her pen and regarded her client. "Joe, remind me why you began coming to me."

"Well," he folded his hands, considering his response. "I'm concerned my tendencies might become self-destructive. I recently had my third divorce. Together, they've cost me over a hundred-fifty million dollars and interfered with my other interests. I reasoned it might be useful to examine the pattern."

Mildred nodded. "You've changed the subject. The pursuit of thrill may be the crux of the issue."

He ignored her comment, sat straight, and grasped the chair's arms. "I don't understand what went wrong. I'm a superb lover, rich, still have my hair, and own the best of every toy imaginable. Yet, three women have left me."

"You've told me your marriages lasted for—what was it—two years? What happened? How did your marriages come apart?" She sat with her legs crossed and jiggled the toe of her high heel.

He noted her foot and elegant leather shoe but refocused. "I don't know. I'm hoping to gain insight. My wives were gorgeous women who lacked for nothing. My associates marveled at their beauty and the things I own. They're jealous."

"Okay, Joe," Mildred raised her pen to her cheek, "but what of your wives? If they were in this room, how would they characterize their lives with you?"

"Hmm…, Diana, wife number three, told me I was too controlling. I don't think my wives appreciated me or all I did for them—and kept trying to intrude on my interests—wanted too much of my time."

"Isn't that what married people do? Spend time with each other?"

"I spent time with them… while they were with me. My wives were always on my arm at the many social events my position requires."

"Have you considered periods when you were 'with them'? A time they were not 'with you'? I'm not talking about sex, but the intimacy derived from spending time together?"

"Sure." Joe frowned. "For example,… in the limo going home from an evening event, which we often did, I'd share my innermost thoughts."

Mildred sighed and brought her pen to her mouth. "But what of Diana's feelings? Did you ever share those? Perhaps Diana was right. What you are describing is control, not intimacy."

"Control makes my accomplishments possible."

"Um." Mildred removed the cap from her pen and scribbled a note. "Is having a woman an accomplishment?"

Joe paused for a moment. "Sure. A beautiful woman signifies success, same as the limo or Maserati."

"But you put these achievements on the line when you pursue ever-higher thrills. Are your other close relationships affected by raising the stakes?"

Joe answered without hesitation, "People do what I say, or I fire 'em."

Mildred remained relaxed. "I find it hard to believe you find such interactions satisfying. Hundreds of people rely on you. Do you appreciate how your exposure puts them in danger? Do you have any loyalty toward them?"

"Hell, no. Fuck 'em. They're well-paid adults who get to make their own choices."

Mildred paused without smiling and jotted another note. "Heredity determines over 50 percent of any personality trait. An event—traumatic perhaps—set you on this path. Joe, do you recall any early circumstances for this tendency?"

"I don't know." He smiled and pushed into his chair. "My father's leaving was a distressing event. By high school, I was selling tests and writing papers for others. I liked the money, but what I really loved was the kick—the power of pretending to be in the system while subverting it. I loved the control. Dropping out of Stanford to borrow a pile of money for, ah, shall we say 'experimental' technology was not traumatic. It was high risk but paid off well. Persuasiveness has always been one of my skills—making use of others to bet the farm. That I'm smarter than everyone else, though, is their problem, not mine."

"You love the dopamine released by your brain. It provides pleasure, compelling you to come back for more—to find a new, higher point of stress. Each time you do requires a higher thrill to receive the same quantity of dopamine." She wrote a note, put the sheet in the file, and recapped the pen. "Joe, you need to contemplate an endgame for continuing to raise your exposure. I want you to consider whether your thirst for thrill is a way to avoid intimacy. If you continue this trajectory, how does it turn out?"

▪ ▪ ▪ ▪ ▪

Joe sat in his car in the underground parking garage and contemplated what Mildred said. He considered his wives. *I damn well was intimate with them. I was.* He compared the length of his ring finger and index fingers. *Risk-taking, aggressiveness,... goddamn right. Ever-higher hazard for the same dopamine hit? Yeah, I get it. Thrill junkie? Junkies give up control—ain't never gonna lose control. A thrill too far? Shit. Anyway,... off to see the wizard...*

4
SEATTLE

February 24 - Seattle
Jason had made the flight to Seattle many times. First-class passengers always acted bored and nonchalant. So did he, but realized it was an act. *Doubt other passengers appreciate this marvel. Suspended thousands of feet in the air, an unimaginable machine transforms my world from provincial to cosmopolitan in a few hours.*

He never tired of gazing out the window through the clear air. Snow-covered rock pinnacles, basking in the sun, stabbed the sky through their white covered forest shroud, then curved away to a ragged fringe of deep blue water. *Love the way tiny communities, set far apart, transition to larger towns nearer each other—smooth the change from the last frontier to urban America.* He grinned at his appreciation of the scene. *There's the haze—nearing civilization.*

The lengthy flight from Sitka to SeaTac provided time to think. Loren's loss left a hole in his life. Anticipation of adventure and money was not filling that hollow.

When the plane's wheels touched down, he turned on his phone, tried Loren again, and heard her familiar voice, "Hey, you. I wondered if you'd call."

"Yeah, well, I'm sure you know I've tried to reach you many times. You kinda set me back there. I miss you."

"Yeah. Sorry about that. You left me alone. I wasn't ready to talk to you."

"Um…, and now you are? I hope it's working out for you. I have the cash I owe you. Just landed in Seattle, but I'll send it now if you need it."

The plane turned onto the taxiway.

"Money isn't everything, Jason. Life has more to it than making ends meet or embarking on a different thrill."

"Yeah, well, money sure seems to make life go better." He glanced at the guy in the next seat, who smiled in sympathy.

"You know I don't care about the money, right?" She took a breath. "It was always about our relationship. You keep pushing the envelope to live on the edge. You're obsessed with excitement and adventure. It'll cause your death someday, and you won't be there when I need you."

"Well, I'll be outside for a week or two. Maybe we could discuss it later?" He stretched for his backpack in the overhead bin.

"Outside for what? See what I mean? Shit. Jason, I can't talk, okay? I gotta go." Click.

He mumbled to himself, "Yeah, well, relationships sure go better if you have money."

Jason entered the din of SeaTac, assaulting his sense of personal space. High ceilings, long corridors, hustling feet, intense conversations, public announcements, weird people, crying children—it was a contrasting world. While descending toward Baggage Claim, he saw a sign with his name held by a frumpy woman in a blue uniform. He smiled and walked toward her.

"Hi Jason, my name is Angie. My associate and I will furnish your ride today." Angie spoke into a handheld radio. "I've got him. Pick us up at the curb."

A dark blue van with only front windows arrived to meet them. Angie opened a rear door—the single access to the back. "Sorry about the drizzle and cold. The sun s'posed to come out later."

"Maybe cold for Seattle. It's nice for Sitka."

"Jason, you'll ride in here. Where we're going is a forty to sixty-minute drive. My instructions require our destination is to stay secret, and I have to take your cell-phone. Our employer will return it to you at our last stop." She held out her hand.

"Ohoo-kay." Jason reached into his coat pocket and handed it over, grimacing with a wary sense of commitment. *Oh, well. Bait's out, might as well fish.*

Angie removed the battery and placed it and the phone in a Ziploc bag. She wrote J.O. on the bag with a black marker pen and stuffed it into her purse.

Jason peered in at a beige colored, tufted fabric compartment with no window. The carpeted floor and ceiling matched the neutral color of the walls and doors. A luxurious black leather armchair, fastened to the center's deck, had an attached reading light. A bulkhead, finished in the same tufted fabric, separated the back from the front. Jason climbed in with his backpack and took the seat. It smelled new.

Angie pointed to a built-in compartment. "There's a box lunch if you're hungry, and there's a headset wired to our sound system." She pointed. "It only plays rock-n-roll from the '60s and '70s. Please fasten your seatbelt." She closed the door.

Secret destination, huh? Like to know where we're going. Can't see, but know Seattle. Start at SeaTac.

After leaving the airport, the hard-left turn onto Pacific Highway, a right corner and acceleration to highway speeds, soft left, and more acceleration—*Ah, must be I-5 northbound.* There was no way to anticipate turns, bumps, starts, or stops with no visual clues. He pulled the seat belt tight. The roar of roughened concrete confirmed his judgment. *Pavement between SeaTac and Seattle always needs a new surface.*

The brakes squeaked every time the van slowed. An odd thing, though: *The momentum—incongruent with the sounds.* The stop-and-go squeaks continued. *We're on I-5.* The sudden thunder of cars and trucks: *We're below the downtown Seattle buildings.* Traffic echoes—*Mercer Street tunnel. Secret location and windowless vehicle won't fool me. As Al always says, if you know you're being made, you're not being made.*

A right turn and the hum of tires on a steel bridge deck. *Freemont Bridge?* Minutes passed, another series of twists, and the sound changed. They braked. Thud. *A speed bump?* The vehicle sped up, rotated right, ran up an incline, down a long slope, a left, a repeat of the Freemont Avenue Bridge—*No momentum. Hmm.*

The vehicle stopped, and an overhead metal door rattled open, resonating like a tunnel. They descended several minutes, slowed, and made a hard-right turn. The reverberation altered—ringing of a sizeable chamber. The wheels made a chatter backing over a grate, then a bump, a clunk, and an overhead door rattled closed. *Ah, arrived. Must be in Ballard.*

The time was 2:30 P.M.

▪ ▪ ▪ ▪ ▪

Joe Cochrane decided his name was Captain Joe Plimsoll for this adventure. He relished the Captain label while in his underground maritime enclave below Ballard. Sitting at a desk on the deck in his climate-controlled dome, he spoke to Doris, his personal assistant. Although he talked casually, Doris knew to take everything literally. His patience with the ineptitude of others had grown thin over the years. Not aware he was autocratic, in the tug between being decisive and fear of being wrong, decisive always won. He refused to conceive he could be wrong.

"... and it'd be cool," Captain Joe continued, "if, during the transition, we play that part of *2001: A Space Odyssey* soundtrack when Dave's landing on Jupiter. It'll fade out in a few seconds, so let's start it at 15 seconds before 'Mark.'"

"Yes, sir." Doris stood awaiting instructions, sharing his stare at the moored sailing ship. "I believe that's *Atmospheres* by György Ligeti. I'll have it played."

They regarded the schooner riding before them in a tranquil artificial salt-water basin. Taut mooring lines kept her suspended in the center of the pool, surrounded by a circular wooden quay. Joe's engineers designed a concrete wharf, but he felt the cement looked too industrial. He ordered wood laid over the concrete, judging the smell of creosote added authenticity and improved the sound-absorbent qualities. Joe saw this as another movie set for his life's journey.

However, even with a wood cover, the resonance was still too high, so he ordered the deck carpeted with light gray carpet squares. The carpet improved the acoustics, though voices continued to evoke a sense of vast space. He wished for a more intimate area, but the openness of the dome and water reflection made some echo inevitable.

His sparse modern desk appeared forlorn on the raised wooden platform facing the boat. Forty feet to his right was a glass wall separating the control room from the dome. Visible through the thick green-tinted glass, his employees in white Tyvek coveralls were implementing the countdown. Banks of computer racks had tiny flashing lights. To his left stood a grid of six computer monitors on a portable stand, three above three, but his attention focused on his desk laptop. From this location, he managed all aspects of his current interests.

It warmed his heart to be a puppeteer controlling the strings of people and power, like the cover of Mario Puzo's *The Godfather. Ah, command. My technical talents made this possible, but my personnel management brought it together. I do well in getting people to believe my best interests are their best interests. They become my unwitting accomplices—a skill that's worked well. People trust me without knowing I don't trust them.* Joe beamed, feeling no remorse.

He stretched his lanky frame out from his chair, smoothed his hair, and clasped his fingers behind his head. Custom-tailored jeans and a navy-blue turtleneck added the right flair to set off his shiny black hair and angular face. Not a perfect mimic of Steve Jobs, he found the style satisfying. He surveyed his dome of creation and smiled to himself. Things had progressed well.

"Wa-da-ya think, Doris? This gonna be cool or what?"

"Yes, sir. Way cool."

The dome—or as he referred to it, The Hangar—a semi-spherical concrete structure with a radius of 150 feet—left plenty of space above the mainmast. Design requirements included powder-coating the entire interior in matte black before installing the hollow cone-shaped, melon-sized Gravity Wave Actuation Devices—G-WADs. G-WADs protruded from the roof's surface to the wharf edge. Attached to its face, except for the bearing band, they continued to the wet line. A soft amber glow from the G-WADs did little to change the dome's somber effect.

A one-foot high white bearing band encircled the entire harbor edge with ten-inch black markings. Numbers with angle labels in ten-degree increments, one-degree hash marks, and large capital letters denoted North, South, East, and West—a protractor on a grand scale.

There was an opening in the wharf equal to one-sixth of the circumference. This portion of the dome kissed the water's surface, suggesting an exit for the boat. Light beyond the shell made an afternoon sun appear to shine through the emerald water. A clean gravel bottom, illuminated by the water-filtered fake sunlight, was visible several feet below the keel.

An overhead hydraulic crane supported the gangway, and stage lights bathing the boat. The crane, on rails, would disappear behind its dome door, also covered in the G-WADs.

An extreme modern schooner faced away from them. The 316 stainless-steel hull formed into the compound curves necessary to maximize her performance had been expensive. But it meant she could sail fast, stand up to heavy weather, and not corrode in saltwater. At 114 feet overall, 82 feet at the waterline with a 20-foot beam, she displaced 150 tons and drew 13½ feet. With her extended overhangs, robust underbody, and well-turned bilge, she was all he had hoped for in the compromises between speed and rough weather stability. Below the waterline, her polished, blackened skin would slip smoothly through the briny deep. An arc of gold letters emblazoned her stern: *SERENDIPITY*.

Above the waterline, everything, except her deck, was matte black, including her spars. She had a four-inch white Mylar stripe along her sheer under the gunwale. Captain Joe ordered the fake cannon ports stowed. He did not want the white rectangles with black circles to alarm the crew. Both the thin polyester film stripes and white socks for her boom ends were easy to remove or install, allowing her to accent or decrease visibility according to circumstances. The Alaska state flag hung limp at the top of the mainmast, and the spreader flag halyards were empty.

"Doris, did you catch how the steel pilothouse is so low and sturdy? A wave could sweep the entire ship without harm."

"Are you expecting a wave to sweep the ship, sir?"

"I don't know what to expect, but I believe in being well-prepared."

The deckhouse trunk had several portholes with deadlights to prevent light escapement at night. She had a pleasing sweep to her shear and well-proportioned tumblehome. The oiled teak deck added a nice dash. They laid it over rolled steel, a necessary structural element to prevent severe damage from a cannonball. A black anodized aluminum cowling covered the automatic weapons stand, port side, aft of the foremast. They located it there to give visual balance to the whaleboat launch mounted to starboard. It failed. The designers spared no expense to make sure the winches, fife rails, and other gear left the deck uncluttered, functional, and graceful. A rigid inflatable dinghy hung from

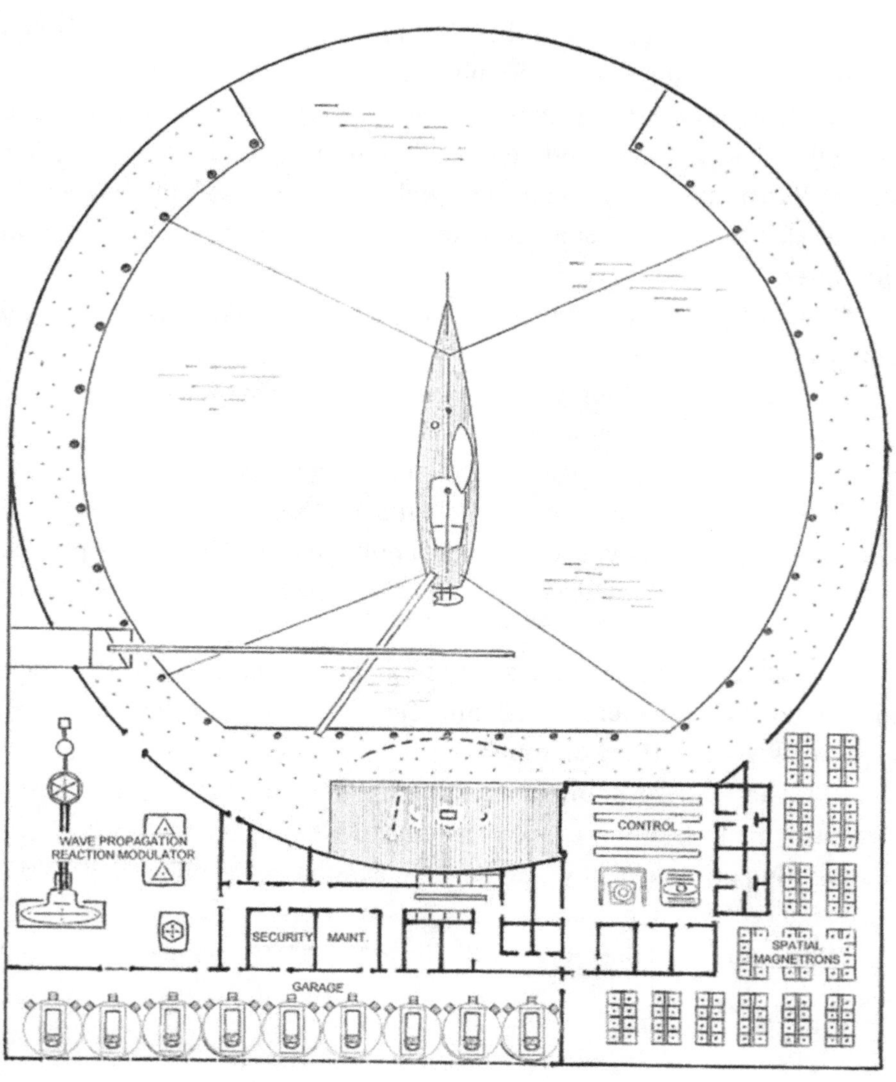
WAVE PROPAGATION
REACTION MODULATOR
CONTROL
SECURITY
MAINT.
GARAGE
SPATIAL
MAGNETRONS

The Hangar

stern davits.

Joe scrutinized his baby. "Is the whaleboat too large?"

"It is out of scale, sir, but the size is necessary to satisfy the design parameter of seating eleven men plus the coxswain in a seaway."

The launch had sweet lines, partial decking forward, aft, and along her gunwales. She, too, had removable white Mylar stripes along her sheer. With a small diesel engine and well-placed ballast, she was reliable and sea-kindly. The staysail boom and electric winches could put her in the water.

"What do you think of the radar?" Captain Joe stroked his chin. "A tad out of scale, too, maybe?"

He had the seven-foot wide, complex apparatus mounted high on the mainmast with a heel actuated gimbal.

"Frankly, sir, I find it ugly—unlike anything I've ever seen."

"Yeah, it is hideous, isn't it? Well, it's another invention of mine. It provides accurate images at 120 miles out—over the horizon. I plan to market the technology after our return. I expect it's worth billions of dollars."

The schooner's utility lines sagged along the gangway to the dock. Joe's mind excluded them, envisioning *Serendipity* waltzing on the waves.

"Doris, is everything on time?"

"Yes, sir." Doris's phone dinged for a text. "They have picked up the last crewman, and he is experiencing a shortened version of the disorienting protocol. They'll arrive in two minutes. I'm on my way to the garage to receive them."

"Okay. And pass the word for Phillip and Bill, oops, I mean Bones and Berg."

▪ ▪ ▪ ▪ ▪

Jason's van stopped, and the motor turned off. Several other engines continued running, then all but one became silent. He heard radio chatter but could not make it out.

Angie opened the door, revealing a gray steel stair leading to a concrete floor, and pointed. "Please stand here until otherwise directed."

As Jason climbed down with his backpack, Angie put his phone bag on the platform, returned to her van seat, and closed the door.

Although the light was dim, he could see his van rested on a turntable with a lane wide conveyor belt facing a closed overhead door. The belt had a steel grate surface with a speed bump ahead of the front wheels. Men exited the rear doors of seven identical vans on similar apparatuses on both sides of him. Two men got off one van and one each from the other six.

The vehicle three rigs away continued running on its rough road conveyor belt and tilted turntable. Road and traffic noise emanated from both the machine and garage speakers. The device turned and twisted, imitating driving except for stop-and-go momentum. An attendant in the same attire as Angie stood looking puzzled at the mechanism's controls.

A green-uniformed workman burst from a door in the wall facing the vehicles. He rushed to the console in front of the running van and pushed a series of buttons. The belt stopped, hydraulic arms retracted, and the bay fell silent. He returned through the door without a word or a glance sideways.

The attendant got into his vehicle. Jason and the prospective crew stood by their stairs and shared a look: "What the fuck?"

Garage lighting was low, but good enough for Jason to see many weirdly shaped speakers lining the high walls.

Shit. This setup—sounds, twists, and turns—generate feelings of travel without moving. Don't know where I am.

To his right, across the hall, was a gray steel door with a light over it and a sign: WAVE PROPAGATION.

"Over here, please." Doris, clipboard in hand, stood under a door light. A slim early thirties woman, the single lamp accented her short blond ponytail. Attired in a prim gray pantsuit and heels, she appeared professional.

Five sentinels, at each garage end, stood at parade rest. The guards wore the same gray jumpsuits and hats with SECURITY inscribed on their fronts in large white letters. Each man carried a black automatic pistol in a brown leather holster, strapped to his chest—Doc Holliday style.

As Doris spoke, one guard from each end walked toward her, gathering the plastic phone bags from the platforms, and put them in a sack. The men gave Doris the sacks and returned to their stations, having not spoken or made eye contact.

"Gentlemen, welcome to The Hangar. I'm Doris. Please follow me."

Ushered out of the garage darkness, they traveled down a hall into a bright fluorescent-lit locker room of glazed white tile. Jason smelled Lysol. Doris stopped and waited for the nine men to assemble. Large wire-mesh lockers with names on them lined both sides of the room. A polished maple bench ran through the center. At the end was a room enclosed by a green chain-link fence. Inside, a smiling man leaned on a built-in counter. A hall extended to the right.

Bet there're showers around the corner.

"Gentlemen, I'm handing each of you a name tag," Doris stated. "Put them on, and use that name. These names allow you to keep your anonymity if you do not go on the cruise."

Jason eyed his nametag—Mr. Decker—put it on and viewed the others. Except for *Gunn,* the names—*Sails, Chief, Cook, Steward, Handy, Rode,* and *Masters*—implied crew responsibilities. *Handy's young. Masters, older. Sails and Rode… my age—intelligent… temperate.*

Doris spoke, "Come this way, please." She led them through another door into a hallway. All in, she closed the door with an ominous click. At the other end, she undogged a watertight steel door and led them into the hangar/dock.

5
ANCHORAGE

February 24 - Anchorage

Loren leaned on the table, holding her head with both hands. The musty odor of the dilapidated mobile home hung in the air. Dim kitchen lights, sagging drapes, and the low ceiling matched her mood. Eluk lay at her feet, his head between his paws.

How'd I get into this? She had dropped out of UC San Diego. A degree and a career track in an office whiling-away her hours on a computer screen might pay the bills but not offer much excitement. Career men, likewise, portended a comfortable but dull future enmeshed in corporate culture. *Knew those guys would leave me alone. Wanted more vitality. Had to get out.*

A book on Alaska with pictures and stories of The Last Frontier enticed her. She envisioned a life of adventure with an unconventional guy. On a whim, she bought a plane ticket to Anchorage with little knowledge of where she was going.

Her seat next to Yashee, a native woman of similar age, was pure luck. They struck a candid conversation about men and life. Yashee described living in Sitka, its virtues, limitations, and men. They became friends. An offer of a place for Loren to stay tipped the scale. With only a carry-on bag, it was easy to deplane in Sitka.

That was two years ago. The vibrancy of living close to nature seemed an exotic contrast to her old world. She enjoyed inhaling the energy required to prosper in a hostile natural environment. The men had a make-it-work attitude. She did not appreciate her good looks: black hair combed back, voluptuous in a close-fitting sweater, skintight jeans, western boots, and a soft, weathered face.

Then she met Jason, spirited and exhilarating. He worked on local fishing boats for cover while maintaining an intricate network of pot dealers throughout Southeast Alaska. *Yeah, exciting, but pushing the margins of excitement versus risk—too much tension.* When he got busted, the money disappeared. She loaned him what he needed before he started work on a Bering Sea crabber. Then she was waking up in a silent, empty bed.

Mad at him—left me alone. But I wasn't fair. I should have left a note. Never told him how much I dread abandonment. S'pose he doesn't have a crystal ball for what I need or want.

It was two months into the season when Bud appeared at the Pioneer Bar, known as the P-Bar. A civil engineer working on the Airport Improvement Project, he struck her as handsome—a novel Alaska man. *Wish I had a better perspective on passionate sex with men. His 'lovely Anchorage home' seemed enticing.*

It was another whim. Things disintegrated fast. Bud's lovely Anchorage home turned out to be a decrepit trailer in Spenard, a poor neighborhood trying to be bohemian. And it became clear he was an alcoholic, hiding it while in Sitka.

Enormous mistake—not working. Thinks I'm property. Got to control relationships. Rotten luck. Ah, Alaska—chance to start again. Adventure isn't always what it seems. Shit. Shoulda finished my degree. Damn, miss Jason—at least he's not a phony.... Great sex... when he's there.

She remembered his cabin—lying on his warm arm—her cheek against his bicep, the musk scent, and the thump of wet snow landing on the ground from the hemlock branches. She shook her head. *Couple o' months ago....*

Loren's phone sounded. The caller ID read Jason. *Jason again?* Her eyes sprang into focus. *Have to take this. Maybe a chance.*

They had spoken for less than a minute before she heard Bud's truck in the driveway. Ka-clunk. Bud ran into the trashcan.

"Shit." Loren shuddered. *Drunk again.* "Jason, I can't talk, okay? I gotta go."

Wham! The truck door slammed. She ended the call, stuffed the phone into her purse, and turned to face the front door. It erupted, and Bud staggered in, bringing the smell of liquor. Spittle coated his chin—

reddish eyes, oily black hair, the old stained parka hanging open—*disgusting.*

She dreaded the inevitable altercation and braced herself. Bud had not responded to her attempts to reach him.

He glanced at the kitchen, "You fuckin' useless whore. Where's my goddamn supper?" He bumped into the wall and slammed the door.

Loren retreated toward the living room. Her voice was shrill and defensive. "You don't tell me when to expect you. You don't answer my texts or calls. I don't know when to have food ready. You don't give me any consideration."

Bud swung his arm and smacked her cheek. "Whack!"

Loren flinched, her eyes closed. A searing pain flashed through her face. She let out an anguished howl and fell over the cheap coffee table, landing hard between it and the couch.

Eluk snarled and lunged at Bud, hit his chest, and knocked him to the floor. Bud scrambled back, pushing himself along until his hip struck the door. Eluk jumped toward Bud's face. He raised his left arm to ward him off. Eluk grabbed the parka's sleeve and shook it, growling. Bud slugged Eluk in the face with a hard-right hook, forcing the dog to release him. Eluk readied for another attack. Bud grabbed the door handle, pulled himself up, slipped out, and slammed the door.

With one arm on the stinking sofa and one on the table, Loren started crying. *Can't believe this—what was I thinking?*

Eluk barked at the closed door, turned, and came to her for reassurance. The warmth of the dog's body, imploring eyes, and soft pant consoled her.

Loren, getting a hold of herself, scratched his head. "Okay, boy." *Dog's love's hard to beat.* "Somehow, I expect my looks to protect me from such assholes."

She moved each limb gingerly to feel for broken bones, then picked herself up and headed for a mirror, continuing to talk to Eluk. "Damn, that hurts. There'll prob'ly be a bruise." Despite the throbbing pain on the side of her face and the red glow, her skin was okay. He missed her eye. She straightened her sweater, went to the refrigerator, grabbed a package of frozen peas, and held it against her cheek. Her hand still trembled. She returned to the couch and contemplated her position in the old dim trailer.

Bud took his truck, leaving her abandoned and alone again in Spenard. Outside it was black. The recent thaw left the snow dirty, splattered with grit and road grime from the constant cadence of vehicles splashing through the puddle out front.

Not my vision after that first night. Imagination got the better of me. Hot-dog engineer and his beautiful Anchorage home... bullshit! Another grab at a dream. Guess there ain't no Prince Charming going to save me.

She strode to the middle bedroom, eyed the dog cage, and grabbed her carry-on bag.

Ah, Jason... on-again, off-again nature of commercial fishing... gone a lot. Thirst for thrill might get him. Hazy prospects. But smart, honest. Not legal, but honest. Never violent toward me. Said he'd return in a couple o' weeks. Hmm. Bud's a fake... got me wrong if he thinks I'll put up with this shit. Could come back any minute—gotta get outta here... back to Sitka 'fore it's too late.

She pulled her iPhone and pushed Recents for Yellow Cab.

6
MUSTER

February 24 - Seattle

Jason emerged into the hangar's lofty expanse. A familiar fragrance of seaweed and saltwater replaced the locker room's sterile smell. Such a vast chamber made even slight noises resonate. He heard a faraway fan's muted whir. A black-hulled schooner floated on a yellowish-green pond. Light from the setting sun permeated the depths from outside where the dome met the water, making it glow a deep emerald. *Must be sea level.*

He glanced up and gasped at the massive dome. Thousands of hat sized cone-shaped protrusions glowing amber covered its surface. A tall man in a blue turtleneck stood behind a desk on the dais, and his face lightened as the crew entered. Two men stood by seats at his sides. Nine comfortable armchairs spread in an arc facing them.

"Welcome, gentlemen. I am Captain Plimsoll. You may call me, Captain. Please take a seat."

Computer lights blinking behind a thick green-tinted glass wall at the side of the platform caught Jason's attention. Workers in white coveralls were scrutinizing them.

▪ ▪ ▪ ▪ ▪

Jack Wilson ignored the purr from hundreds of server fans in the Computer Control Room as he looked out the window at the incoming crew. He glanced at Paul Gorken, his Operations Manager and Transition Coordinator, then nodded in the dock's direction, squinting over his reading glasses. "Here comes the fuckin' posse. Those boys don't have a goddamn clue of what they're gettin' into."

His beer-belly pressed against his wrinkled Tyvek coveralls. An aroma of the unbathed followed him like a shadow. Jack relied on the Control Room's thick, green glass to obscure his unshaven face and casual demeanor. With no regard for Joe's tobacco prohibition, an unlit Lucky Strike hung from his mouth. He delighted in carrying myriad details in his mind. It made him feel indispensable to Joe's operation. His unique comprehension of gravity wave dynamics allowed him a cocky familiarity that Joe would not tolerate in another employee.

Paul Gorken's gangly frame, tailored white coveralls, and trimmed goatee contrasted with his boss. He spoke while staring at a computer display in one of the racks. "If Cap'n Joe catches you with that in your mouth, he'll have you keel-hauled."

"Shee-it. Cap'n can't live without me. In three days, I'll either be a goddamn unassailable hero or a criminal on the lam. Still and all, it's hard to imagine what crime I'll have committed. Time-travel without a permit, maybe? Is the wave trajectory simulation still showing green?"

"Yes, everything's 'go.' The Spatial Magnetrons are 100%, the Wave Propagation Reaction Modulator curves are optimal, and the crews are ready for the SCL power taps." He looked at the three clocks mounted on the wall. SEATTLE read above the first, GREENWICH above the second, and SHIP above the third. Below the dials were two digital date displays, labeled SEATTLE and SHIP. They both read Feb. 24.

▪ ▪ ▪ ▪ ▪

As the crew filed in, Captain Joe moved to the front of the desk, leaned against it, and folded his arms. His smile widened to a grin. "First, thank you all for coming. Doris, please pass out the envelopes. In each is another envelope with the cash I promised you for showing up, and a document revealing the amount I propose to deposit in your account. I have promised each of you a different sum, and I expect you to keep your number confidential."

Rustling paper echoed as the crewmen opened their envelopes.

"The payment I promised for joining me on this cruise, I now double."

Murmurs rose from the team. They repositioned themselves in their seats and exchanged glances.

"That's right—twice the amount of my original offer. Also, if everything goes well, there may be bonus money. You are the entire crew. I ask—well, actually require—we all refer to each other by the name on our identification tags. I wish to preserve our anonymity option. We will all use alternate names."

Jason peeked into his envelope. There was a document of intent to deposit $50,000 in his account and another wrapper full of new $100 bills. He heard grunts from the others. *Shit. Harder to pass up. But what's he buying? Loren right? 'Obsessed with excitement and adventure?'*

Captain Plimsoll clasped his palms together. "Okay, some announcements before I get started. Please use the locker restrooms until we get underway. If you wish bottled water, let Doris know. So, what I have in mind is an adventurous voyage of six days, including today—five sea days. We'll leave this dock and return to this dock. And I assure you, our little cruise has nothing to do with drugs, contraband, or anything illegal.

"Now, gentlemen, I insist you address each other with 'Mister' to get into the habit. Use this title with each other henceforth. I believe the convention encourages respect, so I require it. It's part of the deal. After introductions, you may go aboard to assess the ship. Open the lockers and cabinets, run any of the equipment except the radar. Microwave transmissions within the hanger would affect my other electronics, so I have locked it out. Otherwise, talk to each other, discuss the situation—whatever.

"Brief introductions first. These are my officers." He opened his hands right and left. "To my right is Mister Berg, second in command, and Senior Vice President of several of my interests. I have complete confidence in his decisions if I am unavailable for any reason. He is an experienced seaman and expert celestial navigator." He noted the raised eyebrows. "I know, I know." He raised his hands and shook his head, casting his eyes downward. "We are all used to our GPS navigation systems. I'm fond of the old ways. They are reliable, and it makes me comfortable having an alternative. Mr. Berg…?"

Shorter than Captain Joe, Berg had bushy red hair, a chiseled jaw, and a sculpted beard. His double-breasted dark blue sports coat with polished brass buttons and a colorful silk pocket kerchief fitted his trim form over an elegant shirt. Creased taupe slacks and bright white docksiders completed his ensemble. He smiled with a slight bow. His eyes gleamed.

"Gentlemen, I am pleased to serve with you. I have known Captain Plimsoll for many years, and I assure you we'll be embarking on a well-planned voyage. I am confident we'll have a marvelous time and return to this dock in six days, safe and sound."

Berg sat, crossed his legs, relaxed, and leaned an elbow on the arm of his chair. He turned toward Captain Plimsoll, signaling his remarks had concluded.

Jason considered Berg. *Hmm. Not used to workin' with this kind o' guy.*

"Thank you, Mister Berg. I appreciate the endorsement. On my left is Mister Bones. He is a Doctor of Medicine and my friend of many years. He is a qualified saltwater sailor, having served on two Transpacs. Besides his maritime skills, his presence assures us of prompt, professional attendance in the unlikely event of a medical emergency. Mr. Bones…?"

Bones appeared older than Captain Joe. His trimmed silver hair and beard added an air of dignity to his physical frame. The crisp white jacket and smart trousers formed the image of someone sent from central casting for a doctor's role. His warm grin added to his self-confident demeanor.

A flag raised in Jason's mind. *Doctor? 'Nother aspect of some danger involved.*

The doctor began in a slow, deep voice, "Gentlemen, I am happy to join you on this cruise. I expect it to be one of the greatest thrills of my life. Medical facilities aboard are the best possible, and I will address any health issues that arise. I will also pull lines, handle sail, stand watch, and whatever Captain Plimsoll requires."

Bones lowered himself to his seat, stretched his legs, placed his elbows on the chair's arms, and steepled his fingertips together under his chin. He turned to Captain Plimsoll with the confident beam of someone quite at home.

The Captain resumed, "You are the entire ship's company," he waved his arm at the seated men, "except for Doris, who won't be joining us on our brief adventure. You are all qualified in your area of expertise. Mister Chief, please raise your hand."

Chief casually raised his hand. More than hefty, he reminded Jason of a short half-back with no neck. In his mid-30s, with blond hair in a ducktail, he had a weathered, well-tanned face with crows-feet eyes. Expressionless and wearing a long-sleeve hickory logging shirt, khaki cargos, and Redwing work boots, he sat unmoved. No frown, no smile—a poker face.

"Mister Chief, if he agrees, will be in charge of the mechanical systems. His dossier shows many years managing complex equipment as Engineer on supply boats in the Gulf of Mexico. I'm pleased to have found someone with Mister Chief's skills. Mister Chief, once aboard, start the engines as you see fit. My staff has connected the exhaust ports to the external evacuation ducts. Check the tools and investigate anything that piques your interest. Mister Chief, say a few words?"

"Ah, ah," he shifted in his seat, "I have little to say. It's a blank slate for me. I imagine the job is easier than hauling gear in the Gulf. But, I wish I knew what this cruise is about." Chief folded his massive arms, stretched out his legs, and put his right foot over his left. He frowned. His head did not move.

Jason eyed Chief. *Competent. Good.*

"Mister Chief, in a few minutes, you can familiarize yourself with everything on the boat. I'll disclose the nature of the voyage at the appropriate time. Mister Sails, please raise your hand."

Sails looked trim and tanned. He had longish brown hair tied in a ponytail. His muscled arms rippled from the rolled sleeves of the Pendleton shirt. In his late 20s, the glint in his gray eyes suggested contemplation of an inside joke. His face had a trace of a smirk. Sail's arm shot up and down.

Jason brightened. *My kinda guy.*

"Mister Sails, if he accepts, is to be our Bosun—Deck Boss. He'll oversee everything relating to the rigging, including the hull, masts, sails, stays, shrouds, and tackle. If it's a topside issue, it's Sails'. He has worked three Fastnet Races. For those unacquainted with this event, the Fastnet is a biennial six-hundred-mile sailboat race. It goes from the Isle of Wight on the southern coast of England, around Fastnet Rock on the southwest coast of Ireland, and back to Plymouth. Eighteen people died in one race years ago. High winds and continuous low-pressure systems present common difficulties to overcome. Capsizing, dismasting, blown-out sails and all kinds o' mean, nasty, ugly things are challenges to finishing the race. I'll count us fortunate to have Sails as Bosun. Mister Sails, you are free to investigate, manipulate, or otherwise make yourself convinced the equipment is satisfactory. I'm confident you'll find everything's in perfect order. Anything you'd care to say?" The Captain raised his eyebrows and nodded toward Sails.

Sails answered in a rich baritone with a reserved British accent typical of the western European Isles—too loud, but enthusiastic. "Well, this proposition is a tad mysterious, but a well-compensated short cruise out of Seattle compares favorably with the gale force westerlies I expect in August. A well-found boat will be the duck's nuts. And I would have to be bloody daft to pass on this amount of money." He slapped both palms on the arms of his chair.

Jason's grin broadened. *Like him.*

"Thank you, Mister Sails. Mister Rode, please raise your hand."

Rode raised his hand halfway, more a wave than a school hand raise. His broad face, curly black hair, and beard surrounded a sneering mouth. He had just removed his hoodie. The lack of an undershirt allowed a few of his black chest hair to protrude through his faded red plaid flannel shirt—stretched too tight across his chest. His sand-colored pants were dirty, and no socks were on his loafer-clad feet. He was overweight with huge meaty hands.

"Mister Rode's worked many seasons in the New England ground fishery. It's dangerous work. The Bureau of Labor Statistics reports these boys are more likely to die on the job than a cop is on a beat. Such work requires excellent seamanship and the can-do attitude we might find useful if one or two o' the mean, nasty, ugly things that can occur at sea befall us. Mister Rode comes well recommended as competent and reliable. A general deckhand, he brings more help than I expect we'll need, but I favor the added margin such a committed mariner brings to my little enterprise. Mister Rode, comments?"

Rode's voice lacked enthusiasm, sounding half awake. He remained motionless. "Well, winter work out outta Seattle sure as hell's easier than winter work outta New Bedford. I'm 'tween gigs anyway, so what-the-fuck, I'm game."

Hmm. Little crude. Jason turned back toward the Captain.

"Thank you, Mister Rode. Mister Decker?"

"Yep, that's me." Jason raised his hand, then started removing his jacket. However, it was a challenge to focus forward and not twist to view the stunning schooner floating in the quiet harbor behind them. He finished removing his jacket, shifted in his chair, and leaned forward with his forearms resting on his thighs. He meant his earnestness to show.

"Mister Decker is a veteran of the Alaska crab fishery. Do you ever watch the TV program *Deadliest Catch*? He's worked crab, halibut, salmon, and sailed in the Around Admiralty Island races in Southeast Alaska. A distinguished mariner, he's much sought after on the decks of the Alaska boats. I've offered him a general deckhand position. Again, I expect we have more staff than needed, so I hope no one has to work too hard. Mister Decker, observations?"

Jason smiled. "Well, I find the whole situation rather bizarre. I appreciate the money, and, like Mister Rode, sailing out of Puget Sound this time of year has to be a hell of a lot easier than fishing for crab in the Bering Sea. I presume she's a well-appointed yacht. But what's the purpose of this cruise?"

"This short voyage is unique. I can't divulge the cruise's nature until we set sail, but I assure you we will not be smuggling or doing anything illegal. If you can't trust me, you may decline to take part, keep your show-up money, and return to Sitka."

The entire crew turned to Jason for his reaction.

"Okay. I'll examine the boat and consider the circumstances. Provided nothing too weird comes to my attention, I suppose I could do a five-day trip." He folded his hands against his chest, extended his legs, and put one over the other, imitating Chief. His mouth remained flat, wary of commitment.

"Thank you, Mister Decker. Everything is top drawer, and we WILL have a wonderful trip. Mister. Gunn, please signal your presence."

Mister Gunn stood with a vacant expression and gave a half-assed salute. His muscular, tattooed arms, billiard-ball smooth head, fat neck, barrel chest, and narrow waist brought Mr. Clean to mind—except for the tattoos. His faded jeans were crisp and clean, and the brown leather shoes looked old, comfortable, and well kept.

"Mister Gunn is a former Marine gunnery sergeant. A decorated combat veteran, his knowledge of weapon systems is unsurpassed. We're carrying firearms for potential security issues in the remote chance they arise. He has crewed on blue-water sailing yachts out of Oahu. Besides his competent sailing skills, we'll expect him to provide security if it becomes necessary. Mister Gunn?"

Captain Joe offered an open hand, palm up, toward Mister Gunn.

Jason grimaced. *Security issues? Mr. Gunn—Gunny—a mercenary? Ah, here we go with the 'some danger involved' thing.*

"Yes, sir. Well, like Mister Decker there, this job strikes me as weird, but for enough money, I'll do whatever you want for a few days. What weapons are we carryin'?"

"There is a locker for the weapons. Please inspect everything. Do you see the black anodized aluminum cone aft of the foremast port side?" The Captain pointed.

Everyone bent in his chair to study the designated object.

"If you remove that cowling, you'll find a stand for the automatic weapons we carry."

Jason's eyebrows raised, eyes widened, and mouth opened. *Automatic weapons? Oh, shit, more exigent circumstances. Al, what did you get me into?... has the trajectory of my life brought me to this?*

Gunny fingered his chin and stared hard. They shifted in their chairs with an audible rustle.

Captain Joe started again, "Thank you, Mister Gunn. Mister Masters, please raise your hand."

Masters' arm jerked horizontal and flattened into a salute. His posture was military perfect. Creased blue trousers, starched blue shirt with epaulets, and polished black shoes gave him a naval bearing. Older than the others—maybe early 40s—his clean shave, receding hairline, and trim figure bespoke military seasoning.

"Mister Masters comes to us from the Coast Guard in Florida. He has assisted many heavy weather rescues and drug interdictions. I expect his seamanship and command skills to enhance our ability to cope with any eventuality. He will also join us as a deckhand. Mister Masters, remarks?"

"Yes, sir. I appreciate the opportunity to join your excursion. After my separation from the Coast Guard and run of shore duty, I look forward to being at sea on an elegant sailing yacht for a few days."

In Jason's mind, a mental picture of drug interdiction appeared. *Careful there.*

"Thank you, Mister Masters. It is my firm expectation that we will have to rescue no one. Mister Handy, please raise your hand."

Handy, the youngest, slumped in his chair and seemed bored. His hand did a careless flop.

"Mister Handy comes to us from a family of Seattle-based Norwegian fishermen. Is it true you were born on a halibut schooner in the Gulf of Alaska?"

Handy's bright blond hair, smooth complexion, gleaming white teeth, and casual clothing gave him the air of a surf bum instead of an ingrained halibut fisherman.

Ah, youth and energy.

"Yeah, I guess so—that's what they tell me. I bin fishin' off and on with my folks since I kin remember. Some extra cash would be of use, and I wanna do sump'm different."

"Mister Handy will be a valuable deckhand. And, sir, I think you'll find this cruise IS something different. Now our cooking staff, Mister Cook and Mister Steward. The high-end yacht set holds our Chef in high esteem. He and Mister Steward are always a team. Though he has not seen the boat, Mister Cook worked with my designers on the galley layout. He prepared the menus and a list of his needs. My staff has stocked the boat, and it is ready to go. Guys, we will eat well. We carry superb wines, but boys, we will go easy on the vino unless we have guests aboard. Mister Cook, your views, please?"

Guests? A rendezvous?

Cookie stood and closed his forefinger and thumb to his lips, kissing them with an audible smack. A rotund body and smiling pink face matched his somewhat high, quavering voice. "I promise grand meals. My dear friend and colleague of many voyages—who we are now calling Mister Steward—and I will provide healthy, delicious cuisines equal to anything you have savored, at sea or ashore. As Captain Plimsoll stated, I helped design the galley's arrangement—although I have not seen it—

and except for extreme weather, I expect to present sumptuous meals." He turned to his associate. "Mister Steward, care to add something?"

Stew, light brown with slender Anglo features, stood and gestured with his long, thin arms. His short curly hair had gray highlights. He cast his eyes groundward and spoke in a deep voice. "Well, like Cap'n said, we have been a team on many yachts, sometimes in tough conditions. I support Mister Cook in whatever's needed to make memorable dining experiences. I enjoy serving unforgettable nutritious, delicious, and attractive food."

Hmm. High-end yacht fare is something new.

"Thank you, Mister Steward. I have the utmost confidence we will team well together."

"Now, gentlemen, I will introduce *Serendipity*. Please turn your chairs."

The crew swished their chairs on the carpeted dock.

The Captain stuck his thumbs into his belt. "She's wishbone schooner-rigged with tapered aluminum spars, and the finest laminated sails current technology can produce. Such sails will hold their shape and give us the most efficient airfoils possible. With 5,200 square feet of sail, she'll be fast both full-and-by. She has plenty of power. Hull speed with the engine is over twelve knots. As we heel, her waterline lengthens with a consequent increase in maximum hull speed. I'm not sure what she'll do in a broad reach with the gennaker set, but I'd love to find out. You'll be able to set, reef, lower, and hand the sails from the deck with the electric winches. We have spares for her rigging except for the spars. She sports a mainsail, yankee, forestaysail, inner jib, outer jib, and a well-balanced helm. The generators are more than adequate. She'll have a smooth movement in a seaway.

"Now," he opened his arms, "I invite you to inspect her for ninety minutes. When I ring eight bells, come ashore, and we'll continue the meeting."

7
SERENDIPITY

February 24 - Seattle

The Captain and his two officers observed the nine guys troop aboard.

"What is it," Captain Joe mused, "that makes them appear so athletic?"

Bones responded with an offhand gesture. "Only one of them has a belly. Except for the galley crew, they have an ass and walk with square, upright shoulders. Notice how they carry themselves—no consideration of balance—an aura of self-confidence. Their movements are complex—heads turning, bodies twisting, arms swinging—even in my younger days, I was never that fit."

"Well," the Captain smiled, "let's check out my laptop and watch the action."

▪ ▪ ▪ ▪ ▪

Sails led the crew, spreading out along the deck. "Well, chaps, I suggest we split up to examine our areas of responsibility—or whatever. Let us meet in the salon in sixty minutes to discuss what we have learned and our position, okay?"

Everyone grunted except Gunny, who replied, "Copy that."

▪ ▪ ▪ ▪ ▪

Captain Joe, sitting at his desk, put on his earphones. Bones and Berg moved their chairs closer to Joe, positioning them near his laptop and slipped on their headsets. Tiny cameras with microphones allowed them to see and hear conversations throughout the boat.

Joe spoke in a low tone. "How do you like my crew?"

Bones responded in an intimate tenor. "I rate them able, a competent and an adventurous sort. I worry Mister Handy might be too young. If a plight arises, he's the one most likely to lose his composure."

Berg chimed in with a more academic tone. "After one has achieved a certain level of contemporary mariner competency, the most important skill on a boat for an extended cruise is the ability to get along with your fellows. They are sober and have considerable sea time, encouraging me to believe they have gained this essential skill. They are no doubt able and have an ingrained acceptance of working long hours with little sleep. But I'm not sure they'll go for it. The entire scene may be too strange. The inclusion of Gunny for security may give them pause. I hope this hasn't been an enormous waste of time and resources."

Joe remained relaxed. "No sweat. If they don't go for it, we'll find a new crew who will. Course, I'd rather not reschedule—that could create all kinds o' mean, nasty, and ugly logistical issues. The confluence of events for grabbing a gravity wave is not entirely under my control. Anyway, we'll know soon. Except for Mister Sails, they need money, and I'll bet on greed every time. Let's view the monitors and see how they're doing."

▪ ▪ ▪ ▪ ▪

Sails, Rode, Masters, and Handy strolled forward to start a tour around the deck before going below. Gunny checked the black aluminum cone and started removing it to examine the automatic weapons stand. The other four headed to the wheelhouse.

Cookie and Stew glanced at the pilothouse and headed below. Jason and Chief stopped to examine the lavish appointments.

Jason plopped himself in the helmsman's seat. "Oh, look, it swings. The person steering can stay vertical regardless of heel angle." He twisted around. "We'll have superb visibility while protected from the weather." *Al would like this.* His eye caught an elegant wood cabinet with an angled top and swing-arm drafting machine. "Check out the chart table."

He strode over and examined a drafting machine with a protractor head and engineer's scales. He opened the top chart drawer. On top was British Admiralty chart 2717. He had never seen an Admiralty chart. *The Mediterranean?* He closed the drawer.

"Yeah," Chief reacted, "and these controls are awesome. The engine displays, panel, nav, and com systems—major-league command and control. Man, they spent a lot of money on this." His arms akimbo, he took in the entire enclosure. "There's room for several of us.... Well, guess I'll check out the mechanical systems."

They both headed below. Jason stopped in the cabin. Chief continued to the engine room.

▪ ▪ ▪ ▪ ▪

Captain Joe turned his laptop to the mechanical room camera to check out Chief. He took his dossier from the stack, glanced at it, and passed it to Berg. "This data is the latest." He watched Chief check the oil, start the generator, and switch from shore power to the genset. The lights on the boat flickered when the power shifted to the generators. A few moments later, he started the main. There was a low hum.

Berg read the report.

(CHIEF) Hamilton, Michael (Mike)

SUMMARY: Mike Hamilton; 01/08/1978 Port Arthur, TX (Candid photo) 5'-11", 188 lbs.

FAMILY: Parents deceased. No siblings. Philanderer. Divorced twice. **EDUCATION:** High school. **METAPHYSICS:** Ardent Christian fundamentalist. **POLITICS**: Conservative. **FRIENDS**: Few close, but loyal to those. **WORK HISTORY:** Seventeen years engineering on Gulf supply boats. Skilled, but not popular. **VICES**: No known drugs. Drinks, but rarely to excess. No arrests. **REFERENCES**: Competent and reliable, but difficult. Has problems with authority. **MISC**: Occasionally violent. Concealed carry permit. Master Diver. Needs money.

He passed it back. "Mister Chief's conservative extremism, problems with authority, and an occasional tendency toward violence might prove awkward. But, I understand how hard it is to find a qualified person to fill the position."

"Yes. He has the requisite skills and is available. He was the best we could do." Joe switched his laptop to view Jason in the salon and passed around his dossier.

(DECKER) Oliver, Jason

SUMMARY: Jason Oliver; 04/26/1986 Northville, MI (Candid photo) 6'-3" 195 lbs.

FAMILY: Parents deceased. No siblings. Feels profound loss by girlfriend's recent departure. **EDUCATION:** High school. **METAPHYSICS:** Vociferous atheist. **POLITICS:** Liberal. **FRIENDS:** Many. Highly regarded. Loyal. **WORK HISTORY:** Draftsman before Alaska. Six years on Alaska fish boats. Successful pot dealer until arrested. **VICES:** Drinks but not known to be drunk. Uses tobacco (snus) and marijuana. Marijuana bust is pending before the Alaska Supreme Court. No convictions. Must violate bond to join the crew. Enjoys living on the edge. **REFERENCES:** Reliable. Smart. Doesn't work to potential. **MISC:** Well read. Capable of violence, but only with reasonable justification. Stays cool in stressful situations. Needs money.

Bones reviewed the data. "I find it interesting Mister Decker would violate the terms of his bond to take part. Maybe a thrill junkie?"

Joe's eyes widened at the term.

Bones persisted, "I hope they all go for it—the situation's marginal. I'd prefer running them through a Myers-Briggs personality profile before we become shipmates. But I appreciate the time constraint, trip duration, and our situational control."

▪ ▪ ▪ ▪ ▪

Oh, WOW! Jason's eyes lighted at the polished blond hardwood trim and bright white paneling of the salon and galley. The LED lights provided brilliant illumination. To port, the galley contained stainless-steel appliances, granite counters, a wood inset cutting surface, and white rubber dot flooring. It was well lit and sparkled.

Jason watched Cookie and Stew examining equipment and supplies. Then Masters and Handy descended the companionway, and he switched his attention. "Nice, aye guys?"

Handhold rails extended from the ceiling, running fore and aft. The twenty-foot beam and height between the deck and coach roof created openness. A large flat panel TV mounted on the forward bulkhead was dark. Two lavish tables, in line to starboard, could seat fourteen men in comfort. Natural leather seats and backs lined the sides and ends. The polished teak and holly tabletops matched the deck.

Jason pointed to the tables. "They're separated in the middle. Even with the seats filled, only the center person against the hull would disturb his neighbor to enter or exit. Damn cool."

"Man, this ain't the Coast Guard," Masters quipped. He grabbed a handhold out of habit and twisted around to absorb the view.

Handy, wide-eyed, raised his voice an octave. "Yeah, and it ain't no halibut schooner."

Jason noticed the salon/galley was a separate module within the hull. It sat on visible rails, formed into perfect arcs extending along the hull beyond 90 degrees. A digital electric device on the aft module panel labeled Galley Angle Control showed zero. He considered the apparatus for a few seconds. "Look at this." He tapped the zero. "The whole galley module rotates to compensate for the boat's heel. We'll be able to sit level even with a lee rail buried. Fan-fucking-tastic."

He gazed aft to see the port and starboard teak cabin doors labeled Mr. Bones, and Mr. Berg—larger compartments. Right aft, a cabin door, marked Captain Plimsoll, stood out with a carved curved top and intricate wood detailing. The boys opened the doors and peeked in but did not enter. The Captain's cabin, sparse by luxurious yacht standards, could still function in a gale, unlike a typical ostentatious owner's cabin.

Chief had left the engine room watertight door open amidships. A light showed, but the only sound was a soft drone. Forward of the galley and salon were cabins and lockers. Steel bulkheads separated four areas of the boat. To traverse the central corridor meant passing through a watertight door if closed—an unusual safety precaution in a yacht.

The entrance to each stateroom had a brass plate on it with the name of a crewman. They looked into the first cabin. The made-up berth looked comfortable. The high bunk boards and tie-downs portended heavy weather. The narrow closet, a chair attached to the deck, a computer desk, and attractive lighting completed a cozy compartment.

Handy quipped, "Ain't like no cabin I ever seen." He laid on his bunk. "Hey, this bed is way more comfortable than my dad's boat."

They examined the two heads, one to port and one to starboard.

Masters stood in the port head and stroked his chin. "Glazed white tile and a Hollywood shower—eight side heads, two overhead—damn!"

Gunny came below, swiveled his head, but continued through to the weapons locker.

▪ ▪ ▪ ▪ ▪

Joe turned his laptop to the weapons room. He pulled Gunny's dossier from the stack and passed it to Berg. Berg read it and gave it to Bones.

(GUNNY) Richert, Brian

SUMMARY: Brian Richert; 10/04/1977 Biloxi, MS (Candid photo) 6'-0" 195 lbs.

FAMILY: Mother in managed care. Father unknown. One sister—estranged. Unmarried. Serial girlfriends of short duration. **EDUCATION:** High school. **METAPHYSICS:** No religious affiliation. Racist. Morally flexible. **POLITICS:** Conservative. **FRIENDS:** Unknown. **WORK HISTORY:** U.S. Marines, Master Gunnery Sergeant. One tour in Iraq, two tours in Afghanistan, additional work in Africa, location unknown. Competent on all weapon systems. **VICES:** None known, but disappears for periods. No arrests. **REFERENCES:** Quintessential mercenary. Those who know him would not talk. **MISC:** Works out excessively. Always armed. Needs money.

Bones returned it to the Captain. "He's perfect."

"Yeah. Let's check on how Mister Sails is doing." Captain Joe adjusted his laptop to view the sail locker. They saw him inspect bag labels, remove the ends, feel the fabric, and examine the laminations.

Captain Joe passed his dossier. "I think he's an excellent choice for bosun."

(SAILS) Bartholomew, Harold

SUMMARY: Harold Bartholomew; 03/20/1986 Falmouth, UK (Candid photo) 6'-2" 180 lbs.

FAMILY: Wealthy. Father, a successful London Barrister. Mother, a successful playwright. **EDUCATION:** Oxford. **METAPHYSICS:** Humanist. **POLITICS:** Liberal. **FRIENDS:** Many friends. Well-liked. **WORK HISTORY:** Spotty. Trust fund supports a sporting life. **VICES:** None known. No arrests. **REFERENCES:** Reliable. Trustworthy. **MISC:** Driven to do well in his undertakings. Doesn't need money.

Joe switched to the camera in the salon/galley.

▪ ▪ ▪ ▪ ▪

Cookie and Stew inspected everything in the galley—cabinets, drawers, freezer, refrigerator, range, other appliances, and food stocks. Cookie closed the knife drawer and grinned at Stew. "Good. Everything is like the plans. Somehow, I had envisioned more external light, but this," he extended his arms, "will work out well."

Jason, Masters, and Handy continued forward, examining lockers containing food, mechanical spares, and bosun supplies. They found everything well supplied, stowed, and labeled. An infirmary, aft of the sail locker bulkhead, was large and extended the boat's full width.

After sixty minutes, the engines shut down. The lights flickered back to shore power, and they gathered in the salon. Jason took an outboard seat on the forward table, across from Sails.

Sails spoke first, "Mister Chief, how are the engine and mechanical systems?"

"Great!" Chief spoke with a slight Texas drawl. "The main propulsion is a Cat C-12 with a hundred and twenty-four hours on the meter. Two Northern Lights 25 kW gen sets—we've plenty of power and an enormous battery bank. Fuel filtration is exceptional. We've got both heating and air conditioning. I reckon two thousand gallons of fuel and maybe fifteen hundred gallons of water—the water maker's good for a thousand gallons a day.

"There is a gyroscope in the engine room labeled Salon/Galley spinning with a hum. Y'all prob'ly noted these rails." He pointed to the two steel rails on which the salon/galley sat. "The entire room 'ill rotate automatically with the ship's roll. Within the arc limits, we'll have pitch, but no roll. There's a long water hose and pump for transferring water. Whaddaya suppose that's about?"

Sails interrupted, "Yes, a lot of strange details. Considering the peculiar aspects individually, they are only unusual. However, taken together, they add up to,... I do not know what. Is it just me, or is something here a bit skew-whiff?" Sails waited for reactions.

Chief caught Sails' eye, bent forward in acknowledgment, and continued. "The engine room is pretty—powder-coated white, well lit, with adequate space to work on everything. The engine's well-balanced. I put my hand on it and couldn't feel any vibration. The sound insulation is the best I've ever seen. With the wet exhaust setup, the engines are so quiet, we could come alongside someone, and they wouldn't hear us. The tool systems and spares are more than adequate. They're well stowed for heavy weather and easy to grab. The electrical systems appear to be in perfect order—well labeled and protected. She's ready."

Chief nodded to pass the conversation back to Sails.

"Well, she IS wicked and tidy topside. We have six sets of sails plus spares. Light air, working, and storm sets in both white and black. The light air sails include a gennaker—a kind of cruising spinnaker. They are well-packed and organized. With a black hull, black spars, and black sails, we will be bloody hard to see at night."

The hands exchanged glances without speaking.

Sails continued, "We have two Reckmann manual/hydraulic furling systems, ten electric and five manual Lewmar winches. The windlass is hydraulic, and the ground tackle is stout and new. A shakedown would reveal her characteristics, and I expect they are blinding. I love her shape and the curve of her shear. To see her sails taught in a brisk breeze and the lee rail buried in foam is a vision I would like to experience.

"The cordage is bonnie and the thimbles, splices, snap shackles, and so forth appear in perfect condition. The masts and booms appear strong and well supported. We have spares for most of the lines and working hardware. The flag locker baffles me with many I do not recognize, but I have to agree, considering only one hour of examination, I pronounce her ready to go." He placed both palms on the table and turned to Jason. "Mister Decker, what is your opinion?"

Jason collected his thoughts. "First, a comment on the rigging. It's a yacht, and I'm sure everything is fine for a brief trip. However, having worked on fish boats for many years, I can't help noticing the shrouds and stays size. On a typical commercial boat of half the length, the cables are twice as thick. A storm is a storm regardless of whether it's a yacht or a workboat—just an observation. Anyway, I spent most of my time on the nav systems and equipment. We have a variety of gear lockers, including one for diving gear, which I find interesting. Is anybody here a diver?"

"Yeah," Chief raised his hand, "I have a cert plus underwater welding."

"Hmm," Jason resumed, "So, what about that? A treasure-hunting expedition? We have a curious crate labeled DRONE. Whaddaya suppose that's for? Notice we have three clocks mounted above the screen," he pointed, "labeled SEATTLE, GREENWICH, and the larger one marked SHIP. The big one strikes ship's bells and shows three hours and thirty-two minutes earlier. Why's that?

"And, so, okay, the boat's fabulous. Navigation, communications, vessel management, safety gear, they're marvelous. But that's not the point. Is anybody else concerned with what-the-fuck's goin' on here? He said we wouldn't do anything illegal, but sump'n's goin' on that ain't kosher. This whole setup makes me uneasy."

A murmur of agreement rumbled through the cabin. The men shifted in their seats and exchanged looks.

Jason canvased their faces. "Mister Berg and the doctor seem competent enough, but we don't know shit about the qualifications of our Captain. Who is he really? Then there's Mister Gunn," he pointed, "our 'security' person. That strikes me as a tad ominous. I'm no mercenary. So, Mister Gunn, what do YOU have to report?"

Gunny pulled a toothpick out of his teeth, studying and twirling it between his fingers. "Okay, I have to admit, it's freaky. The firearms locker has munitions for significant engagements. They're locked, but there are a dozen stainless Kimber 1911s—match-grade pistols with checkered rosewood grips, worth around fifteen hundred a pop. We have a dozen M4 carbines—you know, the military version of an AR-15—with splendid sights. We have two McMillan TAC-50s, capable of destroying enemy equipment and people over a substantial distance—I mean a little over a mile. There's an M134 Vulcan minigun set for 3,200 rounds a minute—the optimum rate of fire for this weapon. At close range, it'll mow trees. And there's a Mk 19-40 mm grenade launcher with an effective range of 1,600 yards. Both weapons are attachable to the topside stand. We also have a sealed fiberglass crate labeled 'J.' I don't know what's in it.

"I mean, I dig the toys, boys, but what-the-fuck? I have an active imagination concerning military action, but I can't envision how any of this is useful on a five-day trek out of Seattle. So, yeah, what-the-fuck?"

Rode had been slouching with his legs out straight and his head bent, viewing his twiddling thumbs. He straightened but continued staring at his hands. "Okay, it's money versus mission. What'll ya do for enough money? To me, it's a lot of money, but whatever the story is, there has to be a chunk o' bullshit to justify the money and secrecy. There's a con goin' on. Son-of-a-bitch is sinister. I don't trust 'im. Yeah, yeah, the boat's terrific, but I'm not sure I wanna go.

"Have ya noticed we're all from diverse backgrounds, making it unlikely we got buddies in common? Why do ya s'pose that is? A local crew would o' made more sense. There're plenty o' talented guys in Seattle. And how come we don't use our actual names? We don't even know who this goddamn Captain is...." He looked around at the crew. "Anyone else notice there's no door outta this dock? Or that this ain't real tidewater? There ain't no tide stain, and this ain't Puget fuckin' Sound."

▪ ▪ ▪ ▪ ▪

"Shit." Captain Joe pushed himself back in his chair and dropped his mouse in disgust. "Fuck! I should have thought of that. I could have had a false door painted on the goddamn dome and a fake tide line on the dock face."

▪ ▪ ▪ ▪ ▪

Rode shifted in his seat. "And what's this 'unlikely event of attack' and weapons systems bullshit? And what's with these armed guards? And deadlights on the portholes? Black sails, deadlights, shee-yit. No destination, weapons up the ying-yang, no clue where we're goin' or what we're gonna do. The snot-soaked brain fart that dreamed up this shit sandwich can kiss my ass. I'm gonna take my show-up money, score some dope, and kickback. My old lady can suck the chrome off a trailer hitch. Think I'll hang around Fairhaven and wait for spring. You boys go if ya want, but count me out."

No one commented.

Cookie broke the silence, "Would you care for a galley report?" Everyone swung to his pink, happy face.

"The galley is 100% stocked and ready to go. We're provisioned way beyond what I asked for—and I've planned elaborate meals. The equipment appears in perfect order. Everything I requested for the menus is fresh and well stowed. I don't get why I have to be ready to seat fourteen—there are only twelve of us. But all I care bout's the cooking. The refrigeration and freezer lockers contain way more than we'll need. And several of the supplies mystify me, such as the quantity of to-go containers and a bunch of god-awful canned goods. We also have a liquor locker, including cases of fabulous old Madeira and Port wines.

"Yes, the situation is just short of la-la-land, but we've worked for eccentric owners in strange circumstances before, and they have turned out well for us. You all decide what you want, but if this boat leaves, Mister Steward and I'll be on it to prepare and serve the meals." He shifted to view Stew.

Steward ignored the conversation and smiled. He approached the table with a carafe and mugs. "Coffee's done. Cup anyone?"

Everyone grunted.

Masters, peeling an orange, had been contemplating his fellows. He popped a piece into his mouth then delivered his measured response in an even tone, without emotion. "Umm. Good orange. We have a locker forward full of oranges and apples. I mean FULL—in neatly packed plastic totes. Must be some 200 oranges and apples. We appear to be delivering fruit somewhere. We have an infirmary with a large pharmacy cabinet and a lamp for performing operations. I find that a bit unsettling. Do you suppose they are expecting injuries? But she's well found, and I love the layout. Yeah, the situation is goddamned bizarre. And I agree with Mister Rode that this proposition is a 'money versus mission' issue. But for me, the money tips the balance. Consider me bought. I will take the deal."

Handy, the youngest, had deferred to the others before he voiced his opinion. "I gotta tell ya. I don't give a shit. The money works for me. Whatever this story is, I'm in."

Jason considered his response. "I agree the issue is money versus mission. But the money is outstanding, and I can't believe we can get into much trouble on a five-day round-trip from the Emerald City. What with the Coast Guard, military bases, and constant air traffic, anything overt is too stupid to take seriously."

Masters raised a finger, "But no cell-phones."

"Yeah," Jason resumed, "but whatever the fuck this guy has in mind, it sounds like a grand adventure. I understand we'll have the money deposited in our accounts before we leave—paid in advance! I don't know 'bout you guys, but payment before performance is unheard of in my end of the world. If I hate the guy, I never have to see him again. If I don't do well on a fish boat, the captain won't invite me back. This command structure is comparatively loosey-goosey."

▪ ▪ ▪ ▪ ▪

"He's identified an important issue," Berg observed, staring at the monitor.

"Yeah," Joe shoved his chair and clasped his hands behind his head. "but I'm confident they'll understand they've no choice if they're to revert to their lives. Once they understand the situation, they must follow orders and take care of the ship."

▪ ▪ ▪ ▪ ▪

The team studied each other across the galley table.

Jason considered his fellows. *Discount Cookie, Stew and Rode... six versus three.* "I mean, without payment or the next season hanging over our heads, how rigid can command be? Also, I admit to a certain level of respect for the person who put this together. I'm curious to hear the end of this story, and I have a bit of free time. I'm game."

Sails crossed his legs and took hold of his mug. "I want to go sailing. This boat is the finest, best-found vessel I have ever seen, and the money is great. Whatever wonky voyage this punter has in mind, I will do my best to have fun. I am in too."

Chief sat vertical but relaxed into his seat. "I can keep the systems runnin' fine for five days. Trip seems more vacation than work. Count me in. Jesus will protect me."

Jason's face remained blank. *Yeah, right. Oh, good. 'Nother Jesus Nazi.*

Gunny stroked his chin, swung sideways to the table, and crossed a leg. "I try to be prudent about my missions. But, for enough money, I don't give a flying fuck. I won't allow innocent victims on my watch—and boys, I mean it—but if someone attacks me or my boat, I'll kick the livin' shit out of 'em. I don't foresee that on a five-day cruise out o' here. And the money works for me. I'm goin'."

Ding-ding, ding-ding, ding-ding, ding-ding: eight bells.

8
READY

February 24 - Seattle
Jason joined the party trundling across the gangway, bouncy with their combined weight. The echo in the enormous dome was the inverse of the cozy conversation in the boat's salon. The sun was setting, and the water turned dark. The amber glow from the canopy bathed them in red-yellow light. Six security men stood at parade rest near the door. Equal in height, they stared with blank faces. Black semi-automatics protruding from their polished brown chest holsters contrasted with their tailored gray jumpsuits.

Captain Joe stood and faced the ship's company until they had seated themselves, then turned to Doris. "Please give Mister Rode his envelope and accompany him to his van. Mister Rode, I appreciate your showing up, but upon consideration, I've decided we are one crew member too many. We'll pass on your services for this trip. Thank you very much for coming to our meeting." He signaled the security detail with a glare and raised a finger.

Rode raised his eyebrows in shocked disgust at having Captain Joe beat him to the punch. "Man, you're one crazy motherfucker. I wish you all luck. Y'all gonna need it to get your butts out of this jam." He followed Doris out with a security detail in front and behind.

The steel door closed with a thud of finality, and the dog wheel spun. Captain Joe turned back to his gang.

Jason exchanged a perceptive glance with Sails. *Listening device?* He lifted a hand. "May I ask a question?"

"You want to know where we'll be going and what we'll be doing. If I don't explain, you'll assume there might be a reason not to go. Sorry.

There are reasons to keep it a secret until an appropriate time. We'll be doing nothing illegal or immoral, and we'll safely disembark on this dock in five days.

"Look, I prefer you all to accept my offer, but either you do, or you don't. If you don't, Doris will arrange a van ride for you to your pickup point, and that'll be it. The time to speak is now." He opened his hands and extended his arms to include everyone.

Shit. Jason squirmed.

Silence.

"So, may I assume you all accept my offer?"

No one disputed the assumption. They twisted in their chairs and surveyed each other with blank faces, understanding whatever this was, they were in it together.

"Well," said Captain Joe, "I'm pleased you've chosen to join my little cruise. Here's how this will work. Go to the locker room," he pointed at the door, "sign your non-disclosure agreement and get your gear. If the size information you gave Doris was correct, everything will fit. How many of you brought your original offer letter?"

The men glanced at each other. Everyone raised a hand.

Jason writhed in his seat. *Damn, should have made a copy.*

"Good. Give the letter to Doris with your signed NDA. I am providing everything you'll wear, carry, or use, including clothing, toiletries, hardware—whatever. The dress of the day is the gray jumpsuit, tailored from the information you supplied. Remove your clothes and belongings and store them in the locker with your name on it. Everything is safe in this facility. I'll have the money wired to your account and that of your sponsor. My attendant will return your phone for you to verify the deposit—but only to confirm the deposit."

"What about jewelry?" Chief thumbed the crucifix hanging around his neck.

Nobody wore a wedding ring.

"Your crucifix is okay." Captain Joe hesitated, annoyed at the disruption in his discourse. He stared at Chief for a moment.

Ol' Chiefy slipped a notch. Jason suppressed a grin.

The Captain slowed his pace and increased his enunciation. "I will suspend the phone signal block for the time necessary for you to check your bank accounts, but you may do nothing else. Do not take pictures, make calls, or send texts. Leave your cell-phone and any other belongings in your locker. Security will observe there are no violations. If you have an individual requirement, tell my clerk."

Masters interrupted, "Can I bring my reading glasses?"

Captain Joe's tolerance for interruption wavered. "Yes. Anything else?"

"Can I get a can of Copenhagen Long Cut?" Handy straightened from hunching in his chair and raised his head.

"Yeah, sounds good. Can I get one, too?" Jason had quit using tobacco for a year and a half, but, under the circumstances, he welcomed the opportunity for an extra kick.

"Sure." Tolerance served Joe's interests. "See my clerk. But if you spit on my teak deck,... I'll be unhappy." Captain Joe narrowed his eyes in a penetrating stare toward Jason.

"I am issuing each of you a Citizen Chronomaster watch, Military Steiner Binoculars, Bolle Marine sunglasses, an LED flashlight, and a Spyderco knife. After the cruise, you may keep these items and any other goods distributed that does not have the boat's name on it. You may take nothing aboard but what I supply or otherwise allow."

After a pause, he resumed, "Showers and restrooms are around the corner if you wish before dressing. My clerk has warmed towels. After dressing, come to the dock, go aboard, and stow your gear." He pointed to Sails. "Once stowed, Mister Sails will direct you in bending the black working sails. Raise them, lower them, and secure them. I don't want a single sound from those sails when the first wind hits us, d'ye, hear me, thar?"

He tried to sound like Captain Aubrey from the Patrick O'Brian novels. The joke failed. Except for Sails, their faces were blank. Sails smiled.

Captain Joe checked his watch. "It's now 5:15. Once you've stowed your gear and bent the sails, come ashore for dinner. My staff will serve buffet-style on the dock. You may each have ONE glass of wine." He raised his right index finger. "I have selected a 2012 Silver Oak Cabernet of which I am very fond. Henceforth, Mister Cook will prepare our meals. I'll determine when we leave after dinner."

■ ■ ■ ■ ■

The crew filed into the locker room. Jason found the gear in his cubbyhole well arranged. Shoes, boots, and the equipment promised were on a shelf. A large blue canvas bag lay on the floor in front of it. A navy-blue blazer with bright brass buttons hung on a wooden hanger. *SERENDIPITY* and Mr. Decker emblazed the pocket in gold thread. Next to it hung a red *Stormy Seas* jacket with Mr. Decker sewn above the *STORMY* logo.

Jason rested on the bench and opened his bag. On top was the gray coverall. He removed his clothes, put on new underwear, the one-piece garment, and buckled the attached belt. Tailored to perfection, Mr. Decker and *SERENDIPITY* embellished the left chest pocket. He surveyed himself in the mirror with the satisfaction of Fonzie. "Man, we're gonna look good."

He continued through the bag. On top was a dark blue hat with CREW stitched under an arc of *SERENDIPITY* embroidered in gold thread. There were three shirts—light blue, navy blue, and tan. Each had double chest pockets with snaps, button-down collars, and epaulets. Below them were Navy blue and black military-style sweaters with reinforced shoulder and elbow patches. He checked a label—100% unbleached wool. *Nice.* Underneath them were three pairs of pants in navy-blue, black, and khaki. Toiletries were in a separate, compact plastic container. Rain gear, gloves, underwear—everything needed was there. *Didn't pack this much shit for an entire season afloat.*

An attendant returned his phone in its plastic bag. Jason installed the battery and checked his bank account. It showed a deposit of $50,000. He glanced sideways, noticed a security guard followed his every action, turned his phone off, and forced it into the right toe of his shoe on a locker shelf. Bending to tie his new shoe, he leaned toward Sails, doing the same. "How do you suppose the Captain knew Rode would bail?"

Sails, aware of security in his peripheral vision, pressed his finger to his lips before replying in a low tone. "Yes, mate, I got that, too. A listening device is the obvious explanation and adds an interesting dimension. Have to keep that in mind." They exchanged knowing glances.

Jason extended his wrist toward Sails. "That's a two-thousand-dollar watch we get to keep."

Sails nodded. "The other gear is first class, too. A dodgy situation with cool tools."

Handy approached the clerk at the counter. "Can I get two fresh cans of Copenhagen long cut in a plastic can?"

Jason overheard this and called out, "Yeah, me too for one can."

The clerk spoke in a voice devoid of emotion. "I'll have them in thirty minutes. However, I can't guarantee the plastic can. I advise you not to spit on the deck."

Jason spoke low, "Yeah, probably good advice," and joined the crew straggling aboard. His cabin had ample room to stow everything. He closed the door and sat in the chair. Quiet. He contemplated the situation. *Better or worse, I'm in. What's Loren doing? Explain this to Al....*

On deck, he joined Sails, Masters, Handy, and Gunny in getting out the sail bags and bending the sails. Everything set without difficulty on the first try. The crew furled the limp sails and secured them so they would not flap in a breeze. Sails tied the halyards out to the shrouds to keep them from clinking against the masts. The galley became quiet. Chief returned from having changed the fuel filters on the main and general tinkering. They filed off.

They had set up a table on the dais where a chef carved a smoked prime rib. The smell set Jason's salivary glands flowing. Au jus, horseradish, scalloped potatoes, asparagus with grated hard-boiled egg and crispy prosciutto chips, fresh salad, and a crème brûlée dessert spread before them. He grabbed a cloth napkin wrapped utensil packet, a delicate china plate, and worked his way down the table. Taking his wine in an elegant crystal glass, he returned to his seat with the group.

Gunny took a mouthful of food and eyed the Captain at his desk. "So, Cap'n, when we goin'?"

Captain Joe smiled wryly. "Boys, it'll become clear soon. We'll be leaving later tonight, or more accurately, tomorrow morning. Once you finish eating, I want you all to board and get some sleep. Tomorrow will be a long day. Keep your jacket handy. I'll roust you at the proper time."

At 10:00 P.M., Sails sat alone in the dark salon wishing he had a cup of coffee. The rest of the company were in their bunks. He heard an occasional foot drag from Captain Joe, Berg, and Bones sitting in the wheelhouse, but otherwise, it was silent.

The Captain pecked at his computer, turned to Berg, and spoke softly—almost a whisper. "Remove the gangway and point the helm at 45°. Odds are, the wind will hit us from the northwest. I believe we'll start on the port tack."

Berg opened his laptop computer and started tapping keys. The crane, with a hushed whir, removed the utility connections first, then the gangway. The dock team, having practiced these maneuvers many times, quietly turned the boat, so it pointed northeast by the numbers on the white bearing band.

"Gentlemen," murmured Captain Joe to Berg and Bones, "remove the spar socks, sheer stripes, and single up. We'll be arriving before dawn, and we might find ourselves in an awkward position exposed to all kinds o' mean, nasty, ugly things. I don't want to attract attention. And put on your jacket and hat." He pointed to their gear and slipped on his own.

Berg removed the port side white shear band, and Bones removed it from starboard and both sides of the whaleboat. They pulled the three white spar end covers and quietly stowed them in an inset deck locker. After disconnecting the lines from the cleats and lowering them into the water to avoid a splash, the boat remained motionless.

Berg returned to the wheelhouse and whispered, "Cap, we're up and down."

Captain Joe, Berg, and Bones surveyed the dock teams. To keep from interfering with the transmission, they removed the ropes, desk, monitors, and everything else in the dome with rehearsed, muted efficiency. The door for the crane opened with a hum, and the crane rolled quietly out. The panel closed with a soft click. The area sat empty and silent except for a faint distant fan. *Serendipity* floated motionless in the center of the pool.

Captain Joe spoke in a soft tone to Berg, "You'd better get below to handle the crew. Bones, take the helm. Start the radar antenna turning but don't transmit until after the transition. I'll stand by to address whatever crisis occurs first."

He turned toward the Control Room, made eye contact with Jack Wilson, Manager of Engineering, and spoke low into a handheld radio. “Okay, Jack. I'm bettin' the farm. I've given you the tools, you bullshit, or are we on track for ten-twenty?”

Jack ignored Joe's sarcasm. “At exactly twenty-two-twenty hundred hours, you're gone.”

The music *Atmospheres* played. Captain Joe punched a key on his computer, releasing the keel chain, keeping them centered in the hangar pool. The amber cones on the dome's surface increased their glow. A low buzz coincided with energizing the G-WADs.

Too excited to sleep, Jason joined Sails in the dark salon. The boat was silent. The only light came from various galley appliances and the salon angle control indicator. They both listened to a strange hum above deck, and the weird music, increasing in volume. *Loren nailed it? Adventure going to sink me? Have to change.*

Sails spoke to Jason across the table. “Guess we are getting ready to leave.”

Berg left Bones and Captain Joe in the pilothouse to go below.

Surprised to encounter Sails and Jason, he whispered. “I expected you guys would be sound asleep. But, since you're up, I have to ask you to remain silent and stationary for the next few minutes.” He reached the electrical panel and turned on the salon's red night-lights.

Amber light pulsated through the pilothouse with increasing intensity, concurrent with a growing low-frequency purr. The generator started, then the main. It became bright outside with throbbing golden light. The purr became a mumble, then a medium pitch whir, turning into a high pitch squeal. A gravity wave produced by a pulsar explosion swept over the hangar. The hull started vibrating with a deep thrum.

Jason started feeling tingly over his entire body. “Man, I don't feel right. I have this prickly sensation and ▯ I'm star▯t▯▯g to 00▯▯ fe▯▯l wo0Θzy and 000▯▯▯ m▯▯y 00 b0ΘԿ 000 is ▯▯ siη00kᶅ0ng & mΘʊ!Јɋ 0000000▯▯▯▯▯▯▯……”

The lights in Seattle dimmed, and all Wi-Fi connections north of the Ship Canal died for two seconds from the power consumption.

9
AWEIGH

February 25 - West of the Strait of Gibraltar

"......□□□□□□000000 & r⊙0ЖKing & bΘƱηCⴳng and pitching and, shit, we're at sea!"

The rush of water and dash of waves along the hull replaced the high-pitched squeal of the dome. *Serendipity's* sudden pitch and roll rousted everyone, and the smell of the ocean breeze wafted through on the abruptly chill air. The crew rushed to the main cabin.

"dzzit... dzzzit." The cabin hummed back and forth with the ship's roll.

Captain Joe went below to address the crew from the foot of the companionway. Eight wide-eyed men assembled aft to face him. The red night-lights cast an eerie glow.

"Be cool." The Captain spoke in a soft but urgent manner, patting the air with his left hand and grabbing a ceiling handhold with his right. "Everything's under control."

"Clang." The radar alarm sounded, signaling a nearby object. Bones, at the helm, flicked the switch to shut off the signal. The Captain looked up, and Bones leaned down, speaking in a low, urgent voice, "Captain, we have what appears to be a corsair 1,600 yards to leeward off our starboard beam heading northeast."

Captain Joe's response was both calm and authoritative, "Very well, Mister Bones. Turn us into the wind and increase the distance between us. Are our sails flapping, and what's the weather?"

"The sails are quiet, and it's dark. No moon. Stars are fading. There is an inkling of daylight to the east—temperature 54. Barometer has dropped from Seattle. Wind is gentle, force 3 out of the northwest. We have large wavelets and a few breaking crests—scattered white horses."

"Are any other targets on the radar?"

"Several, but not dangerously near. The only potential threat appears to be a polacca or xebec. I'm viewing her through the Stabiscope. She's three-masted, lateen-rigged. I estimate maybe a dozen gunports—a bird of prey. Probably out of Algiers or Tripoli. I don't think she's spotted us yet."

"All right. Close the deck door to eliminate any light from below and keep us into the wind dead slow. Maybe we'll slip away in the dark. If she reacts, let me know."

Serendipity responded to the helm. The roll decreased, and the pitch increased. The crew, agape and stunned, looked at their Captain for an account of what was happening.

Captain Joe changed handholds and spoke in his calm, commanding tone. "Okay, I owe you all an explanation and an apology of sorts. I've misled you somewhat. Have a seat, check the monitor, and I'll explain the situation."

The crew took seats around the tables, bewildered and alarmed. The boat pitched gently into a three-foot swell. Berg tapped his iPad. The large flat screen switched on and showed Admiralty Chart 2717, the Strait of Gibraltar, east to the Balearic Islands. With the deadlights closed, even the monitor's minimal light would not be visible from outside the vessel. The gleam from the screen added a creepy pall, with swishing waves and whirring wind the only sounds.

Captain Joe moved forward, grabbed a handhold with his right hand, and pointed to a spot west of the strait with his left. "We're right here at 7 degrees west longitude and 36 degrees north latitude.

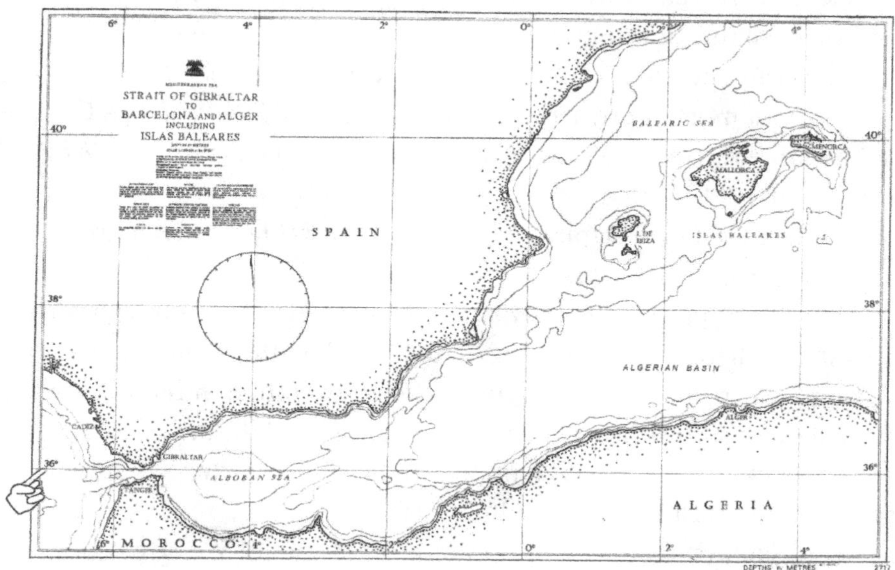

"Also, the time is," he pointed to the bigger clock labeled SHIP, "5:57 A.M., Sunday, February 25 of the year 1798. Please set your watches to match that clock. I'm sure you noticed we have three clocks, Seattle, Greenwich, and this one. Ship's time is local time. We had to know the local time to calculate our arrival before dawn."

Holy shit, what've I done? Jason squirmed in his seat, twisting his head from side to side, trying to grasp the circumstances. His stomach felt rubbery. He and the crew exchanged expressions of dismay.

Captain Joe and Berg checked their watches. Jason and his fellows in fearful confusion set theirs. Someone's nervous foot tapped the deck, awaiting the Captain's explanation.

"Ah, Captain?" Bones cracked the door and uttered below, "Radar bearings show we hit our latitude on the dot but cut out longitude at six degrees fifty-eight minutes—two minutes east of our target."

"That's not a problem."

Bones closed the door.

Jason considered. *Ship's time is off.*

"Okay, so here's the story. Those little amber glass cones covering the hanger dome? They're an invention of mine. I call it a Gravity Wave Actuation Device or G-WAD. Their properties and, ah, well, with a little chunk of borrowed power from Seattle City Light, we've moved in time and space to this time and this place."

The crew sat a-gawk, wide-eyed, their mouths open.

"So, you must appreciate certain things, RIGHT NOW." The Captain pointed to the group. "We are in a war zone. D'ye, hear me, thar? We ARE in the year 1798."

"Bullshit!" Handy slapped his hands on the table. "That's crazy."

"No, Mister Handy, it is not bullshit, and it's not crazy."

A sudden splash—the boat split a breaking crest, the bow prancing upward with the wave passing under the length of their ship—lent credence to the Captain's assertion. The crew shifted in their seats and straightened their backs. Groans and rustling filled the air.

"Well mates," Masters quipped at his fellows, "we've sure gone somewhere." A sad frown engulfed his face.

The Captain resumed. "Allow me to continue. We are flying the Alaska flag, and we're susceptible to attack by anyone in these waters."

"Hold on there, Cap." Jason interrupted, raising a finger and leaning forward to make eye contact. "You claim to have instantly fuckin' shanghaied us halfway around the world to 1798?"

The crew turned from Jason to Captain Joe.

"Well, not instantly, but yes. And Mister Decker has a point." The Captain signaled Berg to get coffee, released his handhold, folded his arms, and adjusted to the vessel's motion. "Shanghaied is not an inaccurate term, except, unlike the days of yore, you're well-compensated, and it's only for five days. And, c'mon, you must have known something was in store. You didn't think you would get this kind of money for doing nothin', did you? Oh,... and regarding payment, Doris will make an electronic transfer of an additional $100,000 to each of your accounts at 10:00 A.M. today, Seattle time."

The crew swapped glances.

"Fact is," he knocked his knuckles on the table to emphasize the point, "NOTHING can get us back for five days—our next gravity wave interval. So, like any shanghaied crewmen, you need to make the best of it until we return to the hangar. Got it?" He looked at each of his crew individually.

Jason tried to wrap his mind around the concept. Captain Joe's explanation turned into background chatter while he tried to process what had just happened.

Chief broke into a broad grin, "Poppycock." He slapped both hands on the table and leaned forward. "Biggest piece of drivel I ever heard. What is this, some kind of cockamamie reality TV show?" He cast around for signs of a TV camera and the reaction of the other crew. No one smiled.

"No, Mister Chief. I'm afraid you must accept my explanation. To manage our ship in these conditions requires the best efforts of all of us if we're to return safe and sound. And that includes you."

"Huh." Chief droned in the timbered tenor of a disk jockey. Dismay distorted his face. "So, how DO we get back?"

"Yeah. How DO we do that?" Jason creased his temple, crossed his arms, and faced the Captain. *Sure as shit transported somewhere.*

"We have to be at a certain rendezvous point, within precise latitude and longitude limits, on an exact time in five days to catch the next gravity wave in our ripple set."

Masters raised a hand. "Do we have radio contact?"

"No, Mister Masters, we do not. We'll have no contact of any kind with the twenty-first century until we re-transition. In the meantime, we'll rely on a combination of Mister Berg's celestial navigation and radar to determine where we are. We have accurate charts from our own time. There ain't no GPS in 1798."

"And, what are those coordinates?" Chief drawled, failing to conceal his internal churn.

"I am the only one who knows, and I ain't tellin'. You got that?"

Chief remained motionless. "Neither Mister Berg nor the Doc knows the coordinates?"

"Right. Y'all wanna resume your lives? Do what I say for the next five days. Under the circumstances, we must trust each other to do our duties. If we don't, we're all fucked."

"And you're sure we can make it back?" Jason raised his eyebrows. "You've done this before?"

"Well, no. Humans have never done time-travel before. We have transferred solid objects, but not people."

A shiver ran down Jason's spine. He considered his fellow crew. *Must believe him—can't get back without the coordinates. Mutiny's not realistic—got us by the short hairs.*

The men exchanged frowns and twisted lips but exhibited no panic.

Steward, sitting across the table from Cookie, searched his face for a hint of reaction. Cookie remained calm, accepting the situation as another wealthy employer indulging in an eccentric whim. He mouthed the words at his friend, "No sweat."

The coffee maker signaled it had completed its cycle. Berg passed around mugs and poured for everyone while the Captain spoke. The boat pitched with an occasional splash into the yard-high waves. The sudden seas made the Captain's explanation plausible. The crew remained silent in rapt attention.

Sails blinked twice and broke the silence. "Let me understand this—you claim to have moved us to a different bloody century to a location just west of the Strait of Gibraltar?"

"Right."

"Blimey!" Sail's face turned ashen. He stared at the table and clasped his hands together.

Gunny raised a hand. "Why are we flying the Alaska flag?"

"I like the Alaska flag. Any flag is better than no flag. No flag makes deception too obvious. Everybody cheats, though, hence our large flag locker. Wartime protocol only requires the correct flag before going into action."

"Is it your intention to go into action?" Gunny narrowed his eyes, wrinkled his forehead, and peered hard at Captain Joe. His teeth were visible through his clenched mouth.

"No, Mister Gunn, I do not intend a military confrontation. If attacked, however, I am prepared to defend my boat and crew. Under the circumstances, claiming to be an American vessel is a bit of a stretch. But we ARE an American boat with all the responsibilities inherent therein.

"We are also the only craft in the current world with an engine, electricity, radar, and automatic weapons. We can sink anything afloat from outside the range of the largest naval guns. Only *Serendipity* can go straight into the wind without rowing. No one else has radar. After five days in these waters, we'll return to our Seattle hangar—all safe and sound. However, we must be diligent. If an enemy gets close enough, one of them ol' cannons could cause all kinds o' mean, nasty, ugly things and prevent our return. Let's not allow that to happen."

"So, Captain, what's this about?" Jason's question elicited buzz from the crew. "Why are we doing this?"

"Because it'll be fun." Captain Joe grinned. "I expect this trip to be a thrill-and-a-half. We are a classic example of good versus evil. A guy is 'good' to the extent of the evil he overcomes. The Greatest Generation, who won World War II, was great in direct proportion to the evil they had to overcome. Superman only defeats supervillains. Good is relative to evil. I have put us in a perfect position whereby we get to be the good guy defending ourselves from an attack of what is clearly a bad guy."

The crew stiffened in their seats. Their faces reflected a palpable uneasiness. The splash of bow spray from a breaking wave bolstered the Captain's reality pronouncement.

Jason focused on the Captain's eyes. "Okay, assuming what you say is true, what about the 'butterfly effect?' Won't interaction in this time affect outcomes in our own time?"

"No. That's the beauty of it." His smile widened. "Nothing will affect our Seattle lives. Everything here is a parallel existence stream. Once we return to our reality, everything will be the same except the wear and tear on our good ship and crew. Try to imagine: You're strolling down the street in our own time, and a nanosecond later, the buildings and people change because of something we did in 1798? It's not conceivable."

Jason's mouth dropped open. "We just traveled two hundred years in time, and you're arguing the butterfly effect is not conceivable?"

Gunny grimaced. "If we kill someone here or we get killed, what happens to their or our reality stream?"

"For us, dead is dead, Mister Gunn. The reality stream of a dead person ends. Let's not get killed, okay?"

"And, who exactly is the 'bad guy?'" Jason scoffed.

"Look, we're just yachtsmen out for a leisurely cruise in the eighteenth century. If someone attacks us without provocation, that's an evil act. We are within our moral rights to defend ourselves against any such dastardly deed. Our most likely antagonist, however, is a Muslim corsair. These Barbary pirates operate out of the North African states of

Morocco, Algiers, Tunis, and Tripoli. A portion of their ill-gotten gains goes to the Ottoman Empire in Istanbul as an homage. They believe it is a religious duty to pillage and enslave non-Muslims for ransom. They use these men as slaves. That's cheap labor until they receive the extortion they demand—which the United States can't afford. So, they love capturing American vessels. These dudes are our principal danger, except for Morocco."

The Captain pointed east-southeast. "That's Morocco right over there. We made a deal with the ruler of Morocco twelve years ago, in 1786, but he died in 1790. His son took his seat but didn't fill his shoes until this year. He may waver in his support for Daddy's treaty, so we must be wary of him too. The Barbary raiders are technically legal—empowered by the Ottoman Empire to raid the ships of Christendom—part of the eternal war of Islam to foster their point of view on everyone."

The boat angled up and down on the oncoming waves, swaying them in unison, forward, and aft. The wind hummed in the rigging.

"Not unlike the interminable mission of Christianity to do the same," Jason quipped.

Chief glared at Jason.

"Well, Mister Decker," Joe went on, "be that as it may, these boys are not pirating per se, albeit from our perspective there isn't any difference. They consider themselves to be privateers operating under a legal license for sending a portion of their booty to Constantinople. And if they die in an attempt, they get various quantities of virgins in paradise. In the last three hundred years, they captured and enslaved a million Christians. Think of it as battling ISIS. Same shit, different century. If you don't believe what they believe, it's their duty to kill you."

Chief scowled, "They're enslaving Christians for being Christians?"

"No. They're enslaving Christians for not being Muslims. It's an age-old economic model. Religion has a history of being an excuse to rob nonbelievers. In this world," Joe swept his hand, "the European powers are more concerned with their internal Christian wounds than external Muslim scratches. Being an American sailor in 1798 is a low occupation, exposed to Barbary enslavement and the usual vagaries of the sea."

Jason contemplated a sailor's life in the eighteenth century. *Brutal, wet, dark, and short—not romantic.* "Captain, could you have gone to any time of your choosing? I mean, if I got to select, I'd pick being the first Europeans in the South Pacific meeting beautiful bronzed bare-breasted women eager to fuck."

Masters and Handy grinned. The rest remained stoic.

"Well, there are technical limits to playing the hero."

Jason asked, "Why did you pick this date and location?"

"It offers the most clear-cut historic opportunity to confront immorality within the range of a predicted gravity wave event. And these ARE evil guys. In 1785, they attacked the American ship, Dauphin, off the coast of Portugal. They seized the boat, stripped the crew naked, sent them to Algiers, and paraded them through the streets to a stone slave pen. They broke rocks to build a breakwater until last year when they got released because of a combination of negotiation, handouts, and an extorted promise of more money."

Jason spoke in an even tenor, gazing into the distance. "So, let me get this straight. You've taken us, without our permission, on something like a life-or-death hunting trip. Now we have to kill some dumb charging bear or rhino or whatever out of self-defense? The risk seems high, and the moral ground low."

"Sure, there's a risk, but we don't get to occupy the high moral ground without risk. And we have all the advantages—we're playing with a stacked deck, no pun intended. Once we return to our hangar, everything we'll have done becomes a parallel reality stream, except we'll be five days older."

"What if we don't make our rendezvous?" Jason's voice took on a sharp tone. He leaned forward, put his arms on the table, and folded his hands.

"Then we're fucked. So, it behooves you to follow my orders." The Captain tilted his head forward to emphasize the point.

"And," Jason said, "all we have to do is hit a certain location on time? We need no further action to transition out?"

"Right. Seattle handles the switch." Captain Joe showed no emotion, considering everyone's reaction. The crew fell silent. "So, we have three primary political realities with which to contend. You must grasp this." He tipped his hand, scowled, and pointed at the crew.

"The first is the Barbary raiders, perhaps the vessel astern of us. Algeria has assembled four frigates, a twenty-gun brig, and many galleys to attack American shipping in these waters. Our second problem is Europe, where the French revolution is what's hap'nin'. France, her allies, and the Barbary States of North Africa is at war with us. France is fighting Britain and the remaining monarchies of Europe. Napoleon, having conquered Italy and defeated Austria, will now turn his attention toward Egypt.

"The United States made a treaty three years ago with Britain, so they shouldn't open fire on us if we're flying the American flag. But we have friction with jolly ol' England. They believe it is their right to press—that is, kidnap—sailors from American vessels for the British navy. They were—are—always short of qualified sailors. They're pressing American sailors to blockade American ports. Forced labor against ourselves grated hard on American pride. They'll stop us if they can, figuring to take anyone they want. Such an affront to our sovereignty is an element of our War of 1812—our second revolution."

Sails blinked, trying to comprehend. "Captain, it was not so simple. What you people call the War of 1812 was a sideshow for us Brits. While we were saving democracy in Europe from the tyrant, you Yanks stabbed us in the back, trying to take Canada. I argue you owed us better. In 1812 Napoleon marched on Moscow. Three and a half million people died in the Napoleonic wars. Your 'second revolution' hardly registers with the British public."

"Well," the Captain said, "the United States tried to remain neutral in Napoleon's conflicts with an eye toward the considerable profit potential of trading with all sides of the warring nations."

Berg tried to break the seriousness. "Ah, profit. A fine American tradition."

Joe ignored him. "But we found the mass executions of the French Revolution abhorrent. Execution by guillotine of sixteen nuns for refusing to repudiate their vows was especially repugnant."

"They cut off the heads of nuns?" Handy's facial muscles twitched. His eyes grew wide.

Chief's brow furrowed.

"I'm afraid so. The nuns ascended the scaffold one by one, singing a hymn before laying their heads over the slot and having them cut off."

"Holy Jesus!" Handy blurted.

Chief turned and gave him a blank stare.

"Such atrocities—and there were many—caused the United States and France to fall out with each other. The French revolution put France at war with Great Britain, so our post-revolutionary war treaty with the English to reopen trade pissed off the French revolutionaries. Then we refused to pay the debt we owed France for their help with our war for independence. We figured we owed it to the French monarchy who'd helped us, not a French government that overthrew their king and killed thousands of innocent people. Kinda like our getting a four hundred million down payment from the Shah of Iran for military hardware we didn't deliver. We didn't return the money for thirty-some years because his replacement is anti-US. Remember that minor incident?"

"Yeah, I remember," Masters sniped. "We landed a plane with four hundred million worth of foreign currencies. A friend of mine watched the Iranian revolutionary guards unload the pallets. He'll never get over it. Me, either."

"Anyway, at our time in February 1798, we've turned against France, and they've turned against us. By June of what is now last year, France captured over three hundred American ships. This coming June, Congress will rescind our treaties with France and build a new navy. Meanwhile, any American vessel in these waters is pretty much fair game for the French and their allied countries.

"The third political reality is the dilemma of the United States. We became an independent nation only fifteen years ago and don't yet have a navy on the high seas. We're poor. We can't afford to build a navy, pay the Barbary extortion, or lose trade profits. We, this ship, can't count on anyone to be a friend out here."

Berg tapped keys on his iPad, and the screen changed to a live plot of *Serendipity's* location on the chart. It also showed a near radar target to the southeast, and additional blips spread out within its range.

Bones steered with his back to the wheel. He peered through his binoculars at the officers on the corsair, their telescopes pointing at him.

▪ ▪ ▪ ▪ ▪

Captain Brahim Madjer was always on his xebec's poop deck at dawn to take advantage of any opportunity as night resolved to light. He had learned his trade under Hamidou Reis, admiral of the successful Algerian corsair fleet. Baba Hassan, Pasha of Algiers, had rewarded his loyalty and achievements with authority in his name. At two meters in height and 115 kilos, he towered over his shipmates. Bushy black hair stuck out from his turban, adding more size. A curly beard and the spark in his dark penetrating eyes left an indelible impression on those who met him. His intensity frightened many at a first encounter.

Hakim Sayoud, second in command, stood at his side and fixed his glass on a mysterious object to the northwest. A curious "clang" had alerted them. "Captain, there's a vessel sitting in the water with no sails set. That's strange."

Captain Madjer paused before commenting, sustaining his stare through his glass to the northwest. "Mister Sayoud, all sail, sheets hard aboard. We'll tack up to her. God willing, we'll close in short order. And call my son. Picking this swine's bones provides a perfect learning opportunity."

▪ ▪ ▪ ▪ ▪

Bones cracked the door and spoke in a hushed tone. "There's now a slight twinge of light in the eastern sky, and she appears to have spotted us—just tacked to the north, close-hauled. Course there's no way she can sail directly toward us—we're straight upwind."

Captain Joe strode aft and looked up at Bones to reply. "Very well. Adjust speed on your judgment, but ride easy until I finish my briefing."

He swung to the crew. "So, let's set the watch." He passed around laminated schedules, then posted one next to the companionway.

"We'll do four-hour watches with the change at eight bells. We'll keep two men on Prime watch and two on Backup. Prime means either on deck or in the wheelhouse. You must be immediately available to handle anything needed. Backup means on-call to the deck at a moment's notice.

Otherwise, Backups may remain at rest. Stay on deck, sit in the wheelhouse, read, play video games, movies—whatever.

	Start	Finish	Start	Finish	Start	Finish
Hours	**2401**	**0400**	**0401**	**0800**	**0801**	**1200**
Officer	Captain		Bones		Berg	
Prime	Sails		Gunn		Masters	
Prime	Decker		Chief		Handy	
Backup		Gunn		Masters		Sails
Backup		Chief		Handy		Decker
Sleep	Berg		Captain		Bones	
Sleep	Masters		Sails		Chief	
Sleep	Handy		Decker		Gunny	
Hours	**1201**	**1600**	**1601**	**2000**	**2001**	**2400**
Officer	Captain		Bones		Berg	
Prime	Sails		Gunn		Masters	
Prime	Decker		Chief		Handy	
Backup		Gunn		Masters		Sails
Backup		Chief		Handy		Decker
Sleep	Berg		Captain		Bones	
Sleep	Masters		Sails		Chief	
Sleep	Handy		Decker		Gunny	

"But you must be instantly available if the officer of the watch calls 'Backups on deck.' The men on Backup move to Prime in the next four-hour period. I don't want you to jump out of bed to go on Prime. Mister Bones is now Officer of the Deck, and Mister Gunn and Mister Chief are Primes."

The Captain pointed at Gunny and Chief. "Grab your jackets, a hat, and be ready to go. Mister Masters, Mister Handy, you're Backup, now until 0800. Check the schedule for your assignment. If you head on deck, wear your jacket, you got that?" He looked at each person to be sure they got it.

"Now, if someone yells 'all-hands-on-deck,' I expect all hands except the galley staff unless explicitly included in the call."

Bones opened the cabin door. “Primes on deck, please. Captain, she's hoisted everything she has and is bearing forty-five degrees to the wind, tacking toward us. With no sails set, I'll bet we appear disabled. I think she intends to assault us.”

10
EVIDENCE

February 25 - Juneau

The snow had turned to drizzle. Frank smushed through the slop down Gold Street in Juneau's early morning gray. The hiss of traffic through the slush and the drip, drip of melting snow filled the air. To Frank, Juneau did not have the feel of a state capitol—more like a lost city clinging perilously to a tiny piece of land between the moody mountains and a black sea.

In his office on North Franklin, he removed his rubber boots and put on his law office shoes. Shackleton and Bayer's weekly staff meeting would begin in fifteen minutes. Frank knew he was up first. Jason's case was at the top of the list.

"Mister Atherton," Frank's secretary extended a file folder as he headed toward the conference room, "here are the papers you requested."

Maurice Shackleton, the managing partner of Shackleton and Bayer, closed the conference room door. That signaled the beginning of his weekly staff meeting. "Okay, Frank, what's the status of your cases?"

Frank straightened his stack of papers and lifted his head. "Well, we have moved the Jason Oliver case up on the docket. Jason made a drawing of his cabin, showing the floor plan and a cross-section. I couldn't use it as evidence because it also shows the dope. However, it did purport to show the police could not observe the weed from outside the dwelling. If they could not view it from his porch, game over—they had no right to enter. If the police observe a suspicious substance, that constitutes a reasonable justification for obtaining a search warrant, not entry without it. I have an excellent chance of prevailing and keeping the evidence suppressed. I might meet with the D.A. to discuss this sketch informally."

Maurice raised an eyebrow and dipped his head. "Sounds risky."

"Jason claims they once both smoked pot in the same room at a private party. The District Attorney wants a conviction on his record and to show support for the police, but he has an honest interest in justice and the larger constitutional issue. I don't have a copy of his sketch. I will reach out to Mister Oliver for a duplicate and arrange a meeting, perhaps early next week, to discuss the situation."

"He's still in Sitka?"

"Yes, I think so. I told him not to leave Southeast Alaska with his case pending. I think he'll appreciate his proceeding has moved forward."

"Okay. On the one hand, I'm skeptical of the public relations value equaling the cost for most pro-bono cases. On the other hand, a successful argument before the Supreme Court enhances our reputation with the paying clients. Give it your best shot, Frank. What else is on your sheet?"

▪ ▪ ▪ ▪ ▪

Frank spoke to his secretary on the way to his office. "Shannon, get me Jason on the phone, please."

A few minutes later, Shannon switched on the intercom. "Mister Atherton, I didn't reach Jason, but I left a message."

"Damn. I need to talk to him. I'll try his contacts. Get me his buddy's number—what's his name—Al Pax something."

▪ ▪ ▪ ▪ ▪

Al sat alone at his galley table reading *National Fisherman*, warming the engine when his phone rang. He looked at the display. *907 Area Code—don't recognize number.* He answered, "Al Paxton."

"Hi, Al. I'm Frank Atherton, Jason's attorney. Can you talk for a minute?"

Al replied tentatively. "Good morning, Mister Atherton. Sure, what's up?"

"Do you know where Jason is? I left a message on his phone and need to speak to him right away. I expect he's around somewhere. I advised him not to leave Southeast."

"Gosh, I don't. If I see Jason, I'll ask him to call you. Is it urgent?"

"Ah... well... yes, it IS urgent. Maybe I'll try his girlfriend—what's her name? Loren Roberts? Did I get that right?"

"Yeah, uh, I think Jason and Loren split up, and she left for Anchorage."

"Well, I want to try. Do you have her cell number?"

"Ah, no, sorry, I don't." Al flushed at the lie.

"That's okay. I have it somewhere in his file. If you hear from Jason, please tell him it's important he calls me."

▪ ▪ ▪ ▪ ▪

Alaska Flight 62 arrived in Sitka. Loren viewed a cold dull rain falling on the drab slush with a smile. Low gray clouds enveloped the town, hiding the mountain tops. The dreary scene differed from her mood, awaiting her baggage and Eluk. The rain turned to snow, but she was home.

She lit up her iPhone and called Yashee. "Hey."

"Yak'éi yagiyee, Loren."

"And a pleasant day to you, Yashee. Well, I'm back. Can you pick me and Eluk up at the airport?"

"Uh, yeah, sure. I'll be there in twenty minutes."

Loren opened the door of Yashee's truck and grinned. Yahsee's bright smile and gushing exuberance contrasted with the slate-colored day. Her shiny teeth gleamed. Her long black hair tumbled out of her old red Sitka Sound Seafood hat. She radiated. Her halibut jacket hung open, revealing the figure of a healthy Tlingit woman.

"Welcome back, Loren. That didn't take long."

"Yeah, it's good to be home."

Eluk peed and jumped into the bed of the old pickup. On the way to the P-Bar, Loren studied the mountain slope, permeating wetness, and enclosed laden sky. "You know, Sitka's a gem—rarely appreciated. Didn't know I'd miss it so much."

Yashee found a parking space across the street. There were no tourists.

Rita greeted them with a warm smile. She had a knack for tracking the undercurrents of comings and goings while balancing congeniality and the bar's interests. She would never unduly interfere in the personal lives of P-Bar patrons. But sharing the knowledge with Al that Loren left town with Bud seemed appropriate.

"Hi, Yashee. Hey, Loren, you back in town?" She noticed the bruise on Loren's face—not well hidden with makeup.

"Hi, Rita. Yeah, glad to be here."

Loren and Yashee slid into a window booth. "Guess Sitka has become part of who I am. The snugness of this ol' bar, the cars splashing on the street," she patted the seat, "even this old duct-taped vinyl seems somehow chic in this context. Look," she waved a hand at the guys at the bar, "the jackets, hoodies, and the stale smell of smoke don't change, do they? I guess these old boat pictures and big brass bell are now a part of my soul."

Yashee put her hands on the table and read Loren's face. "So, ol' Bud didn't work out, huh?"

"Nope, just another drunken asshole in a long line of drunken assholes. People often aren't what they claim."

"I never saw Jason drunk." Yashee mused, then looked down and away.

"Yeah, liquor wasn't his thing. Stoned, but not drunk. And never violent toward me." She reached across to Yashee's hand. "I miss that man."

"Yeah, he's unique in this town. What's with you and younger men?"

Loren gazed out the window. *Warm embrace—shape of his ass....* "I don't know."

"Where you gonna live? I spoze you can't go back to his digs."

"I've no idea. I need somewhere to stay until I find a permanent place, and I'll need a job."

Al strode into the P-Bar with a concerned expression on his face. Tufts of white hair protruded from the old Greek fisherman's cap, and his white beard needed a trim. His oil-stained Carhartt jacket fit right in.

He spotted the gals, slid into their booth, and saw the injury on Loren's face. "Jesus, Loren, what happened?"

"I screwed up, Al. So what else's new?"

"You heard from Jason?"

"Yeah, he called me from Seattle. Our call lasted sixty seconds. He said he'd return in a week or two."

"Did he mention what he is doing?"

"No. We exchanged jibes on values before I had to go. Why?"

"Hmm. Listen, it might be important that few people know he's out o' town. I got a call from his attorney who's lookin' for him and learned he advised Jason not to leave. Please, don't mention to anyone that Jason's not around. His attorney may try to call you. If he does, and you care for him, you know nothing, okay?"

"Yeah, okay. What's this about, Al? What's he doing in Seattle—working on another dope deal?"

"No, no, nothing like that—nothing illegal. But I'm afraid I may have contributed to leading him astray. If anyone in town asks, you don't know where he is, okay?"

"Yeah. Okay. Hey, Al, I just got back to Sitka, and I need a place to stay. Do you know where I could crash until I find a decent crib? Can't go back to Jason's."

"Eluk with you?"

"Yeah, he's in Yahsee's truck."

"I'll take Eluk home with me, and you stay on the boat, okay?"

"Yeah, great. Thanks, Al."

Loren's cell rang. The ID read "Shackleton and Bayer."

11
ASSAILED

February 25, 1798 - West of the Strait of Gibraltar

All hands, including Cookie and Stew, donned their jackets and climbed topside. To leeward loomed a tall ship, barely perceptible in the morning light, close-hauled, sheer strake awash on the starboard tack. She had turned west, to tack northwest toward *Serendipity*. The best she could lie was forty-five degrees on the wind.

Berg suppressed a grin, braced against the stern rail. Bones remained stoic, concentrating on the helm. Captain Joe stood next to the pilothouse, assessing the situation. He followed the ship through the night vision binoculars—then switched to the Steiners. Tall and erect, his slender build and captain's peaked hat evoked a distinguished visage, even in the dim light. Everyone waited for him to speak.

"We're out of range for anything she's likely to carry. Probably too light for anything over a six-pounder, yet she might have a long brass six chaser. If well handled, such a cannon might find us, ah, how shall I describe it,... structurally embarrassed. She probably has nothing over a four-pounder along her sides, and she'd have to turn to give us a broadside, anyway. But, beyond 1,500 yards, we're safe."

"A six-pound gun can hurt us?" Handy's inflection showed doubt.

"Well," Captain Joe intoned, lowering his field glasses and turning toward Handy, "it's called a six-pounder because the cannonball it shoots weighs six pounds. When you consider the ball is three and a half inches in diameter and comes at you at over 1,200 feet per second from a six-foot barrel—yeah, it can hurt us. Large naval guns can throw a forty-two-pound ball a good mile. I don't figure to get too near one of them bogeys."

■ ■ ■ ■ ■

The xebec crew came alive and cleared for action. They sent everything loose below, then doubled the sheets and halyards. The boarding party crouched 'tween decks, out of the way of the sailors managing the ship. There they loaded fresh powder in their pistols and refreshed the edges on their axes and swords.

Captain Madjer grasped a shroud and listened to his vessel. The grunts of the crew performing their tasks and the vessel's creaks whispered in his ear. He sensed the stress on his boat as if it were on him.

He turned to his lean son, wide-eyed by the excitement of a voyage with his father. It was an opportunity to teach the trade and how to wield power and authority. He pointed toward the maintop. "That's a suitable spot to observe the impending action. Stand there."

He resumed staring at the strange vessel through his telescope, then addressed his second in command, "You may try the chaser, Mister Sayoud. I doubt she's in range, but her captain may prefer a safe capture rather than the inevitable deaths in battle. She's not large."

■ ■ ■ ■ ■

Serendipity's crew beheld an explosive flash against the dark southeastern sky from the xebec's foredeck, followed by "BOOM!"

The corsair's shot, well-timed with the vessel's pitch, missed astern, and fell 100 yards short with a hissing splash.

"Mister Bones, a little more throttle, please. Don't let her get any closer."

"More throttle, aye." Bones, confident in his control at the helm, used an arm movement to tap the throttle lever with his palm to increase the rpm. The engine labored for an instant and died.

Captain Joe turned to Bones. "What?"

Bones shrugged, his hands turned upward, eyes wide with alarm. "I dunno. It just died." The tachometer read zero. He cast around, trying to imagine what caused the engine to quit, then glanced to the southeast in the predawn light. The corsair was gaining.

The Captain turned to find Chief.

Chief headed below. “Shit!” He mumbled to himself. *Filter change—line air.* He glanced at Bones before disappearing in a rush. “Don't put 'er in gear till I tell ya.”

The Captain spoke in a commanding tone, “Mister Sails, prepare to hoist and to get us underway on the port tack. Mister Bones, keep us into the wind while we have way on.”

Sails turned to the crew and pointed. “Mister Masters, Mister Berg, the mains'l if you please. Mister Handy, the fores'l.” He indicated the foresail halyard. “Mister Decker, the stays'l. Leave the yankee furled. I will handle the jibs. If you have questions, sing out. Look lively now.”

They had to loosen the well-tied sails before hoisting, but the crew hopped to it. The mainsail raised with no difficulty, but when Handy raised the foresail, the halyard shackle came loose. The sail dropped. Handy grabbed the sail's head and stared at the hardware in his hand. The halyard streamed aft in the wind.

Jason grasped what happened. He cleated the staysail halyard, leaped on the automatic weapons cover, grabbed the dangling foresail line, and landed on deck.

Handy unhanked the shackle from the foresail head and handed it to Jason.

Jason tied a halyard bend to the shackle and gave it to Handy.

Handy clipped it on and hoisted the foresail.

Sails nodded toward Jason. “Marvelous piece of work.” He exchanged a look and a bob with Masters and Gunny.

They stared at the corsair. It had gotten closer, but *Serendipity* was drawing well on the port tack. The raider tacked north to follow but could not lie as close to the wind.

▪ ▪ ▪ ▪ ▪

Chief flung open the Freeman watertight door, flipped on the lights, and jumped down the stairs to the engine room. The polished diamond plate deck helped make the room bright. He removed his jacket, stuffed it into the space between the stair treads, and turned to tackle the problem. *Warmth feels good.*

He closed the main fuel valve, placed absorbent pads, and opened the filter air bleed plug closest to the fuel tank. The smell of diesel fuel was an old pal. He reopened the fuel valve and pumped the priming lever until there were no more bubbles.

"Boom!" Another cannon shot reverberated through the hull.

Getin' closer. Focus. He repeated the process for the secondary filter, fuel pump, lines to the injectors and tried the engine. It started but burped and belched. He shut it off and began bleeding the injection lines, adjusting to a sudden starboard list. Water gurgled along the hull. *Under sail. Good.*

He used two wrenches to keep from twisting the steel tubes, loosened each injector line on half the cylinders one turn, and cranked the engine. It popped. He tightened the injector lock nuts one at a time. In a few seconds, the air in the remaining injectors bled out. The engine returned to its low purr. He tightened the other nuts and then called the bridge on the intercom, "Okay, put 'er in gear."

He put the fuel pads and cleaning rag in the red container marked Oily Rags, grabbed his jacket, headed topside, and closed the watertight door.

▪ ▪ ▪ ▪ ▪

Bones re-engaged the propeller shaft. The helm responded.

"Mister Bones, put us into the breeze, dead slow—steerage only. Mister Gunn, let's get the grenade launcher. It's the best choice if it becomes necessary to take out that son-of-a-bitch. We'll set up for a shot port side and come about to fire."

Gunny eyed Captain Joe. "Yes, sir. I will need help with the gear. Mister Handy and Mister Masters, okay?"

Captain Joe nodded at both men.

Gunny turned and addressed them. "Follow me."

Sails and Jason cleated the sheets amidships, but the sails flagged loudly.

They checked the other ship. It turned north, on the port tack.

Captain Joe led Gunny, Handy, and Masters below to the weapons storeroom with keys in hand. Passing through the pilothouse, he switched on all the below deck night-lights.

Masters saw Handy wince. Jerky movements and quick grunts made his agitation clear. “Mister Handy, a moment, please.” He pointed to Handy's cabin and ducked in. Handy followed.

“Hey, take it easy. The situation's under control. Take a deep breath and grab your binoculars. Everything will be all right, okay?”

Handy took a breath and collected himself. “Yeah, okay.” He grabbed his binoculars and a can of Copenhagen. “Cap'n's right about one thing. This cruise IS sump'm different.”

▪ ▪ ▪ ▪ ▪

Captain Joe entered the weapons room and unlocked the Mk 19 grenade launcher. “Mister Gunn, you got this?”

Masters and Handy joined them in the room.

Gunny looked at the gun and his help. “Yeah, we got this.”

Captain Joe headed topside.

▪ ▪ ▪ ▪ ▪

The Xebec officers studied their quarry through their telescopes. First Officer Sayoud snarled, “Light! They're showing a light!”

“Yes, I see it.” Captain Madjer answered in an even tone. “He's one dumb son of a whore—probably desperate. But,… is it only my impression, or is he moving straight into the wind?”

▪ ▪ ▪ ▪ ▪

Captain Joe spoke to no one in particular. “Gentlemen, I suggest you grab your binocs. This incident may prove interesting. And when below, dog the bulkhead doors.”

Jason, Sails, and Chief bounced below to grab their glasses. After emerging from their cabins, they understood they were alone and faced each other in the salon.

Jason eyeballed both men and grumbled, "I guess we're all mercenaries now. Cap'n's got us by the short hairs."

Sails placed his binocular strap around his neck. His low baritone resonated, "Go easy—it is cock-up all right, but well-planned. Except for getting back, we are under control."

Chief grabbed a handhold when a more substantial wave bumped their bow. "Well, at least I didn't sell out cheap."

Jason and Sails nodded and followed him topside.

Cookie's eyes widened at Stew in a forward corner of the pilothouse. His pink face turned ashen.

Stew recognized Cookie's concern, stopped wiping a cup, and spoke low on an in-breath, "We're gonna be all right, ain't we Lance?"

In a blink, Cookie comprehended his responsibility and collected his composure. "Oh, yeah. I'm sure Captain Joe's prepared us for anything. All we have to do is keep the meals coming and let the guys handle it. We must serve breakfast soon. Remember," pointing for emphasis, "we don't let the owner's hobbies interfere with our duties. And please," checking no one noticed, "don't let anyone hear you use my actual name. Call me Mister Cook or Cookie. I want to leave this affair behind once we get home and disappear into the usual yacht set."

Jason and Sails emerged from the cabin and followed Chief forward but stopped next to the launch's bow to have a few words. They exchanged a grimace of comprehension—no way out. They must continue to return home.

Sails groused in his full-throated British manner, "Well, mate, I expected something unusual, but I am gobsmacked at this state of affairs. Perhaps Mister Rode had it right—we WILL need good luck to get our arses out of this jam."

"Umm." Jason nodded with a low grunt.

Chief turned to make eye contact with Sails and Jason. Signaling to have listened with a nod, he returned to his glasses without comment.

▪ ▪ ▪ ▪ ▪

Handy and Masters' eyes expanded, and their pulses quickened at the array of munitions. Sidearms, M4s, support gear, and crates of other ordnance gleamed in the amber light. Gunny instructed them on removing the grenade launcher from its cradle and opened the magazine for ammunition. Pointing to the ammo can, he left them to it and ascended the midship companionway. The hatch was near the weapons cowling.

"Mister Gunn," Chief stood with his left hand grasping the top of the whaleboat stem, "you got the wherewithal to take out the heathen Moor?"

Gunny spoke, moving the cowling aside. "Cap'n says so, an' the gun don't jam, I'm gonna rack me up some rag-heads."

Handy and Masters hefted the 80-pound launcher to Gunny through the hatch and followed with the ammo can. Handy, with illumination from well-placed night lights, helped place it on the stand. Gunny positioned himself behind the gun, secured the ammo can, and fed the belt with quick, expert movements. He set airburst fuses for the first two rounds at 1,500 yards, pulled the slide, pressed the butterfly trigger, and yanked the slide again.

Gunny turned toward the Captain. "I'm ready. You tell me, I'll send those cocksuckin' camel jockeys to their fuckin' virgins in pieces."

Captain Joe acknowledged the comment with a nod, appalled at the boorish racism, but refrained from checking the impulse. "Mister Bones, bring our port beam to bear."

"Yes, sir. Ready about." Bones turned west. "Helm's alee."

Jason cringed at Gunny's comment and lowered his glass to exchange a pained expression with Sails. *'Nother fuckin' racist.* His stomach churned.... *get back? Al and I duped. Ah, Loren....*

As they fell off, the sails filled with a pop. *Serendipity's* pitch frequency decreased, and the wind on her sails steadied their roll. A flare of fire, the cannon's report, and a visible splash—reality emerged.

Captain Joe repositioned himself behind the gun at Gunny's left side. "Mister Gunn, I'd prefer not engaging until we've acclimated ourselves to our time-travel situation." Nodding in the corsair's direction, "It would be nice if yon Captain and I could ignore each other. But it isn't practical to lose the bugger by sailing away in the dawn, and I don't want him to dog us on our brief adventure. Capturing people is how he survives. I'd hate enslavement. So, let's try shots behind and ahead to discourage an attack. Perhaps I can coax him into trying easier prey. Fire when ready."

Serendipity swung, giving a clear shot to leeward. Even with pressure on the sails, *Serendipity* rolled in the moderate waves. But the ship's sway was steady as the waves passed beneath them.

Gunny, timing the pitch and roll, pressed off a round. Nothing happened.

"Shit." He jacked in another round, waited for his chance, and pressed the trigger again. Nothing. He glanced at the ammo can and noted the seal was missing. He kicked the box. Water sloshed. He looked at the corsair. It was getting closer.

"Mother-fuck! Handy, get me another ammo can right fuckin' now."

Handy bounded below. He grabbed another canister and took it to Gunny, who checked the seal—intact. He opened the can—dry. He set the fuses and loaded the belt, yanked the slide, pressed the trigger, and pulled the slide again. Ready to fire, he timed the pitch and roll, pressed off one round, waited for a wave to pass, and triggered a second.

The smoke of the grenade's arc disappeared into the darkness. The first explosion discharged behind the xebec and caused no damage. The second grenade detonated in front, also causing no harm. *Serendipity's* crew viewed the Corsair through their binoculars, waiting for her reaction.

■ ■ ■ ■ ■

"BLAM!" An orange-yellow flash of roiling fire burst in the sky above the water behind the Muslim ship. The sailors turned their heads to view an explosive flash astern, followed almost instantly by the concussion. Still staring aft, a second blast detonated ahead. The fiery eruption illuminated the deck, a stark contrast to the dark western sky. They turned forward then at each other. Their ears rang—the only effect—no further damage. A cheer rang out.

Captain Madjer grinned. "Praise Allahu. She's armed, whatever she is, but couldn't hit a lake from the dock. Bring us alongside, Mister Sayoud."

■ ■ ■ ■ ■

Captain Joe was grim. "Mister Gunn, let's do that again. Perhaps a second demonstration will change his mind."

"Goddamn cock-sucker." Gunny concentrated on the motions, distance, and bearing of the two vessels. He sent two more rounds with the same precision. The shots curved away into the southeastern predawn light.

■ ■ ■ ■ ■

The second set of flash-bangs did not startle the Barbary crew. They regarded the shrapnel splash as harmless fireworks. Another cheer rang out, "Allahu Akbar."

■ ■ ■ ■ ■

Serendipity's crew continued to study the xebec, hoping it would turn away. She did not. Her officers, on the foredeck and poop, kept their telescopes pointing at them, unmoved.

Captain Joe lowered his glasses, continuing to fix his stare on the Corsair. "Damn! You'd think such a demonstration would deter her. Well, fuck this shit. We can't afford damage by a desperate raghead's lucky shot. If he believes his options are to take us or die, let's give him death. Mister Gunn, send them to Allah."

Gunny exchanged a nod of understanding with the Captain and switched his attention to the corsair. He reset the fuses for impact ignition on eight rounds. Timed with a wave, he took careful aim and squeezed off four quick shots. As the roller passed, he lobbed four more.

The grenades blanketed the xebec with blasts and enveloped it in flame. One hit the foredeck ahead of the mast. The entire bow exploded in a blinding blaze of splintered wood. Another hit amidships and blew the boat apart. Fragments of flaming wood flew into the air, and the masts rolled sideways in different directions. Debris rained and splashed into the water. Her spine broken, she split in half and sunk fast, leaving the wounded struggling in the water. Their cries were just audible in the distance.

Jason stared wide-eyed through his binoculars. "Jesus, fucking Christ! Captain, will we save those men?"

"No. Sorry, Mister Decker. We don't have accommodations for prisoners. We can't have our existence known to the Barbary Coast without creating all kinds o' mean, nasty, ugly things, and it won't matter, anyway. Besides, what do you think your fate would have been if one of those cannonballs had smashed us, and we became prisoners? 1798 may be an exciting place to visit, but I don't want to live here. Killing them was an act of self-defense. They got what was coming."

Jason continued to peer through his binoculars. "How many do you suppose there are?"

"Oh, I don't know—quite a few, probably. Their boats are typically over-maned to overwhelm their prey. They can do that when they are near a port. At least that's their standard modus operandi. That guy won't be enslaving any more Americans or report our existence to any other Ottoman corsairs.

"Mister Bones, have the crew hand the black sails, bend the white working sails, and install the white markings. And add the fake gunports and open the deadlights. Mister Gunn, secure the launcher with Mister Masters and Mister Handy's help, then return to the deck. I'll address everybody with additional details on our current situation. Oh, and move the Alaska flag to the stern flagpole and run up the stars and stripes from bin fifteen."

The American Flag in 1798 – 15 stripes and 15 stars

Bones turned and pointed to Chief, Jason, and Sails. "Okay, let's git-er-dun."

The sun peeped over the eastern horizon, making the occasional spray sparkle and turning the sea from gray to deep green. The galley staff went below with grim faces. The crew performed their tasks in silence. Bones turned her into a freshening breeze, making the foredeck pitch. The team unhanked the black sails, stuffed them into their bags, and packed them into the sail locker. Then they bent the white working sails to the masts, booms, and stays, and ran the American flag from 1798 to the main truck.

Gunny, Masters, and Handy removed the grenade launcher and disappeared below. Their tasks completed, they returned topside to view the deck crew at work, knowing they might have to accomplish a similar sail change at night in a storm. Handy's movements were jerky and indecisive. He took the can of Copenhagen from his pocket, cut the seal, and took a dip. Chief scanned the wreckage through his binoculars with pursed lips.

With the sails hoisted and sheets started for a broad reach on a port tack, *Serendipity* headed east toward the Strait. The boat rode with a gentle undulation and a slight starboard list, heading away from the carnage she had wrought. Under Berg's direction, the topside crew installed the white sheer stripes and white spar end socks. Then they removed white rectangles with large black circles from the deck box.

"What the hell are these?" Masters inquired.

Berg took one, pointed to a pre-mark on the hull, and put it in place. "From a distance, they'll look like gunports. You'll find pre-marks on both sides. Let's appear to be able to defend ourselves, okay?"

Bones shut down the main.

Serendipity transformed into a living thing, prancing on the rolling waves of a quartering sea. The crew's attention switched from the recent crisis to the bright orb in the east. The sunrise was turning from orange to yellow. The wind increased to a moderate breeze, and the waves became longer with intermittent white horses. The sails were taut.

The crew spread out along the high side of the cabin. Captain Joe stood aft with Berg, behind Bones, to address the hands. Even with the wind freshening, everyone could hear the Captain's booming voice.

Jason took a comfortable spot on deck along the windward rail. He stared at his hands, contemplated his position, and said to no one in particular, "Shit. Guess we will earn every bit of our money."

Jason and Sails exchanged a look.

Sails leaned toward Jason, "What is with this 'all kinds o' mean, nasty, ugly things?'"

Jason slanted toward Sails. "It's a quote from *Alice's Restaurant*, an old Arlo Guthrie tune. My dad used to listen to it over and over. The Captain must have an affinity for the '60s."

Jason turned to assess the rest of the crew. Berg, Bones, and Captain Joe showed no emotion mumbling together aft.

Captain Joe's gaze settled through the pilothouse to the companionway. "Mister Cook, when will breakfast be ready?"

Cookie popped into the Captain's line of sight. "I'll have breakfast ready in thirty minutes."

Joe nodded to Cookie, then turned his attention to the crew. "Okay, listen, we're all short on sleep. I'm afraid the jet-lag—in this case, time lag—will haunt us for a while. But it's in our best interests if you understand what's goin' on here—what could affect our getting back to Puget Sound in five days."

Bones interrupted. "Captain, there is a strong blip twenty miles to the east."

"What's her heading?"

"Due east—maybe six knots, I'd guess."

"Very well, Mister Bones. Head for the blip."

Gunny and Chief adjusted the sheets for a broader reach to the east and returned to their spots to windward. They could not yet discern the blip from the deck.

Cookie returned to the Captain's line of sight. "Captain, with the wind holding steady and nothing happening, may I feed everyone at one sitting?"

The fragrance of fresh crumpets and ham drifted from the galley.

Captain Joe checked the sails, tell-tails, weather, and crew. "Yeah, sure. If the wind doesn't change, we shouldn't need to touch a line for quite a spell. Gentlemen, let's adjourn to the cabin. I have a tale to tell."

12
ACCEPTANCE

February 25, 1798 - Heading East toward the Strait of Gibraltar

Bones stayed at the helm. Waves had increased to five feet. The crew gathered around the galley table. "dzzzit... dzzit." The salon continued to rotate. Captain Joe seated himself at the head of the aft table with Berg to his left. The rest of the team returned to their previous seats. A sad silence prevailed.

The smell of melted butter, eggs, Cajun spices, and fried meat filled the cabin. Galley sounds of clanking plates mingled with the rush of waves passing beneath the undulating boat. They headed east on the northwest breeze. Bright light streamed through the portholes.

Stew had installed fitted white tablecloths. Polished stainless-steel dinnerware glimmered in the warm cabin light. Each setting had a linen napkin rolled inside a woven rope ring. The coffee mugs were thick and pre-heated. A coffee carafe sat in the center of each table. Crystal glasses of fresh-squeezed orange juice and water stood by each place with practiced exactness.

Jason was unsure how to react to fine food while sailing away from cries for help and floating bodies. No one spoke.

A flight of hollandaise-covered eggs benedict appeared in front of each man—Black Forest ham, Sardou with creamed spinach and artichoke, and sautéed shrimp with a Cajun sauce.

Jason grabbed both sides of his plate and leaned over it to savor the fragrance. *Wow. Great food.* He peered at Cookie and around at his mates. Cookie and Stew continued their tasks without a smile. Captain Joe and Berg concentrated on eating. Stew took a serving to Bones with a refilled coffee mug. Chief folded his hands and bowed his head in prayer.

Jason stiffened. *Oh, great. Praying. Bet the guys we killed did the same thing. Didn't do them any good either.*

Masters noticed Handy fidget and the anguish on his face. He turned to Gunny. "So, Mister Gunn, it's been some time since I've seen such a weapon. A Mark 19, huh?"

Gunny's eyes lit. He held his fork suspended. "Yeah, a Mark 19 forty-millimeter grenade launcher designed by Naval Ordnance. Never used one from a rolling vessel before, but it's been effective in land operations where I kicked a lot of ass."

"Captain," Gunny crooked to his right, "I'm concerned with the dipshit who packaged and stowed the ammo. If we're gonna defend ourselves, the weapons gotta work, know what I mean?"

Captain Joe knitted his brow and nodded. "Point taken. Believe me, when we get back, I'll find out who was responsible."

Masters interjected, "Considering the variables, those were amazing shots." He grinned. "I saw a grenade launcher used once in the drug wars, but not from a boat at sea. Hard to beat for short-range animate and inanimate collateral damage."

Jason assessed his silent shipmates. Except for occasional grunts and eating noises, they were trying to merge the situation's shock and the concept of collateral damage. *Shit. Masters and Gunny look enthralled. Killin' doesn't bother them at all. Handy's freaked. Chief... can't tell. Sails... perturbed. Bad.*

Stew whisked away empty dishes and replaced the carafes with freshly brewed coffee. The crew quietly awaited Captain Joe's tale.

Captain Joe crossed his legs, stirred cream into his coffee, leaned back, and considered his men. *Return coordinates, my ace, still adequate.* He glanced at Berg. *Bought long ago. He's mine, whatever comes down. Lavish living—indiscretions—won't stray far from the well.* He turned his head to scrutinize Bones through the open door on the helm. *Occasional independence streak. Scruples, Ha! Self-esteem is the key. Play him like a vi-o-lin.*

Joe fixed his eyes on Gunny and suppressed a smile. *Confident, even cocky. Racist—moral flexibility. Good mercenary. Perfect fit. Finder deserves a chunk of cash.* He took a sip of coffee and considered Chief. *Jesus thing... hmm. Problem? He and Gunny... fit watch mates.*

Joe put his cup down and studied Masters and Handy. *Masters... glad to be at sea. Steady. Splendid match with Handy—supportive. Handy... young—out of his element—difficulty adjusting, probably malleable. Accent adventure—he'll go with the flow.* He stroked his chin and analyzed the body language between Sails and Decker. *Different. Intelligent, confident, leadership... hmm—valuable. Excellent team—afternoon watch—boarding party.*

Their broad reach with wave action on the stern port quarter continued the ship's gentle twisting roll—mitigated by the salon/galley's rotation. The crew, having eaten, relaxed a little, trying to adjust to the circumstance. Jason took out his can of Copenhagen and started cutting the seal with his knife.

Ding-ding, ding-ding, ding-ding, ding-ding: 0800 ship's time.

"Gentlemen," Captain Joe announced, "change the watch."

▪ ▪ ▪ ▪ ▪

Berg scooted from his seat and headed for the helm. He closed the deck door so he and Bones could have a confidential conversation.

Bones handed over the helm. "Steady as she goes. With the wind freshening, we'll be up to the target blip by mid-day."

"Roger." Berg took the wheel, checking the heading and sails trim—an easy broad reach to the east. "Oh, hey? We haven't talked since we arrived at the hanger. What are your thoughts on having missed our arrival longitude by two minutes?"

"Not much. The important thing is our departure coordinates." Doc removed his gloves and stuffed them into the pocket of his coat.

"Yeah, well, it means ship's time is wrong. I'd have to calculate the distance error. Two minutes of arc at 36° is a different distance than two minutes at the equator. Course GMT is always GMT. Has Joe shared the departure coordinates with you?" Berg spoke, checking the compass, radar, and depth sounder.

"Nope. Did he share 'em with you?"

"No, he hasn't. If anything happens to him, we can't get back."

"Yes, that is precisely the point."

Berg assessed the weather, then turned to Bones. "You buying this alternate reality thing?"

"Hey, man, I'm in. If he's right, he's right. If he's wrong, he's wrong. Whatever. I hope for the best, but we're all going to die of somethin' sometime."

"Hmm. Fairly fatalistic. I s'pose you're right, although I think it prudent to improve my chances if I can. Anyway, I'm in, too. Chief's a problem, but the others are okay. Get some rest."

"Before I go down, I gotta ask ya," Bones paused before opening the door to go below, "you heard anything about Joe ordering a hit on someone for infringing on one of his patents?"

"Ha! No. Joe may entertain such fantasizes, and I know he'd do it if he believed the situation warranted it and sleep like a baby. But I have a hard time imagining a circumstance rising to such a level. Nobody beats his legal team."

"Hmm. Okay. Heard... never mind. Just had a notion.... Have a wonderful watch." Bones proceeded below.

▪ ▪ ▪ ▪ ▪

Captain Joe kept on. "Mister Masters and Mister Handy," he pointed, "you two are Primes now but stay seated. Have another cup of coffee. I will enlarge our historical context. You must understand our current situation and appreciate life in these times. It would be a shame for you to come to 1798 and not dip a toe in the political waters where we swim."

Chief raised his head. "Fuck the political waters. I didn't sign-on for no killin', an' I ain't ready for ol' Davy Jones. Only wanna get back."

Captain Joe remained at ease. "Well, we're heading toward the rendezvous point now. You'll be home in a few days. You have no alternative, anyway, so get used to it."

"Yeah, well, I don't like it. I'll tell you what I'm used to—sleep. It's been a long day, and I'm on watch in less than four hours." Chief got up from the table. "Unless there's an emergency, don't disturb me." He headed down the corridor.

"Captain." Jason viewed his fellows then back at the Captain. "I'd love to dip my toe into the political waters where we swim. But I expect I speak for all of us," he opened his hands to the crew, "when I state that the most important issue at the moment is not the 1798 geopolitical situation. We just witnessed many people killed. We need to deal with that."

Sails, Masters, Handy, and Gunny turned to Jason and nodded in agreement.

"Okay," Captain Joe folded his hands, "look, THEY attacked us. What were we supposed to do? They'd follow us if we tried to run, and we must head into the Mediterranean to reach our rendezvous point. Once in the Med, they could link with the entire corsair fleet. Even with our superior firepower, we'd be at risk. While this expedition IS a grand adventure, I wanna get back too."

Jason pointed west. "Did you figure there'd be a Barbary pirate waiting for us when we dropped in from the twenty-first century?"

"I didn't know," Joe's demeanor turned defensive, "but I was aware of the possibility. I expect the best but prepare for the worst. You've got to admit time-travel is a hell of an experience. You're here, that's a fact. Aren't you curious about it?"

Jason lifted his head. "I am. I presume if you can get us here, you can get us back. These circumstances are so bizarre I'll even entertain your 'parallel universe' theory. We have no choice but to subscribe to this weird world, anyway. Yeah, it IS a hell of an adventure."

Sails smiled. "Yes, I agree with Mister Decker. It is a journey like no other."

Captain Joe leaned forward. "That blip twenty miles to the east might be a French or British man-o'-war, another raider, or a merchant attempting to get rich or die tryin'. Napoleon will depart Toulon, France, in three months with 40,000 troops and hundreds of ships to attack Egypt and threaten India—maybe push England into a peace deal."

Bones turned to the Captain. "I've heard this story, and I, too, need to rest before my next watch."

"Sure. No problem."

Bones left his cup and edged aft into his cabin.

Gunny watched him go and raised a hand. "I want to catch a bit of shut-eye, too. I'm due on Backup in four hours, and I'm more worried about an attack tomorrow than in the past. Know what I mean?" He rose from the table and strolled off.

■ ■ ■ ■ ■

"Tap-tap." Gunny knocked on Chief's door and looked to be sure no one noticed.

"Shit," Chief grumbled, having closed his eyes, and sunk into the rhythm of the boat. He rolled out, got up, and partially opened the door. His hand remained on the handle.

"Sorry," Gunny said, "I hoped we might exchange a few words before we sack out. May I come in?"

Chief peeked out and glanced aft to see everyone engaged in conversation. "Sure. C'mon in. Let's make it short."

Gunny slipped in and quietly closed the door. Light from the passageway filtered through the door's louvers.

"Chief, you gonna handle this okay? I mean, on the bizarre scale, we just popped off the chart."

"Yeah, sure, it's off the chart, but I recognize there's nothin' for it. Cap'n's right, we're stuck. Sorry about the engine glitch. I'll keep the mechanical systems operating, and you keep the bad guys at bay. Let's hope the Captain knows what-the-fuck he's doin' in gettin' us back. Chance favors the well-prepared. Best thing right now is rest—be ready for our watch."

"Yeah, I guess that's true." He observed Chief had calmed. "Okay, we're on call in four hours."

Gunny opened the door, observed no one paying attention, stepped out, closed the door, and glided along the darkened corridor to his cabin.

■ ■ ■ ■ ■

Joe picked up where he left off. "The British Admiralty is trying to figure out what-the-fuck Napoleon's doing. They are aware he is assembling a fleet in the south of France, but they don't have a clue of where he intends to go. They will dispatch Horatio Nelson in a month to join Old Jarvie, admiral of the fleet off Cadiz. Jarvis will send him with a small British squadron to recon Napoleon's intentions in Toulon."

"Who's Horatio Nelson?" Handy's voice rose a note.

Sails' jaw dropped. He turned to stare at Handy, raised his eyebrows, and dipped his head. "You do not know of Horatio Nelson? He commanded—wait, will command a fleet of twenty-seven ships of the line to defeat Napoleon's thirty-three French and Spanish ships in 1805. We call it the battle of Trafalgar. The French and Spanish lost twenty-two ships, and we lost none. That battle established British naval supremacy—seven years from now if this bloody bullshit time-travel thing is real—as, apparently, it is. Do you realize that Cape Trafalgar is a few miles northeast of here?"

"Oh." Handy's face was blank.

Captain Joe resumed, reveling in lecturing his inferiors. "Thirteen ships of the line will soon join the British Mediterranean fleet, but they lack recon frigates. The brass doesn't have any idea what the hell Napoleon's planning. So, I expect there'll be a lot of traffic through the Strait. Note that, on land, bulk freight moves by a team of oxen. Most cargo goes by sea in small boats—ain't no container ships.

"Try to imagine life if you are living onshore today," he pointed north toward the Spanish shore. "Night is dark unless you have many candles. If you're rich, you might have a whale-oil lamp. You believe vapors—whatever those are—cause diseases. You think bathing's unhealthy. Garbage, shit, dead animals, and trash of every kind lie abandoned in the streets to rot. Creeks and rivers are the sewers. Cities stink.

"Your heat is by coal or wood. City air is unhealthy to breathe. Ninety percent of people—most likely, you—work on a farm. Your life revolves around the seasons and sunlight. In summer, you work from sunup to sundown. In winter, you spend a lot of time sitting around getting drunk. You'll probably die at forty-something. The industrial revolution has scarcely started. Transportation on land is by foot, horse, or ox. Horseshit's everywhere. There ain't no trains."

Jason considered the ramifications of using his coffee cup for a spittoon.

Joe carried on, "So, here's the current political situation. The French Revolution has morphed into the Napoleonic Wars. In a strict sense, it wasn't just a French rebellion. France was at a confluence of historical forces. The industrial revolution had begun, which put pressure on the class structure. Reason displaced the dictated doctrine of the Church or whoever was king. The logic of science produced verifiable truths, and the value of reason rose. Reason became the source of authority and legitimacy. It replaced religious dogma. Napoleon harnessed these forces for his personal ends."

"Ah, the age of reason." Jason put in. "I regret the loss of reason based on verifiable truths. Religion and reason are at odds. It amazes me how so many people are proud of being unreasonable. Is it necessary to suspend critical thinking to have a moral ethic?"

"Well, we will not resolve the differences between religious faith and reason in our time any more than they did in theirs. And, damn, it was a violent time—populism run amok. The Revolution caused chaos throughout France. Armed masses attacked the entire system of ownership and distribution. They were killin' nuns an' priests an' women an' children an' doin' all kinds o' mean, nasty, ugly things. Known as The Terror, it lasted two years and killed 17,000 'enemies of the revolution.' One enthusiastic Jacobin filled floats with 1,500 men, women, and children in the Loire River, then scuttled the boats to watch them drown. Paris saw 2,700 executions on the guillotine. The people desperately needed something to restore order."

"Yeah," Jason declared, "I've noticed if people have food, clothing, shelter, and security, they'll tolerate the damnedest tyrants. If they lose those elements, they'll embrace anything to restore them."

Captain Joe smiled, "That's true. The French government failed to provide these things. Something had to change. Napoleon happened along at the right time to take advantage of the situation. He distinguished himself in a battle for the French Republic, so the elected Convention made him a Brigadier General, assigned to the army at the Italian border.

"Two-and-half years ago, in October 1795, Napoleon was in Paris. A royalist army—supporters of a monarchy—prepared to attack the seat of the Republic. Napoleon saw an opportunity for advancement and offered his services. They gave him the command. He defended the Directorate with artillery, killing over 300 Parisians in 45 minutes—and quelled the rebellion. The government made him Commander of the

Army of the Interior, then Commander-in-Chief of the Italian Army—that's the French army at the Italian border. He was 27 years old. That's where we are today."

Handy took his Copenhagen from his pocket and concentrated on twisting the cap off without spilling tobacco.

Sails twirled his finger inside the handle of his mug on the table. His mind was elsewhere. He grabbed the remote control, clicked to the menu, and changed the screen to Admiralty Chart 142. They were not yet this far east.

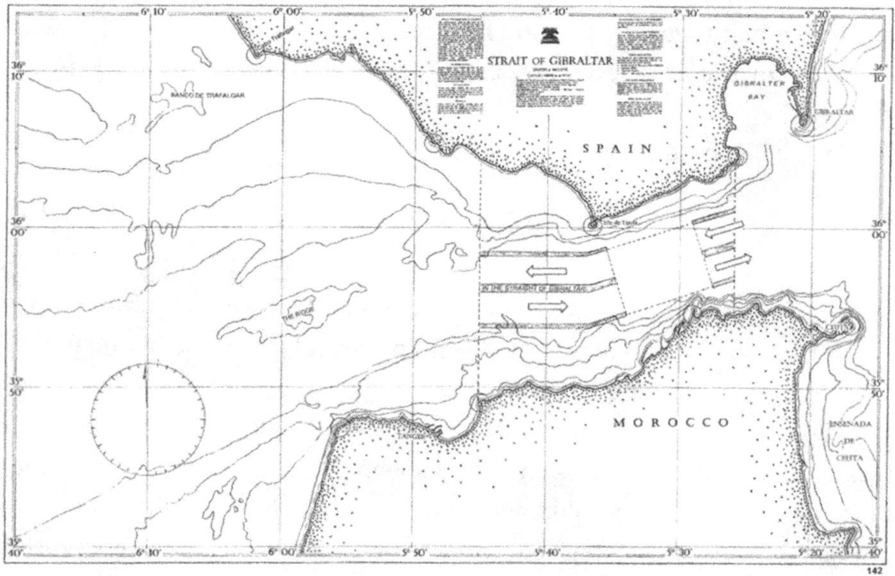

A high breaking wave gave Masters an opening. "Captain, I may be of use on deck."

"Yeah, okay." The Captain focused on Handy. "I suppose you want to go, too?"

Handy sensed a chance to escape. "Yes, sir."

Masters turned in his seat and put on his jacket. Handy followed Masters' lead.

▪ ▪ ▪ ▪ ▪

Masters and Handy, with a nod to Mr. Berg, made their way forward on deck, checking the sails and adjusting sheets. After a show of 'one hand for the ship,' they leaned against the launch's outboard bow where Berg could not see them. The rush of water along the hull and the wind in the rigging prevented overhearing.

"You okay, kid?" Masters sensed Handy was close to losing it.

"Yeah, I guess so." He gave Masters his full attention. "This job is more 'n I bargained for. I get we ain't got no choice but to make the best of it 'til we're back. Takes some gettin' used to." A twinkle appeared in his eye, along with a perceptible grin. "Truth is, my life was dull, and this scene is kick butt. But I do wanna get home."

"Affirmative. I don't think we are in any genuine danger, considering our tech advantage. The Captain has this under control. We need to work together for the next few days. Let's try to relax and keep cool. Can you do that?"

"Yeah, I can do that."

▪ ▪ ▪ ▪ ▪

Jason spit in his cup, trying to be inconspicuous. "Well, Captain, I got to agree this jaunt is an adventure like no other. If I get home in one piece, I can't imagine how I'll explain it."

"You can't. You tell this story, people will think you are a kook, and treat you like those who claim to have been abducted by little green men in flying saucers. And you'll have no proof it ever happened."

Sails' gaze suggested comprehension. He checked the weather through a porthole.

Cookie and Stew had only half listened while clearing the galley. Finished with their chores, they headed forward in the corridor without a word.

"Anyway," Captain Joe concluded, "I presumed you would appreciate what we might be up against if we encounter other vessels."

Jason and Sails exchanged shrugged shoulders, not sure what to do. There was an awkward silence.

Jason retreated into thought. *What I'll tell Al? I'll have no credibility. Shit. Loren didn't sound right. In trouble?* Masters and Handy broke his reverie, clambering below to grab their sunglasses.

As they passed through, Masters remarked, "There's a square-rigger ahead, hull-down, but we're gaining fast. She's headin' for the Strait with every rag hangin'. They are watching us from her maintop. The wind's freshened, and the sun's out. Y'all may want to come topside and check this out."

Jason and Sails jumped at the chance. They moved from the galley table to their cabins, grabbed their sunglasses, and headed on deck.

13
BUGS

February 25 - Seattle

"Ah-ooo-gah! Ah-ooo-gah!" The klaxon signaled from Jack Wilson's laptop in the G-WAD control room. He frowned and adjusted his dark-rimmed glasses. All trans-time engineering responsibilities were his. Captain Joe's Security Nazis had not spoken a word or even made eye contact, but they were always a cloud lurking in the corner. If anything went wrong, they would blame him.

Jack turned from his keyboard to his mobile computer stand. A mangled, unfiltered, unlit cigarette dangled from his lips. He started punching keys. The folds in his belly jiggled beneath his unzipped disposable coveralls. The tech room staff assembled around his office door. They wanted to be near enough to grasp what was happening but not close enough to affect his concentration.

Paul Gorken was first to speak. "What's goin' on, Jack?" Second in command, his tailored Tyvek suit conformed to his slender body, contrasting with his unkempt boss.

"Shit." Jack studied a computer screen of complex mathematical formulas—able to grasp the implications of the variables. "Ah, well,... I hacked into the Laser Interferometer Gravitational-Wave Observatory and established an account. I get a klaxon signal if an event threatens my gravity wave formula. It appears an incident has dislodged a gigantic muthafuckin' piece of shit, now zingin' through space at five million miles an hour."

"Gravity wave generator?" Paul leaned over Jack's shoulder to better view the computer screen, but not too close to his boss's greasy hair and foul odor.

"Yep, or at least the result of a wave-generating event."

Watching Jack tapping keys was like seeing splattering raindrops on dry pavement—too fast to follow.

Jack carried on, "The probable culprit is an intense gravity wave outside the predictability algorithm. Goddamn universe. Another fuckin' bug. What I know, compared to what I don't know, ain't much. Shit suckin' black holes and the immensity of potential interactions of so goddamn much mass is just too fuckin' hard to predict. Pisses me off."

The staff scrutinized Jack's monitor in silence. Screens and windows flashed in and out. The people turned to each other. They did not understand the intricate details of the physics, but they comprehended the stakes. All Ullage Enterprises personnel had accepted big money for high risk. With less than five percent of the universe's matter explained by modern physics, much could go wrong in tampering with mass-based time-travel. If the Captain and crew's retrieval failed for any reason, they would be outcasts in the industry, their reputations ruined, and the bonus money lost. Nothing had gone wrong during the gravity-wave time-travel experiments, and the technology had seemed a good bet. Now, not so much.

"Mass and energy are different configurations of the same goddamn thing," Jack mumbled. "They're transposable. But by using photons, which have no mass, I can line-up on the wave shoulder of an impending gravity wave at the exact spot necessary for a kick out at a predictable time and place. This puppy's prob'ly the collision recoil from two super bitchin' black muthafuckin' holes of dissimilar sizes. Such an event generates gravity waves like ripples in a pond. Somethin' dislodged this bad boy and sent it through space. Bad news—this fuckin' wave's a gnarly bomb. Good news—I can predict the wave interval and ride the son-of-bitch. Terrible news—the wave pattern may interfere with my 1798 set."

Paul Gorken furrowed his brow and stroked his goatee. "So,... can the system handle it?"

"I dunno. Give me a minute to run an analysis curve." His eyes narrowed to the screen, and he tuned everyone out.

▪ ▪ ▪ ▪ ▪

Gary and Pete, from Seattle City Light, surveyed the University substation. "You ever seen anything like this, Pete?" The rain had stopped, but they raised their collars against the wind. Gray steel columns supporting improbable gray apparatus and an overhead wire grid did nothing to ease the bleak day. A precast concrete fence encircled the crushed stone yard. A low-level hum infused the air, and the wet rocks crunched under their boots. Burn marks on the ground were the only visible evidence someone had tapped into the grid.

"I never heard of anything like this. It's the same as Canal." Pete spoke, looking around at the marks on the stones. "Whatever happened, they organized it well. No damage other than the burn marks—no sign of a break-in or cable connection. How on earth did they not leave any other evidence?" He raised his head, scanned the entire yard, and stroked his chin. "Gary, pull the map out of the truck. Let's look for a pattern."

"UFO, you think? An alien spacecraft needing a shot for refueling?" He got the map roll and handed it to Pete.

Pete ignored Gary's ridiculous theory. He wiped the truck hood with his sleeve and unrolled the power distribution map. He pulled a pen from his pocket and circled the two substations they had surveyed so far, University and Canal—north of the Seattle Ship Canal and west of I-5.

"Hmm," Pete spoke, intent on the map. "A major 'quickie' at the expense of the public. Someone around here wanted an enormous piece of power without paying for it. So, who, why, and how? Well, let's check the Vineland/Hoffman site. Maybe we'll find a clue somewhere."

▪ ▪ ▪ ▪ ▪

10:00 A.M. Seattle time.

"Ping." Doris's iPhone signaled a calendar event. She glanced at it, knowing it was time to perform the $100,000 transfers to each of the crew's accounts and payments to the crew facilitators. It only took a few seconds.

▪ ▪ ▪ ▪ ▪

Keith Larken, Power Supply Manager, whispered into Paul Gorken's ear, trying not to disturb Jack's concentration. "Paul, a nanny cam has alerted us to an SCL investigation team at one of our power tap sites."

Paul turned away from Jack and followed Keith to another computer. Keith tapped the keys. A black-and-white scene replayed SCL's investigation at the University transformer yard. Paul and Keith watched for several minutes.

The recording ended, and Keith stroked his chin. "It's clear they don't know shit. Their names are Pete and Gary. They've visited two sites so far."

Paul nodded. "Yeah, our boys did a superb job of covering their tracks. I presume our investigative unit has dossiers on both. Pull their files and tell me when they complete their survey of the last site—regardless of whether they find anything. I'll be in the control room somewhere."

The tech crew disbursed to their desks. Jack's actions were impossible to follow, and they did not want to interfere with his concentration. Any distraction might hinder a successful outcome.

An hour passed.

Jack's eyes lit. "Okay, here's the score." He assumed someone was listening. "After considering the earth's spin, tilt, wobble, orbit around our star, the sun's movement within the Milky Way, and our galaxy's trajectory relative to the expansion rate of the universe, I've calculated we have a 62.5% chance to get 'em back. Course, it would be nice to know the exact Hubble constant. I'm using a value of 67.5 kilometers per second per megaparsec, but hell, it could be 85.

"Anyway, our extraction window has narrowed. The gravity wave will cross our transmission in three dimensions, not including time, but after the extraction—if they're on time. They'd better be at the exact fuckin' coordinates at the exact fuckin' time I told 'em or face a brief life in a horsey world with no lights. And we'll need another shot of power from SCL. Paul, start the power tap protocol."

Someone on the engineering staff spoke in an undertone, "We have a three-in-eight chance of wiping out on a gravity wave."

14
ADRIFT

February 25, 1798 - Ninety miles north of Casablanca
The first concussion saved Captain Madjer by knocking him backward, over the stern rail of his Algerian corsair into the sea. He did not panic when he hit the chilly water, just kicked off his boots, dropped his sword, and made his way to the surface. He kept his knife and recovered his turban, a symbol of rank, and floated to spend little energy. Flames, crackling wood, and wounded men heaved on the dank sea in front of him against a bright dawn. A large broken spar floated within reach, and he pulled himself over and straddled it, trying to minimize his exposure to the sea. He yelled for his son several times, his deep voice unmistakable through the chaos of the wreck. He neither saw nor heard his son anywhere. Soon the screams of injured and panicked men faded to groaning and cries for help. He could do nothing except pray for guidance. Braham Madjer called to Allahu.

The sun lifted over the horizon. Captain Madjer rode the floating spar, dipping and rising on the building seas, and scanned the skyline. He would not forgive the loss of his son. The ruin of his ship was a scar to bear forever. Burning revenge kept him warm.

The sun continued its ascent. It reflected off a small lateen sail coming his way from the south. *Hmm. Probably out of Rabat or Casablanca.* He waved but did not waste energy yelling. Someone on the boat waved back. Sweeps appeared, and the boat's course altered.

Hoisted over the side, he straightened his body and adjusted his turban, trying to maintain his dignity. He towered over the fishermen of his salvation and nodded toward three of his sailors, also pulled from the sea.

"As-salāmu ʿalaykum." (Peace be upon you) Captain Madjer's voice was sharp.

"Waʿalaykumu as-salām," (and upon you, peace) responded the fisherman.

"Praise Allahu for our deliverance. I am Captain Braham Madjer, Vice Admiral of Alger. Captain, I shall see you rewarded for saving us, but I must commandeer your vessel." He twisted around—sizing up the fishermen and his rescued crew.

The captain of the fishing vessel, his hand on the hilt of the sword, regarded the fierce man standing before him.

The recovered crewmen, dripping and shivering, overheard their Captain. They came to attention and stood erect, exhibiting their obedience.

"Captain Madjer, my boat and crew are at your disposal."

"Good. Make it Tanger. And get us dry clothes, water, and food."

After several hours, Captain Madjer sighted a sleek square-rigged xebec coming out of Tanger. He smiled. It was perfect for a chase—new, light, sizeable sail area, and able to row.

"Captain, turn your flag upside down and head for that boat. And bring me a quill and paper. I will write two notes for delivery in Tanger. You are to carry them in my name to the Alger Vice Counsel immediately upon landing. The first is of utmost urgency. The second will arrange your reward."

Feb. 25

Vice Admiral Braham Madjer: Admiral Hamidou Reis. As-salāmu ʿalayka. Praise Allahu. Attacked by American schooner headed east. My vessel destroyed. Lethal weapons. Commandeered 20-gun square-rigged xebec. Suggest fleet convergence and attack at noon, approx. 2° E., 37-1/2° N. on Feb. 27.

B.M.

ض

Feb. 25

Vice Admiral Braham Madjer: Alger Vice Counsel, Tanger

As-salāmu ʿalayka. Praise Allahu. The bearer of this message saved me and some of my men. Please reward him.

B.M.

ض

He numbered the messages 1 and 2, then sealed them with wax and his signet ring.

▪ ▪ ▪ ▪ ▪

The square-rigger captain stared through his telescope at the turbaned man standing proudly on the bow of the approaching boat. He recognized Braham Madjer. "Mossli Krarzi, if that isn't trouble headed my way."

▪ ▪ ▪ ▪ ▪

The fisherman came alongside the xebec. Captain Madjer climbed aboard. He loomed over the sailors and spoke in his most resounding voice, "As-salāmu ʿalayka. Do you know who I am?"

The youthful xebec's captain responded, "Waʿalaykumu as-salām. Yes, sir. I encountered you in Tripoli and Alger."

"Good. I assume command in the name of Baba Hassan, Pasha of Algiers. Captain, head toward the Strait at maximum speed." He gestured toward the cabin. "And meet me in the cabin for a full accounting of ship's condition, armament, supplies, and the proficiency of your gun crews."

The captain's eyes flamed. Then he looked down and away. To question the power of Baba Hassan or the Vice-Admiral was too dangerous. He would acknowledge the authority of Braham Madjer and do as directed.

15 ASPIRATION

February 25, 1798 - Twenty-five miles South of Cadiz, Spain

"Ahhhh." Jason exhaled and smiled, stepping from the pilothouse to the deck. The swish of white-crested waves and salt spray still stirred his soul, even after all his time at sea. The clear weather and bright sunlight struck a pleasant note compared to the ponderous history lesson below. He examined the sails. *Drawing well.*

Sails checked aloft and considered the wind's strength and direction. "Mister Berg, we might set the gennaker to advantage."

Berg glanced aloft. The wind was steady. He nodded toward Masters, "Okay?"

Masters acknowledged the command with a wave, then dipped his head toward Handy. "Let's git-er-dun."

Eager to display their competence, they bounded below to the sail locker.

The square-rigger's gray sails ahead were easy to pick out through their binoculars in the morning sun. Jason saw she was not large and will soon be hull-up. He took a seat to port, leaning against the cabin outside the pilothouse.

Captain Joe stood aft of him. "So, Mister Decker, you regret the loss of reason, do you?"

Jason turned his head toward the Captain. "Yes, I do. In former times, when so much of how the universe works was unknown, it made sense to believe fantastic explanations for the unexplainable. But science—unlike faith—is not dogma, or at least shouldn't be. Data supporting a conclusion is logically actionable unless or until proved incorrect."

"You're talking about religion, I suppose."

"Of course. Suppression of religion may be reasonable, but it's untenable, as the French Revolution eventually discovered. People are weak. A religious crutch helps them be happy, or at least deal with their misery. Belief without evidence, though, is unreasonable.

"But I regret the loss. Once you discard reason in one sphere of life, it's easy to discard it in others. I mean, you either subscribe to reason, or you don't. If you do not, it's a small step to choose the data you want to ignore—such as human activity causes global warming. Avoiding inconvenient facts is not a viable survival strategy. There are no alternative facts. Along with regret for losing reason, I mourn the loss of consensus on what constitutes facts."

"Hmm." Captain Joe considered Jason's remark. "Why did you accept my offer?"

Jason focused on the distance. "Well, I wouldn't have done it without the money, but I must confess that I sensed a compelling adventure. It makes me feel alive. I worry, though, that seeking excitement gets me into jams I can't get out of—like this one."

"Ah, yes. Sounds familiar. You and I have similar tendencies. Jason, may I see your right hand?"

Jason raised his eyebrows, grasped the pilothouse rail with his left hand, and extended his right. "Sure. What for?"

Joe held Jason's hand flat, palm up, and considered his ring and index fingers' lengths. "Have you ever noticed your ring finger is longer than your index finger? A man whose ring finger is lengthier than his index finger is more likely to be a risk-taker." He released Jason's hand. "You and I both have the finger trait." He smiled at Jason. "What will you do with your money?"

Jason looked Joe in the eye, then gazed again at the horizon. "Well, I want to buy a fish boat. If I could make a good living in Sitka, I might get my girlfriend back. She left me while I was crabbin' in the Bering Sea."

"Yeah, I'm familiar with being left. Where would buy such a boat?"

"Dock Street Brokers in Ballard. They're the best."

"Umm." Captain Joe moved aft to stand behind Berg.

■ ■ ■ ■ ■

On the foredeck, the crew was ready to set the gennaker.

"Okay," Masters turned to Handy, "pop the chute."

The cruising spinnaker snapped open. The backstays tautened with an audible squeak. The power surge was immediate. Masters and Handy adjusted the sheets for maximum effect. The increased hiss of water along the hull lent urgency to the chase. The boat's motion on the quartering seas changed from a gentle undulation to a longer ride down the wave's backside.

Jason, at the stern, soaked in the scene along the curve of the teak deck. An occasional wave surged on the stern port quarter. Diffused sunlight glowed through the new white sails, and froth, bubbling on the backs of the seas, marched away toward the horizon. He took a deep breath. *Ah, motion under sail—harmony.*

The brig was now hull-up. A smart ship and beautiful to behold with all sails set high and low.

"Fast under the circumstances," offered Berg at the helm. "She must be close to six knots. With what's likely a foul bottom, them boys know their business."

"Yes," the Captain responded, studying them through his binoculars. "Seasoned sailors, no doubt."

■ ■ ■ ■ ■

"Holy Mother, what was that?" Captain Angus Allen spoke to his first mate, Laurence Chaderton.

They sat on the American merchant ship *Aspiration's* maintop, staring through their telescopes, studying *Serendipity*. The vessel gaining on them popped open a sail, unlike anything they had ever seen. Both men sported black, untrimmed beards. Their long-braided pigtails rocked with the ship. The bright white sails of their pursuer reflected the sun.

Aspiration was eight weeks out of the West Indies and low on supplies. They knew the most critical part of their journey lay ahead in the Mediterranean Sea. Barbary corsairs, the French navy, and a host of unsavory characters would love to relieve them of their valuable cargo and sailors: Barbary pirates for ransom; the British for seamen; the French for a war prize; and everyone else for the booty.

Captain Allen observed, "She is approaching too fast for us to outrun her even if we jettisoned everything—a most prodigious sailer. She must do two miles to our one. Thy eyes are younger than mine. Canst thou make her flag?"

A lengthy silence passed. First mate Laurence Chaderton concentrated on holding his glass steady. He waited for the flag to flap at an observable angle. "Bless my soul, Captain, I believe she's flying an American flag."

"Hmm," Captain Allen contemplated the situation. "Strange... possibly false colors to lessen our guard. We need to be ready. Run out the guns. Prepare to repel boarders."

They slid down a backstay to the quarterdeck.

▪ ▪ ▪ ▪ ▪

"What do you make of her, Captain?" Berg had his hands full at the helm.

The on-deck crew tensed and studied their quarry, waiting for Captain Joe to speak.

"She's a brig flying an American flag—dangerous for her in these waters. Must be a valuable cargo to be worth the risk. If she flew false colors, she'd pick a different flag. We'll view her hail port on her stern as we close." He lowered his binoculars.

"Okay, here's the drill. Remove and stow the fake gunports. We'll pull even on our port beam, out of cannon range, and send the launch over with supplies. I'll take the helm here. Mister Berg is in charge." He turned to Berg. "Mister Sails and Mister Decker will join you. Snap a pulley on the boathook, run a line through the sheave, stand it in the forward brackets, and run up a white flag. Take the handheld radios and keep in constant contact. Use the bullhorn to speak to her captain at a reasonable distance. Our goal is to establish amicable relations. I will issue sidearms and one extra magazine to the three of you. Please note your coverall's right leg pocket has a built-in holster and harness to transfer the weight of a forty-five to your coverall belt. Keep your weapons concealed. You are only to use them in dire self-defense. And I mean DIRE, d'ye hear me thar? I mean a life-threatening kind o' mean, nasty, ugly thing." The Captain considered Jason and Sails before continuing.

"If he just completed an Atlantic crossing, he'll appreciate fresh fruit, and he may be desperate for clean H_2O. You guys get to be Santa Claus. Load one tote each of apples and oranges. I want to strike a friendly tone, get close, equal his speed, and transfer fruit and water."

Captain Joe punched two buttons on the intercom. "Galley crew to the companionway, please."

Cookie and Stew stumbled from their comfortable beds and traveled to the companionway.

"Mister Cook, we will soon have an American merchantman on our beam. I want to encourage their friendship with a meal. I reckon she has a crew of, say, sixteen. What could you prepare for these guys?"

Cookie looked up to the pilothouse. "How long do I have?"

"At least ninety minutes. More likely, two hours."

Cookie turned and spoke to Stew, considering his larder. "I'm thinking of a box lunch… maybe thaw those bacon burgers in the microwave. We could whip up a potato salad and coleslaw in short order. We have lettuce, tomatoes, onions, pickles, buns, mustard—all the fixings. Let's make burgers and send them over in containers. We can make enough to cover lunch for us, too."

"Captain," Cookie answered up the companionway, "we can do that."

"Good. Make it happen."

▪ ▪ ▪ ▪ ▪

Captain Allen asked his first mate, "Laurence Chaderton, what dost thou make of this?" Relying on his number one's keen eyes to track the oncoming vessel, he checked the set of his sails and preparations for an attack. Cutlasses in their holders, muskets under the railing, boarding axes at the ready, and the cannon crews loading fresh powder. He nodded with a grunt.

Aspiration was now silent except for stretching cordage, squeaking timbers, and splashing sea.

First mate Chaderton followed *Serendipity* in his glass. "Captain, she's out of range but reducing sail and spilling wind to equal our speed. I detect no armament. Whatever she is, she's not a Corsair. She appears to be putting a launch in the water. Canst she intends to row over while we are under full sail? The launch dost not have a sail. Wait,... the mother ship has dropped her sails,... but continues to move at the same speed? I don't understand how that is possible. No one is rowing the boat,... now it is moving with no visible means of propulsion—a white flag hangs from a pole—on a heading for an intercept. There are only three men. Captain, the black hull dost not appear to have planks." He snapped his telescope closed. "Could be the Devil's work."

■ ■ ■ ■ ■

Berg spoke into his handheld radio. click "Captain, she is *Aspiration* out of Boston." click click "Roger. Once you hail him, leave one radio in transmit mode so I can follow the conversation." click click "Copy that." click "Mister Sails, that's your job. Keep a transmission channel open so the Captain can hear. And your British accent may cause alarm, so, please, stay out of the conversation unless you can't avoid it."

"Okay." Sails checked his radio. click "Radio check. You got me, okay?" click

Captain Joe clicked back, "Got you, five by five. Thanks." click click Sails held his radio in transmission mode.

■ ■ ■ ■ ■

Aspiration's crew alternated between manning the guns and managing the ship. Captain Allen watched the strange self-propelled boat approach. His stomach became queasy, and he paced the deck.

. . . . .

Berg called through the bullhorn, "Ahoy *Aspiration.* Captain Joe Plimsoll from the vessel *Serendipity* sends his compliments."

The crew jumped from the rail, shocked at hearing electronic amplification.

Captain Allen stood his ground, mindful of the necessity to maintain command. He raised his speaking-trumpet and spoke to the launch, "Avast, there. What be your intention?"

Berg responded through the bullhorn, "We've fresh oranges and apples for a fellow American vessel if you're interested, and freshwater too if you're short. Permission to come alongside to speak?"

"Permission granted to lie near, but if thy intention be evil, prepare to meet thy Maker."

"Mister Sails," Berg spoke in an undertone, "open a tote of oranges. Toss them a few, then pass one to me and eat one yourself. You too, Mister Decker."

The launch ran parallel to the brig, thirty feet from its stern starboard quarter. Sails lobbed half a dozen oranges, one at a time, to the sailors, then tossed one each to Berg and Jason. *Aspiration's* crew caught them suspiciously. The launch crew bit a portion of their orange's skin, peeled it, separated the sections, and popped them into their mouths.

Captain Allen followed the scene. One of his crew tossed him an orange. He saw the boat crew eat their oranges, smelled his orange, opened it, and tasted a piece.

"Umm." He smiled at his crew. "Good orange. Go ahead."

"Start tossing oranges," Berg growled. "Once everyone has one, start the apples."

"Thanks to thee for the fruit. We're *Aspiration*, Captain Angus Allen, out of Boston, eight weeks from the West Indies, and out of fresh provisions. I believe an account of what we see is befitting, sir."

"We're the American vessel *Serendipity*, Captain Joe Plimsoll, out of Seattle on a brief excursion to these seas."

Captain Allen turned to Laurence Chaderton and spoke low. "Have thou heard of Seattle?"

"No, sir, I have not."

"And what sort of vessel is that?" The deep voice of Captain Allen could carry in a storm.

"It's difficult to explain, sir. But I assure you we are friends. As you can see, we do not rely on the wind for propulsion. Are you short on water?"

Angus Allen and Laurence Chaderton exchanged a glance and raised an eyebrow. Their water became critical after a storm broke three tierces and tainted the other in the crossing. Desperate for water, gaining this essential store changed the value of the eerie encounter. They would not trust this peculiar wayfarer, but the chance to relieve the parched crew made a significant shift to their risk/reward calculation.

"Yes, we find ourselves a little short," Captain Allen offered. "Canst thou spare some?"

"We have a pump on *Serendipity* capable of sending you a thousand gallons in fifteen minutes. If you allow us to approach your leeward side, working together, we'll rig a hose from our staysail boom to your yardarm and deliver the water. You will not have to slow or alter your course. Would a thousand gallons be sufficient?"

Laurence Chaderton turned aside to the captain. "It's impossible to pump that much water so quickly. But it is also impossible to move through the water without wind or rowing. Let's assume they can deliver what they claim. While they are getting their vessel in place, we'll move the hogsheads and ready the larboard and starboard tuns to receive. More water would get us to Palermo without stopping."

Captain Allen did not need his speaking trumpet at this range. "Sir, I accept your offer. You may bring *Serendipity* close enough to transfer water."

He turned to his number one in a lowered voice, "Keep the cutlasses at the ready. Let no one aboard without my permission. This situation leaves a pit in my stomach."

"Captain," Berg bellowed, "If you rig a whip from the yardarm, we'll send these totes of oranges and apples for you and your crew then return to our ship to assist in the water transfer operation."

Berg turned toward Sails and spoke toward his radio. "You got that, Captain?" click "Got it." click

Captain Joe turned the wheel, increased the rpm, and started closing the distance between them.

Aspiration's crew rigged a single whip off the main yard. Berg moved the launch close enough for Jason to grab the tackle. *Natural fiber rope, wooden blocks—wonder what these guys would think of a Hydro-Slave pot hauler.* He looped the first tote yoke on the hook and looked up at the crew lining the rail. They appeared unhealthy, wincing from apparent pain. With a wave of his hand, they hoisted the box aboard. The sailors unhooked it and returned the tackle to Jason. He hooked on the second tote. When it lifted aloft, the launch headed away to *Serendipity.*

▪ ▪ ▪ ▪ ▪

Captain Joe knocked, then opened Chief's door, having left Berg at the helm. "Sorry, Mister Chief, but I will need you for a water transfer to an American vessel out of Boston. You'll be on Backup in a few minutes, anyway."

"Yeah, okay, no problem." Chief raised to the edge of his bunk and rubbed his face to clear the cobwebs. "I know where the hose is and the pump connections. Someone else 'ill need to run the hose. I'll handle the pump and valves."

Once alongside *Aspiration,* Joe concentrated at the helm to maintain speed and not draw any closer than the twenty feet now separating them. The bulkier vessel shielded *Serendipity* from the wind, damped the waves, and changed the steering dynamics. With the sails furled and the staysail removed, it was easy to use the staysail boom for a derrick. Sails rigged a special hose pulley at the boom's end. Jason tied a duplicate pulley to a heaving line, pointed at *Aspiration's* main course yardarm, and tossed it.

The New England crew pulled it aboard, tied it to the main course reefing line, rove a pull line, and ran the hose pulley to the reef-tackle block at the end of the yard. Jason retrieved the heaving line, attached the capped hose, and threw it back. The Bostonian crew pulled the tube across, tied it to their pull line, and dragged it through the hose pulley down to the deck. Eager hands, mystified by the clear plastic, passed it through the hatch to the water tier. A wind eddy from the larger vessel caused the smell of cooking burgers to waft across. The crew lifted their heads at the scent of frying meat. Alert and alarmed, their stomachs grumbled.

"Captain," Joe called out, "the weight of the water coming across will require you to secure your end to keep the hose from dropping into the sea."

"Aye, Captain." Captain Allen nodded to his first. The situation was obvious to men who spent their lives at sea. They had an intuitive understanding of the physical forces at work.

He gave the schooner a full scan. Myriad unique details overloaded his senses. The smooth black hull, thin black masts and spars, tiny capstans, sail material, braided cordage, an unwieldy spinning apparatus near the top of the mainmast, twisted steel shrouds and stays, equaling their speed with no sound—it was too much. He shook his head.

"Ready." Laurence Chaderton signaled his Captain with a wave.

"Ready." Angus Allen bellowed.

Captain Joe spoke through the intercom. "Okay, Mister Chief, start the pump. Also, start the water maker to replace what we send. I want to preserve our trim."

Captain Joe changed *Serendipity's* vector to compensate for the water's weight in the hose to draw the two vessels into each other. Water surged through the hose. In ten minutes, *Aspiration*'s crew had filled three tuns and four hogsheads. After filling the last barrel, they let the water overflow into the bilge. Laurence Chaderton signaled Captain Allen.

"Cut." Captain Allen signaled *Serendipity* with a wave of a finger across his neck.

Joe used the intercom. "Mister Chief, stop the pump."

Chief turned off the pump and closed a valve, an additional precaution to the check valve, ensuring the hose water would not run into the freshwater tank.

The water stopped flowing to the brig. A crewman untied the lashing, and the hose pulled out of the yard block and dropped into the sea. *Aspiration's* men removed the wide block from the yardarm and tied it to the heaving line.

Serendipity hauled it in and edged away. The deck crew retrieved the tubing, drained it, rinsed it with a deck hose, and stowed it.

Captain Joe relaxed a tad. "Mister Cook, how are the lunches coming?"

"They are ready to load into the containers. We'll pass them along in a few minutes."

Captain Joe yelled, "Captain Allen? We have prepared hot meals with fresh meat for you and your crew. I guarantee the quality of the food. If you are interested, we'll bring them over. Perhaps you and I might have a private word."

Aspiration's crew turned in unison toward their Captain. They had eaten little more than hardtack, salt pork, pea soup, and spoiled cheese for the past few days. Anything was possible, considering the bizarre nature of what they witnessed so far.

Captain Allen knew the crew's opinion on the matter. "We thank thy kindness. There are fifteen of us if you please. And Captain, with my compliments, come aboard if thou wish. I would like a word, if convenient."

"Ding-ding, ding-ding, ding-ding, ding-ding." *Serendipity*'s ship's clock chimed noon.

Captain Joe's voice was firm, "Mister Berg, can you stand another watch while I go across?"

"No problem, Captain." Berg moved to the helm.

"Once we arrive, call me in an hour. Tell me there is a situation that requires my presence. If no actual problems have occurred, tell me it's situation forty-two. If an issue needs my urgent attention, tell me the situation is nine." He turned to *Aspiration*. "Yes, Captain Allen," Joe yelled. "I'll be across shortly." He hurried below to grab a forty-five.

16
SCURVY

February 25, 1798 - Forty miles West of the Strait of Gibraltar

Captain Joe returned to the deck. "Mister Berg lay off a hundred yards. Mister Masters, Mister Handy, bring the launch alongside, then get your rest. You're on Backup in four hours. Mister Bones, Mister Sails, and Mister Decker, you're in the launch with me. Mister Sails, you will remain in the launch. Maintain our pace somewhere between both vessels and listen to the radio. Pick us up at my call. We'll keep our sidearms concealed. Mister Decker and Mister Bones will board with me. When we board, salute the flag to allay their fear."

Jason passed the lunch tote loaded with nineteen Styrofoam containers to Sails, bobbing alongside to leeward in the launch. He nodded at the slight bulge in Sails' leg pocket. "You know how to handle that thing?"

"Oh, yes. I am proficient. I checked the magazine, and it is ready. But I am not sure a weapon adds to our security or lessens it."

"Yeah, I know what you mean. But seamen in 1798 may not recognize a nineteen-eleven to be a weapon. It bears no resemblance to an eighteenth-century flintlock. Anyway, they'll never know I have it in my pocket, and I feel better having one."

Sails steered the four of them alongside *Aspiration*. He opened the tote, took a lunch container for himself, and pushed the box toward Jason. Jason attached it to the whip. The whiff of cooked meat grew more potent as they went aboard. Captain Joe went up the side, followed by Doc, with his bag over a shoulder, and Jason. Each gave the flag a smart salute.

"Captain Plimsoll, welcome aboard. Allow me to name Laurence Chaderton, my first."

"Thank you, Captain. Allow me to introduce Mister Bones, our doctor, and Mister Decker, my aide-de-camp."

Aide-de-camp? That's a first. Jason glanced aside to Captain Joe, then smiled at Captain Allen.

Captain Joe continued, "I'll bet you have some concerns. We have little time to spare. Perhaps we could answer your questions and eat the meals we brought aboard?"

Bones noted one of *Aspiration's* crew vomit over the side. Several men grasped their stomachs and looked weak. One moaned with abdominal pain and walked with an awkward gait.

"Yes, my cabin, please. Laurence Chaderton, light along the wine with the yellow wax. Doctor? How timely. We have scurvy aboard. My men are exhibiting fatigue, irritability, and bone pain. I expect thy apples and oranges will help us resolve this affliction."

Jason connected the black flat-brimmed hats, black vests, and black coats. *Ah yes, colonial New England. Al would love this. He should be here instead of me. Thy and thou....* Jason whispered to Captain Joe, "Quakers."

They ducked into the Captain's stern cabin. The overhead was low, permitting them to only stand between the deck beams, but they sat at a long table illuminated by an overhead skylight. Curved windows of small panes splayed across the transom and sides. Dappled sunlight reflected off the waves and lit the cabin. Jason's view astern framed a straight wake streaming away to the west in the bright sunlight. The groan of hemp rigging, creaking wood, and the odor of tar added a Disneyesque quality to the scene.

Captain Angus scrutinized his guests, opening their Styrofoam containers and taking a bite of their burgers. He tried his. "Umm. Amazing fine food, Captain. What dost thou call this?"

"We call it a burger in honor of its inventor, a prosecutor who lost all his cases against a lawyer named Perry Mason. It's an old story whence we come."

Jason straightened a bit, turned to Captain Joe, but kept a straight face. *Perry Mason?*

"Well, we thank thee. It goes down well. We are Friends on this ship and warm to kindness when we receive it. I must ask, what is the nature of thy vessel? The powerful voice device, the lack of visible propulsion, no hull planks, the material of the boxes, the hose you sent aboard, thy ability to transfer water, so many things—my crew worries this be the Devil's work." Captain Allen narrowed his eyes, staring deep into those of Captain Joe.

"Sir, we are not the devil. I cannot explain to you our unique circumstances in the time available. We can only stay aboard a short while. Then we must be off. However, allow me to attest, we are a fellow American vessel and mean you no harm."

"Thou appear to be unarmed...." Captain Allen tilted his head to one side, considering the possibility of taking *Serendipity*. He had a flintlock within quick reach under the table. There was much to gain, but such an aggressive act would harm his Quaker standing.

Laurence Chaderton caught his captain's drift. He tightened his left hand on the scabbard of his cutlass.

"Looks may be deceiving. I guarantee you we are well-armed. We have potent weapons and can blow anything afloat out of the water." Captain Joe leaned forward, tapping his finger on the table for emphasis.

Oh, shit—these guys going to drawdown? Jason eased his hand onto his pistol in his right pocket.

"Captain Allen," Bones interjected, "I'm not sure what you have is scurvy. If you permit me to examine your crew, I believe I can diagnose and treat their apparent ailments."

"Oh?" Captain Allen appeared to relax. "Yes. Laurence Chaderton, please conduct the doctor on deck to examine the crew."

Bones took another bite of his burger and followed Mr. Chaderton, who brought his meal with him.

Jason removed his hand from his pocket.

▪ ▪ ▪ ▪ ▪

"Mateys," First Mate Chaderton called for the crew's attention, "this here's a doctor who might treat what ails ya."

Bones took charge. "Gentlemen, Captain Allen mentioned you might have scurvy aboard. By your demeanor, I suggest your problems may be more serious. If I may examine you, I can identify your malady and treat it. You, sir," Bones selected a sick man and pointed to the hatch cover. "Please take a seat."

The man looked at his mates with alarm, took an enormous bite of his burger, and slumped forward to sit in a humble posture, continuing to chew. Bones beheld a swollen face and inflamed eyes. He opened his bag, removed a stethoscope, and listened to the man's heartbeat—more for show than a diagnosis. His lungs were not well, but the men nodded and grunted at the purple tubed stainless-steel instrument.

"I'm listening to your heartbeat. Would you like to hear it?"

Bones removed the stethoscope from his head. He placed the ends in his subject's ears and held the diaphragm against the man's chest. The sailor's eyes widened.

"Sir, that's your heart beating." Bones removed the instrument and addressed the man, "Do you have diarrhea, abdominal pain, and vomiting?" The man appeared shocked at the doctor calling him Sir.

"Aye, your honor, I 'ave."

"Are you experiencing fever or muscle pain?"

"Why, yes, sir, I am."

"Do you have a rash anywhere?"

"Aye, it gnaws on me somethin' awful."

Bones took the man's hands and examined them carefully. He observed small hemorrhages resembling tiny splinters under the fingernails. He released the hands, folded his scope into his bag, and addressed the entire crew. "Any others experiencing this?"

"Aye." Mumbled many of the men.

"Well, gentlemen, I believe you have something other than scurvy. What kind of meat have you been eating?"

"Why, sir, we ain't had nothin' but hardtack an' salt pork for many a day, now."

"How many of you have been experiencing diarrhea, abdominal pain, or vomiting?"

The men studied each other. Several hands raised.

Bones raised his radio to his mouth. click "Captain, I'm going across to get medicine to treat the crew for trichinosis. Mister Sails, you copy?" click

■ ■ ■ ■ ■

Captain Allen's eyes widened. He jerked in shock at the voice from the Captain's pocket.

Captain Joe pulled his radio. click "Roger, doctor. Mister Sails, Mister Berg, you got your ears on?" click

■ ■ ■ ■ ■

The crew on deck made a collective inhale and lurched from the talking box.

click "I will be right there." click Sails started toward *Aspiration*. click "Roger, Captain." click Berg's voice was unmistakable.

"Gentlemen," Bones addressed the crew, "I'm going to my boat to get the medicine to make you well."

The crew stood with their hands on the rail in silence, watching Bones and Sails motor away.

■ ■ ■ ■ ■

Sails piloted Bones across and waited, bobbing in the launch. The Doctor scrambled below. Trichinosis was among the possibilities he had foreseen and stocked Albendazole. He considered the average weight of his subjects. *Hmm. Probably 80 kilos each, 5 milligrams per kilo a day for only twelve men for a week.* He loaded 170 - 200-milligram tablets into a brown plastic bottle. He wrote out a label: **2 tablets per day per sick man. Take after dinner.** He grabbed two white jars of multiple vitamins, put on his white coat, and headed on deck.

"Mister Sails, secure the launch and help me load two totes of canned meals. Those boys have been eating poorly cured pork and are sick with a parasitic worm. It's easy to treat, but they will have to change their diet. We will take them a supply of canned goods. Compared to what they've been eating, it will seem rather good."

They loaded the totes, including two can openers, and returned to *Aspiration*. Eager hands helped the doctor over the side. They hoisted the totes aboard on the whip, staring at his white coat.

He passed the bottles to Laurence Chaderton. "Gentlemen, you have trichinosis. It is a parasite that comes to you from having eaten infected meat—meat not adequately cooked. No more hardtack for you. Throw it over the side. You are to eat the meals in these cans until you get fresh provisions."

He brought out a can opener, opened a 20-ounce can of Dinty Moore Beef Stew, and passed it around for them to smell. "Heat the contents of each can until it is hot. If you're experiencing diarrhea, abdominal discomfort, or vomiting, take one pill in the brown bottle after your meal every day for a week. I promise you'll have more energy, the pain will go away, and you'll feel better."

The crew murmured a mix of approval and suspicion.

"Also, the entire ship's company is to take one pill per man per day from the white bottles while they last. These pills will restore what your bodies are lacking. Do you understand?" He gestured to the crew, then to Laurence Chaderton, who nodded.

▪ ▪ ▪ ▪ ▪

Captain Plimsoll, Jason, and Captain Allen remained seated in the cabin.

"Captain," Captain Joe uttered, "if you don't mind my being forward, I have questions, too. When I consider these political waters, I wonder what cargo's worth the risk?"

Captain Allen continued chewing for a moment, swallowed, and took a drink of wine. "Sugar. Refined sugar. A most welcome commodity in Europe."

"Huh. May I assume you are an abolitionist?"

"Thoust may. No man may enslave a fellow human. No Friends would descend to own another."

"I see. Hmm. Now, the sugar comes from West Indies plantations, is that right?"

"Aye, it is true."

"And slaves make the plantations viable, isn't that so?"

"Well, I suppose so...."

"So, it appears you have less hesitation with the fruits of slavery than actual ownership. Anyway, I was curious."

Captain Allen put his burger down, leaned back, and lowered his eyebrows. His mood darkened. He took offense at the negative sentiment and considered his response.

Oh, shit. Jason reached into his pocket and put his hand on his pistol. *Here we go again.* "Captain, we mean no disrespect." Jason leaned forward and opened his left hand in a conciliatory gesture. "We're just trying to grasp the economic forces you have to deal with."

▪ ▪ ▪ ▪ ▪

Gunny and Chief, on Secondary, sat muttering at the galley table. Light streamed through the open portlights. Masters, Handy, and the galley crew had turned in. With the boat under power, they remained below.

"You know what?" Gunny confided to Chief. "If anyone on board is carrying a weapon, I want one in my pocket, too."

"Yeah, I know what you mean. Most everyone I know in the Gulf carries somethin' somewhere. You're familiar with the weapons locker. What would it take to get one of them forty-fives?"

"A key, a good lock-pick, or a bolt-cutter."

"Well, I'll tell you what." Chief slapped his hands on his thighs and leaned forward. "This ain't the deal I signed up for. I don't need this guy for nothin'. If I get back, I'll already have the money, and if I don't get back, the money won't matter. Fuck it. How 'bout I go get us each a gat?"

"You know they'll notice two roscoes ain't on the rack."

"So, fuckin' what?" Chief got up, went below to the engine room, grabbed the bolt cutters, returned to the cabin, and padded down the corridor to the weapons locker.

▪ ▪ ▪ ▪ ▪

A low audible alarm from the motion detector in the armaments room sounded on Berg's laptop, sitting on the pilothouse table. Alone at the helm, he tapped the keys and got a picture with sound. He moved the computer closer and turned the volume lower.

A cable ran through the trigger guards of the pistols secured by a brass padlock. Chief cut the lock, removed the wire, grabbed two guns, and handed one to Gunny. They both checked the butt—no magazine. Gunny cut the padlock on a case labeled .45 ACP, removed four loaded magazines, and handed two to Chief. They each popped one in and hammered it home with the heel of their left hand. Each stuck their pistol and the extra magazine in their leg pocket with long faces without working the slide.

"What about the rest?" Gunny pointed at the lock on the cable through the trigger guards of the M4s and TAC-50s.

"Let's leave 'em for now. I'm satisfied. If anyone's carryin', I'm gonna carry, too." He grabbed the cut locks and put them in his left pocket. "I'll drop 'em over the side first chance I get."

They wandered out of the camera's view. click "Captain," Berg spoke through the radio in an urgent tone. "Sir, we are experiencing situation nine." click

▪ ▪ ▪ ▪ ▪

The call got Joe's attention. He picked up his radio. click "Copy that." click

"Captain Allen, I'm afraid I must cut our conversation short. If you would be so good as to return the empty fruit and food boxes, we will wish you well and be on our way. Mister Decker, get the totes and see them loaded into the launch." click "Mister Sails, pick us up starboard side." click

"Captain Allen, I bid you farewell."

With that, the men stood, shook hands with a slight bow, and climbed on deck.

Once gone, Captain Allen turned to his first mate. "Even if blessed with the fruit, water, meals, and medico, I'm glad to see them away."

"Aye, Captain."

▪ ▪ ▪ ▪ ▪

In the launch, the Captain and Bones settled forward, and Jason sat aft. Sails steered with his knee and opened both his hands at Jason to convey, "What happened?"

Jason made a tiny shake of his head and mouthed the words, "Not now."

■ ■ ■ ■ ■

Once aboard, Berg conferred in a lowered voice with Captain Joe on the bridge. "Captain, Chief and Gunny cut the locks on the forty-fives. They took pistols and magazines. I was a fly on the wall to their conversation. They figured if we armed anyone, they should be too."

"I see. Thank you, Mister Berg. I relieve you of the helm. Get your sleep. But first, remove the weapon locks. They have a point, and, under the circumstances, everyone ought to at least have a sidearm if they want one."

"All the weapons?"

"Yes. It's clear we're all in this together."

"Joe, are you sure about that? If you allow them arms, you won't be able to disarm them."

"It won't matter. They need me to get home."

17
BARANOF

February 25 - Sitka

A truck splattered slush with hollow thumps, driving by their booth in the P-Bar.

Loren's phone rang. She raised it to her ear and exchanged eye contact with Al. "Hello?"

"Hello, Miss Roberts? I'm Frank Atherton, Jason Oliver's attorney. I have an urgent matter to discuss with him. I've tried his cell-phone and left a message, but he hasn't returned my call. Could you help me get in touch with him?"

"Gosh, Mister Atherton, I just returned to Sitka, and I haven't seen him." She focused on Al. "If he's not answering his cell, he may be out of range somewhere around here."

"Yeah, maybe. Listen, I understand you and Jason were close. Do you know of a drawing he prepared showing his place at the time of his arrest?"

"Sure, I've seen the bust drawing." She held Al's eyes and spoke so he would know the subject. "He drew it at the drawing table in the living room of his cabin."

"Well, if you encounter Jason, please tell him I need a copy. I may use it to help his case."

"Okay. If we talk, I'll let him know."

"Super. Thanks. How's the weather on Baranof Island?"

"Winter."

"Yeah, here too. Well, I hope you have a wonderful day."

Loren put her phone away. She gave Al a skeptical smirk. "Okay, Al, what's going on?"

Yashee kept quiet but joined Loren's leery look.

"All right, but you have to keep it secret. I mean, there's a lot at stake here, and you can't share it with anyone. I think there are heavy people involved. I mean it. Except for Jason, we three are it, okay?"

Loren and Yashee exchanged subdued smiles, then turned to Al with sincere nods.

"Jason's in Seattle crewing on a fancy sailing yacht. I don't know where the boat is going or what it's doing, but the owner's paying an unreasonable amount of money for a short cruise. The situation must be more complex than I imagined. I arranged this little shindig, and I'm feeling uneasy. If I had known his attorney warned him not to leave Southeast, I'd never have gone along with it. He had a first-class ticket paid for by the client and checked in online with only a carry-on. I dropped him off right before the flight to reduce his exposure to people knowing he left town."

The girls checked each other in their peripheral vision but didn't change their expressions.

"I don't know where he's goin' or what he's doin'. But, having facilitated this affair, I'd like to help cover his ass. What's this about a drawing?"

Loren glanced at Yashee then to Al. "He prepared a drawing showing the pot was not visible to a cop standing on his porch. In his usual OCD manner, he drew it to scale."

"You know where he keeps it?"

"Not exactly, but it won't be hard to find. You know his cabin. I can't get into his computer, but I'm sure he wouldn't trash the hard copy."

"Well, what do you say we find this drawing and send it to the attorney pretending it's from Jason? It'll take the weight off 'im until he gets back."

They glanced at each other, slid out of the booth, and nodded to Rita.

Rita, behind the bar, tucked dirty dishes on a shelf, aware something serious was going on with her friends at the booth. "You kids stay outta trouble, ya hear?"

Al held the door for the women. "Thanks, Rita. We'll try."

▪ ▪ ▪ ▪ ▪

The wind whispered through the tall, dense hemlocks surrounding the winding drive to Jason's cabin, nestled into the mountain. The yard light did little to dispel the sullen afternoon twilight. There were no tire tracks in the recent snow. Eluk jumped out, happy to be home, and ran into the woods. Yashee turned her truck around, so it faced down the driveway. Dripping water from the trees overhead pecked at the snow.

Jason's unmistakable '49 Chevy pickup with the vice mounted on the left front fender sat forlorn, covered in the wet white stuff. Loren retrieved the hidden key and opened the door. She turned off the security alarm, opened a secret panel, shut off the cameras, and turned on the lights. Al and Yashee followed her in.

"My best guess is it'll be in his desk file in the bedroom."

Al tried the drawer—locked. "Shit. Yashee, you got any tools in your truck?"

"Sure. Behind the seat." She and Loren sat silently in the living room.

Al walked to the truck, located a well-stocked tool bag, and took it into the cabin. He placed it on the floor, sorted through it, and found a wood chisel. It was a simple matter to hammer a chunk out of the drawer above the lock and cut the steel latch using a hacksaw blade in his gloved hand. The files hung perfectly aligned with printed labels in hanging folders. He pulled a thick one labeled BUSTED. In it, he found a drawing on vellum and stepped into the living room.

"Loren, this it?"

"Yep, that's it."

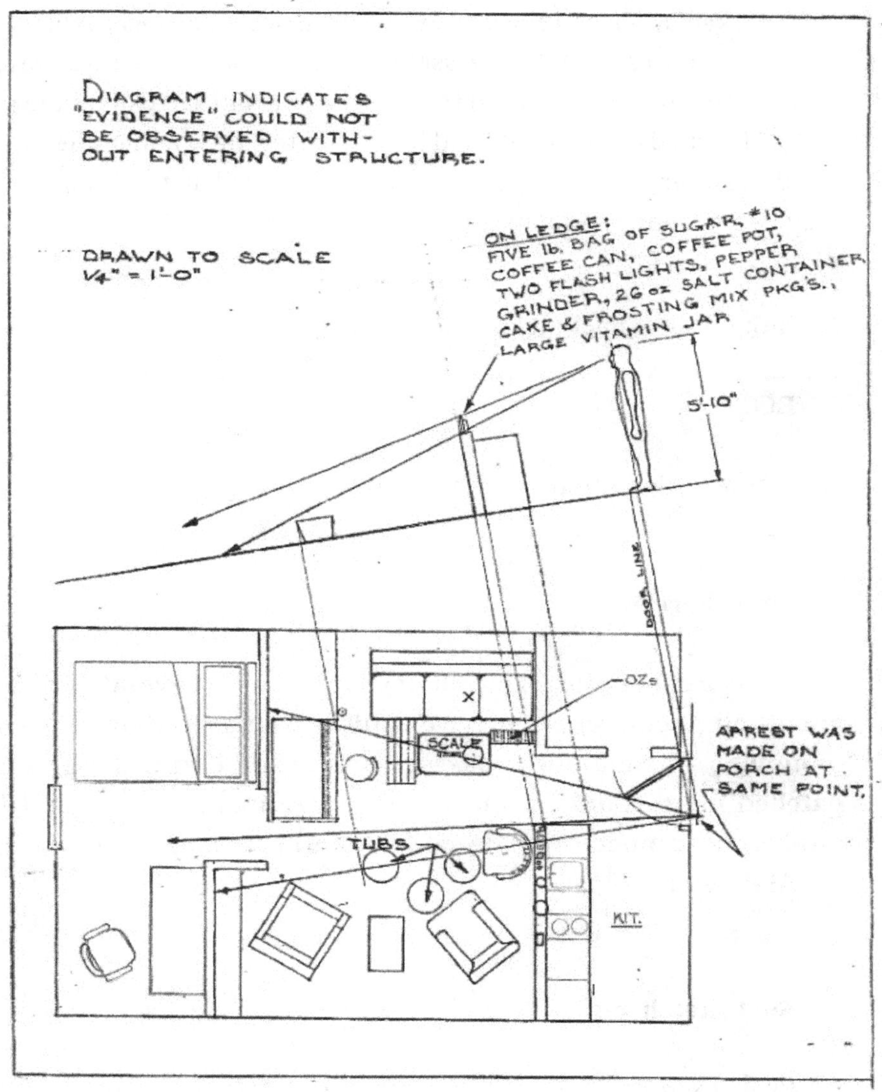

Loren left last. She glanced at the bed, *his body against hers... good times,* before turning the security system on and the lights off. She took Jason's truck key, locked the door, returned the house key to its hiding place, and called Eluk. He came running and bounded into the passenger's seat of Jason's truck. She cleaned the snow off the windshield, started it, and followed Yashee down the driveway.

. . . . .

They parked at Eliason Harbor and walked along the dock, avoiding the dog poop, to Al's boat. The vessel rocked a little as the three of them stepped aboard. They entered the warm cabin and sat around the galley table. Al turned on the lights and his computer. He scanned the drawing on his printer, built into a cabinet niche, saved it to a pdf file, and prepared to send an e-mail.

To f.atherton@shackeltonandbayer.com X

CC/BCC

Subject Jason's sketch

Mr. Atherton -

I took a chance Jason was at anchor in a cove beyond Peril Strait, out of cell-phone range, but reachable by radio. I radioed a friend of mine who was making a passage and asked him to try Jason. He patched me through. Jason told me to retrieve his sketch. I have attached a scanned copy. He said he would return in a few days.

Al Paxton

Bust sketch .pdf

"Ting-tong." Al's phone signaled activity on his bank account. He entered the access code. The display showed a deposit of $12,500. He exited the program while maintaining a poker face. *Damn. Awful. Guilty.*

18
DINNER

February 25, 1798 - Gibraltar abeam

The wind had increased to a moderate breeze. Waves were longer with frequent white horses—breaking waves with crests reminiscent of a horse's mane and the low thunder of hooves.

"Mister Sails," Captain Joe raised his eyes, "will the gennaker hold? I want to see *Aspiration* drop over the horizon."

Sails considered the wind speed, direction, and forces on the rigging. He placed his left hand on the main port backstay. It was as tight as a steel rod. "We can dispense with the gennaker. It is pressing the bow. With this breeze, we will make hull speed with the main, staysail, foresail, and yankee, balance okay and run down our easting like a racehorse."

With the sails reset, Jason stood abaft the foremast. The warmth of a bright afternoon sun penetrated his jacket. Even recent events could not suppress his exhilaration of rushing along on the steady quartering seas. Green water swooshed along the lee chainplates. Sparkling white wave tops tumbled away in a splendid splash and background growl.

■ ■ ■ ■ ■

Ding-ding, ding-ding, ding-ding, ding-ding. 1600 hours. Bones relieved the Captain at the helm.

Berg, Masters, Handy, Cookie, and Steward were already up, having forced themselves awake at 1545.

The Captain grabbed a ceiling handhold standing aft by the companionway and addressed the ship's company. "Everyone, gather around the table before we change the watch. I have some announcements."

Everyone took their former seat.

"dzzzit...... dzzzzit." The salon continued to rotate with the ship's roll.

"Gentlemen," he grinned, "I imagine we've had enough fun for one day. So, we will take it easy until morning. Here's the plan. Tonight, we'll continue east under power. All hands, except Mister Cook and Mister Steward, are to go on deck and furl the sails. Leave them on, but tie 'em down tight. I will be unhappy if I hear a single sail or halyard flap tonight. Let's be silent in the dark. Dinner at four bells, Mister Cook?"

"Yes, sir. Dinner will be ready."

"Good. Once you've tied the sails, do what you wish until dinner. Sleep, play games, whatever—same thing after we eat. Mister Bones, Mister Berg, or I will take the helm. The posted schedule will resume at 0800. Tomorrow's uniform is blue trousers, light blue shirts, and blue sweaters. Breakfast at 0730 hours."

The crew exchanged brief smiles, exhaled, and widened into their seats.

"Now, only some of you have pistols. That's unfair. I have ordered the weapons and ammo unlocked. If you want a Kimber forty-five for the duration of the cruise, please help yourself."

Chief and Gunny read each other with flushed faces, trying to suppress a guilty grin.

"And, Mister Gunn, check the ammo to ensure we don't have a repeat of the problem with the Mk 19, okay?"

"Yes, sir." Gunny cast his eyes downward in apparent contemplation, then at Chief with a slight jerk of his head and eye movement toward their cabins.

Cookie and Stew glanced at each other, then returned to their galley tasks. Cookie mumbled to Stew, "Weapons aren't my bailiwick."

Masters winked at Handy, got up, and headed to the weapons cache. Handy followed close behind.

Masters held out a forty-five to Handy. "You know how to operate this?"

"Oh, yeah. I been shootin' sharks since I 'us ten." Handy took the gun in his right hand, pointed it away from anything vital, and cracked the slide to verify there was nothing in the pipe. He cocked the hammer, popped in a magazine with a confident smack, and racked the slide. It was ready to fire. He transferred the gun to his left hand, holding it with the ejection port facing up, and racked the slide again. The cartridge popped into the air. His left thumb clicked on the safety. He caught the ejected bullet after it bounced off the ceiling and placed it between his teeth. He took the pistol in his right hand, dropped the magazine from the grip, caught it with his left palm, and put the .45 in his pocket holster. He removed the bullet from his teeth and replaced it in the magazine. He pulled the pistol from his right pocket and shoved the magazine into the grip. Cocked and locked, he stuck it back in his pocket. Comfortable with the additional weight, he grinned at Masters. "Fuckin' with me ain't healthy."

▪ ▪ ▪ ▪ ▪

Stew slunk toward Cookie and muttered. "Lance, this ain't like the other jobs. We gonna be all right?"

Cookie whispered, "Don't call me Lance. The walls have ears. We'll be fine. This trip has turned into a strange military thing, but it isn't any worse than the Saint Kitts gig. Remember that? Drunks with guns. These guys have lots of guns, but they're not drunk. And the Captain is well-prepared. Think of the money. We'll be able to pay off your mom's losses and the condos. Concentrate on getting the potatoes and broccoli ready, and don't worry."

▪ ▪ ▪ ▪ ▪

Gunny and Chief moseyed along the corridor to Gunny's cabin. After a brief check that no one was noticing, they ducked in. Gunny sat on his bunk, elbows on knees and hands folded.

Chief relaxed into the chair. "I've done nothing like this. This situation ain't no problem for you?"

"Well, obviously, I've never traveled in time before, but I get paid big bucks to protect my client's interests, whatever they may be. And when it's them or me, I'm fairly good and making sure it's them. You handle a pistol?"

"Yeah, sure. It's a tough scene in the Gulf, although we rarely get 'round to shootin' each other. I don't know shit about the other weapons we carry, including the M4s. You check me out on one of those?"

"Sure."

▪ ▪ ▪ ▪ ▪

Ding-ding. 1700 hours.

"Gentlemen," Bones called from the helm, "The Rock of Gibraltar is abeam. You should see this."

The boys grabbed their binoculars, lined for the companionway, and followed the Captain up through the pilothouse. A deep blue sky framed the scene to the north, and they spread out along the deck. The famous rock appeared on the port beam. Its pondering form stood distinct against the monochromatic air. A rotor cloud was forming in the distance to the east.

"Wow!" Jason expanded his arms to embrace the promontory. "It's not what I imagined. I expected the Prudential Insurance logo. I did not appreciate its extent."

Sails turned to Jason. "Sure jumps out compared to everything around, does it not?"

Jason considered the panorama. "Yeah, sure does. Views I've seen conceal most of it. Isn't it interesting how the camera angle makes a scene more vivid?"

White canvas sails dotted the distant water, but none were substantial, near, or on an interception course. Once they furled the sails, the boys went below.

Captain Joe, Berg, Masters, Handy, Chief, and Gunny returned to their cabins. Cookie and Stew continued in the galley. The late afternoon sunlight sparkled off the waves and danced around the cabin—more reddish than the earlier brilliant white.

Jason sat across from Sails, alone at the table.

"Mister Sails, I noticed a chess set behind my seat. Whaddaya think? Looks like we'll get a full night's sleep tonight."

"Sure." Sails folded his hands on the table, awaiting the pieces.

Jason moved a roll-up Staunton chess set to the table. "Wow. Wonderful pieces. Well weighted with felt bottoms. Somebody knows chess."

They set up the board. Sails played e4. Jason played the Sicilian with c5.

"It seems," Sails remarked, "Napoleon viewed European politics as a chess match." He played f4.

Jason responded with d5, the Tal Gambit. "I get the allure of comparing chess to the challenges of diplomacy by other means, but it doesn't hold up. Non-nuclear warfare has too many pieces and squares for accurate analysis. The options are so many that winning requires luck. Chess is strategy and tactics, not luck. The possibilities are many but finite. Unfortunately, analyzing over two or three moves ahead is beyond me."

Sails moved exd5. "Well, Napoleon played a lot of chess, but I doubt he was an exceptional player. I understand his openings were weak, but he would come alive for complex combinations in the middle game. I'll bet beating him was a dangerous career move."

Jason saw an opportunity for confidential conversation if they kept their voices near a whisper. He waved his hand over the board to get

Sails' attention, then covered his mouth. "Let's not forget the hidden microphones, okay?"

Sails nodded.

Jason resumed, "We may be in deep doo-doo. But the Captain's right about eighteenth-century weapons killin' potential. I get the Captain's adrenaline rush—it IS a hell of a thrill. But it's all lost if we die. Death may be an exception to this parallel universe shit, but those men we killed this morning looked darned dead to me. We've made a bad deal. You should have seen him on *Aspiration*. I was afraid of a shoot-out. Whatever problems I face in the twenty-first century, they usually were not life-threatening, know what I mean?" He moved Nf6

Sails covered his mouth and maintained the undertone. "We are in for the full monty. The yacht is a delight to sail, but I would rather battle forces that I understand. I comprehend the weather. Eighteenth-Century naval tactics—not so much. Four more bloody days of this, and I am afraid I will lose the plot. The Captain snookered us, all right. I did not figure on tickety-boo, but this borders the shambolic. Perhaps a good night's sleep will improve my perspective."

"Yeah, I'm ready to crash, too. I joined to improve my lot. Now I've lost my old lady, stuck my neck out with the law, and am in danger of being killed by an adrenalin junkie halfway around the world where sailors eat hardtack and salt pork."

"Balderdash. You joined for the adventure and the money, just like the rest of us." Sails raised his eyebrows, nodded his head, and moved a bishop to B5. "Check."

"Ding-ding, ding-ding." 1800 hours.

▪ ▪ ▪ ▪ ▪

Stew set an elegant table again. The forks, knives, and spoons gleamed in the well-lit cabin. Water glasses stood next to Waterford wine goblets with a large old English S engraved on their faces. He set each place with measured exactness.

Captain Joe slowly poured a 2012 Napa Valley Silver Oak Cabernet Sauvignon into a decanter for each table, careful to leave the bottle's sediment. The aroma of sautéed mushrooms and onions mingled with the grilling ribeyes. A Royal Copenhagen plate arrived in front of each man: Thick steaks smothered in a Worcestershire laced mushroom sauce with a sprig of fresh thyme, bubbling scalloped potatoes with caramelized fennel, roasted broccoli, and parmesan.

Steward passed a tray with a napkin-wrapped utensil package up to Bones at the helm.

The doctor accepted it with a smile. "Thank you."

The Captain poured a glass of wine for Gunny, Chief, Berg, and himself, then consumed the incredible food as if it were normal.

Chief leaned over his serving, inhaled the aroma, and broke into a broad grin. "Man, this ain't nothin' like the grub I been eatin'. Mostly I scarf fast food in front of a TV. This stuff's great!"

Joe observed Chief gulp his wine—no appreciation for its complex character.

Handy regarded his serving with trepidation. He had little exposure to fine dining and was unsure of the etiquette. He watched Masters.

Masters' military training stood him in good stead. He understood he was setting an example and poured wine for Sails, Jason, Handy, and himself. He eyed Handy, took his napkin from its ring, and placed it on his lap. With his fork in his left hand and his knife in his right, he cut a single bite, transferred the fork to his right hand, wiped it in sauce, and put it in his mouth.

Handy followed Masters' lead.

"Mister Cook," Jason offered, "that was a superb dinner. Any chance at a cup of coffee?"

"Yes, sir." Cookie was already filling the carafes.

After a sip, Jason put his cup down and addressed the Captain, "Cap'n, I want to return to my charging bear metaphor."

Captain Joe stared at the table with a blank expression, stirring his coffee. He removed the spoon, laid it on the table, and took a sip.

"I have a friend in Southeast Alaska who makes his living guiding foreign industrialists on bear hunts. These guys pay big money to be in a position where a bear might threaten their life. It's a great adrenaline rush. Then they shoot the bear—charging or not. Incidentally, my friend takes a step back to the side and shoots the bear at the same time as his client to ensure a kill. His customers—charged with 'buck fever'—never notice."

Joe put his cup down, listening intently.

Jason continued, "Now, I suppose you'll argue, 'What am I supposed to do, let the bear kill me?' But the bear is just doing what bears do. A human with a superior intellect has created a situation where he feels justified in killing the bear. He has intentionally placed himself in a defensive position. The bear does not know it has no protection against a high-powered rifle. This hunter-bear encounter is unfair."

The crew turned from Jason to the Captain, whose face remained blank.

Jason persisted. "Our situation is analogous. These eighteenth-century dipshits can't possibly grasp the disparity between their weapons and ours. Even though they would kill us if they could, the situation is basically unfair."

The Captain droned, "Well, Mister Decker, people who have dedicated their lives to killing and enslaving others are not bears. They're terrorists. There is an enormous difference between the intelligence of a bear defending territory or her young and a human intent on killing you for money. And a bear doesn't invent a religious excuse."

Chief looked at Jason, shocked. "You don't believe in huntin'?"

"Sure, I believe in hunting for food. All mammals get their energy from consuming other living things. But you don't hunt a bear for food."

"And," the Captain interjected, "the Barbary Muslims aren't hunting for food either." Captain Joe picked up his spoon and pointed it at Jason. "A cannonball heading toward you at a thousand feet per second isn't a foul-tempered bear wanting you gone from its territory. It's a distinct form of aggression. If you're walking through the woods and a guy attacks you with a knife, do you think you're not justified in shooting him with your pistol?"

"Yeah," Jason conceded. "You got a point, there."

"Hear-hear." Gunny raised his glass and took another drink.

"Look," the Captain said, "I get your argument. But the Barbary states are hunting us—the United States. It's a special case. It is the single most extreme example I have found of justifiable self-defense within gravity wave time-travel limits. Further back in time reduces the mass I can send.

I need that mass to maintain technological superiority to ensure our return. I'd rather bring a gun to a knife fight than a knife to a gunfight. And, hey, y'all shoulda known the amount of money you're getting would entail some adventure."

The crew stared into space without reacting.

After dinner, the crew split up. Bones continued his watch at the helm. With *Serendipity* under power, he could manage the ship alone. The crew, except for Gunny, ambled off to their cabins.

Gunny headed for the weapons. The lights in the locker were bright. Gunny opened all the ammo cans and checked for water. *Dry.* He inspected twelve M4s, and the two TAC-50s lined vertically on a rack. *Loaded? Need a training session if they're gonna be useful.* He removed a magazine from the 5.56×45mm case and pressed the top cartridge. There was a little give. *Twenty-eight rounds loaded—right.* He checked the magazines. *Loaded.* He took an M4 and checked the chamber. *Empty.* He fitted a magazine, clicked on the safety, and looked through the Trijicon scope. *Ah, Dual-Illuminated ACSS Reticle—nice.* He checked each of the M4s, put in a magazine, ignored the charging handle, and stuck them on the rack. He hefted a McMillan TAC-50, examined the pipe, and peered through the Nightforce scope. *Minute angle-based reticle—cool.* He pressed in a five-round magazine and put it on the rack. *Training tomorrow morning.* He checked the minigun's ammo. *Ready.*

▪ ▪ ▪ ▪ ▪

Captain Joe nodded toward Berg. "A word with you in my cabin, Mister Berg?"

Bill followed the Captain aft to his cabin, stepped in, and closed the door. Captain Joe sank into his comfortable leather desk chair and gestured for Berg to sit across from him. He switched on the green glass desk lamp and the similar sconce lights around his cabin, crossed his legs, and leaned back into his seat.

"Mister Berg, what is your assessment of how we're doing?"

"You won't use my name in the privacy of your cabin?"

"I will not use it on the boat; I will not use it with a goat; I must maintain our little sham; I do not like green eggs with ham."

"Okay, okay. So, tell me what happened on *Aspiration*?"

"Captain Angus Allen, a Quaker out of Boston, is running refined sugar out of the West Indies to Palermo. His crew was sick with what he believed was scurvy. We had a conversation in his cabin. He liked his burger, appreciated the water, and admired our technology. As our relationship became less formal, Captain Allen appeared to contemplate our lack of visible armament. I think he considered a try to take *Serendipity*. Fortunately, Mister Bones interrupted, having observed *Aspiration's* crew was suffering from trichinosis, not scurvy. His offer to treat it changed the subject, and he went on deck.

"Captain Allen, Mr. Decker, and I continued our conversation in the cabin. Sugar is a high-value cargo made profitable by slave labor on the plantations. The proceeds are probably akin to running dope out of Columbia. Quakers are abolitionists, but it doesn't seem to stop them from taking advantage of slavery to make money. When I made that point, it struck a nerve—then you called. It was a great slice of eighteenth-century life. I loved it."

"Um. If I may be a little bold, are you sure about this parallel reality stream concept? Any chance we will return to a changed world because of our interaction with people in 1798?"

"Well, not in theory. There must be a transition moment. That makes no sense. Try to imagine—you're ambling peacefully down the street, and instantly everything changes. No, it doesn't conjure. I am certain we can't do anything to alter events in our own time."

"So, if we slay someone here in 1798, there's no effect, but if they kill us, we're dead? Not much of a deal, huh?"

"Look, it will not be boring. I hate boredom. The risk keeps it from being mundane." The Captain uncrossed his legs and leaned forward. "Mister Berg, I have taken great care of you over the years. I have protected you and made you rich. I appreciate your management skills, and I expect a long and mutually beneficial relationship. I need you to uphold your end on the boat. I will be unhappy if the crew senses you have any doubts. You going to be okay for four more days?"

"Yeah, Captain, I'll be fine. I'll adapt." His eyes drifted to his folded hands. "I find the violence a little much."

▪ ▪ ▪ ▪ ▪

At 0400 hours, Captain Joe spoke as Bones relieved him at the helm. "No problems. *Aspiration* has dropped off the radar astern. Berg said he got a star sight and fix at midnight—practice in case anything goes wrong with the radar. The wind has been steady out of the northwest at fifteen knots. We just passed north of the Alboran Islet. I'm delighted with how well the boat rides. Significant red radar blip way out ahead—a bogey is coming toward us. It's all yours. I'm going to bed."

"Roger. I got it until 0800."

19
MÉCHANT

February 26, 1798 - The Algerian Basin

As the sun peeked over the horizon in the mid-morning watch, Bones was more concerned with the red radar target coming toward them than the inflamed orb rising in the east. He fidgeted over another encounter on the next watch.

Jason awoke after a good night's sleep, took a shower, and laid out the uniform of the day: blue trousers, blue shirt, and the blue military sweater. He unfolded the shirt, found a stitched opening under the armpit on the left side, and rolled the slit between his thumb and forefinger. *Oh, shit. Concealed shoulder carry setup.* He checked the sweater—same vertical slot, but broader.

By 0730, Jason and the gang were ready for breakfast. After soft fried eggs over finely cut spiced potatoes, covered in hot salsa and cheese, squarely set slices of avocado with just-squeezed orange juice and fresh ground coffee, he felt refreshed. At 0800, he and Sails followed Masters and Handy on deck.

The sun was bright, and the temperature warming. A briny smell floated on the breeze—backing to the west-northwest. Azure waves took a pronounced long-form with breaking crests and spray.

Berg relieved Bones at the helm and called to the salon. "Captain, the vessel heading directly toward us is a full-rigged ship."

Captain Joe was studying a chart. "Very, well, Mister Berg. Keep *Serendipity* to windward. I want to reserve our fight-or-flight option."

Bones passed through the cabin on his way to his bunk. "Captain, I hope it's flight. I need to sleep."

The gray sails to the east became more defined by the minute. The on-deck crew studied the oncoming vessel through their binoculars. Her hull came into view, leaning far over in the fresh breeze.

"Captain," Sails called down, "she is a single-decker, a frigate flying French colors on a bowline. I'll bet she cannot bear up another point. The waves are probably lapping her lee chainplates. She has not cleared for action. Her gunports are not open, and they have not chained, or pudden'd their yards. I estimate she is a hundred and fifty feet, maybe a thousand tons. I count fourteen guns per side. Whatever mission she is on, I doubt that it is peaceful. Make her name: *Méchant*."

Jason turned to Sails. "Chained or puddened?"

"In the old days, ah, well, in 1798's nautical parlance, ships going into an action chain the yards or tie them to the masts to prevent them from falling if their supporting ropes get blown away."

Captain Joe returned to the pilothouse, raised his binoculars, and studied the frigate. "Gentlemen," his voice had a sharp tone, "when we get even with her, we will come about and run parallel. If we can entice her to chase us north, *Aspiration* could slip through to the south. She's dangerous. The French build excellent ships, and she could carry eighteen pounders. Such a cannon will blow a hole in all the oak hulls afloat at close range. Farther away, though, they are less effective. I reckon a range of sixteen or seventeen-hundred yards at maximum elevation—pretty goddamn unlikely with this sea running. That's a break. If she were a ship-of-the-line, she'd carry heavier cannon in her lower tiers. According to Patrick O'Brian, a forty-two pounder can pierce two feet of oak at seven hundred yards."

Jason glanced at Sails, shrugged his shoulders, and whispered. "Who the fuck is Patrick O'Brian?"

"He was a British author," Sails whispered back. "Wrote a series of stories set in the English navy during the era of Napoleon, the time we are in."

Captain Joe lowered his binoculars. "Maybe she'd be up for a workout, but we don't want to let her practice on us. Then again, if she has an appetite, perhaps she'll salivate enough to chase us."

. . . . .

Baudouin Laurent, *Méchant's* commandant, stood at the windward rail on his quarterdeck, surveying the American schooner through his telescope. He wore the wig, cravat, broadcloth coat, and linen breeches befitting a French frigate captain. Clovis Durand, his lieutenant de vaisseau, studied the same scene from a position near the binnacle. "A most comely lady, Mister Durand. She'd be a thrill to whisk around the dance floor."

They watched *Serendipity* come about within her length. It was clear she could sail rings around the French frigate. She was too small to offer any threat—her gunports were ridiculous fakes. She offered little monetary value as a war prize, and her position to windward made it impossible to close within cannon range.

On a mission to Mauritius in the Indian Ocean, any opportunity for a prize along the way was welcome, but he would have to pass on this one. Lucky to sail out of Toulon through the British blockade, Gibraltar still lay ahead. Any engagement that slowed them was out of the question. The upside potential was not worth the downside risk. His attention returned west-southwest.

. . . . .

Captain Joe uttered, "She ain't taking the bait." He studied the French ship through his Steiners. "Damn. She'll sight *Aspiration* before sundown."

Captain Joe lowered his binoculars and cogitated out loud. "She'll encounter and take *Aspiration* unless we prevent it. I feel obligated to protect a fellow American. The only weapon we have with a range outside their guns is a missile, and it's too soon for their use."

Jason turned to Sails and raised his eyebrows. *Missiles?*

"Mister Berg," Captain Joe ordered, "please call Mister Gunn on the intercom. I need his help."

"What's up?" Gunny moved to a seat in the pilothouse next to the Captain.

"Mister Gunn, I seek your advice. See that French warship over there?"

Gunny turned and gaped. "Holy shit, I'm livin' in an eighteenth-century movie set."

Captain Joe explained, "America is in a quasi-war with France. There's justification for conflict, but it won't last. France and the United States haven't formally declared, but it's being fought on the high seas, anyway. French warships are seizing our merchant ships in the Caribbean Sea, and our privateers are returning the favor.

"But neither of our governments want the United States to join the conflict. If we take England's side, France won't be able to purchase our goods. And they're desperate for what we can supply. If we ally with France, the British navy will overwhelm us, and the French won't get shit. If we remain neutral, we can make a lot of money by trading with both sides. So, the cooler-headed politicos will eventually make a deal and sweep this whole little-undeclared war under the rug."

Gunny crossed his arms and scowled, "They're seizing American ships?"

"Yeah, that's right. By this time last year, the French had taken over three hundred American merchant ships and are now cruising our entire east coast at will."

"Well then, fuck 'em."

"At the moment, our friends on *Aspiration* are in grave peril. Let's assume the Frenchie's armed with eighteen pounders, a worst-case scenario. They have an effective range of a thousand yards and a maximum range of, oh, probably eighteen-hundred yards. His bow and stern chasers won't have such a range, but they're a little more accurate and higher. It won't be long before he sees *Aspiration*. She stands no chance against such a ship. I would like to aid our fellow Americans to pass the Frog safely. But I haven't figured a way to get close enough to dissuade a frigate without using our missiles. Any ideas?"

"We have missiles?" Gunny raised his eyes, creasing his forehead.

"Ah, yeah. I guess I didn't mention that. We have four FGM-148F Javelins with launchers. You know how to use those?"

"Ah, the fiberglass crates. Sure. They'll do the job if you want to blow it in two. The 148 Javelin has a range of a little over a mile and a half, and the F version has a naturally fragmenting steel warhead—pretty much be all she wrote. You say so, I'll splash the frog."

"Well, I don't want to 'splash the frog.' I have an underlying sympathy for the French position."

"Why's that?" Gunny raised an eyebrow.

"Well, unlike the Muslim pirates, the French are not devoid of moral justification. Fighting for the Rights of Man is a noble cause. I mean, it was Rousseau, a French-Swiss philosopher who debunked the class system and envisioned government as a social contract. Another Frenchman foresaw the separation of the congressional, executive, and judicial branches of government. These are the principles of our Declaration of Independence and Constitution. We owe a great debt to the French enlightenment. What I'd like is to do enough damage so *Aspiration* is not in danger—something that leaves her with steerage but unable to attack."

"Hmm." Gunny considered the situation, riveted on the beautiful tall ship off the port beam through his binoculars. The sun lit the ship's gray sails against a blue sky. Small, occasional wispy clouds passed in the distance.

"If I get close enough with the minigun, I could cut up her rigging something awful. It would mean getting me within less than a thousand yards. She could repair the damaged parts, but she couldn't attack *Aspiration* at the same time. We can go faster and turn sharper. If we maneuvered behind her without allowing her stern guns to set, I could chew the rigging out of her in a few seconds with a raking action."

Sails offered, "I suggest you do not underestimate her potential. That is not a yacht, nor is sailing their hobby. French ships were typically well-manned. Their sailing characteristics and gunnery proficiency might shock you."

"Well, if we made a quick tack behind her," Captain Joe intoned, "she has two options to bring a broadside to bear. Option one is she comes about clockwise through the eye of the wind. That means turning through roughly seventy degrees or missing stays—tough to aim a cannon under such circumstances. Option two is she wears. That takes longer and requires more space. And turning counterclockwise means we are going opposite directions, also making it difficult to aim the guns.

"Keep in mind the French navy's a mess. The qualified officers were members of the nobility and supported the king. After the Revolution, they either split the scene or faced a guillotine. It's a good bet their officers aren't the A-team, and their discipline is probably dicey. Jacobian equality doesn't fit well with military discipline. The crew might have spirit, but their competence is iffy. Let's go with option two. Mister Gunn, you good with that?"

"Sure. I'll do whatever you want. But, keep in mind, you must tack again, once we get behind her, so our port side will bear. When we do, her stern chasers will have a clear shot, and we'll be within range."

"I don't see a problem. We'll jig enough so they can't line up with this sea running. Set the minigun."

"Mister Handy, give me a hand?"

"Right." They headed below.

Jason held a shroud with one hand and leaned against the launch. He glanced at Sails. *Oh, shit. More exigent circumstances.*

The minigun weighed more than the grenade launcher, but Handy and Gunny had no trouble bringing it through the midship hatch. Custom modifications to its base made attachment to the weapon's stand simple and easy. Gunny looked around for the electrical motor connection.

Captain Joe stood on the aft deck seat, saw Gunny trying to find the electric outlet, and spoke over the coach roof, pointing to a weatherproof outlet at the base of the mast. "It's on the foremast."

Gunny glanced at the Captain, spotted the outlet, and plugged it in.

"Hmm," Gunny rubbed his chin. "we'll need a lot of ammo. The minigun needs a sustained feed."

He spotted a bronze deck plate next to the gun stand, ideally located to feed the 7.62 mm NATO cartridges in a disintegrating link belt.

"Mister Sails, you got a wrench?" Gunny pointed at the deck plate.

"Yes, sir. Right away."

Sails ducked into the pilothouse. Berg handed him the deck plate wrench. He unscrewed the plate and returned both the disk and wrench to the cabin.

"Mister Handy," Gunny pointed, "I will show you how to connect the disintegrating link feed through this hole."

Handy nodded without a word.

They went below to the weapons locker. Gunny opened the lid of several crates built into the floor labeled MINIGUN 7.62 MM 10,000 ROUNDS and showed Handy how to pass the initial connection through the deck plate hole. "You got this?"

"Yeah, got it." Handy started raising the belt out of the ammo canister.

Gunny returned to the deck, accepted the ammo belt through the opening, and loaded the gun.

Sails considered the impending maneuver while they continued close-hauled west, parallel to the French warship. "Captain, considering the freshening breeze, I suggest we reduce sail, furl the jibs and yankee and put one reef in the main, stays'l, and fores'l. If we come about clockwise to the north onto the port tack, we can continue around until we jibe into a starboard tack to pass his stern. Once we get across, we can switch to the port tack to give Mister Gunn a clear shot, port side. Some sail will dampen the roll, and we might confuse them a bit."

Captain Joe agreed. "Outstanding idea. Make it happen."

"Okay, ready about." Captain Joe exclaimed.

Serendipity spun through the wind to a broad port reach, heading east-northeast, the opposite direction. Rhythmic waves dashing against the starboard bow suddenly changed to the quiet undulating heave of traveling with the wind. She continued to curve behind *Méchant*, then jibed to the starboard tack, turning fast with the engine engaged. The French maintained their west-southwest, heading toward the Strait. *Serendipity* fell in behind her.

▪ ▪ ▪ ▪ ▪

Commandant Laurent stood at *Méchant's* starboard rail, considering what lay ahead at the Strait.

Maître Favre, supervising the mizzen sheets, addressed Lieutenant de vaisseau Durand deferentially, "Capitaine? Sir, the American schooner has tacked in behind us. Perhaps we might bloody the bugger's nose."

Lieutenant Durand pivoted to see *Serendipity* twist to a new heading. "Commandant," he pointed, "the American has turned to cross our stern. She may be a minor distraction, but we might poke the arrogant Yankee's eye with a well-placed ball from our stern chasers."

"Eh?" Commandant Laurent turned from their course in time to catch *Serendipity* slant across his stern. Somehow, her speed and wake did not correspond with her sails. "Yes, Mister Durand. A tough shot, I believe. Her pace is remarkable, but you may try."

The smell of slow match permeated the aft cabin. It did not bother the Gunner's mate. A lengthy pigtail confirmed his experience. With both the deck and target in motion, his perception of distance, direction, angle, and timing came together. He stood behind the first cannon, sighted down the barrel through the open stern window, instructing his crew. He put the match to the touchhole and moved to the second cannon.

▪ ▪ ▪ ▪ ▪

Serendipity's team surveyed the frigate. Two bright flashes appeared, three seconds apart, followed by the cannons' report. The first shot hit the water short, in their wake, and skipped harmlessly into the distance. The second shot flew with a high-pitched whizz, like a hummingbird's wings, ending in a far splash.

Captain Joe passed *Méchant*'s stern, waiting until her port broadside came into view, closing the distance between them.

FLASH! Another shot followed by the cannon's roar. "Smack!" A hole ripped through the reefed mainsail, leaving the fabric ends trailing in the wind, blue sky beyond contrasting with the white translucent sail. The on-deck crew instinctively ducked, then peered at the hole.

Jason's face flushed with alarm. He bent from his crouch to view the Captain. *Fuck. Attack thing isn't one-sided. Captain—a deep-seated death wish? WAY too risky.* He turned to Sails, crouched, holding a hand on a shroud, calm, but squinting at the hole.

"How's the range for you, Mister Gunn?" Captain Joe remained motionless, with a wry smile and sparkle in his eyes. His voice was bland but raised with a stern tone.

"At the rate we're gaining, we'll be 'bout right on the tack." Gunny remained calm, showing no emotion.

"Okay. Ready about. Helm's alee. I'm going close-hauled on the port tack. Sheets hard amidships." Captain Joe put the throttle to the wood.

The boat wheeled through the northwest wind. A fourth shot splashed the water with a deep 'ploop' where they would have been, had they not tacked.

Gunny sat behind the minigun, waiting for the tall ship's stern to swing into view. *Serendipity*'s pitch increased, but the roll dampened with the wind pressing the sails. He waited until she bore at 10:30 off the port bow, and the distance closed before spraying bullets.

"Sitidididididididit." Gunny marched a burst with tracers every five rounds—53 per second—down the port standing rigging and sheets. Mizzen lines split with a "pop" and flew to leeward, followed by those of the main and foremast—all but a few forward lines shredded.

"Jesus." Jason jumped from the rattle of 3,200 rounds per minute, the minigun's firing spin, and the clatter of spewing ammo links, hitting the deck and bouncing into the sea.

Gunny turned to the starboard standing rigging. "Sitidididididit." His second burst left only a few lines visible. The masts, no longer having side-to-side support or back bracing, fell. Another spurt focused on the mizzen mast above head height, cut the lines leading to the fife-rail. The yards tumbled down. When the mizzen sails dropped, the starboard side opened to view. He had a clear shot at the mainmast halyards and prepared for another burst until Captain Joe spoke.

"That'll do, Mister Gunn."

▪ ▪ ▪ ▪ ▪

"Mon Dieu!" *Méchant's* Commandant and crew ducked below the railing, hearing the splat of bullets striking the rigging, sails, and masts. The top hamper and crosstrees emitted an explosive 'crack,' splitting from their partners at the topmasts' junction. The lack of side support combined with the wind toppled the mizzen and main topgallant masts. They, in turn, brought down their topmasts. The yards and sails crashed to the deck with the sounds of splintered wood, smashed tackle, and ripped cordage. Men's cries pierced the air as they fell from the tops. With no backstays, the fore topgallant and topmasts twisted and toppled forward in sickening slow motion. Only the main and fore courses remained, flapping in the wind.

Commandant Laurent hunkered on the deck, red-faced and wide-eyed at Lieutenant Durand. The spanker boom broke from the mizzen and fell across the rails, protecting them from the falling mizzen topmasts and rigging. A double block, the size of a cannonball, smashed through the covering sail into the deck between them with a thud, rope streaming around the sheaves. The sun glowed yellowish through the sails, settling over the mass of broken spars. The smell of slow match, oakum, and rent wood permeated the air.

"Mère de Dieu." Lieutenant Durand uttered, fear making his voice quaver. He turned to his Commandant. "Qu'est-ce que c'est que ça?"

▪ ▪ ▪ ▪ ▪

"Well done, Mister Gunn," declared Captain Joe. "She's in no condition to attack a herring buss. Let's increase the distance between us. Gentlemen, I want to point out he fired first on what had to appear an unarmed American."

Gunny snickered at the damage. "That'll teach the fuckin' Frog o' messin' with the big dog."

The shooting had lasted less than sixty seconds.

Distant cannon reports and cascading cartridges reverberating through the hull awoke the below-deck crew. They jumped from their bunks and headed topside. A hint of acrid smoke drifted on the air. They stared at the French vessel floating sideways in the moderate sea. Yells of men trying to make order out of rigging all ahoo faded into the distance.

"Ding-ding, ding-ding, ding." *Serendipity*'s ship's clock chimed five bells. It was 1030 hours.

"Mister Berg, head due east. When we are well out of range, turn into the wind and replace the damaged mains'l. Then head east-northeast."

Berg pointed to Masters, Handy, Sails, and Jason. "Okay, boys," a trace of disgust in his tone, "prepare to hand the mains'l, and hoist the rest. Let's get away from here. Several blips on the radar, over the horizon, signal more adventure to the east."

20
POST-MERIDIAN

February 26, 1798 - Further into the Algerian Basin
At 1200 hours, Joe took the helm from Berg. A steady breeze out of the west-northwest allowed him to remain alone. The radar revealed his location. He smiled, thrilled with his craft, conditions, and locale. White horses danced away from the starboard bow. *Serendipity* undulated on the quartering seas heading east-northeast in the Algerian Basin. High, thin clouds had moved in to cover the sky to the horizon. The gauzy light made soft shadows from the masts and sails. The air grew more chill. His jacket felt good.

The crew sat at the tables in their matching navy-blue military sweaters awaiting food.

"dzzzzit.... dzzzzit." The salon continued its steady roll.

The fragrance of Chicken Veracruz permeated the cabin. Cookie had baked shingled potatoes until the edges turned golden, and his seasoned chicken became browned and crisp. He poured a mixture of tomatoes, cinnamon, and oregano over the chicken and sprinkled it with scattered olives, shallots, and sprigs of oregano. It was not enough to overcome the gloomy atmosphere.

Cookie and Stew resumed their tasks with long faces. Berg glanced to his right. Bones' head rested on his clasped hands, lost in reverie. The crew ate in silence.

After lunch, Chief stared at Gunny for a time before breaking the silence. "Mister Gunn, that cannonball was too fuckin' close. Money ain't worth dyin' for."

Berg snapped to attention. Bones abandoned his reverie. The Captain listened from the pilothouse through the open door.

Gunny studied Chief. "Yeah, I get it." He looked aft to Berg. "You know, defending against attack is one thing—and they fired first, even though we could not have appeared to offer much of a threat. I will have a problem, though, of attacking without provocation. Now, I understand," he waved a hand to dismiss the notion, "the French are killin' Americans in the Caribbean Sea. This quasi-war," he made quote fingers, "might be political bullshit in hindsight, but I'll bet it's not to those guys losing limbs, lives, and livelihoods in the West Indies.

"Don't get me wrong, I'll always defend America's interests—in the twenty-first century, the eighteenth century—I don't give a fuck." He shifted his position and eyeballed his coffee cup, turning it in his fingers. "My mind ain't easy, though. If a cannonball hits me, I'll be dead. Wonder how my epitaph would read...."

Chief nodded, grasping Gunny's point of view.

Masters quipped, "How's this for an epitaph:

On two twenty-six, seventeen ninety-eight,
An untimely demise came to pass that date,
A cannonball took a good man called Gunny,
Here lies what's left, and it ain't very funny."

Gales of laughter broke out. Handy rolled in his seat. Gunny grinned, and his face reddened.

"But," Sails interjected after a suitable pause, his British accent implying curiosity, "was America's singular interests threatened?"

Jason considered Sails' comment for a brief interval. "America must pay off her Revolutionary War debts by expanding trade. The Captain was right about protecting *Aspiration*. If we did nothing, she had no chance against the French frigate. But, I, too, am having a hard time balancing the realities of the 1798 political situation with potential death. I mean, this parallel universe thing is hard to grasp. If it's true, it's only a death match for us—I'm not sure what it is for them. I saw actual people killed. Our plight is not a video game. I'd prefer to go to our rendezvous point and hang out until we get the hell out-a-here." He turned to Berg.

"Gentlemen," Berg responded, "making sure we are still in one piece when we reappear in Seattle is worth a strong defensive posture."

Jason raised an eyebrow at Berg. "Attacking the French frigate was defensive?"

"We will defend American interests no matter what, when, or where." Berg tapped his forefinger on the table. "You must understand, like it or not, we ARE here. We will do whatever is necessary. It's just for another couple o' days. Did you suppose you would not earn your money?"

Gunny changed the topic. "Okay, listen up. There might be more action. If so, I want y'all familiar with a carbine. Before anybody sacks out, I think we should do weapons training on deck. You must be competent in your use of an M4 and have confidence in each other's use, okay?" Gunny turned from the crew to Berg.

Berg punched the intercom button for the pilothouse. "Captain, weapons training okay?"

Joe had been listening. He pressed an intercom button. "Yes, go ahead, but I want everyone except Mister Cook and Mister Steward set up with a shoulder holster first, and give me one."

"Okay." Gunny pointed at Masters. "Give me a hand. Guys, hang loose for a minute. Before we go on deck, I'll get everybody lined out with shoulder carry."

Masters followed Gunny to the arms locker. Gunny opened a drawer and removed nine custom forty-five under-shoulder packages and put them in a sports duffel. He took two M4s out of the rack and pulled the magazines. He put the magazines in the duffel, added several more from the ammo case, handed it to Masters, and carried the two carbines to the salon.

Gunny laid the guns on the forward table, put the duffle on the aft table, and removed the holsters. "Gentlemen, you may have noticed the slits in your shirt and sweater. I expect those openings will accommodate these little goodies." He tossed a holster to each of the crew. Berg flipped one up to Captain Joe. "Here's how they work."

He took his .45 from the back of his pants, placed it on the table, and removed his sweater and shirt. He opened a package, unclipped the holster from the harness, and swung both arms through the straps over his t-shirt.

"Adjust to fit your body. Help each other with this. Extend the horizontal band across your chest and clip it to the other side." The snap made a crisp click. He slipped back into his shirt. "Push the metal holster clasp and tie-down strap through the vertical slot, re-button your shirt, and snap the strap to your belt."

After putting his sweater on, he drove the clip through the armpit aperture, hooked on the holster, and jammed his .45 in the black leather assemblage. Thwack! He raised his hands. "That's it. If you're wearing a jacket, no one will know you're carrying unless you're pretty goddamn careless."

The crew stood up, and the salon transformed into a locker room with shirts and sweaters hung on seats and laid over the tables. They helped each other adjust the straps, eventually got it right, put their sweaters on, clipped the holsters, grabbed their forty-fives from many spots, and popped them in.

Gunny pumped his fist in the air. "Good. Put on your Stormy Seas, and let's go on deck—check everyone out on an M4." He grabbed the gear and headed on deck.

As they passed through the pilothouse, Captain Joe spoke in an appeasing tone. "Look, guys, I don't expect anyone except Mister Gunn to have to use a weapon. But we are, in fact, in a war-zone, and we can't get home for a couple more days. Radar shows we're approaching traffic on both sides. If you look carefully, you'll make out a sail peeking over the horizon ahead, off the starboard bow. And the radar reveals smaller targets off the port bow. I don't expect you to use these weapons, but it's prudent everyone has a fundamental idea of how in case of an emergency. Also, before we start the weapons stuff, set the gennaker. I want to take advantage of what wind we have."

The air blew with a gentle breeze, and the temperature continued to cool. Occasional breaking crests with glassy foam paraded away from the starboard forequarter with a whispered swish. Silvery clouds to the horizon did not entirely conceal the sun. The crew gathered around, holding on to whatever was handy.

Sails and Jason, on watch Primes, set the gennaker. The strain of the large sail tightened the backstays.

"Okay, listen up." Gunny removed a magazine from the duffle. "Who's familiar with an AR-15, M4, or an M16?"

Berg, Masters, and Handy raised a hand.

"Okay, who's competent with an M4?"

Berg and Masters raised a hand. Jason, Sails, Chief, and Bones frowned.

"So, Mister Handy, you're acquainted with an AR-15, I take it?"

"Fuckin' A," Handy quipped. "Smoked a lot o' drift shit up north."

"Well, the M4 is the carbine version of the M16—a fully automatic version of an AR-15." He slid the slide enough to verify it was empty, tapped it closed, and passed it around. "To the left is the safety. The ejection port is right. Don't point it at anyone."

The carbine arrived back, and Gunny raised a single index finger. "Rule one, never, ever point your gun at anyone or anything unless you intend to use it." He looked at everyone individually to make sure they got it.

Poker faces concealed their disgust with such condescension. When Gunny turned away, the boys exchanged glances. Everyone on deck was a gun guy.

Gunny's soliloquy consumed his attention. "Rule number two, keep your finger above the trigger until you're ready to fire." He showed with his finger. "Rule number three, if you're not ready to fire, keep the gun on safe. So, once done firing, I want to hear that safety click. Did everybody get that? Here's an acronym to remember: SPORTS S-P-O-R-T-S. S means Slap." He slapped upward on the magazine to make sure it's seated. "P means pull the charging handle. O means Observe. Make sure the chamber is clear. R means to release the charging handle to feed a fresh round, but don't ride the charging handle. Let it snap back. T means to tap the forward assist to verify it's seated. And S means Shoot."

Gunny loaded a magazine, slapped it in place, pulled the charging handle, checked the chamber was empty, let it snap forward, tapped it, raised the weapon to his shoulder, and fired a three-round burst.

"Blam-Blam-Blam."

He removed the magazine and pointed to Chief. "Mister Chief, you're first."

Everyone took a turn. Its weight surprised Jason. *Thought it would weigh more.* He fired his shots. "Blam, Blam, Blam." Loud. The recoil jerked the barrel. Ejected casings bounced on the deck, then into the sea. Excitement overcame the blasts and recoil. He handed the gun to Gunny. *Fuck. What have I done?*

The breeze turned light. Wave crests became glassy and no longer broke. The off-watch guys headed to their cabins. Jason, Sails, Gunny, and Chief studied a topgallant sail above the horizon through their binoculars. They were gaining on her.

21 SEATOWN

February 26 - Seattle

Mother Nature dealt Seattle another gray, wet, wintry morning—trying to keep Seatown down. She failed. Pete and Gary were at the Seattle City Light Canal substation, site of the first power intrusion. They were oblivious to the weather. Pete drove the crew-cab pickup inside the enclosure. Gary locked the gate behind them.

"Gary," Pete pointed, "you check the sides. Look high and low for small anomalies. Something ain't right—too well organized. Whoever it was must have known we'd be aware of the stolen power. They've gone to considerable effort to keep us from knowing how. My gut tells me they will return. If they did it once, they'd do it again. Maybe they left something—some indicator."

"Like what?"

"I don't know, a clamp, a wire scrape, something that doesn't belong."

They both pulled out their Maglites and started their inspection, light in one hand and a to-go coffee cup in the other. The flashlight would be a decent cudgel in a pinch at fifteen inches long and two and a half pounds.

"Hey, Pete?" Gary called from over by the street barrier. He shined his light on what appeared to be a littered coffee cup stuck in the square pattern wire fence. "Come, look at this."

Pete hustled over. "Whatcha got, Gary?"

"Well," shining his light into the cup, "see, there's a little white electrical gizmo stuck in that cup."

Pete removed the cup from the fence and examined the device—a little white plastic box with a small glass eye and a white wire wrapped around the inside.

"Hell, it's a nanny cam." He rolled the gizmo in his fingers. "Somebody has been watching the yard."

"You gonna report this?"

Pete poured out the rest of his coffee, shook the cup clear of fluid, placed the camera inside, and stuck it in the fence. He took Gary by the arm along the fence line, out of sight from the camera.

"Gary," Pete spoke in confidence, "we will not file a report until we know if it involves anyone else at City Light. Okay? This attack was well-organized. It needed help from someone inside SCL. Before we go through regular channels, give me a day to go through a backchannel—see if it might involve anyone upstairs, okay?"

"Jesus, Pete, how we gonna explain why we didn't report this right away?"

"It's only one day. We can 'find' it tomorrow, can't we? Come on, Gary. Let's consider the integrity of the entire system."

"Oh, shit. Okay, Pete. But it 'ill piss me off if I get my butt in a jamb over this."

■ ■ ■ ■ ■

Paul Gorken, Operations Manager and Transition Coordinator, checked the time and date displays as he arrived at the G-WAD control room. The Seattle clock read 0755. Both the Seattle and Ship date displays read Feb. 26. He peeked in on Jack Wilson, Manager of Engineering. Jack was staring at one of three computer monitors rubbing his neck. His lab coat draped over his chair back, and his coveralls were more crumpled than usual. "You okay, Jack?"

"Yeah." He was unshaven, and his eyes were red. "Our chances haven't improved—still around five-in-eight."

"Shit." Paul walked by the tech crew cubicles to get a sense of their morale. Their coats laid around, but no one was in his seat. He stopped outside the Coffee Room to listen to the low chatter.

"If this doesn't work, I'm screwed. I don't relish doing maintenance on some bullshit website."

"Yeah, if we get the chance. I'm not sure a certain amount of notoriety is avoidable in the event of a failure. If Joe Cochrane and Bill Stratton disappear, there'll be an inquiry. I'll have to get a CDL license."

"Well, I'm not giving up yet. I'm bettin' on Jack Wilson."

Paul retired to his office and slumped into his chair, staring at a black screen.

Keith Larken, Power Supply Manager, approached Paul. His hand shook, and his voice quivered. "Paul, the two SCL guys from yesterday, found a nanny cam at Canal."

Paul frowned. "Huh? Okay." He returned to the moment. "Is the second cam operational?"

"Yeah, it's continuing to transmit. I've been listening live. I have also loaded the conversation into a file if you want to hear it yourself."

"Have they reported their find upstream?"

"No, they have not. Pete, the Foreman, wants to go through a connection of his inside SCL to determine if someone in management is part of a conspiracy."

"Just the same two guys?"

"Yes," Keith handed Paul two SCL dossiers.

"Okay. Yahoo, here we go. In for a dime, in for a dollar." He punched a number on his phone.

▪ ▪ ▪ ▪ ▪

Rolf's cell-phone started ringing. He recognized the phone number. "Hi, Paul."

"Hi, Rolf. I got a hot one for you. It needs immediate action. Two guys from SCL have found one of our nanny cams. We need another shot of power. Pete, the leader of the two, has figured we might return for another infusion of kilowatts. I want you to intervene and convince them to sit on it. I'm sending their vitals to you right now. The billing code is 'all kinds o' mean, nasty, ugly things.'"

"I'm on it." Rolf hung up.

▪ ▪ ▪ ▪ ▪

Pete and Gary stopped at a Starbucks in Ballard on their way to Viewland/Hoffman. They used the bathroom, got coffees to-go, and headed to the truck. Two enormous well-dressed men came toward them chatting, apparently headed to Starbucks.

Pete climbed in the driver's seat and Gary into the passenger side. The two approaching men suddenly split, jumped into the seats behind

Pete and Gary, grabbed their collars, and stuck pistols with silencers into the back of their heads.

"Aaagh!" Pete and Gary screamed and tried to jerk forward in their seats.

"Sit up. Don't move, and you won't get hurt," the suit behind Pete ordered. Pete turned his head right toward Gary. Even in the dim light of the cab, he saw a massive man with a dark complexion, scruffy black beard, and black hair holding a gun at Gary's head. The man showed no emotion.

Gary twisted left to see a clean-shaven silver-haired man aiming a gun at Pete's head. The man smiled and spoke calmly like this was normal. "Do nothing stupid, and everything 'ill turn out fine. Hand me your phones and don't look back."

Pete glanced at Gary, then peeked at the Maglite next to his seat, considering its weapon potential. *No chance.* They exchanged a glance and passed their phones.

"Okay, don't speak. Not a word. Drive to the Fremont Troll, and I'll tell you where to park. You are about to receive an obscene amount of money."

"So, Pete and Gary." The driver's side suit passed each man a folder. It contained their SCL employee's data with pictures. "We know who you are, where you live, who your wives are, where they work, who your kids are, and where they go to school. Pete, we know your Mom's schedule in the home. Gary, we know where your sister is, and needs your help with your asshole brother-in-law. So, here's the score: You have option A, option B, or option C.

"I like option A where you each receive approximately two-hundred thousand dollars. I'll bet you don't even remember going in together on two one-dollar lottery tickets, do you? Well, you did. It was a donation to an organization called SAVE! DON'T PAVE! Congratulations. I have your winning entry ticket stubs right here. SDP is a legitimate organization maintained by our client for situations where it is necessary to pay off people secretly. Your prize is an all-expense-paid trip to Las Vegas for you and your wives."

"Oh, shit." Pete winced.

The suit resumed, "You'll fly first-class. An escort will meet you, and you'll stay at a designated casino in a first-class suite. At that casino, you'll bet as directed with money supplied to you. Each of you will win at least $250,000. You will pay the taxes. While in Vegas, you may take in any show of your choice at our expense—part of the prize. Then you go home. The amount each of you receives will vary. Sorry 'bout that, but we must have a semblance of reality.

"Option B is you agree to this arrangement but reveal it to someone. Someone means anyone—police, wives, co-workers, bartender, cab driver, that barista you've been flirting with, Gary, over on Alki—whoever. Then, we hunt you down, kill you, and everyone listed in the file you have before you.

"Or option C, the option whereby you decline our offer, and we kill you right now and leave."

Pete and Gary looked at each other, shook their heads at the futility, and moaned.

"But wait. There's more. You guessed it. Our client needs another hit of power. You will aid this endeavor by finding no initial evidence of how we did it. You will also report any problem you encounter that might hinder our client's mission to a cell-phone number I will provide. I assure you this will be our last power heist. Also, you need to appreciate it will cause no permanent damage to the system. After the next shot of power, you are free to find the cameras and follow any lead—except to tell anyone what you know.

"So, now you must decide. Option A, option B, or option C?"

▪ ▪ ▪ ▪ ▪

"Bringg." Paul's caller ID displayed Rolf. "Hey, Rolf. They give you any trouble?"

"Not really. It was a nice carrot with a big stick—an offer they couldn't refuse. You're all set. You've got a green light."

"Okay. Thanks."

22
BETWIXT

February 26, 1798 - 2,638 meters on the depth sounder

Serendipity rocked on a low, slow swell, continuing east-northeast. Small glassy yellowish-green waves no longer broke. A weak sun showed through the dull afternoon sky, and the dying wind carried a damp chill.

The watch crew clustered in the pilothouse and stared at the boats ahead through their binoculars. With the gennaker asleep, they continued to gain on a large square-rigger. Her flag was not yet visible on its stern or masthead. Two three-masted corsairs farther north were on a similar heading. One was all lateen-rigged. The larger had a lateen sail only on the foremast. Both had gunports along their sides. Outboard of them were two galley consorts—smaller craft rowing in a slow, steady rhythm besides their single lateen sail.

Captain Joe started the engine. "Gentlemen," he spoke offhanded, "provided the sails stay asleep, we'll give them help. I intend to keep the corsairs to port but maintain our position more than a mile windward of the ship. We'll slip betwixt and between. I will not allow *Serendipity* to get within range of that ship's cannon."

Everyone trained their binoculars on the ship. Eventually, the flag swayed enough to reveal the Union Jack in the first quarter on a red field.

Captain Joe let his glasses hang. "She's a British man-o'-war. Hmm. Now then, we are not at war with the British, but they view American vessels as a labor source and, without a doubt, will have designs on us."

"Why's that?" Chief asked.

"The war with France has made the English desperate for sailors. Rule Britannia requires a lot of men. Since the United States doesn't have an effective navy, the Brits have made it standard practice to take

American seamen out of our vessels anytime they want. We won't let that happen. However, I wish to befriend them—a delicate situation."

As they got closer to the ship, its port side, painted yellow with blue top works and a blue stripe between the yellow and waterline, came into view. Two rows of gunports ran along her side. Additional cannon apertures appeared on her upper decks.

"Captain," Sails declared, continuing to focus, "I make her a fourth-rate… *Centaur*—maybe sixty guns. Out of Gib searching for Napoleon, I will wager."

Jason focused his Steiners on the corsairs and galleys bearing northeast. *Serendipity* was edging away from the man-o'-war to keep out of cannon range but toward the four raiders. He saw many flag hoists exchanged. *Oh, yeah. Pre-radio.* Their courses changed in unison to intercept *Serendipity*.

▪ ▪ ▪ ▪ ▪

The British masthead lookout shouted, "On deck, there. American schooner gaining port side."

The watch officers stood on the quarterdeck, training their telescopes on the approaching schooner with the strange headsail. Captain Callum Clayton, distinguished by the single epaulet on his right shoulder, was a Post-Captain for fewer than three years. He dressed well, wearing a blue coat with white lapels and a high collar. Not a flag officer, he wore his cocked hat fore and aft. His posture was perfect.

He ran a tight ship. His crew sported white duck trousers with horizontal black-and-white striped shirts under their red vests. Many had neck scarfs and donned blue waistcoats in various states of decay, their regular wear. Several wore shoes. The ship was trim and well provisioned. Decks, holystoned daily to a light tan, pleased both eyes and feet. New sails were light gray and supple, holding their shape in the fading breeze. Number one manila running rigging was nearly white, that ideal stage in their life with stretch and shrinkage out, yet sturdy and soft.

"A strange sail indeed." The Captain spoke to his first lieutenant, sipping his coffee. "Her speed is excessive, considering the light air. Perchance, Mister Northcott, she may offer a suitable man or two for which we could find useful work. With the breeze dying, perhaps the dispatch of the pinnace might avail us of what she offers."

■ ■ ■ ■ ■

Serendipity's crew observed the nearest corsair change her flag hoist. The breeze died, and the sea became glassy. The pirates lowered their yards, and sweeps appeared through their hulls. All four vessels started rowing toward an interception, but it would take time. The two galleys began pulling ahead of their mother ships. The gennaker fell flaccid. Sails and Jason dropped and stowed the large sail, then raised the foresail. The Captain tapped the throttle, moving faster than necessary to maintain steerage. His wake bubbled away.

■ ■ ■ ■ ■

The course change by the lateens was not unnoticed aboard *Centaur*. The officers studied the scene from their port rail.

Lieutenant Nye Northcott addressed the men preparing the boat. "Belay the pinnace there. Captain, I'm afraid the American is in serious trouble. Those galleys will overwhelm her in short order. Our launches cannot protect her, and with no wind, we cannot intervene. She's too far away for our cannon to cover her with any effect."

"Very well, Mister Northcott. I believe you are right. However, even with no wind, she has headway. How...?"

■ ■ ■ ■ ■

Jason continued to stare through his binoculars at the flotilla's formation. Their course would intercept *Serendipity's* before long. He could see dozens of men armed with swords and pistols crowding their bows. "Captain, I believe an attack is imminent."

Captain Joe and Bones exchanged a furtive glance. "So, Mister Decker, do we let the charging bear kill us because that's his nature, or do we defend ourselves? Never mind, the answer's clear."

Sails lowered his binoculars. "Captain, I appreciate your patriotism. Your impulse to defend American interests, regardless of when or where, is commendable. But, Sir, you must understand my loyalty to British pursuits is equally patriotic. I will take serious offense should you order any action that would harm a British vessel."

Captain Joe smiled and adjusted his hat. "No problem, Mister Sails. I hope to establish an amicable relationship. If so, I want to exchange two men for dinner. Wouldn't that be a thrill? Could you have dinner with a fellow Brit who lived over two hundred years ago and not do anything that would compromise our situation?"

Sails narrowed his eyes and glanced sideways. "I believe so. But how could I compromise our situation? I mean, if what they learn only exists in a parallel universe and will not affect our own time, what is the risk?"

"It's true there's no risk to our own time. But keep in mind, they are warriors. I wouldn't want you to do anything to jeopardize our boat and crew. And,... we have problems to overcome."

Bones gave the Captain a surreptitious glance, hoping his parallel universe theory was correct.

"The first hurdle is the British navy during this period. They have no respect for American ships. In those days—these days? Anyway, your ancestors felt, or feel, it's their right to impress American seamen into the British navy. Impressment's a serious issue. We must satisfactorily address this problem before establishing affable relations."

"The second challenge and the most urgent is the impending attack by Muslim pirates." He pointed at the vessels rowing toward a point to cut them off. "Fortunately, a solution is at hand. By demonstrating our power in overcoming the pirates, we will ensure the British afford us proper respect. Then we can approach them for a gam."

The Captain turned to Gunny. "Mister Gunn, it appears an attack without provocation is upon us."

Gunny lowered his glasses. "Yes, it does."

"So, take the launch with the coxswain of your choice and our javelin missiles. Blow the two larger Muslim vessels out of the water. That should convince the two galleys an attack is futile. It will also show our capabilities to the British. I want the Brits to understand we pose a greater threat to them than they do to us. Can you do that?"

"You bet your sweet ass."

"Now, let me be clear: I do not want to destroy the galleys if you can help it. Non-Muslim slaves probably man those boats, possibly Americans, poor chaps. I want the galleys to see that an attack on us would mean certain death. Okay?"

Gunny lowered his head and put his hands in his pockets. "Yeah, okay. I'll take a TAC and a Colt in case it's necessary to pick individual targets or protect us from unforeseen circumstances."

Captain Joe pointed to Sails and Jason. "Get the launch in the water for use by Mister Gunn."

Gunny turned to Chief. "You run the boat, and I'll snuff rag-heads."

"Sure." Chief went below with Gunny to help load the missiles and command launch unit. While he was there, he slung an M4.

▪ ▪ ▪ ▪ ▪

The launch ranged ahead, giving the British an unimpeded view of events. The fifteen-star American flag flew off the stern. Gunny positioned himself with his back against the engine cover and his feet against the hull. The launch tube rested on his shoulder over the engine housing, aiming to port so the backblast would go safely to starboard. He used the command launch unit's infrared (IR) targeting system to set a track box around the closest corsair. Nothing showed up—no IR signature. The galleys were getting closer, not yet within range of the M4s. The larger ships were not far behind. "Damn." He had a fiery flash inside his Stormy Seas.

▪ ▪ ▪ ▪ ▪

"Mister Bones, please take the helm." Captain Joe considered the vectors for a probable outcome. "Mister Decker, you're with me. I need your help in setting up the drone to establish communication with *Centaur*."

They hustled below to a forward locker, unpacked the drone, brought it on deck, and prepared to launch.

▪ ▪ ▪ ▪ ▪

"Hullo, what is this?" Lieutenant Northcott followed *Serendipity's* launch proceeding under power through his telescope and offered a narrative for the crew's benefit. "The schooner has dispatched a boat. There is no one rowing. How is that possible? Two men—one steering—must be eight knots. Strange gear aboard. Red jackets, blue hats, blue pants—match the schooner. One of them has crouched in the hull and placed a strange tube over his shoulder, pointing it toward the Moors. I cannot imagine what that will do. The galleys will hit them in minutes."

With the sails limp, the men lined the port rail. The crew murmured while watching the launch move through the water. They could see no means of thrust.

▪ ▪ ▪ ▪ ▪

Flash,... Boom! A cannon fired from Gunny's targeted vessel. The splash was not near.

Gunny grinned. "Perfect." The cannon shot left a sharp infrared target. He placed brackets around the image in the command launch unit and established a lock.

"Here we go. Fire one."

"Swoosh." The missile flew straight as a light beam.

A roaring explosion turned the lightly built wooden boat into an orange-yellow fireball, raining fragments over the sea.

▪ ▪ ▪ ▪ ▪

Centaur's crew took a collective breath. The concussion resonated across the calm sea. Aghast at the sudden and complete devastation, they stood away from the rail. The crew broke protocol, talking aloud. "Holy Mother." "Bloody beastly." Such a weapon could threaten them.

"Silence on deck there." Captain Clayton brooked no deviation from naval decorum. "Mister Northcott, you may beat to quarters and clear for action."

Lieutenant Northcott turned to his second Lieutenant. "Mister Bickerton, beat to quarters." Then he returned to his telescope and continued his narrative. "The galleys have stopped rowing. They are having a conversation—seem to argue whether to continue or turn back. Yeah, I would turn back too if I were you. The American in the launch is pointing his tube at the other corsair."

■ ■ ■ ■ ■

Serendipity's crew saw *Centaur's* gunports open. A low rumble emanated as the cannons ran out. Their black muzzles appeared through the holes.

■ ■ ■ ■ ■

Gunny loaded a second missile and returned to his firing position. He changed from the day viewer to the wide field-of-view to acquire an IR target.

Chief squirmed. The other vessels continued toward them. "Any time now, Gunny."

Gunny did not reply. He awaited another shot. An orange flash appeared from the side of the remaining corsair. He switched to the narrow view and locked on the hot cannon.

"Fire two." The missile swooshed toward its target. The cannonball splashed astern. The second corsair erupted in another orange-yellow blaze. A thunderous roar poured forth.

■ ■ ■ ■ ■

Centaur's crew executed their clear-for-action drill, trying to follow the conflict on their port beam. The smell of slow match drifted in the air. The other corsair exploded in a semi-spherical inferno. The blast in the distance caused them to pause.

Captain Clayton uttered, "It would appear the Americans have developed a potent destructive weapon." His officers, starring through their telescopes, made no response.

■ ■ ■ ■ ■

Gunny put down the launcher, picked up the TAC, and loaded a cartridge. "Hold her steady, Chief. I'm gonna try to take out that tall dude steering the galley to the left."

Chief came around to go straight into a long low lump from the west-southwest with just enough speed to maintain steerage, minimizing pitch with no roll.

Gunny changed his position to a starboard side crouch and shouldered the twenty-six-pound fifty caliber rifle. He concentrated on the helmsman, pushed the stock firmly into his shoulder, breathing, launch pitch, galley roll, aim, aim, his fingertip squeezed the trigger between heartbeats. BLAM! The recoil jerked hard into his body. The helmsman burst into pieces, tumbling over the side. The galley quickly changed helmsman and rowed away. click "Mister Chief? You got me on?" click click "Yes Captain?" click click "That'll do. Tell Mister Gunn to cease firing." The Captain nodded to Sails. "I will send a drone over to the Brits to initiate friendly relations." click

Chief steered while standing. "You hear that, Gunny?"

"Yeah, I heard it. Bullshit. Son-of-a-bitch wants to kill me, he's dead meat." Gunny jacked in another cartridge, made one click on the scope, and aimed at the other helmsman. Even breathing, a smile for calm, anticipating the launch's pitch, galley motion, timing, stock pressed to shoulder, breathe, hold, squeeze. BLAM! Pain telegraphed into his shoulder. The second helmsman's body blew apart. No one took his place. They rowed hard. click "Mister Chief, please pass the radio to Mister Gunn." click

Chief passed the radio without comment to Gunny.

Gunny laid the rifle on the engine cover and took the radio. click "Yes, sir?" click click "You done now? I'd appreciate it if you'd follow my orders for the next couple of days. Can you do that?" click click "Sure." click click "Thanks. Now that the Brits understand our capability, we have an excellent chance of dealing with each other as wary equals. Hold your location and hoist the white flag. Rest the unloaded launch tube on your shoulder and face the Brits, but don't aim it, okay?" click click "Copy that." click click "Does that mean you hear me or that you'll comply?" click click "I hear you, and I'll comply." click

▪ ▪ ▪ ▪ ▪

The man-o'-war attended. The smoke and scent of slow match hung in the windless air.

23
CENTAUR

February 26, 1798 - Latitude Algiers, Longitude Valencia
Captain Clayton snapped his telescope closed, held it in his hands behind him, and rocked back and forth. He made little blowing toots with his mouth, considering the situation. A rocket capable of blasting a ship to pieces, bodies flying apart from a single shot at an incredible range—he had no defense. The crew continued to line the port rail. Their flushed faces and wavering murmurs signaled they grasped the threat. With no wind, *Centaur* was a sitting duck.

▪ ▪ ▪ ▪ ▪

Gunny took the boat hook, attached the white flag to the halyard, and stood it in the forward brackets. Then he got the missile launcher and sat casually on the engine cover facing *Centaur.* They idled peacefully on a long undulation—a leftover lump from a faraway wind.

▪ ▪ ▪ ▪ ▪

The explosions awakened Berg, Masters, Handy, Cookie, and Steward. Once on deck, they rubbed their eyes with looks ranging from bewilderment to fear.

"Good afternoon, gentlemen." Captain Joe smiled. He and Jason continued preparing the drone on the foredeck. "You just missed a marvelous piece of action." He pointed toward the smoking wreckage. "We dissuaded a Barbary attack a few minutes ago."

The men scanned the horizon. *Centaur* lay becalmed a mile away to the south. The galleys were rowing north toward smoking debris in the water.

"It will be eight bells soon, anyway. Take your showers and dress in the day's uniform. We may have company for dinner."

Jason had not seen a drone before. "So, Captain, tell me about this thing."

"It's a quadcopter I had built. These lights," he clutched one end of a quad unit, "will make it easy to distinguish from a distance. It can fly out over three miles and remain in the air for forty-five minutes. It has a loudspeaker, microphone, video camera, and can deliver small stuff." He attached a radio wrapped in instructions. "We'll be able to see what it sees and hear what it hears on my computer. I'm hoping this hanging white flag," he attached it, "will allow us to approach the Brits and establish communication." He took a Citizen Chronomaster AB9000-61E watch from his pocket and strapped it to the radio.

Jason creased his brow at Captain Joe. *A watch?*

Joe discerned Jason's frown. "It's a gift. Accurate time makes it much simpler to determine longitude. I set the watch for Greenwich Time. It is accurate within five seconds a year—and like yours—it's waterproof to ten atmospheres. Any decent navigator in the British navy can determine longitude by lunar distance, but having the correct time makes it simpler. They only have to swing the sextant at noon. The difference between exact noon wherever they are and Greenwich is their longitude. The battery will go dead in five years, and it will become a curious piece of junk for somebody to throw away."

Jason eyed the Captain. *Why would battery life matter if this parallel universe thing is real?*

Eight bells chimed on the ship's clock—1600 hours. The Captain and Jason joined Sails in the pilothouse. With the foredeck clear of jib sheets and no wind, the drone lifted quickly and headed for the man-o'-war.

▪ ▪ ▪ ▪ ▪

Centaur was quiet except for an occasional rigging creak and a final rumble of rattling down. The odor of slow match continued to drift from below. Those who were able contemplated the schooner and launch to port. The small boat maintained its position. The shooter relaxed on the center box, continuing to hold the peculiar tube. A white flag drooped from the jury-rigged pole. They switched their attention to the schooner and the strange whine of the drone. It lifted off and headed for *Centaur* at a hundred feet above the water. The crew made a collective draw for breath and, again, stood away from the rail.

"Marines ready," Captain Clayton ordered.

Lieutenant Northcott announced while staring through his telescope, "Captain, the curious flying machine has a white flag hanging."

"Hold your fire." The Captain raised his left arm. "Do not fire unless I give the word. D'ye hear me thar?"

The blades whirred with the sound of a hundred bees. The impossible mechanism slowed and descended to an elevation twenty feet higher than the officers on the quarterdeck. Then it halted its advance and hovered thirty feet from *Centaur's* stern port quarter.

▪ ▪ ▪ ▪ ▪

Captain Joe turned to Sails. "Mister Sails, please introduce me. Your British accent may help decrease their fear. Also, you handle the microphone while I'll manage the drone."

Sails reached for the microphone. "Abso-bloody-lootely." Joining Captain Joe and Jason looking at the live feed on the laptop computer, he spoke in his most vibrant baritone, "Greetings, Gentlemen. Captain Plimsoll of the American schooner *Serendipity* sends regards to His Majesty's Ship *Centaur*. Compliments to the Captain."

▪ ▪ ▪ ▪ ▪

Centaur's crew recoiled at the amplified voice. Two men cowered behind the main hatch cover, one shrunk behind the mast. The Brown Bess equipped marines cocked their flintlocks. Fingers trembled next to triggers.

Captain Clayton pulled his pistol but pointed it down by his side. "Hold your fire unless I say the word." His gruff tone traveled through the otherwise quiet ship.

"Captain, we mean you no harm," Joe declared, seeing the frightened crew prepare to fire. "Quite the opposite. I'm sure you've noticed we possess unique equipment. For example, I can give you a wrist compatible waterproof chronometer set to Greenwich time accurate within five seconds a year under any sea conditions. If you allow me, I'll bring my flying machine over your vessel and drop the clock attached to a communication link. It will facilitate conversation between our two ships. I have a gadget whereby I can see and hear you speak to my flying machine. But it cannot stay aloft for long. To whom do I have the honor of addressing, and may I approach your ship?"

Captain Clayton hesitated and grumbled to his first lieutenant, "What's a gadget?"

Lieutenant Northcott shrugged.

Captain Clayton weighed the risks. *Serendipity's* weapons, abilities, and the bizarre flying contraption left him astounded. But the apparent friendliness of the American seemed sincere. Playing along to see how events unfold seemed best at the moment. He shouted, with a slight quiver in his voice, "I am Captain Callum Clayton of His Majesty's Ship *Centaur*. You may approach, but at the first sign of hostility, I will blow you to hell."

"Very well." Joe piloted the drone to approach slowly, then hovered ten feet over the aft deck. The crew shrank away at the whizz of the rotors. Joe lowered the speaker volume. "I will drop you a small handheld object we call a radio with the chronometer attached. It is delicate. Will you agree to catch it?"

Captain Clayton pointed at Lieutenant Northcott.

"The radio will allow us to communicate directly from our respective ships. I will hear you, and you will hear me." He dropped it over Lieutenant Northcott, who caught it, then backed the drone off several feet.

"Nice catch. Here's how it works. See the button on the left side? Press it to talk. Speak directly to the device. Release the button to listen. Only one of us can speak at a time. Please read the printed instructions. Press to talk and release to listen. Now try it."

The Lieutenant fearfully handled the queer object. He had never seen plastic before. He turned it over in his hand, unstrapped the watch with the printed radio instructions, handed the clock to his Captain, and the instructions to Lieutenant Bickerton.

Captain Clayton took the watch, surprised by its lightness. His eyebrows raised, and eyes widened. The calendar date showed in a tiny window, and the polished metal hands contrasted with its blackface. The second hand went tick-tick. He nodded to Lieutenant Northcott.

The radio fit well in his lieutenant's hand. He identified the button at the side and pressed it tentatively. click

From the drone: "Continue to hold the button in. Say something into it and release the button to hear a response."

"Hello?"

"Release the button to listen." click

Captain Joe handed his radio to Sails and nodded, continuing to control the drone. Sails put down the drone mike and held the radio button for Joe to speak. click "Good afternoon. May I ask your name, sir? Press the button to talk and release to listen." click

Lieutenant Northcott, shocked at the voice coming from the object in his hand, dropped it. click

Captain Clayton frowned and pointed at the radio.

Lieutenant Northcott gingerly picked it up, put it near his mouth, and pressed the button. Click "I am Lieutenant Northcott, second in command." click click "Captain, Lieutenant, gentlemen, I wish you fair winds and following seas. I will now bring my flying machine back to *Serendipity* and continue to converse through that handheld contraption we call a radio." The drone turned toward *Serendipity*, and the whizzing rotors faded. "Sir, I cannot explain the circumstance of the situation we now find ourselves over our communication link. I assure you, we are not an apparition or the devil's work. We are a friend of King George the Third, and we wish the Commonwealth well. Now, when you hear a 'click' on the radio, that means it's your turn to speak." click

Lieutenant Northcott handed Captain Clayton the radio, glad to get rid of it. He took the Captain's pistol in exchange. Many of the crew were within earshot and listened intently. click "Sir, I require an explanation of what the bloody hell is going on here." click click "I apologize, Captain, but an adequate clarification is too complex for a radio conversation. We will disappear after a few days. You and I are both subject to the same laws of nature, but an account of how we became what we are requires a lengthy discourse. As you see, we do not rely on wind for power, and we have other attributes that might astonish you. However, I have a proposal to provide you with answers, although it will undoubtedly seem extraordinary. Would you entertain a suggestion?" click

Captain Clayton looked skeptical. click "I will consider what you have to say." click click "We are planning a delectable dinner with accouterments aboard *Serendipity*, including fine wine. I propose we exchange two men for dinner, of which I will be one. With the radios, we will both be able to keep in contact with our men. I suggest we use my launch to transfer our parties but maintain a safe distance from each other during dinner. I will now turn on our deck lights so you can see us easily in the dark." click

Captain Joe switched on the deck lights, including the spotlights from the spreaders and radar mount.

▪ ▪ ▪ ▪ ▪

The sinking sun touched the horizon. *Serendipity* shone brightly in the distance to the north. A collective gasp emanated from *Centaur's* crew.

▪ ▪ ▪ ▪ ▪

click "I have information you will find of interest," Captain Joe continued. "Admiral Nelson has recovered from his wound. The central ligature from his amputated arm, causing the inflammation and poisoning, came out on its own. He will command *Vanguard* 74 and sent your way next month." click

Captain Clayton exchanged frowns with his officers. Such naval intelligence was impossible to come by, honestly or otherwise. The drone had returned to *Serendipity*, so the radio was the only communication link. He held the radio at his side without pressing the button. "Gentlemen, I invite your comments."

. . . . .

Captain Joe changed channels. click "Mister Chief, you on?" click click "I'm here." click click "C-mon back. We will lie abeam of the Brit. That ends our military action for today." click click "Okay—I'm on my way." click

. . . . .

Gunny put down the launcher and moved to a forward seat. They motored toward their ship.

. . . . .

Centaur's crew stared in silence as the small boat and schooner started toward each other on the flat calm water. There were no visible means of propulsion and no noise. Their wakes rolled softly away, disturbing the reflection of the darkened sea.

Three Lieutenants, three Warrant Officers, and the Master huddled together with Captain Clayton on the quarterdeck. Lieutenant Northcott passed the radio and wristwatch around for examination.

Ambrose Penhale, the Master responsible for navigation, examined the watch. "Captain, if the accuracy he claimed is true, it would be a major advantage for worldwide navigation. With your permission, I will take it below and compare the time shown with our timepieces. I can render an opinion on the veracity of the stated precision."

"Permission granted. Make it so."

"Sir, if I may," Albert Bickerton, Second Lieutenant, assumed his opinion to be of particular value, "there are salient points I wish to draw your attention."

The officers fell silent and turned toward Lieutenant Bickerton.

"The first is that portion of the proposal whereby we draw a secure distance from each other during the swap for dinner. We do not know the effective range of the weapon used to destroy the Moors. There was no arc on its trajectory—it flew flat. The limits of naval cannons are no doubt known to the Yankee. Therefore, he can withdraw a safe distance from us while we cannot be sure we are safe from him."

Grunts and bobbing heads signaled their collective agreement.

"The second is the fact we are at their mercy, anyway. Their weapons are considerably more destructive than ours. I propose we accept the transfer and avail ourselves of the opportunity to learn what we can of the Yank's weapons and machinery."

"Sir, I agree with Mister Bickerton." Lieutenant Northcott joined. "We must use this chance to gain any knowledge possible of potential threats. Besides, it appears they are privy to Admiralty intelligence. It is vital we attempt to glean where such knowledge originated."

Warrant Officer Gideon Harris groused, "I think we shouldn't let 'em anywhere near us. This time o' year, a wind could arrive any minute to get us away from these bloody bastards. I say we prepare to repel boarders and wait for wind."

The other officers exchanged a glance, rubbed their chins, and gazed down.

Master Penhale returned to the deck and handed the watch to the Captain. "Sir, I believe this chronometer has the exact time. It is precisely correct."

"Very well. Thank you, gentlemen. It appears we will have company for dinner. Mister Bickerton, choose midshipman Edmond Kempthorne to go with you." click "Captain Plimsoll? We accept your offer. I propose my Second Lieutenant Albert Bickerton and midshipman Edmond Kempthorne join you for dinner. How will the logistics work?" click click "Thank you, Captain Clayton. I will come over at seven o'clock on the wrist chronometer, if that is acceptable to you, joined by Mister Decker, my aide-de-camp. The launch will return to *Serendipity* with your choice of two men. After dinner, it will return your men to *Centaur* and my aide-de-camp and me to *Serendipity*. Is that satisfactory?" click click "Yes, that would be fine." He exchanged grimaces with his senior officers. "I look forward to greeting you." click click "And I look forward to meeting you. 1900 hours then." click

Captain Clayton turned to his officers with his hands behind his back. "Mister Northcott, tell my cook we'll have one of our geese for dinner."

24
G-WAD

February 26 - Seattle

Jack Wilson slumped in his chair, gazing toward his monitor with the unfocused stare of someone twirling images in his mind. The screen showed a revolving grid, simulating distorted Euclidian space. He knew the mathematics for tracking the gravity curvature of Riemannian manifolds well. Jack's grasp of the noncommutativity of the covariant derivatives and affine connections was unequaled. But making this work in real-time to ride a gravity wave had experimental aspects not entirely predictable. Some of this was just a hunch. It was his responsibility to make it all work.

Paul Gorken, Transition Coordinator, oversaw the eight-member tech crews. He watched the watchers. Hundreds of data points filled two of his four screens in spreadsheet monotony. A blank screen stood to the side of each for detailed views of specific node data. Next to each value was a blinking colored cell. One screen followed the Wave Propagation Reaction Modulator, and the other watched the fifteen Spatial Magnetrons. Everything continued to blink green.

Then, a cell turned to amber on one of the Spatial Magnetrons. It set off an audible intermittent buzz. The blinking stopped, changed to a constant amber, and a sustained hum. He shut off the alarm and expanded the specific magnetron data to the side screen. It showed excessive heat and a loss of pressure—an endomorphism anomaly. He closed the power feed to the affected slots and switched to the primary screen to view the entire array's effect in graph mode. There was a spike, but it was within acceptable operating limits. Spatial Magnetron redundancy was part of the design with three extra capacity units—but they should need none. Something was wrong.

Alyx, the foreman of the Spatial Magnetron group, appeared at Paul's door. "You get the alarm on number two?"

Sometimes his bouncing energy, youthful manner, and gleaming white-toothed smile were too much to bear. Everything was a game to him. Paul appreciated that Alyx was smart, but his freckled face, black-rimmed glasses, and cropped red hair always seemed cartoonish. He had to remind himself of Alyx's talent to take him seriously. "Yeah, I got it. Let's go see." He grabbed his flashlight.

They hustled into the Spatial Magnetron chamber, where the polished concrete floor, ceiling, and walls reflected the magnetron's soft hum. Yellow light from the low-pressure sodium lamps cast a glow on the tron's white steel cabinets reminiscent of winter street lights on snow. The light on Number Two shined amber. They opened the controlling laptop, launched the menu, and clicked on the system analysis display. Two of the eight ioxin slots showed amber. Two more blinked several times before becoming solid amber. Then two more. The light atop Number Two changed from amber to pulsating red. Paul cut the power feed to the entire magnetron. All eight slots turned red.

"Shit." He clicked on the circuit board display. They showed green. "Thank God. The circuit cards haven't fried."

Alyx opened the electrical panel and examined the power connections. "Paul, we have burned ends here on all eight black jumpers from the bus." He studied the hot wires. "Damn. These wires are number twos—the spec called for double ought."

Paul aimed his flashlight at the black wires. Alyx was right. The neutral and ground wires looked fine, but the black wires were smaller, with burned ends. "Hell's bells. How did that happen? Okay." He took a breath, summoning the courage to overcome the problem. "Probably all the trons are alike. We must check each one, but let's assume they have the same error. We have to take each tron offline, replace the bad connectors, and re-energize. Alyx, you and your crew will make the switch-out. Maintenance will supply pre-cut jumpers with prepared ends. That's a hundred-twenty jumpers. I'll get you a hundred-thirty. We have twenty-two hours before the next transition."

As Paul turned to leave, the light on Number Five started flashing amber. "Shit—put up time. Advise me of any additional problems and your progress on the hour. Inform me immediately if you project failure to complete the change-out on time. I'll allocate whatever resources you need. Do you understand?"

"Yes, sir." He flashed a conspiratorial grin.

Paul absorbed Alyx's exuberance in silence. *Sometimes your goddamn smile just grates on me.*

▪ ▪ ▪ ▪ ▪

Paul approached Jack's dim office and found him deep in contemplation. He hated to break his concentration, but it was his duty to keep the boss informed. Jack was stroking his lips and staring into space.

"Knock, knock."

Jack lowered his hand and twisted his head toward Paul without speaking.

"Jack, we have a Spatial Magnetron problem. We can institute a repair before the next transition, but we will have to take them offline one-by-one to make the fix."

Paul sensed Jack's mind switch gears.

Jack winced. "The problem is common to all fifteen? Fuck. How'd that happen?"

"We aren't sure if it's all fifteen, but the probability is high. I don't know how it happened, and the 'how' isn't relevant right now. The important thing is we get the trons restored. The fix is simple but time-consuming. They won't all be off at one time, but we will have a diminished capacity until the repair is complete."

"Fuckin' goddamn, Paul. This morning's wave event already reduced our margin. Any additional problem affecting our G-WAD hardware's reliability will further shrink our chances for a successful recovery. If over three are offline, we won't get the boys back. Can you keep some slots operational on a Magnetron while you fix the others?"

"No. I have to de-energize the bus."

"Is there any doubt they'll all be operational by the next transition?"

"Jack, I'm sorry to report, doubt will remain until we complete the repairs, test the units, and bring them back online. But my confidence is high."

Jack switched his screen to the Wave Propagation Reaction Modulator curves. It showed the predicted optimal curve in green, the current output curve in blue, and the red minimum acceptable output curve. The blue curve registered a downward trajectory of 15%. It dropped another 15% a few seconds later.

"This trend is not good. The output has a direct correlation with my earlier success prediction. The longer we are below the red line, the less chance we have of getting them back. If we are below the line during the transition, we're fucked. Everyone has access to the data, huh?"

"Sure. Our staff can access and interpret the data. And, no, it won't help morale any."

Jack looked at his hands and twiddled his thumbs, weighing staff loyalty, time, technical variables, and ramifications. He returned to his screen. The blue line dropped another 15% to the red line, then stabilized. "All right, do the best you can. Your attitude will affect our people. Keep on the sunny side."

"Yes, sir."

"And tell Keith we'll need a maximum effort for power from SCL."

25
LIMEYS

February 26, 1798 - Becalmed

Jason sat on deck next to a cable rail stanchion. His legs hung over the side, and he draped both arms over the cable. *Centaur* lay stationary, a little over a mile to the south. Its sails hung limp, silhouetted against the clouds blazing red and orange where the sun had just set. Sails sat next to him. The rest of the band were also on deck, sharing the view.

Sails murmured to Jason, "Quite a day."

"Yeah, I'll say—quite an encounter. I've spent most of my adult life seeking adventure in one form or another. Whoever said, 'be careful what you ask for' had an incredible insight. This situation isn't a movie set where we get to do a re-take. If we get back, I'll have had enough adventure."

Sails continued to stare into the distance. "Well, mate, I have to admit to being more chuffed than gutted. My life has been fairly jammy, even though this escapade is a snookered fluke I had not expected. I do not mind the dosh, and this bloke is full of beans, but I will give it some welly."

Captain Joe spoke from behind Sails and Jason. "Gentlemen, it is our watch for rest, but I believe you'll find what we are about to experience worth missing sleep. Mister Sails, I want you to run the boat back and forth. Mister Decker, you will accompany me to dinner aboard an old British man-o'-war. If that doesn't get your blood up, you must be brain dead. We will both wear our blazers and keep our weapons concealed. Mister Berg, you're in charge while I'm gone."

Jason weighed the risks of wearing a hidden pistol—refusing the Captain versus threats aboard: *Shit. Go with the flow.*

Jason and Sails got up, and everyone went below.

"Mister Cook," the Captain inquired, "may I presume you have a suitable dinner planned for our guests?"

The crew stopped and waited for the answer.

Cookie turned and wiped his hands on his apron, having pricked his roast with a knife to see if the juice ran clear. His smile gleamed from his smooth pink face—he was having fun. "I hope my roast suckling pig with black bean soup, saffron rice, and a watercress salad is suitable." He opened the refrigerator and took out a sample dessert. "These are chocolate mousse served in an edible semi-sweet chocolate cup with raspberry sauce."

The men's eyes widened. Only Jason spoke, "Save one for me, please."

"Paired with a Condrieu white wine from the northern Rhone Valley," Cookie kissed his forefinger and thumb then opened his hand, "the Viognier grapes will balance the sweetness of the pig. It has a subtle floral nose with a hint of peach and a complex character that comes alive on the palate. Coffee, and the forty-year-old Taylor Fladgate tawny port."

The crew exchanged nods, grunts, and smiles.

Captain Joe looked pleased. "Excellent. Gentlemen, please wear your blazers tonight and look sharp. Pistols are optional, but if you wear one, keep it concealed. You may get the Brits suitably snockered, but it behooves you to keep yourselves in a relative state of sobriety. Tell them anything you want. Any information you convey will not affect our reality in Seattle. After dinner, we will separate from our British friends. I expect tomorrow to be another exciting day. With no wind tonight, Mister Berg, Mister Bones, and I will run the boat. I hope you get a good night's rest. The watch list starts again at 0800.

"Mister Decker, please load a case each of the Taylor forty port and the '88 Malmsey Madeira."

▪ ▪ ▪ ▪ ▪

As they motored away, Jason sat across from Captain Joe forward of the center console. Joe was holding a large computer backpack and staring at *Centaur*. Jason contemplated the man before speaking. "So, Captain, what are you planning tonight?"

Captain Joe turned toward Jason. "I intend to wow them with a version of the truth. And to do that, I'll need your help. I have a dedicated computer and a large monitor in my pack. I'll provide a history lesson. You hold the monitor."

"You will tell them we're time-travelers?"

"Sure. In the first place, if the Brits tell anyone what they hear, the navy will laugh them off as lunatics. And in the second place, we're in a parallel universe, so it won't matter anyway."

"So you keep saying, but you also hedge, showing uncertainty. You mentioned we couldn't have our existence known ashore without all kinds of problems, and the watch battery will die in five years—why would those issues occur to you if you knew for certain? What if this alternate universe bit is one way? What if we only return to a future year of the universe we're now in?"

"That requires a separate gravity wave than the one we used. The death and destruction in our wake will alter the future of this universe. The odds of managing the same gravity wave event by the ancestors of these people is too remote to contemplate."

"Yet, you have doubt."

"We will all die of something. Let's concentrate on what we know. When we board the Brit, we salute the ship, not the flag. Follow my example and face athwartship for your salute. Note our dinner companions will appreciate your active participation in the conversation, so please join in. My tale tonight may bend the facts a little. I'm counting on you to go along with whatever bullshit I expound."

"No problem." *Oh shit. Missus Oliver, look what your son is doing. If I survive this, I will change my life—no more thrills.*

"Mister Sails," Joe turned his head, "keep your radio on and within easy earshot. Call me every 30 minutes with a radio check. If there's a serious difficulty on either vessel, Mister Berg will let me know, or I'll let him know. In such a case, we'll graciously conclude the night, and I will need you to return fast. Otherwise, I want you to touch *Centaur's* side at 2200 hours Ship's time. Okay?"

"Yes, sir. 2200 it is."

Darkness descended. *Serendipity* was an island of brightness rocking on the long, low lump of the otherwise calm sea. The launch murmured away, its soft light contrasted with the blackness extending to the horizon.

Lanterns on *Centaur* failed to illuminate much of the ship. The yellowish light through two rows of open gunports and the windows across her stern cast an enchanting spell. The brooding dark hull, lantern's glow on the slack sails, and her elongated reflection on the dark undulating sea were like something from a Montague Dawson painting. With darkness elsewhere, the pale haze failed to obscure the moon—a little beyond first quarter—or many of the stars, twinkling above. A bosun's whistle pierced the night.

The air continued to cool, but with no wind, Jason's Stormy Seas, plus his blazer and woolen sweater, was overkill. *I'll sure be glad to leave my float jacket in the boat.*

▪ ▪ ▪ ▪ ▪

Captain Clayton and his senior officers stood at the taffrail, watching the brilliant points of red, green, and white approach while *Serendipity* wobbled slightly in the distance. The Captain frowned, twisted his mouth to the side, and puckered his lips. "Whatever this American is, we cannot get away without wind. Any breeze would be a blessing. Mister Northcott, you may have a knife driven into the Mizzen from the southwest and whistle us up a Vendaval. Let's learn what we can from the Yanks and send them back." He slapped his hands on the rail and turned toward the boarding port.

▪ ▪ ▪ ▪ ▪

Sails shifted to reverse, and the launch made an eggshell landing alongside *Centaur's* starboard boarding ladder. The Bosun whistled *Pipe the Side*. Anxious faces peered over the rail, mystified by the diesel's deep purr, lights, and movement through the water.

"Gentlemen," Captain Joe raised his head to address *Centaur's* crew, "a whip and a small net, please. We have a fine port and Madeira to offer the mess."

A tackle appeared off the mizzen yardarm, and Jason attached the cases. Captain Joe removed his Stormy Seas jacket, put his computer case over his shoulder, and clambered up the side. He stepped aboard, gave a sharp salute to the ship, and the Bosun whistled *Pipe the Side* again. Jason followed his lead. The officer's uniforms' white lapels showed crisp and clean in the yellow gleam of the lanterns. The ship oscillated slowly on the barest whisper of a swell. A rope made a single creak.

Captain Clayton, the only officer with an epaulet, stood closest to the boarding ladder. "Captain Plimsoll, welcome aboard." He stuck out his hand. "I am Captain Clayton." He walked with Captain Joe down the line of his officers. "Allow me to name Mister Nye Northcott, first lieutenant, Mister Albert Bickerton, second lieutenant, Mister Ambrose Penhale, Master, and Mister Edmond Kempthorne, midshipman."

"Gentlemen, I am delighted to meet you." Captain Joe shook hands with each, passing along the row. "Allow me to present Mister Decker, my aide-de-camp. And," opening his hand to the launch, "Mister Sails, a fellow Brit, our coxswain for taxi duty this evening."

Sails smiled. "Hello, mates. It will be my pleasure to provide transportation services tonight." His British accent was unmistakable.

"Oh?" Nye Northcott considered impressment. "As a British seaman, he is subject to naval discipline, I believe."

Captain Joe stepped forward. "Sir, I would take grave offense at such an action."

Captain Clayton intervened. "Belay there, Mister Northcott. We will have a friendly dinner. Let us not have any animosity." He turned his attention to the two men chosen for the dinner exchange. "With your permission, Captain Plimsoll," a slight bow, "I will send Mister Bickerton and Mister Kempthorne to your vessel while you dine here."

"Fine." Captain Joe bent toward them. "You're welcome to board my vessel. Here is another radio," he handed it to Lieutenant Bickerton, "for you to maintain contact. Try it now. Press the button at the side to talk, release, to listen."

Lieutenant Bickerton hefted it with suspicion. Then he tried it. click "Hello? Captain?" click.

The words crackled on the Captain's radio. They nodded to each other and smiled.

"Thank you." Lieutenant Bickerton brought his legs together and inclined forward. "By your leave." He turned, saluted his Captain, and eased down the side, followed by Midshipman Kempthorne.

"Gentlemen," Sails spoke as they settled in the boat. "I believe you will have a splendid dinner and a delightful time. I am Mister Sails, Bosun on *Serendipity*."

"And I am Second Lieutenant Bickerton, and this young man is Midshipman Kempthorne."

They both smiled, shook hands with Sails, and took a seat.

Captain Joe, Jason, and the deck officers watched them away—their lights receded toward *Serendipity*. Then they joined the senior staff for dinner in the cabin below. No one wore a sword.

▪ ▪ ▪ ▪ ▪

Sails regarded his two charges while piloting the launch toward *Serendipity*. They sat erect, staring first at the bright lights ahead, then the mysterious wake. Midshipman Edmond Kempthorne appeared young, maybe sixteen. His eyes were wide with anticipation. He was a robust youth with clean blond hair, outgrowing his coat. Lieutenant Bickerton looked to be in his mid-thirties with ebony hair and a knowing smile. Sails turned on the strip lights hidden from view under the gunwales. They bathed the deck in a soft amber shine. It shocked Edmond Kempthorne. He took a knee, reached under the overhang, and felt it. It was not hot. He rubbed the lens, removed his hand, and looked at his fingers.

Sails used his radio. click "Mister Berg, you got me on?" click click "I'm here. You got guests for us?" click click "Yes, sir. I'm bringing one Second Lieutenant Bickerton and one Midshipman Kempthorne." Sails smiled at both. "We are expecting a fine dinner." click click "Good. Okay, see you in a few minutes." click

"Gentlemen," Sails turned to his two charges, "I believe much will amaze and astound you tonight."

"With respect, sir," Lieutenant Bickerton offered, "we have already seen much that astonishes us. What makes the boat move?"

Sails answered while continuing to steer toward *Serendipity,* "Are you familiar with the word 'engine?'"

"Yes, a mechanical machine. I believe I've read of siege engines, but I have not seen one used."

"That's correct. You see those latches there?" He indicated the fastenings holding down the engine cover. "Open the latches and swing the cover forward."

Lieutenant Bickerton pointed to the clasps for Edmond Kempthorne. The midshipman sprang off his seat, undid the couplings, and rolled the engine cover forward on its hinges. Sails flicked on the engine light. The red two-cylinder Westerbeke diesel hummed much louder with the insulated engine cover off.

Sails pointed to the spinning propeller shaft. "This machine uses the energy of small, controlled explosions to turn that shaft connected to a screw. We are screwing our way through the water."

Their mouths dropped open at the spinning shaft.

"Please close the cover. We're about to come alongside."

Dazzled by the bright lights, the guests stared. Handy received the bow line from Mr. Kempthorne. Sails tossed the stern line to Masters and tied spring lines fore and aft. Sails' charges regarded the well-dressed sailors with matching blue blazers, shiny brass buttons, and corresponding gold thread embroidered hats. The Mid's eyes strained in disbelief. Speechless, they climbed aboard.

"Gentlemen," Berg took charge, "welcome aboard. I am Mister Berg, second in command of the yacht *Serendipity*."

Lieutenant Bickerton paused. *Yacht? Thought this was military.*

Berg extended his arms. "I promise you a delightful evening filled with fine food and confounded by much of what you'll see. Would a topside tour be of interest before we go below?"

Lieutenant Bickerton brought out his radio. "May I check in with *Centaur*?"

"Of course." click "Captain, can you hear me?" click

▪ ▪ ▪ ▪ ▪

Lieutenant Bickerton's distorted voice clattered on his Captain's radio. Captain Clayton eyed Captain Plimsoll. click "Yes, Lieutenant, I hear you well." click click "We are safe and have arrived aboard the American vessel." click click "Thank you, Lieutenant. Have a pleasant evening." click

A long table, set in the large cabin aft, awaited dinner. The deck and sides painted red, and the low ceiling, painted white, returned the golden flames from the lanterns. Windows of small hand-blown panes extended the entire width of the transom. Similar windows with slanted sashes graced the sides next to the stern. The flames' reflections danced off the windows. *Serendipity*'s shined in the distance.

Captain Clayton took the seat at the head of the table and directed Captain Joe and Jason to the first two chairs on his right. Nine men remained standing until Captain Clayton seated himself. An attendant filled the crystal glasses by each place with claret, a light red wine from Bordeaux.

Captain Joe raised his glass. "Gentlemen, President Adams."

Captain Clayton nodded to his officers, and they raised their glasses. "The President." The officers took a sip.

Captain Joe continued, "And gentlemen, King George the Third."

The officers raised their glasses again. "The King." They took another sip, and dinner arrived.

"Captain, if you will permit," Captain Joe interjected, "I believe you will find the port I brought with me will go down well. Perhaps you and the gentlemen might try it. I see the cases sit unopened."

"Very well, Captain." He signaled a servant. "Let's try the American port."

"Oh, it's not American, Captain. It's a 40-year-old Portuguese tawny. The Madeira has aged 25 years in oak, and I think much of it."

"Is that so? Well, we will try to do it justice."

The servant hesitated, having never seen a corrugated cardboard box before. He pulled apart the glue on both cases, picked a bottle of port, removed the cork, and poured it into a decanter while everyone watched.

The Surgeon—known for his deft hand—started carving the sizeable roasted goose. Welsh rarebit, plum duff, and a pease pudding followed close behind, a rare treat for a Monday.

Captain Joe started a conversation. "With your permission, Captain, I'd like to explain to Mister Decker why we make toasts from a sitting position. He is not aware of many British naval customs."

"Very well. It's a noble story."

Captain Joe turned to Jason, "Back in 1600 something, Charles the Second rose in response to a toast in one of his ships and bumped his head on an overhead beam. He pointed at the timber and said, 'Gentlemen, your loyalty is not questioned.' So, to this day, we remain seated for the Loyal Toast."

"Here, here." They laughed and downed a glass.

"Also," Captain Joe resumed speaking to Jason, "we don't clink glasses. The ring of glass means a sailor has died. If we stop the ring, two soldiers die instead. We will ding no glasses tonight."

"Aye," replied Lieutenant Northcott, "but we'll drink to being able to drink."

Laughs all around.

"Captain Plimsoll," Master Penhale inquired, "how's your glass?"

"There's a south wind in it if you please."

The officers roared their approval, and the refilled decanter of port passed to the left.

Warrant Officer Gideon Harris's seat allowed him to view the lights on Serendipity in the distance. Suddenly they blinked out. "Sir, the Yank has disappeared."

"Huh?" Captain Clayton turned to the window and palmed his radio. click "Lieutenant, is everything okay?" click

Serendipity's lights blinked back to their radiating glow. click "Yes, sir. Lights were out to show us equipment that glows in the dark. Everything's fine." click

"And now," Captain Clayton returned to his guests, "I believe an explanation is in order. What's this about Nelson?"

Berg came on the radio. click "Captain, just checking in. All is well here." click

Joe responded, click "Everything is well here, too." click

He continued without missing a beat. "Yes, of course." Captain Joe reached behind to his computer satchel, opened it, turned on the external monitor, handed it to Jason, and opened his computer. "You may have a hard time grasping this, but we came here from the twenty-first century. We will return to our own time in three days."

Chuckles bounced around the table.

The screen lighted and showed a Sikorsky SH-60 Seahawk helicopter lifting off from the aircraft carrier *Gerald L. Ford* with sound. The scene panned away to reveal the mighty ship slicing through a blue, sunlit sea.

"Oh, my God!" The Chaplain shuddered, and his eyes enlarged. "I smell the Devil's breath, warm upon my neck."

The other officer's eyes narrowed and became silent.

Master Penhale jumped from his seat to peek behind the thin monitor. He pressed it between his thumb and forefinger. "Huh!" was all he produced.

Others leaned over to view its back.

Joe grinned, "You're familiar with lightning? A bolt of lightning is what we call electricity in an enormous amount. We have created a way of harnessing electricity in low volume. That's what powers these machines." He pointed to the computer and monitor. "It is also the energy source for the watch I gave you."

They leaned forward in rapt attention.

"Here is the future of the American navy." He aimed his thumb at the *Gerald L. Ford*. "The ship you see is one of several displacing 100,000 tons. It is over 1,000 feet long and carries a crew of 3,700. Its hull is steel and can go worldwide without refueling. The flying machine that took off from her deck fires missiles more powerful than the ones we used on the corsairs. But the British are our friends—two countries separated by a common language."

Several officers giggled.

"The United States and the British government will have difficulties between your time and ours, but our values continue to align."

The video switched to an F-18 Hornet whooshing off the carrier, then in the air over mountainous terrain. It dropped a bomb. The clip changed to detonations in the Afghanistan war, then a napalm bomb video from Operation Rolling Thunder in Vietnam. Joe joined the crew in silence. The flames engulfed the jungle.

"We can kill thousands of people in a few seconds."

Mouths agape and wide-eyed, the officers pushed from the table. Exclamations burst forth. "Blood and thunder!" "Christ, the Savior!" "Beastly!" "Blimey!"

The video switched to a carrier landing from the pilot's point of view.

"This angle is what the pilot sees making a landing at sea. These planes fly at over a thousand miles per hour and can destroy anything we want. I assert you cannot even imagine the destructive force of our weapons. In the future, devastating conflicts, much worse than the Napoleonic wars, will afflict humanity. In one war, over 60 million people die, 3% of the world's population at the time. I'm sorry to report the future contains all kinds o' mean, nasty, ugly things."

Chairs squeaked on the deck, and several glasses of port emptied. No one spoke. A servant refilled the decanter.

"Now, the earth's population is a billion people. In the twenty-first century, whence we come from, the population is approximately seven-and-a-half billion. Our average lifespan is eighty years. Most people are literate, and we have vast libraries. So, we know just about everything in your time by reading history. Your generation kept excellent records."

"Tosh!" retorted the captain of the marines. "It's pork pies."

"No, sir, it is, in fact, correct. I don't mind telling you because if you pass it along to the fleet, your senior officers will label you daft and end your career. But, to answer your question, we know much concerning Nelson, Napoleon, and how the war proceeds. I am happy to report Great Britain wins, and Napoleon loses. He will, however, leave a lasting influence. Western Europe adopted his liberal policies, including Great Britain."

Lieutenant Northcott turned sideways in his chair and jeered. "Poppycock. You're claiming we will abolish Parliament and our Monarch in favor of mob rule?"

"No, not at all. With minor modifications, your governance system has stood the test of time very well. The Napoleonic Code, though, has had a lasting effect. It has inspired the legal systems of over 70 nations. To paraphrase Andrew Roberts—a British historian, I might add—the ideas that underpin the modern world, advancement based on merit, equality before the law, secular toleration, and financial transparency, are legacies of Napoleon. His support for science and the abolition of feudalism was the greatest advancement of civilization since the Roman Empire."

Captain Clayton squinted at Captain Joe. "You support the tyrant?"

"No. In the year 1804, he'll orchestrate crowning himself emperor. I'll never support an emperor. No one is above the law. He used the tenants of the French Revolution to further his ambition—not a noble impulse."

The screen changed to an image of earth from space spinning slowly on its axis.

Captain Joe continued, "This simulation is how our planet appears from space. You're living at a time we call the Age of Enlightenment—when scientific advancement took off to make all this possible." He swung his hand at the computer.

Jason grabbed the opportunity to express his view. "Yes. Science has continued to rollback superstition and religion—essentially the same thing."

The Chaplin narrowed his eyes and glared.

Joe pointed toward the sky. "We have various machines up there in our time circling the earth. They look down, tell us the weather, and facilitate communication between people anywhere on the globe. Unfortunately, we don't have access to that equipment in 1798."

The scene switched to a computer-generated view of the Solar System with Earth in the near ground. It receded from the sun, showing the other planets in their orbits with their moons.

"With the discovery of Uranus in 1781, you know seven planets." The picture continued to move away from the sun. "We now know there are eight planets, five dwarf planets, and thousands of other rocks and comets in our Solar System."

The frame switched to a simulation of the Milky Way, slowly revolving. An arrow showed the location of the sun. "Our sun sits in this galaxy. It contains nearly 200 billion stars. The arrow points to our sun. It's a rather insignificant star. It would take roughly 100 thousand years to travel across the galaxy at the speed of light. There are over a trillion galaxies—that's a thousand billion, or a million, million."

Master Penhale spoke, "The speed of light?"

"Yes. Light travels at a constant speed. It takes light eight minutes and twenty seconds to reach us from the sun."

Joe turned the computer off, took the monitor from Jason, and put them in his bag. The chairs grated, jackets swished, and they repositioned themselves. A low rumble of men chatting to their neighbor rose from the table. Glasses emptied.

Captain Clayton folded his hands, surveying their reactions. He pushed his chair from the table, crossed his legs, and considered his assembly. "You astonish us, sir. But, on a more terrestrial level, what are Napoleon's immediate plans? And, Mister Penhale, I believe the decanter stands by you."

Jason spoke, pouring himself another glass, "If I may be so bold, Captain Clayton, if we tell you what will happen, what will you do with it? Do you think you can sidle up to Ol' Jarvie and say, 'Excuse me, Admiral, but some Americans visited us from the future and informed us of Napoleon's plans. Would you like to know what's going to happen?' What reaction would you expect? They'll treat you like those who claim to have shagged a mermaid. You would do well to consider this an interesting evening's entertainment and keep the information you've learned to yourselves." Jason swung his hand at the officers.

"Hmm." The officers smiled at each other.

"Captain," Joe picked up the story, "Mister Decker makes an excellent point. But that aside, if I may, Napoleon and his fleet will leave Toulon, Marseilles, Genoa, and other ports on May 20 for Malta. He'll take it from the Knights of Malta, replenish his supplies, then sail for Alexandria on June 11."

"Leave Toulon May 20 for Malta and depart Malta on June 11 for Alexandria. Got it." Captain Clayton tapped the table with his finger, looking directly at Lieutenant Northcott.

Captain Joe viewed one man, then the other. "On the night of June 22-23, vessels in Napoleon's fleet will hear Nelson's signal guns, but they will pass each other unnoticed. Napoleon will take Alexandria by July 2. The British fleet under Nelson will reach Alexandria on August 1. There will be a glorious battle called The Battle of the Nile. You win."

"And you don't suppose we can do anything affect this?" Master Penhale asked.

"Hey, it's up to you," Captain Joe responded. "If you believe it's in your best interests to tell your senior officers you know the future, nothing can stop you. It's your decision. The last year has seen much ebb and flow for Great Britain. With Napoleon beating the Austrians last January, Admiral Jarvis' February defeat of the Spanish off Cape St. Vincent, and the French landing in Wales, who knows what to believe? The Spithead and Nore mutinies in April and May and Nelson's loss at Tenerife in July didn't do you any good. But, your victory over the Dutch at Camperdown was a beautiful piece of work."

"I was at Camperdown." Captain Clayton offered with a broad smile.

"Were you?" Jason uttered. "Perhaps you will tell us about the battle."

Captain Clayton leaned over the table and extended his arms. "Oh, yes. It was a great naval battle."

The officers remained mute with furtive sideways glances. They heard the details many times.

"A fresh to moderate breeze blew from the northwest. The Dutch formed their line of eleven ships and eight frigates heading northeast." He arranged leftover pieces of the goose to illustrate. "Admiral Duncan split his squadron into two divisions to attack both ends of the Dutch line. That left the center ships useless."

The deck abruptly heaved and twisted with a sudden wave. Conversation halted. Eyebrows raised, and hands were quick to grab glasses.

SMACK went the sails struck by the wind. THWOOM echoed through the hull as the bluff stern swooned to a wave.

Master Penhale's eyes lit. "The Vendaval!" He jumped out of his seat and headed on deck.

Berg called in. click "Captain, a powerful wind has arrived." click click "Yes, here too. Have Sails come over immediately with our two guests. click

Captain Clayton, Gentlemen. I'm afraid we must cut this evening short."

The British Captain smiled. "Yes, it appears we both must proceed our separate ways."

The officers downed a quick glass then hurried to their divisions with, "By your leave, sir."

■ ■ ■ ■ ■

The launch pitched in the roaring blackness. Sails' expertise was evident as he came alongside *Centaur.* To get close enough for a passenger exchange without being smashed against the larger boat's hull took exceptional skill. Lieutenant Bickerton timed *Centaur*'s roll and leaped to the boarding ladder. The crew hoisted the inebriated Midshipman Kempthorne aboard. *Pipe the Side* whistled as Jason and the Captain climbed down the ladder. The Bosun played it again as Captain Joe jumped into the heaving launch. A wave washed over Jason before he leaped. They turned away toward *Serendipity.*

"Toodle pip," bellowed Sails, taking them away into the storm.

26 DISCORD

February 26, 1798 - Becalmed

Lieutenant Bickerton's radio call to Captain Clayton was loud enough for all to hear on *Serendipity's* deck. The bright lights washed out the stars. Mast lights, spreader lights, radar lights, deck lights—everything was well lit. With no wind, the chilly evening was not uncomfortable. *Centaur's* stern lanterns and a soft glow from her gun decks were all that appeared of the British man-o'-war, a little more than a mile away.

Chief, Gunny, Masters, and Handy were on deck and standing in a jagged line to greet the British sailors. Sails put a reef in the mainsail and sheeted the main, staysail, and foresail booms hard amidships in case of a sudden squall.

▪ ▪ ▪ ▪ ▪

Bones stayed below with Cookie and Stew, who worked on dinner. He rummaged through the movie selections on the bulkhead screen, starting one, then another, listening on his earphones.

▪ ▪ ▪ ▪ ▪

Berg straightened and waved at the ship's company. "Gentlemen, first, I believe introductions are in order. This is Lieutenant Bickerton and Midshipman Kempthorne."

Both men leaned forward in a slight bow. Lieutenant Bickerton replied, "Thank you for having us. We are curious as to the explanation for all this." He turned and waved his arm around the deck. "I am utterly mystified."

"Ah, yes, no one has told you. We—and this boat—traveled in time from the twenty-first century. We arrived yesterday a little west of the Strait. We're here for five days. Then we go back and never return."

"Really...?" The Lieutenant smiled, amused with such bullshit. "How did you do that?" He turned to wink at Mr. Kempthorne, but the Mid was too wide-eyed to notice.

"I don't know," said Berg. "Our Captain is a genius and has devised a way to time-travel for temporary periods riding a gravity wave—whatever that means. Hey, I only work here. But I assure you it's true. What you witness tonight is the state of technology from where we come."

Berg turned to the entire group. "I believe you have already met Mister Sails, our bosun. Allow me to introduce Mister Chief, our engineer, Mister Gunn, in charge of security, Mister Masters, and Mister Handy, distinguished crew."

The Brits proceeded down the line, shaking hands. Berg led them forward on a topside tour. They twisted their heads, trying to absorb the surroundings.

Mr. Kempthorne was in a daze. *All I recognize is the wood deck.*

Lieutenant Bickerton shielded his eyes from the bright lights. Everything on deck was well lit. "How the bloody hell do you do that?"

Berg paused, stumped for the moment to explain it. "You're familiar with lightning, no doubt? We have found a way of harnessing the energy in lightning in small controllable quantities. We can turn it on or off at will."

The Lieutenant smiled. "Amazing." *Codswallop.*

Both Brits stopped to examine a shroud. They had never seen wire rope before, let alone stainless-steel.

Lieutenant Bickerton fingered the polished strands. "Well, bugger me blue."

"Yes," Berg reacted to their mystified faces, "steel rope made from an alloy that cannot rust even in saltwater. Similar steel forms the hull and superstructure. Although less than half an inch thick, it will stop a cannonball." He pointed at the hull and contemplated a hit. *An eighteen-pounder might make quite a dent.*

Handy pulled out his Spyderco knife, kneeled to the deck, and tapped the boat's side. It did not have the resonance of wood, surprising the visiting Midshipman. "Here, you try it." He handed his knife to the young sailor.

Mr. Kempthorne stooped and tapped the hull. "Wow." He stood and handed the knife to Handy.

Handy took the knife, showed opening and closing it with one hand, and gave it back. "Keep it. We have spares below. I'm called Mister Handy. Mister Capthrone? Did I get that right?" Handy stuck out his hand.

"Ah, Edmond Kempthorne, if you please." He grasped Handy's hand and shook it with a broad smile and a slight bow. "Thank you for the knife."

Berg stopped on the foredeck and pointed to the windlass. "That's a mechanically driven anchor windlass. We push a button and crank with enough power to pull five tons. We also have power winches for raising sails." He pointed to a winch by the foremast. "Unless something breaks, we never have to go aloft to manage this ship."

The Lieutenant's eyes widened at the polished chrome capstans gleaming in the artificial light. "It takes sixteen of our crew doing the 'stamp and grind' to haul our number one anchor. How can a small winch accomplish that?"

"I'm afraid I can't explain the workings of a hydraulic pump. You will simply have to accept much of your experience tonight as an inexplicable wonder. I assure you this technology is commonplace in two hundred years. And you'd like these spars." Berg cradled the foresail clubfoot. "We make them of a different metal we call aluminum. It is much lighter in weight than wood or steel, and this alloy will not corrode in saltwater."

Both seamen felt the spar. Mr. Kempthorne tapped it with his new knife. It rang hollow. "It sure sounds different. Is there a cavity inside?"

Berg pondered the two men and stroked his chin. "There is. That's why it weighs so little." He pointed to the masts. "The masts are hollow, too. It reduces weight aloft."

The lieutenant fingered the sail bound to the foresail boom. "This feels quite different from the canvas on *Centaur*. What is it called?"

Berg hesitated on the explanation. "It's Mylar—a thermoplastic polymer resin unknown in the 18th century." He paused for a moment and smiled before continuing. "Let me say just one word: plastics."

"Now, Gentlemen," he pointed aloft, "please direct your attention to that spinning thing on the mainmast." They twisted their heads up to the radar antenna. "That's an object-detection system using different radio type stuff," he pointed to Lieutenant Bickerton's radio, "to determine the range and bearing of anything out there." He swept his arm across the sea to suggest *out there*. "Follow me to the pilothouse, and I'll show you how we use it."

The eight men trooped into the pilothouse. It was warm. Masters, Handy, Gunny, and Chief continued below and closed the companionway door behind them. Berg flicked a series of switches, and the deck lights went dark—sudden blackness outside. Their eyes adjusted, and they noticed the glow of *Centaur's* stern and a gleam of light through her open gunports—yellow reflections on a glassy sea.

Berg said, "I turned out the lights so you could appreciate all this." He spread his arms to include all the instruments facing the helm. "The illumination level allows the helmsman to watch everything without impairing his night vision."

▪ ▪ ▪ ▪ ▪

Below, Chief took the farthest outboard seat on the forward table. Masters sat to his left. Gunny took the position across from Chief.

Chief glanced at Bones, earphones on, and into his movie at the aft end of the aft table, ignoring their conversation. Chief spoke in a muffled voice, anyway. "Fuck this. I've had enough. I say, get the transition coordinates, go there, and wait until we zap out o' here."

Masters turned toward Chief, away from Bones. "How do we do that? Only the Captain knows the answer."

Handy sat silently across from Masters.

Gunny put his elbows on the table with his hands holding his chin. He leaned forward, intent on hearing.

Chief glanced at Bones again, engrossed in his movie, then continued in his hushed tone. "I don't believe our departure location and time ain't written somewhere in Cap's cabin. It's likely on his computer and is prob'ly password protected. But most people keep a password cheat sheet stashed somewhere. If I get his login password, I may find the coordinates. If you," he nodded at Masters and Gunny, "create a distraction after dinner, I'll slip into his cabin and see what I find."

Masters raised his eyebrows. "Mutiny? You're proposing we take over the ship? That's too extreme."

"Maybe, but it isn't even an option unless we have the data. Let's get it, then vote."

Masters demurred, "Even if you don't get caught going through his cabin, he'll know you've searched it. Don't forget the boat's bugged."

"So, what? What's he gonna do, fire me? Ain't no one gonna buy this story back in the world. No one's goin' to the police, an' you'll get MY gat when you pry it from my cold dead fingers."

"Or," Gunny offered, "when you're sleeping. But, hey, I get your point. He's stuck with us, and we're trapped with him."

▪ ▪ ▪ ▪ ▪

The helm's instruments glowed with whites, grays, and colors. Digital numbers shined on the radios and electric panel. The computer displayed a chart. The depth sounder showed a bottom profile. The green line on the radar circled round and round. Berg smiled at the confusion on the Brits' softly lit faces.

"Christ almighty," uttered the Lieutenant. He took a breath and a half step back. "These devices are a far cry from our binnacle light."

"Jesus," cried the Mid.

Berg pointed to the radar display. The sweep, going around, showed Spain and Algeria's shore with many minor blips between *Serendipity* and the land. "That line," he pointed, "is Spain. That point is Cape de Palos. To the left is Cartagena. That line," he touched the screen, "is Algeria, and right there is Cape Aiguille. Those tiny blips are other boats." He adjusted the range setting to two miles. "Here we are," he tapped the center of the screen, "and that's you." He pointed to the other major blip. He turned to the computer screen. "This locates our position on Admiralty Chart 2717 of our time."

The Brits leaned toward the screen. It showed the land in yellow and the sea in white with depth contours in blue. They gaped at each other—astounded.

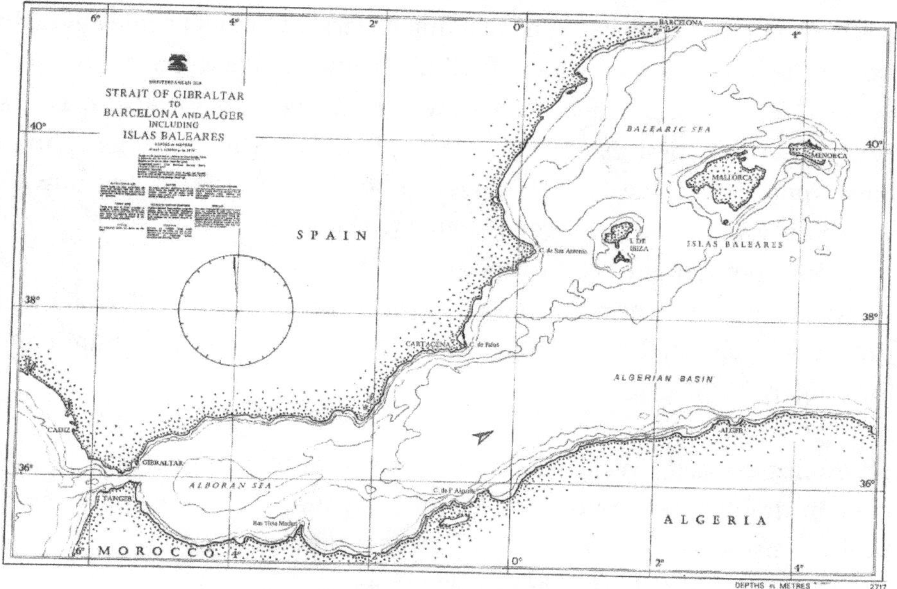

After the lights out demonstration and radio exchanges, Berg opened the cabin door to descend into the dazzling salon. With the sea calm, he abandoned the helm and left no one on watch. The smells of roasted pork and black bean soup filled their nostrils. Bones took off his earphones and stood for the introductions. Masters, Chief, and Gunny stopped their conversation when Berg entered.

"Lieutenant Bickerton and Mister Kempthorne, allow me to present our Doctor, Mister Bones."

Bones gave Berg a wry smile and shook hands with their visitors. "Gentlemen." He smiled, sat back, and started *Master and Commander: The Far Side of the World* starring Russell Crowe.

Bright lights, stainless-steel appliances, granite counters, white rubber dot galley flooring, polished teak and holly deck, matching tabletops, cushioned natural leather seats—the Lieutenant and Midshipman turned slowly at the sensory assault.

Lieutenant Bickerton stopped, and his eyes widened at moving pictures of a British captain at sea on the bulkhead screen. "Blood and thunder!"

Bones picked up his reaction and unmuted the sound. The scene of a double epaulet British captain speaking American English came alive. He was at the bow of a man-o'-war looking through a telescope surrounded by his officers. The scene continued with clearing away for action, ship's bells, and the Captain staring into a fog bank. A yellow-orange cannon flash appeared in the fog. They were under attack. "Everyone down," yelled the Captain on the screen, diving to the deck.

Bones pointed the remote and paused the movie.

Dumbfounded, the Brit's mouths dropped open. They both examined the display, checked behind it, and pressed it between their thumb and forefinger.

The Mid emitted, "Mother of God."

Bones reacted, "We call it a movie, short for moving pictures. I could explain the process to you, but I doubt anyone in 1798 has a frame of reference suitable for understanding this technology."

They nodded to each other in amazement.

Bones placed the earphones on the Lieutenant's head and resumed the movie.

The Lieutenant's eyes widened, and his mouth fell open. The scene raced forward with blasted wood and raked rigging on the deck of the man-o'-war. He stood frozen.

The scene unfolded until Bones hit the pause button.

"Holy mother."

Bones removed the earphones and put them on the table with a nod toward Berg.

Berg continued, turning to the galley. "These are the men responsible for the first-rate meal we expect tonight, Mister Cook and Mister Steward."

Cookie, wearing a full white apron, smiled, holding a large spoon. "Welcome, gentlemen. Dinner will be ready soon."

Steward smiled, waved, and continued chopping vegetables.

Mr. Kempthorne sniffed. He smelled the food and something else… the lack of the usual ship's odors. He shivered and shook his head, "This ship is bizarre."

Berg took the lead and pointed toward the bow. "Perhaps a brief tour would be of interest?"

As the five men moved forward, Bones put his headphones on, moved to the inboard seat, and returned to his movie.

Berg took them to the well-lit starboard head. "Hot showers every day are available, and we have flushing toilets."

He flushed a pressure-assisted toilet. Whoosh! The Brits leaned over, watching it refill.

"This commode is where we shit," Berg explained and turned to the urinal. "This fixture is where we pee." He flushed the urinal. "Incidentally, we still call this the head."

The Brits were dumbstruck.

"Yes," Handy offered, "plenty of pressurized hot and cold water—good conditions even on a high-class boat where we come from."

Berg opened a hot water faucet and stuck his hand under it. "Feel this."

Albert Bickerton tested the water, then jerked his hand away from the heat. "Blimey."

The Mid felt the water, too. "Wow!."

"Hot and cold running water at all times," Berg mentioned exiting the head. "We have two heads for the crew. The Captain, Bones, and I each have our own." Stepping across the hall, he opened the stateroom door and turned on the light. "All crew have a separate cabin."

The Brits peeked in. There was a warmly lit cushy bunk, convenient storage, snug chair, and a desk with a contraption and screen similar to the one in the pilothouse. The white paneling and polished wood trim left them speechless. These accommodations were nothing like living with hundreds of men slung in hammocks on the gun decks.

They looked forward along the bright corridor to a white steel door with a tiny window and a three-spoked wheel in its center. Berg turned and led his entourage aft toward a similar entrance to the engine room. Sails and Handy dropped out of the group and took seats at the tables.

Berg undogged the door, spun the wheel, pulled it open, switched on the lights, and went below into the engine room. His two guests followed.

■ ■ ■ ■ ■

The impression on the eighteenth-century sailors was overwhelming. Brightness, gloss white paint, generator whine, stainless-steel parts, hoses, electrical lines, valves, gauges, ducts, bench, tools, parts storage, and the faint smell of diesel fuel—it was sensory overload. The two guests gradually turned around, bewildered at the equipment.

"Holy bloody hell," blurted the Lieutenant. "What is all this?"

"This room contains our mechanical apparatus. That," pointing to the imposing presences of the Caterpillar C-12 engine in gloss white, "is what powers us through the water if we are not under sail."

Berg pointed at one of the generator covers, humming on its stand. "This machine gives us light."

Berg let them absorb the sights and sounds for a minute, then pointed to the stairs. "Let's go eat."

He followed them up, closed the door, and directed them toward two seats at the right of his. "If you please, Lieutenant Bickerton, sir, and Mister Kempthorne."

Berg took the table's aft end seat, Bones to his left, then Sails. Handy slid in next to the Mid. Bones turned off the movie, tapped his iPad, and changed the display to the ship's location on Chart 2717. Then he split the screen with the other half showing a philharmonic orchestra playing *Rimsky-Korsakov's Scheherazade.*

The usual elegant tables awaited. A crystal decanter of white wine stood on each.

"Gentlemen," Berg grasped the decanter, "wine? You will find it goes well with the dinner Mister Cook is serving tonight." He poured Mister Bickerton's glass, his own, and passed the decanter to his left.

With glasses filled, he raised his. "Gentlemen, King George the Third."

The Brits raised their glasses in unison. "The King."

The crew maintained blank faces but raised their glasses and followed, "The King."

Berg refilled his glass and raised it again. "Gentlemen, I give you President John Adams."

They got it and responded in unison. "The President."

Cookie rolled out a cutting stand with the suckling pig roast and started carving. Stew served the watercress salad and black bean soup.

"What music is that?" Lieutenant Bickerton pointed at the orchestra on the monitor.

"Oh," answered Berg, "it's a piece that was—I mean will be composed a hundred years from now. I am extremely fond of it."

He clicked the orchestra to the full screen and turned up the volume. It showed a closeup of the horns, a single cello, the flutes, and woodwinds. Then a single violin, playing a haunting melody. The Brits sat straight, stunned, staring at the piercing violin.

Soft music from the symphony, serving, eating, and air circulation fans created a background hum conducive to private conversations. Several began at once: Berg with the Lieutenant, Bones with Sails, and the Midshipman with Handy. Deep discussion continued at the forward table. The guests kept stealing glances at the orchestra. The meal progressed, and the wine disappeared, replaced by wide-bottom port decanters and tapered rim glasses.

▪ ▪ ▪ ▪ ▪

"So, Mister Berg," began Lieutenant Bickerton, breaking off a piece of bread, "are you really from the future? I find that hard to believe."

"Oh, yes, I'm afraid it's true. We are all," Berg waved a finger at the crew, "obligated to our Captain. I suspect certain of our crew aren't any happier serving aboard *Serendipity* than many of your crew are working aboard *Centaur*. This trip was a surprise for them."

"Oh?" replied the Lieutenant. "Were they pressed into service? The conditions and accommodations are fabulous, and your ship is unlike anything we have ever seen."

"There are no press gangs in America." Berg twirled the stem of his port glass in his fingers. "We've succumbed to greed and trapped ourselves in this grand adventure." He turned his head right toward

Bickerton. "Time-travel has unforeseen risks. I'd prefer returning safely to our own time and reading an account by someone else."

Lieutenant Bickerton asked, "Where are you are from?"

"Seattle. It's a city on Puget Sound. Have you ever heard of Puget Sound? It's an enormous bay in northwest North America named by Captain George Vancouver of the Royal Navy."

"No, I have not, although I am aware of his four-and-a-half-year voyage. It was a magnificent display of seamanship."

▪ ▪ ▪ ▪ ▪

Handy turned left to the Midshipman. "If you don't mind, I'm gonna call you Eddie, okay? Call me, Handy."

"That will be fine. So, what is this about time-travel?"

"Yeah, it's accurate enough. I'm a commercial fisherman out of Seattle. Been workin' my Dad's boat and wanted something different. I didn't know I was goin' to the Med in 1798."

"Where is Seattle?"

Handy was astonished, grasping the enormous difference in their context. "Ah, that's right. I suppose it didn't exist in 1798. It's a major city on the northwest coast of North America. Where are you from, Eddie?"

"I'm from Plymouth."

"Oh? Where's Plymouth?"

It was Eddie's turn to marvel at their different contexts. He looked into Handy's eyes to judge if Handy was using him for sport and took another drink of port. "You've never heard of Plymouth? It's in Devon County, southwest England."

"I see.... How old are you, Eddie?"

"I'm sixteen. Been at sea for four years and passed for a lieutenant."

"So, you'll be an officer soon?"

"Not bloody likely. The Admiralty can't promote me without an opening in the ranks. I'm struggling with whether I should become a Master's Mate or await a commission."

Handy grasped his pistol under his coat and adjusted how it hung.

Eddie saw him do it. "What's that?"

Handy viewed the others. With everyone occupied in conversation, he opened his coat so that Eddie could see the butt of his gun, then closed his jacket. "It's a pistol—fires bullets as fast as I can pull the trigger. We are all armed." Eddie's eyes flashed. Handy realized Eddie just grasped that he was a hostage.

■ ■ ■ ■ ■

Bones took a long drink and twisted left to Sails. "What was it like on the Limey?"

"It was a movie set without the insincerity. These guys are serious. The chatter and smells of three hundred men living in 150 feet of the gun deck were surreal—the difference between a museum and the genuine thing is striking. I did not get aboard, but there are steps built into the ship's side and handsomely served manropes to aid going aboard. Captain Plimsoll was enjoying himself." His eyes shifted to the Brits to see they were not listening. "Mister Bones, I hope I am not too indelicate, but may I ask you a question concerning our Captain? You have known him for a long time, I presume?"

"Sure."

"Ah,... is the Captain stable, or is he daft?"

"What do you mean?"

"I mean, is he harboring a romantic death wish? If he keeps bringing us to the precipice, I am afraid we will eventually fall off." He flapped his hand at the crew. "I appreciate we were naïve to believe we would receive so much money for a few days cruise on Puget Sound. But he lied to us regarding the risk. Mister Bones, is he trustworthy? Can he bring us home safely?"

"I hear ya. Well, he's the most brilliant man I've ever known. Yes, he needs risk. But, no, it doesn't rise to the level of a death wish. I trust him to get us home safe and sound. You've got to concede this quite an adventure. Keep a level head. Don't let this lead you into a stress disorder. In three days, you'll be on your way home flush with cash."

. . . . .

Gunny tapped his finger on the table to keep the attention of both Chief and Masters. "Our weapons are adequate to protect us from anything in these waters for three more days. And nothing we can do will change our time-travel risk. Even if you have the return coordinates, it won't alter that fact. The upside of your proposal does not equal the downside. Count me out."

"Okay," Chief said, "but can we count on you to keep quiet?"

"Yeah, okay. I ain't no rat."

. . . . .

Cookie and Stew joined the table across from each other. Chief noted everyone at the aft table was engaged in conversation. He nodded to Gunny and Masters, stood indifferently, and wandered into the galley, ostensibly to refill his coffee. He turned toward his mates and took a sip. No one was paying him any attention. He edged a little aft, around the mainmast, and stood by the engine room door unnoticed. He slipped into the Captain's cabin and quietly closed the door.

The skylight allowed illumination from the topside brightness. Chief turned on his flashlight and panned the room. It extended the transom's full width, exquisitely detailed to be comfortable for one person in heavy weather. A carved teak desk and chair, two comfy office chairs, a luxurious bed, and many cabinets presented. The head was port side. He closed the stern deadlights and started going through the desk.

He pulled the center drawer: Locked. Chief put the flashlight in his mouth, picked the lock, opened it, and shuffled through the papers one-by-one. There was a yellow sticky note:

From: The Desk of Jack Wilson
To: Joe
V=H0d

Otherwise: zero. The cubby holes and associated little drawers: naught.

The file drawer contained many hanging folders with printed labels in groups. One folder said, CREW. In it were eleven manila files with name labels. He spotted one marked (CHIEF) Hamilton, Mike. He removed his file.

SWOOSH! A wave lifted the stern. The sails popped AH-THWACK, struck by the wind.

"Shit." Chief stuffed the file back and turned toward the door to leave.

■ ■ ■ ■ ■

The crew's eyes widened, and they grabbed the edge of the tables. A wave boosted the boat. "dzzit…." The salon started rotation.

Berg grabbed his radio. *Dang, the barometer, the barometer….* He had a quick conversation with the Captain and sent Sails to return the Brits and pick up Joe and Jason.

■ ■ ■ ■ ■

Slanted rain pelted hard, and thunder boomed. The lightning flashes revealed blown off wave tops and tumbling water. Sails concentrated, pitching, and wrenching his way from *Centaur*. *Serendipity* jogged into the southwest wind with reefed sails and lights ablaze, awaiting the return of their Captain, Sails, and Decker. Each made the perilous leap aboard. They let the launch stream astern. It soon swamped in the violent seas, but positive flotation kept it from sinking. Tethered by a stout line from the stern cleat, the boat dragged like a sea anchor.

Berg, steering into the blow, felt the tension on the stern. He motioned Captain Joe aside. "Captain, Mister Chief snuck into your cabin and rifled your drawers and things trying to find the time and departure coordinates. It came to my attention right before the storm."

"Ha! I'm not surprised. That's why I didn't write them down anywhere onboard. They exist only in my head. Relax, I've got everything under control."

"Discipline concerns me."

"A discipline problem? I doubt it. I'm sure they'll realize they have no choice. We are all stuck, and only I can get them to Seattle. It'll be fine. Don't worry."

By 2200 hours, the cold front had passed. The barometer rose. The wind backed to the northwest and dropped to a moderate breeze. The crew dragged the launch alongside. The automatic bilge pumps worked well but were not adequate to clear the water sloshing around in the boisterous waves.

Handy jumped aboard the bucking launch to help empty the water and yelled, "Ain't no bilge pump like a five-gallon bucket and a guy thinkin' he's sinkin'."

They soon had it secured aboard. The crew gathered below. Berg remained at the helm and returned to an east-northeast course.

▪ ▪ ▪ ▪ ▪

"Well, gentlemen," Captain Joe announced, "let's call it a day. Misters Berg, Bones, and I will take turns at the helm tonight. We'll start the posted watch again at 0800 unless something unusual happens. Tomorrow's uniform is khaki pants, shirts, and black sweaters. I hope you all have a good night's rest."

There was an unidentifiable mumbling as they turned to their cabins.

27
ELIASON

February 26 - Sitka

Sitka's intermittent snow continued in the late morning gray. With the temperature below freezing and a brisk wind, Bud felt lucky they could land. He picked up his rental car and put his suitcase in the trunk. After looking around to verify no one paid attention, he leaned in under the trunk lid, opened the bag, removed his S&W snub-nose .38 and ammo box. He loaded the pistol and put it in the right-side pocket of his cargo pants. The phone in his left pocket failed to counterbalance the gun, so he hitched his pants and tightened his belt.

He drove into town and strode into the P-Bar, assuming Jason was still crabbing. Knowing Rita was one of Loren's friends, he took a stool in front of her and offered a toothy grin. "Your name's Rita, right? You know where I can find Loren?"

Rita remembered Bud and Loren's bruised face. She connected the dots and continued to work without signaling her understanding. "Sorry, Bud. I haven't any idea where she is."

"Okay. I'll find her." He stood from the stool and left.

Through the window, Rita viewed his return to a car across the street. He got in, paused, then drove away. She called Loren.

▪ ▪ ▪ ▪ ▪

Loren was sipping coffee on Al's boat when her phone rang. She viewed the display. It was Rita. "Hello, Rita. What's up?"

"Your ol' buddy Bud just walked in looking for you. You on Al's boat in Eliason Harbor?"

"Oh, shit! I never thought he'd follow me to Sitka. Does he know where I am?"

"Not yet. I didn't tell him anything but stay out of sight. I saw that welt on your face."

"Yeah, thanks for the heads up, Rita."

Loren called Al. "Hey, Al, I may have a problem. Rita called to say that Bud showed up from Anchorage looking for me. I'm afraid he'll find me."

"Take it easy. I doubt he'll locate you on the boat. I'm in the middle of trying to fix a radio, and I have stuff spread out all over my table. I want to put this together before I leave. I'll call Sly on the boat next door and ask him to keep a weather eye for trouble, okay? I'll come down to the boat later. Is there anything you need?"

"No. I'm good. Thanks, Al."

▪ ▪ ▪ ▪ ▪

Al called Sly Perkins on *Styrke*, the classic wood halibut schooner with whom he shared a finger float.

▪ ▪ ▪ ▪ ▪

Sly and two other skippers were sitting around *Styrke's* galley booth drinking coffee with a smell of rum. Their striped hickory shirts were in various stages of wear. All were in their sixties, with dirty blond hair covered in discolored hats emblazoned with fisheries logos.

"Hey, Sly."

"Hey, Al."

"Izzit blowin' pretty good down there?"

"Yeah, the wind has a bite. What's up?"

"I've got Loren, Jason's former squeeze, stayin' on my boat. That asshole—Bud—she ran off with to Anchorage, hit her. She came back yesterday. Jason's out of town, and she doesn't feel comfortable returning to his place. Bud's just showed up in Sitka and is lookin' for her."

"Loren left Jason? Silly girl. What's this guy want with her?"

"I guess he can't take 'no' for an answer and wants revenge. It's a complicated situation, and I'm kinda responsible for Jason's absence right now. I've got my single-sideband opened up, and I'm tryin' to find a leak. Could you look out for her until I get down this afternoon in case he comes snoopin' around?"

"Sure, Al. No problem. Eric and Elias are sitin' here with me tellin' lies." He turned and smiled at his two friends. "Course, all MY stories are all true." Eric and Elias laughed. "We'll keep an eye on 'er." He winked at the two guys. They got it.

"Good, thanks."

▪ ▪ ▪ ▪ ▪

Bud picked up Loren once at Jason's place, so he knew where it was. He drove out the snow-covered road and stopped at the driveway. The yard light was on. The heavy snow obscured much, but he saw no truck or tracks. *Find Jason's truck, find her.* He returned to town and started driving around. It was snowing harder and sticking. There was little color other than shades of white with occasional signs of humanity. The blowing snow cloaked everything beyond fifty feet. He drove slowly through the parking lots.

South on Lake, west down Lincoln, up Barracks past the Backdoor Café: Nothing. East on Seward, down American Street, left on Lincoln, around St. Michel's Cathedral, up Cathedral Way to Seward Street past Highliner Coffee: Still nothing. *Huh. Try the harbors.* Crescent Harbor, Centennial Hall lot: Nothing. Sealing Cove: Nothing. Past the Pioneer Bar to the ANB Harbor, then Thomsen Harbor: Nothing.

Traction became iffy in the Eliason Harbor parking lot. The wind-driven snow masked the few cars. He spotted the truck sitting alone. The thick snow cover meant it had been there all night. He parked next to it and gave the marina a quick engineer's analysis. *Twelve main floats—a hundred fingers—boats on outer arms, so 250 vessels?*

The tide was low, and the ramp steep, but its open grate kept the snow from accumulating. Bud started strolling the floats, checking for signs of someone aboard.

▪ ▪ ▪ ▪ ▪

Al continued checking continuity on the circuits of his disassembled radio. It was not too hard to find the blown fuse. He identified a filter capacitor to be the culprit. *Great, replace it, and all is well.* He went online and located the part. *Ugh, another account and password to keep track of—or not.* He ordered the capacitor, shut off his computer, put on his hoodie, Carhart jacket, and called Eluk. After cleaning the snow from his truck, they set off for town.

▪ ▪ ▪ ▪ ▪

Bud kept his parka hood up and his hands in his pockets, following the tracks in the snow. Many boats were dark, rocking in the wind. Snow accumulation showed no heat within. He ignored those.

Many skippers had taken elaborate measures to protect their boats with crafted winter covers of Visqueen over wood frames with hinged doors. Occupancy in those boats was hard to determine. He looked for heat coming out of the stacks. Others appeared abandoned to the elements. He was casual, checking every slip—out to the end of a float, around, and a leisure amble back.

▪ ▪ ▪ ▪ ▪

Al stopped first at Market Center to get fresh groceries for Loren. Next, LFS Marine for shoulder length PVC gloves. At Eliason, he parked on the other side of Jason's truck, opened the door for Eluk, and started for the boat.

▪ ▪ ▪ ▪ ▪

Bud stopped at two vessels, sharing a finger float. One was a beautiful wooden halibut schooner, and the other a fiberglass Little Hoquiam combination boat. Both faced away from the main float with Visqueen shelters over the tops of their working decks. Lights shone from both pilot houses, and heat shimmered above the stove stacks.

Loren opened the cabin door of Al's boat to access the deck locker, a good refrigerator this time of year. Her eyes locked on Bud's. "Aieee! Help, help me!" She screamed, slammed the door, locked it, and backed away.

Bud boarded the boat, grabbed the knob, and smiled through the window. "You can't escape me now, bitch. No one walks out on me."

■ ■ ■ ■ ■

The guys on the *Styrke* heard Loren's scream, peeked out the window, jumped up, moved on deck, and stepped to the dock.

Sly Perkins, wide as a door, boarded Al's boat first, his face contorted in a toothy grin. Eric and Elias came aboard and circled aft around the hatch cover. They were between Bud and the dock.

Eric smiled. "Oh, boy. Fresh crab bait."

Sly got into Bud's face. "There a problem here, mister? Cause, if there is, I'll bet I can solve it right quick."

Al strode down the float seeing the commotion on his deck. Eluk picked up Bud's scent and barked. He jumped aboard ahead of Al, bared his teeth, and growled, preparing to attack.

Al swung aboard, took hold of Eluk's collar, and grinned. "Hello, boys. Find some crab bait, did ya?"

Bud reached for his gun. "This ain't none o' your business, mister." He pulled the pistol.

Eric stepped forward, snatched it from his hand, and tossed it in the water without a word—just a smirk.

Bud grabbed his phone from his left pocket.

Eric twisted it out of his grip and tossed it over the side, too.

Al, Sly, and Eluk lay between Bud and the dock. He lurched forward and took a swing at Sly, attempting to get by. He connected thinking, *a solid hit*, but it was all arm and no body.

Sly took the whack and felt his jaw, amused. "That was a pretty good swing there, young feller." He jerked his left foot forward, carrying his entire mass, and planted a left fist in Bud's teeth. His right foot came around with his full weight, rotating for a hard-right to Bud's jaw.

Bud dropped, screaming on the cold deck. Blood gushed from his face.

Eric and Elias stood on Bud's arms. He lay howling. Sly straddled Bud holding his legs together, immobilizing him even as he tried to writhe on the deck.

Al sauntered over, holding Eluk. "Well, boys, whaddya think? Call the poo-lice or administer a little local justice?"

Loren emerged from the cabin and yelled at Bud. "You asshole. Just leave me alone."

Al handed Eluk to Loren and kneeled toward Bud. "How 'bout it, mister? You willin' just to leave town an' forget her, or have the poo-lice handle it?"

Bud left Sitka on the next flight.

28
COLLOQUY

February 27, 1798 - 1-½° east longitude

By 0615 hours, Captain Joe had showered, dressed, and filled his coffee cup. He closed his cabin door and opened the stern ports. Gray daylight peeked in, joined by chilled air and the hiss of his churning wake. He eased back in his chair, put his feet on his desk, pulled his laptop to his thighs, and started tapping keys. Their location appeared on Chart 2717. The compass showed they were on course. The barograph showed a downward slant. The twisting motion of *Serendipity*—with no sails set—had remained unchanged for hours. He no longer noticed the swishing rhythm of passing waves and considered his situation.

The crew knows Chief has searched my cabin. Could face a volatile group at breakfast. Oh, boy! A mutiny?... thrill-and-a-half... ah, Mildred... better review crew files.

He set his computer within easy reach on his desk and pulled his center drawer, expecting it locked. It slid easily. *Oh yeah, Chief....* He opened his file drawer. Chief's file in the CREW group was askew. He removed all the dossiers and put them on his lap. Each folder label had a pseudonym and name. He picked the one on top. *Let's see what we got here.*

(COOKIE) Lewis, Lance

Sumptuous meals. No problems. Wonderful choice. Joe laid the folder on his desk without opening it and moved to the next.

(STEWARD) Nicolescu, Nicholas

No problem. He put the file on Cookie's. *Ah, here we are. Chief.*

He reviewed Chief's file, noting his Christian conservative leanings, "problems with authority," and "occasionally violent."

Hmm. Captain Joe stroked his chin. *Be an exciting day. Essential skills, but unhappy. Most likely to lead an insurrection. Need to make this work. Have to be tough, though.* He put the folder on his desk and picked the next.

(GUNNY) Richert, Brian

A rare find. He glanced at the summary. "Morally flexible" caught his eye. *Need to keep track of his whereabouts and remember to pay his finder a bonus.* Captain Joe stacked it on Chief's, took a sip of coffee, and opened the next.

(DECKER) Oliver, Jason

Ah, yes. Mr. Decker. I'm familiar with his file. Likes a thrill, huh? Young Jason and I have a common issue. He closed the folder, placed it on Gunny's, and took another sip of coffee. *Jason grasps history and thinks logically—right about his bear analogy—never hear that from me. Align with Jason more than Berg. Like him, more than anybody I've found in a long time. He'll keep his cool.*

He stacked the folder on Gunny's and pulled the next.

(MASTERS) Prichard, Peter

SUMMARY: Peter Prichard; 02/23/1971 Toms River, NJ (Candid photo) 5'-11" 175 lbs.

FAMILY: Father in (FL) managed care. Mother working in Orlando. **EDUCATION:** High school. **METAPHYSICS:** Nonreligious. **POLITICS:** Conservative. **FRIENDS:** Few. Military associates shun him. **WORK HISTORY:** Twenty years in Coast Guard. Experienced in Caribbean Sea drug interdiction. Competent with weapons. Forced to retire as Chief Petty Officer for malfeasance. Charges dropped. **VICES:** Drinks occasionally to excess. No convictions. **REFERENCES:** Reliable crew. **MISC:** Has been at loose ends since leaving the Coast Guard. In search of a new identity. Needs money.

Captain Joe scanned the details. *Guy's no leader—go with the flow, whatever's happening.* He closed the cover, put it on the stack, and grabbed the next one.

(HANDY) Olsen, Eric

SUMMARY: Eric Olsen; 09/11/1994 Seattle, WA (Candid photo) 5'-9" 160 lbs.

FAMILY: Family fished for generations. Father is a highly respected halibut fisherman. **EDUCATION:** High school. **METAPHYSICS:** Religious, but doesn't attend. **POLITICS:** None, doesn't pay attention. **FRIENDS:** Two close, but have gone away to college. **WORK HISTORY:** Commercial fishing boats from an early age. Highly skilled. **VICES:** Drinks, but not excessively. Uses tobacco (snus). No arrests. **REFERENCES:** Loyal. Hard-working. **MISC:** Bored with commercial fishing. Expert with a pistol. Needs money.

Reliable seaman. Least mature. Might lose control. Follows Masters' lead, though. Likely to suck along. He placed the folder on the stack and picked the next.

(SAILS) Bartholomew, Harold

Know his file, too. What a find. Right guy, right job. In for the count.

Captain Joe put the files in the drawer. He started going through his center drawer for anything that might leave him vulnerable to Chief's search. There was a small sticky note from Jack Wilson addressed to Joe. *Shit. He's learned my real first name and has Jack's tag. Careless. Damn.* He turned off his computer, checked the magazine in his .45, stuck it in his holster, put on his blazer, and walked into the salon.

▪ ▪ ▪ ▪ ▪

0730 hours. Bones continued at the helm, and the crew took their usual spots around the tables in somber silence. Everyone had on black sweaters with their Kimber .45s hanging in their holsters.

"dzzit.... dzzzzit." The salon sustained its relentless roll. With no sails set, the boat twisted on the swish of each passing sea.

Cookie prepared another spectacular meal. The secret was Spanish smoked paprika. Each plate contained crisp dark Yukon gold potatoes mixed with separately fried onions, covered with a poached egg that settled to their base's shape. To the side was a seasoned hanger steak, cooked rare to medium-rare, how each person liked it. Cookie sprinkled the food judiciously with paprika and black pepper.

Jason smiled and inhaled the aroma. His mouth watered. The fabulous food eased his melancholy mood.

But not Chief's. He wolfed his breakfast, gulped his coffee, and smacked the cup on the table. "Cap, I'm callin' bullshit. I don't give a fuck about the money. I jus' wanna get home. I think we should go to the rendezvous point an' jus' hang out—away from trouble until we transition out." He turned to the crew for support.

Captain Joe raised himself erect in his seat. "Call me Captain Plimsoll or Captain."

"Fuck that shit. And we're beyond this 'Mister' crap. Your actual name's Joe, right?"

The others at the table stiffened.

"Yeah, I'm aware you rifled my desk. Look, only I can get us back. So," he pointed at Chief, "take your attitude and your fuckin' gat and stick 'em up your ass." He waved his hand at the others of the crew. "Day after tomorrow will see you found, flush with cash and safe in the Sound. If y'all want to return to your 'normal' lives, you'll do what I tell ya. Anyway, our present heading is toward the transition point."

Chief pushed back in his seat, folded his arms, and stared into the captain's eyes, "Well, it better work, or I'm gonna cap me a Cap."

Captain Joe chuckled, smiled, and placed his hands behind his head. "It'll work if you'll keep your cool and do what I tell ya."

Gunny tilted across toward Chief, "Take it easy, Chief. We're in no particular danger right now. If Joe," he pointed, "leads us into another life-threatening encounter, I'll join you in trying to persuade a more conservative approach. Okay?" He turned and focused on the Captain. "Whaddaya say, Joe? Can you avoid putin' us at risk for a couple o' days?"

Jason gave Sails a scan, then turned to the Captain. "Yeah, how about it, Cap? It could be a delightful day. Can't we just cruise to the embarkation point? I mean, couldn't you at least tell us how far we have to go, so we have confidence this will work out?"

"No. I will tell you nothing. If you want to get back, you'll follow my orders. And upon our return, my security force will meet us to deal with any unpleasantries. Got that?" He looked at Chief, then to each man.

Berg jerked his head back, and he turned to Captain Joe. His face reddened, his earlier exhilaration gone.

Masters viewed Handy, then raised his hand. “If I may offer my two cents. Joe, right? Joe, you need to understand, we're scared. There are two problems here. In no particular order, we're afraid of not getting back, and we're worried we'll get killed in one of your adventures. Attacked twice by pirates and once by the French in two days at sea, we think it's too dangerous out here.”

“No one's injured. You're well-fed, rested, and paid beyond your wildest dreams. I feel no remorse and apologize for nothing.”

“Yeah,” Masters wiped his mouth with his napkin, “well, even busting drug runners didn't put me at such risk. You seem confident we'll get back, but you have to realize, we've no idea how this all works.” He turned his palms up. “It's naturally upsetting to lose control over our lives. We're sure guilty of being fools to buy into this wacky scene, but you're guilty of deliberate fraud. If something happens to you or we get shot, we can't call the Coast Guard.”

“Yeah, I get that. Just hang tight. We're heading for the transition point, but we're still in pirate waters, so I can't guarantee there won't be an attack. However, I won't go looking for trouble, okay?”

Masters tipped forward. “Yeah, okay, but I'm done with the ‘Mister’ shit, too. My name is Peter, okay?”

Jason knocked his knuckles on the table for attention. “Hey, if you all want to reveal your names, that's up to you. But I'd prefer remaining anonymous. Ain't no one gonna believe this story. I want to take my money and resume life the best I can.”

Sails joined in, “Yeah, I am with you. We can drop the Mister, but you may continue to call me Sails. It will not bother me if we go our separate ways upon return to Seattle.”

Murmurs circulated the table without comment.

▪ ▪ ▪ ▪ ▪

0800 hours. The moderate breeze out of the northwest was strengthening. The sun had arisen in a thick red haze. The waves had increased to six feet and were breaking all around. The air was 53°.

“Anything to report?” Berg relived Bones and surveyed the horizon.

"Not really. Course 67°. Everything's running fine, but the barometer's dropping fast. Check the radar. Quite a few blips look like they will converge on our course in a few hours. It's strange. Anyway, I'm ready for some sack time."

Masters and Handy put on their jackets and joined Berg in the pilothouse.

Berg changed his focus from the weather indicators to his deck crew. "Gentlemen, forestaysail, staysail, and reefed main, please. Even with worsening weather, we'll have a downhill run."

▪ ▪ ▪ ▪ ▪

Masters tightened the halyard on the reefed mainsail, then returned to a personal tone with Handy. "Okay, so, shall I call you Handy or something else?"

Handy coiled the halyard and hung it on the cleat. "Let's stick with our assigned names, okay? This whole situation is jus' too fuckin' weird. I'm not sure what to do. You figure Chief's gonna go off the deep end? We need the Captain to get home."

"Nah. He and the Captain are all bluster. Ain't nothin' gonna happen to any of us. His 'security force' don't mean shit. This scene is so far outside the law that he has too much to lose to make any serious trouble. If we get back okay, we'll be able to go our separate ways."

"Yeah, but if I have to choose between the Captain and Chief, I'm gonna choose Captain. And Mister, I can shoot."

▪ ▪ ▪ ▪ ▪

Berg shut down the main. The boat became quieter. The 15-knot wind pressed the sails and changed Serendipity's motion from twisting over the waves into regular oscillation with a slight heel. Chief and Gunny set out for Chief's cabin, leaving Captain Joe, Jason, and Sails at the tables.

"Captain," Jason took a sip of coffee. "I want to expand on your parallel universe theory a little more."

Captain Joe smiled and waited.

"You've argued nothing could alter our own time because it is unimaginable—people, buildings, and streets instantly changing because of something we did in 1798."

Captain Joe nodded but remained silent. Sails focused a curious gaze at Jason.

Jason expanded his thought. "But what if people exist in an altered reality without being aware they have switched tracks to a parallel universe? The altered history would be normal for them."

"Yeah, we considered that. Before committing myself, I sent a series of devices to the past to check the effect. I could discern no difference."

"But if your device changed history, in that instant, wouldn't we only be aware of the changed record?"

"Hmm. Well, if so, we'll be the only ones conscious of it. Our brain's neuron connections won't change, either while we are here or during the transition to the hangar."

"If we return. If we've altered the past, maybe your hangar won't be there."

Sails shifted out of his seat and put on his coat, "Too deep for me. You might as well argue about angels sitting on a pinhead. You guys work it out. It is what it is. I will be on deck."

▪ ▪ ▪ ▪ ▪

Chief perched in his cabin chair.

Gunny followed in, closed the door, sat on the bunk, and leaned forward. "Look, Chief, we need both of you. We need you to keep the mechanical systems operational to arrive at the transition point. And we need Captain Joe to get us to that point. I'll back you, and the crew will back you if the Captain flips out. But until we see there's no return, ain't nobody gonna let anything happen to the Captain. So, try to tone down the threats, okay? Unless the crew sees we won't make it back, if they have to choose between support for the Captain or support for you, they're gonna go with the Captain."

Chief folded his arms and pursed his lips, considering what Gunny said. He took out his .45, jacked a shell into the chamber, flipped off the safety, put it in his holster, and cast his eyes to the floor. "Yeah, okay."

■ ■ ■ ■ ■

1000 hours. Berg studied the radar. It showed twenty blips converging on an intercept point in roughly two hours. Sails, Masters, and Handy scanned the horizon with their binoculars, although it was apparent none of the vessels were close enough to see.

"Captain," Berg called below, "check the radar."

■ ■ ■ ■ ■

Joe got his computer and returned to his seat. He pecked the keys and superimposed the radar image on Chart 2717. Sure enough, twenty red pips showed collision courses. Echos of varying brightness meant vessels of several sizes. A quick calculation showed convergence at 37-1/2° north and 2° east in two hours.

"Huh. That's peculiar." Joe hurried to the pilothouse, followed by Jason. Gunny and Chief heard the commotion, came out of the cabin, stopped to check the monitor, then joined them.

■ ■ ■ ■ ■

The wind and wave heights had increased with occasional spray. The barometer continued to descend. The sailors stared at the radar screen in silence, adjusting their stance to the pitch and roll without effort.

Berg broke the quiet. "What do you make of that, Captain?"

"I don't know. It's too bizarre for a coincidence. Well, boys, they're on our path to the transition point. I told you I wouldn't go looking for trouble, but I expect every man to do his duty if it comes looking for us. Whaddya think, Gunny? The minigun?"

Gunny peered at the radar, sea, sky, and then to Captain Joe. "Yep. Let's get it mounted before the weather worsens."

29
ENGAGEMENT

February 27, 1798 - 2° east longitude
1100 hours. The barometer continued to fall, and the blow increase. Waves became longer and more pronounced. Frequent foaming tops from the northwest produced more spray. Wind, from abaft the beam, drove *Serendipity* east-northeast with a comfortable roll under a reefed mainsail, staysail, and foresail.

Captain Joe, Jason, Sails, Gunny, Chief, Masters, and Handy peered through their binoculars at the approaching boats. A slate-gray sky enveloped their world. No one complained that their sweaters and jackets were too warm. The minigun was ready, covered with a tarp.

▪ ▪ ▪ ▪ ▪

"dzzzit.... dzzzzit." The salon/galley continued its relentless swivel. Preparations for engagement had become clear to the galley crew. Cookie's face was solemn. He stopped wiping a glass and turned toward Steward. "We have to make lunch. I doubt the crew will come to the salon. We'd better start on something for them to eat on deck—and soon. Let's do chickpea and cheddar quesadillas. The secret for on deck consumption is how we put them together. We'll layer the center with cumin-scented chickpeas covered by melted cheddar. Then we'll fold the tortillas with five folds, so the ingredients stay in the center. They can eat them with their hands. I want to warm the boys and keep them fueled. Get the blender for me, please, and start the tortillas. I'll start the chickpeas."

Steward moved close to Cookie. "We gonna be all right, ain't we, Lance?"

"Sure, Nick," Cookie lowered his voice. "These guys have it under control. And don't call me by name. After this trip's over, I don't want any of them coming to find us, okay?"

"Yeah. Okay. Sorry. Corn tortillas, is it?"

▪ ▪ ▪ ▪ ▪

Gunny let his binoculars hang and turned to Captain Joe. "If this is a coordinated attack, and we must assume it is, our setup on deck presents a problem. The launch and foremast make the minigun ineffective to starboard. The mast is a given, but the launch increases our profile and our exposure to a lucky shot. We must get the launch off the deck or defend to starboard with the M4s."

Sails, staring through his binoculars, voiced his opinion, "I, for one, prefer we keep the launch aboard. Streaming it causes drag, and we do not need any drag."

"Me, too." Jason piped in. "Another option is to cut it loose, but I am not in favor of that. It's our lifeboat."

Grunts from the others, except for Chief.

Chief flinched. "Couldn't we go upwind until we lose them in our lee and circle to the north?"

"No," Captain Joe retorted. "We must be at our transition point on time to catch our return gravity wave. If we go around, we'll risk missing our departure coordinates. I regard a Muslim attack to be a lesser risk. Sorry, boys, but I guess that quashes the concept of staying out of harm's way."

Sails interjected, "I recommend we keep sail on to minimize roll. However, prudence requires we change to the black storm sails. Let us not make ourselves an easier mark than necessary." He glanced from Captain Joe to Berg.

Berg did not need convincing. "Splendid idea. Get 'er done."

Steward donned his Stormy Seas, came on deck, and passed out the chickpea and cheddar quesadillas. He also carried napkins, a large carafe of coffee, and mugs. "Gentlemen, how about a hot meal?"

"Well," Jason grimaced, holding a cup for Steward to pour, "I'll tell you what, the pirates may kill us, but we sure as hell eat well. Thanks." He placed his mug on the launch's gunwale, took a big bite of the quesadilla, and raised his binoculars to his eyes.

Masters and Handy joined the somber tone. "Yeah, thanks, Stew."

Before going below, Steward scanned the horizon. Sails were now visible from the deck with a naked eye, and they seemed to converge from all directions. The vessels were of various sizes, but four were much larger than the rest. Steward frowned but did not speak. He went below.

Berg wondered aloud, "How do you suppose they could organize such an attack? And why?"

Jason replied while staring through his binoculars, "I'll bet their coast-based point-to-point semaphore communication was more sophisticated than we give them credit." He lowered his glasses and spoke without looking, "My guess is someone from that corsair attack two days ago survived and is really pissed."

"Hmm, maybe," Captain Joe murmured. "Hey, Gunny, we have two Javelin missiles left. How about taking out those two bigger bitches once they get within range?"

"Yeah. Sounds good to me. Also, let's get everyone armed with M4s. Chief? Give me a hand with the missiles?"

"Sure."

■ ■ ■ ■ ■

Gunny led the crew to the munitions cache and started passing out M4s and magazines. "Boys, in the interest of safety, don't load the magazines until we have a brief review on deck, okay?"

Handy's voice was confident. "How 'bout more .45 clips?"

"Yeah," voiced the others in unison.

Gunny handed out the additional .45 clips each person wanted, filled a black canvas tote with M4 magazines, and headed on deck.

Masters scanned the locker before leaving. "Captain, don't we have another stand for the grenade launcher?"

"No, I'm sorry to admit, we don't. I did not expect this much action." Joe put the strap of a TAC-50 over his shoulder and headed topside.

. . . . .

Gunny's voice carried over the wind and waves. "Remember S-P-O-R-T-S. S—slap the magazine." He showed on his M4, "P—pull the charging handle. O—observe the chamber's clear. R—release the charging handle—let it snap. T—tap to verify it's seated, and S—shoot. Put your weapon on safe. Set your switch to semiautomatic." He showed how. "Now load and take a few shots. And keep your goddamn guns pointed away from the boat."

Shots rang out, cartridges clattered to the deck and bounced into the sea.

"Good. Now listen up. We'll be facing hundreds of shooters. Their accuracy is bad, but with volume, shots will hit us. So don't just blast away. Stay on semiautomatic and aim your shots."

Jason stared through his Steiners. A European rigged brig, xebecs, polaccas, and galleys were on collision courses with *Serendipity*. Signal flags raised and lowered on all the vessels, but he could not tell which one was in command.

Gunny reverted to military protocol. "Mister Masters, station yourself at the minigun. I'll take out the brig with a Javelin."

"Yes, sir." Masters removed the tarp, sat on the deck, and took hold of the handles.

Gunny sat far forward, near the foresail tack. With the target closing in from the southeast, the backblast would clear *Serendipity*. He set the targeting system track box in the command launch unit around the two-masted square-rigger. The infrared signature was not enough. Then it blinked to 'lock.' "Shit! Hope the lock holds. Okay, here we go—fire one."

"Swoosh." The missile zoomed through the air and smashed into the brig with a roar. The ship exploded into a yellow-orange plume of debris that rained over the water. The sea's maw swallowed the wreckage.

Gunny saw the other vessels kept coming. He pointed, "Chief, hand me the other rocket."

Gunny reloaded and picked the next largest vessel—a three-masted xebec to the north, coming fast on a broad starboard reach. The infrared signature was even weaker. "Shit. I hate to wait until he fires to get a good lock, but I need a better image."

A dash of spray felt cool on Gunny's face. He licked his lips, tasting salt. The wind continued to increase, and the waves were extending and becoming more uniform.

Bones appeared in the pilothouse.

Captain Joe was in full authoritative mode. "Mister Bones, an attack is imminent by a flotilla of Barbary corsairs. I want you safe in the infirmary."

Bones paused. Many boats were on a collision heading. All were under sail and some rowing besides. "Yes, sir." He retreated below.

Jason, Handy, and Chief rested their M4s on the launch's inboard gunwale, covering the downwind approach. *Serendipity's* starboard heel gave them clear shots.

The three-masted xebec fired, its bow cannon making a bright flash followed by a boom and the fizz of the ball—a little high and ahead.

"Good." Gunny locked on and fired.

"Swoosh."

The missile flew true. It pierced the bow, blowing both sides outward in an instant flash of fire. The boat disappeared into the waves, smoke trailing where it had been.

All the Moors started firing with cannons and muskets, making hundreds of flashes against the darkening clouds.

Now in range, Masters opened fire with the minigun, and the boys started plinking with their M4s. Musket balls pierced *Serendipity's* sails and bounced off the hull. One shot penetrated the outboard side of the launch with a thud.

Gunny looked around to assess *Serendipity's* defense. Masters' management of the minigun was deadly. Attackers collapsed in jumbled heaps of fractured bodies. Tracers every five rounds streaking orange in the fading light made it easy to identify his targets. Several ignited fires on the attackers. One hit the magazine on an approaching galley. It blew up, raining boat parts. Sails fired from the bow. "Bonk." A cannonball hit *Serendipity's* hull to starboard, forward of amidships. Gunny peered at the dent, then looked astern. Captain Joe had braced his back against his cabin's skylight aft, aiming his TAC-50 at a sizeable bearded man at the bow of an approaching xebec.

▪ ▪ ▪ ▪ ▪

Captain Braham Madjer had pressed his crew hard to catch the American schooner. Well supplied and able to row during the recent calm, he closed the distance on a broad reach. Now, he was finally within range. He stared at *Serendipity* through his telescope—unmistakable with its black hull. A man with a peaked hat, pressing his back against a skylight, pointed a strange musket at him.

He grinned, tasting his revenge. "Praise Allahu. There he is." He closed his scope and sighted down the bow chaser. With a mallet, he made final adjustments to the cannon's breach wedge. He waited for the pitch and roll to be right, holding the slow match above the touchhole.

▪ ▪ ▪ ▪ ▪

Captain Joe watched Braham Madjer watching him. The bearded man closed his telescope and prepared to fire. Joe adjusted his telescopic sight, timed the pitch, and squeezed off a round. "Blam!" The kick made the image jerk, but as he recaptured the view, his adversary exploded into pieces.

Gunny grinned. "Nice shot, Captain."

Sails lay flat, forward of the minigun, shooting at boats off the port bow.

Berg, alert at the helm, had started the engine and kept them on course.

The ship's clock struck eight bells.

Berg got up, and Captain Joe took the wheel. Berg peeked above the coach roof to get a sense of the external action. A bullet grazed his scalp, knocking him to the deck, bleeding.

"Bones!" Joe yelled into the intercom. "Bill's wounded and needs your help. Quick. Get something to stop the bleeding."

Hundreds of bullets were in the air. Jason joined Handy and Chief lying prone below the launch, firing to starboard. He hollered to his shipmates while continuing to pick out targets, "It's getting dark, and the storm's increasing. Maybe we can disappear into the night."

Six galleys were rowing hard into the wind but losing ground.

Windward boats were coming fast. "Clunk." Another cannonball struck the hull—this time from the north.

"Crash." A cannonball smashed through the launch, missing the engine but spraying hull parts to leeward. Jason checked his fellows. Everyone was okay.

Bullets whizzed in a constant hail. One struck Masters. He rolled to his left in agony, grabbing his upper arm with blood running through his fingers. "Shit, my arm."

Gunny took his place at the minigun. "Get below quick." He pressed the Vulcan trigger and ripped the boats to port with a stream of fire and death.

The wind increased. The sea was heaping. White foam from breaking waves blew off in streaks. Jason fired at a Moor to starboard. With too much sail, its foremast broke above the deck and dropped over the side. It wallowed away in fifteen-foot waves.

A cannonball struck Serendipity*'s* foremast waist high from the south with a resounding "clank." The main headstay separated from the foremast at the shackle, leaving it blowing wildly in the wind. Berg shut off the radar to keep the dancing wire from wrapping around the antenna. The foremast bent with an agonizing screech to leeward and hit the water, dragging the foresail and the headstays with it. But it did not separate. The sail settled over Jason, Handy, Chief, and the launch.

"Fuck!" Chief grasped the danger of losing the ability to steer. "Gotta cut away the mast."

He climbed from under the sail, jumped below, and returned topside with a pack of tools. Shots continued to buzz. He cut away the shrouds, stays, and halyards with a cable cutter, then the mast with a cordless Sawzall. It crashed to the deck.

Jason and Handy helped shove the total mess into the sea.

Chief turned to the launch and cut the tie-downs. Jason and Handy aided Chief to boost the useless boat over the side—the wrenching screeches masked by the screaming wind and roaring sea.

Sails retrieved a five-eighths thimble from the deck box, hooked on a snap shackle, and spliced it into a five-eighths three-strand rope. He took the end and climbed the mainmast, unfolding the mast steps as he went. When the errant mainstay swung by, he grabbed it and attached the shackle. Jason brought the line forward and fastened it to the anchor windlass, and pulled it tight.

Captain Joe took in his crew's performance and smiled. *Excellent work. Saving mainmast—a lucky break. Lose it, lose radar and navigation—no return.*

Down from the mast, Sails turned to Jason, "We have to set the forestay tight. Get a double tackle from the deck box and a carabiner." He took a piece of dock line and joined Jason on the foredeck. After tying a small bowline on both ends, he made four wraps around the new forestay. After the fourth wrap, he brought the tails even, crossed the lines in front, then again behind the new head stay. He joined the ends in front and clipped them together with a carabiner to make a Valdotain Tresse knot.

The high-pitched wind screamed, contrasting with the deep rumble of breaking waves.

Jason attached one end of the tackle to the anchor cleat. A bullet punched a hole through the sleeve of his jacket. He glanced at it. Sails bound the other end to the carabiner. They heaved on the line together, stretched the forestay taught, and tied the tackle fall to a deck cleat. Jason undid his previous forestay cleat—now loose—and refastened it tight. Sails then untied the tackle fall. The forestay relaxed a bit. They bowed to each other and returned to their weapons in the deepening gloom.

Captain Joe turned them into the wind and pushed the throttle to the wood. *Serendipity* passed between the attackers. When one bore near, Handy pulled his .45 and started shooting with deadly effect.

Then they were through, crashing into the waves, taking green water over the bow. The mainsail's flap punctured the air. The crew grabbed whatever was near to brace against the rush of water.

The weather became wild. The corsairs had to attend their ships and faded to leeward. *Serendipity's* black hull and sails disappeared to windward in the darkening sky and erupting storm.

The crew turned their attention to the ship. Gunny detached the power from the minigun and dropped the link belt through the deck feed. Sails refastened the deck plate. Jason, Sails, and Handy collected the loose gear and secured the deck.

"Before you guys go below," the Captain directed, "furl the mains'l and yankee. We'll turn soon and proceed under power for the duration of this storm." He switched on the radar.

The weather got worse. The wind increased to 40 knots. Waves, now over twenty feet high, were longer. The edges of the crests were breaking into spindrift with foam blown away in well-marked streaks. *Serendipity* rose and dipped into the oncoming seas, awash with rushing spume. Rain pelted the deck.

Captain Joe checked their position on the radar and continued northwest, into the wind.

30
TEMPEST

February 27, 1798 - 54 miles South by East of Cape Berberia, Formentera Island

1500 hours. The northwest wind continued to increase. The sea rolled. Waves grew higher with dense streaks of foam blown away in a gurgling roar. Rain and spray painted the view gray. *Serendipity* pitched and rushed into the looming darkness.

Captain Joe sat alone at the helm with the deck door closed. He had turned east-northeast, figuring he was far enough to windward of the corsairs. With the launch gone, his view was unobstructed. Dim lights from the radar, binnacle, and instrument panels glowed in the dark wheelhouse. He concentrated on steering. Waves passed beneath the boat, alternating between lifting it abruptly to a crest before surfing to a trough.

▪ ▪ ▪ ▪ ▪

Bones' eyes had adjusted to the infirmary's bright lights glaring off the white cabinets and tile floor. The antiseptic smell was a familiar companion. His two patients lay in beds, tied securely against the boat's pitch and roll. Now with a following sea, Bones no longer lofted when *Serendipity's* bow dropped over a high wave.

He wrapped a bandage on Berg's head. Berg was conscious but shaken and confused. Bones continued his conversation with Masters in the other bed. "You were both lucky. A fraction of an inch more, and I'd have an awful scene down here. The bullet didn't break Mister Berg's skull. His disorientation continues, but he'll be okay."

He cut the final wrap with scissors, turned to Masters, and changed the dressing on his arm. "You will not be using this arm for a while. The bullet didn't hit a bone or a major blood vessel, so you will be okay too." He smiled and put Masters' arm in a sling.

"Thanks, Doc," Masters groaned. "This trip was a terrible bargain. The money ain't worth shit if we don't get back or get a permanent injury. Two more days is too much. I agree with Chief—we should go to the transition point and hang out 'till we get the fuck out o' here."

Bones completed the bandage and bent toward Masters. "Yeah, I gotta agree. You've lost blood and need to lie here quietly. I'll have a word with the Captain, okay?"

■ ■ ■ ■ ■

"dzzzzit.... dzzzzit." The salon's rotation ground away. Gunny, Chief, Handy, Sails, and Jason sat around the galley tables, drinking coffee. Cookie and Stew worked without a word on preparations for dinner.

Gunny relaxed and stroked his chin. "You boys were magnificent. That was a good fuckin' job anytime, anywhere. Handy, I've never seen a better hand with a .45. You're one fuckin' dangerous dude with a pistol."

"Thanks." Handy strode forward to check on Masters.

Sails hunched over the table and turned to Chief. "Chief, your clearing away the damage was prompt and efficient. You pulled a blinder there. If you had been slow or bumbled it, we would be shaking hands with Davy-Jones."

"Yeah, well," Chief replied, "your fast work on the forestay," he nodded to Jason, "is what allowed us to go upwind from those raghead bastards without losing the mast and radar. But, I gotta tell ya, I ain't gonna take two more days o' this." He took a drink of coffee and gazed into the distance. "Me an' da Captain gonna come to an understandin', one way or da other."

Gunny's eyes narrowed in on Chief. "Whaddaya mean?"

"I mean," he turned to Gunny, "if he wants to continue breathin', we're gonna go to the transit point and hang around until it's time for our return."

"Chief, you can't threaten the Captain. He's the only one who can get us home."

"Bullshit. I'll threaten anyone I want." He returned Gunny's stare. "I want the when and where. Ain't no reason to keep it a secret. I want to hang out there 'til we get the fuck outta here. I don't need no more excitement."

▪ ▪ ▪ ▪ ▪

Captain Joe called the infirmary on the intercom. "Hey, Bones, can you talk?"

"Yes, sir." The speaker allowed Bones to talk and work.

"How are our patients doing?"

"The bullet missed the bone on Masters. It's a clean slash. He won't be using his arm for a while, but he'll be fine. Bill, oops, I mean Berg, took a nasty swipe to his head, but the bullet didn't penetrate his skull. He's confused and out of action, but he should mend okay."

"Well, that's splendid news. No more deck duty for you. Your job is to take care of our injured crew."

He switched the intercom to ALL. "Mister Chief, and Mister Gunn to the wheelhouse, please."

▪ ▪ ▪ ▪ ▪

Gunny and Chief entered the wheelhouse. Chief closed the door.

"Boys," Captain Joe smiled and pointed at the clock, "you will be on watch in a few minutes and—."

Chief pulled his knife, flipped it open with one hand, and pointed it at Joe's chest. "Fuck that shit. I wanna know where and when."

"Oh, shit!" Gunny pulled his .45, clicked it off safe, and aimed it at Chief. "Take it easy, Chief. I can't let you harm the Captain."

"I'm not gonna harm him. He's gonna tell me where we gotta be and when we gotta be there. So,..." He pressed the knife closer to Joe. "I won't need to harm you, will I, Captain?" He thrust the blade even closer to Joe's chest.

A pall passed over Joe's face. He started up from the helmsman's seat just at the boat lurched over a breaking wave. He pitched toward Chief and stumbled into the knife with the full force of his body. The knife jabbed into his chest. His eyes widened.

"Shit!" Chief pulled the knife out, shocked. His eyes filled with terror. "Oh my god, what've I done? Damn, I didn't mean to hurt him."

Blood spewed, and Captain Joe collapsed. Chief dropped his knife, caught Joe, and lowered him to the deck.

"Goddamnit, Chief! You stabbed the Captain. Are you out of your fuckin' mind?" He put the gun in his holster, kneeled, and helped Captain Joe lie to the deck, pressing a hand on the cut to reduce blood loss.

"Ahaaa, aha," Captain Joe groaned.

Gunny punched the intercom. "Doc, Chief's stabbed the Captain. Come to the wheelhouse right now!"

"It was an accident! I only meant to threaten—didn't mean to stab 'im."

"Well, now you've done it." Gunny removed his jacket and placed it under Captain Joe's head.

Jason and Sails raced to the pilothouse. Gunny, on his knees, held his hand on Joe's oozing wound. Waves passed under the boat, swaying their bodies in unison. Sails took the helm and continued what he judged their approximate course.

Chief's face was pale and hapless. "It was an accident—really. I didn't mean it."

Bones came carrying a small bag and kneeled beside Joe. Handy peered from the companionway. Bones didn't look up, intent on triage, not blame. He opened Joe's jacket and shirt. "Give me the knife—how deep did it go?"

Chief picked up the knife and held it out for examination.

Bones checked the blood on the blade. It had run a bit, but he judged it penetrated an inch and a half. He grunted and taped a large gauze bandage over the cut.

Captain Joe grimaced in pain and spoke in a sinking voice—but loud enough for the men to hear, "I give command of the boat to Jason—Mister Decker. He is in charge until further notice. East-northeast." He passed out.

Jason straightened and glanced around. *Holy shit. Can we make it? Can't show fear.... Must get coordinates—somehow.*

Bones scanned the crew, too, then to Jason. "You gotta do it. Somebody has to, and I have my hands full. Both Captain Joe and Berg are out of commission. You're now in charge." He shifted to the crew. "Gentlemen, we need to put Joe into his bed—very carefully. Handy, get the stretcher from the infirmary. It's rolled up and tied to the corridor wall near the ceiling. I'll treat him in his cabin."

"Okay," Jason announced. He took in a deep breath, pointed, and spoke to Sails. "East-northeast. I'll go with the Captain and try to get the departure coordinates."

▪ ▪ ▪ ▪ ▪

The roar of the sea lessened in the Captain's cabin, rising, twisting, and falling with the waves. Jason sat in the Captain's desk chair with grim concentration.

Joe lay on his bed. Bones cleansed the stab wound with gauze and carefully examined the gash. "Good. There's no active arterial bleeding. A pressure dressing will do the job." He took several pads from his kit and maintained pressure to stop the bleeding. He wrapped Joe's chest tight with a bandage and examined the pads. Little blood appeared. "Whew. We're fortunate. It didn't hit his heart. He will be all right."

Bones hurried to the infirmary, returned, and started a saline IV. "I think the knife nicked his pericardium. Joe's out of action and needs to rest. Another eighth-inch would have cut his heart."

Jason leaned forward, clasped his hands together with his elbows on his thighs, and stared at Captain Joe. "Doc, I must talk to him."

Captain Joe's eyes opened, and he gazed up, unfocused. "Jason?"

Jason leaned over the bed. "Yes, sir?"

"Jason, 7:32 P.M. ship's time tonight... transition... 38° north... 2°, 30' east."

"Tonight? I thought we had two more days."

"No... lied... figured... necessary for control." He closed his eyes. "May have fucked up." He fell unconscious.

Jason turned to Bones. "Did you know about this?"

"No, I did not. He didn't share the information with either Berg or me."

"Damn.... Okay. I have to tell the crew."

■ ■ ■ ■ ■

Jason moved to the Captain's salon seat where the intercom was within easy reach. "dzzzzit.... dzzzzit." The salon ground away on its axis.

Jason pressed ALL on the intercom. "Hey, everybody. Listen, I've got news. We transition tonight at 7:32 ship's time. That's right—the Captain lied to us—1932 tonight provided we're at 38° north and 2°, 30' east. Meet me in the pilothouse."

Masters and Berg remained strapped to their beds. The galley crew continued to work on dinner. Gunny, Handy, and Jason gathered around the radar in the pilothouse. Sails continued to concentrate on steering. With no GPS, no stars, and daylight gone, navigation to a precise point in an unmarked sea would be challenging. *Serendipity* twisted over the enormous waves from the northwest. They headed east-northeast in the howling wind, radar providing their means of navigation.

"So," Sails questioned, steering to meet a wave, "where the bloody hell are we?"

Gunny laid out Chart 2717. Jason and Handy stared at the edge of the green line on the screen, going round.

Handy twisted the radar's protractor edge dial, so zero was north, matching the compass. "Alger bears 132°." He read off the angle.

Gunny used the drafting machine to align the angle from the compass rose, transferred it to Alger, and drew a pencil line on the chart.

Handy said, "The western cape on Formentera Island lies 346°."

Gunny drew another line.

"Cabrera Island at 36°."

Gunny drew a third line. "That puts us here," he pointed at the chart, "37°, 45' north, and 1°, 47' east." He did a quick measure. "We have four hours to travel forty-three miles east-northeast." He twisted the drafting machine on the chart. "I make the course seventy degrees east of north."

"Roger. We are on course." Sails continued steering. "Four hours, forty-three miles, at over ten knots—with this sea pushing us, we will overshoot. That is good. We will come about and turn into it to jog to our target position."

The men exchanged nods.

Jason addressed the crew. "Gentlemen, remember Bones reporting we arrived two minutes east of our projected longitude? An error of two arc minutes coming in means two-minutes going out. We need to be two minutes east of the Captain's coordinates, at 2°, 32 minutes. Is everyone on board with that?"

"Jesus," Handy uttered, "I hadn't thought of that."

Sails spoke, turning the wheel to compensate for the force of the next wave. "Two minutes of longitudinal arc at 36° latitude is not the same distance as two minutes at 38°. Is the error in distance or angle?"

Jason grabbed the wheelhouse table fiddle to steady himself against a giant passing wave. "Two minutes is two minutes, regardless of the latitude. We must choose one or the other. It's more than a mile, but I don't know how to calculate it. Can anyone figure the distance of a minute of arc at a specific latitude or have a reason to choose distance over the angle?" No one spoke. "Okay, I choose angle."

Gunny continued to concentrate on the chart. "Right, we go with angle. At the transition time, we need the east cape of Formentera Island to bear 311°, Cabrera Island at 15°, and Alger at 165°. I've marked them here."

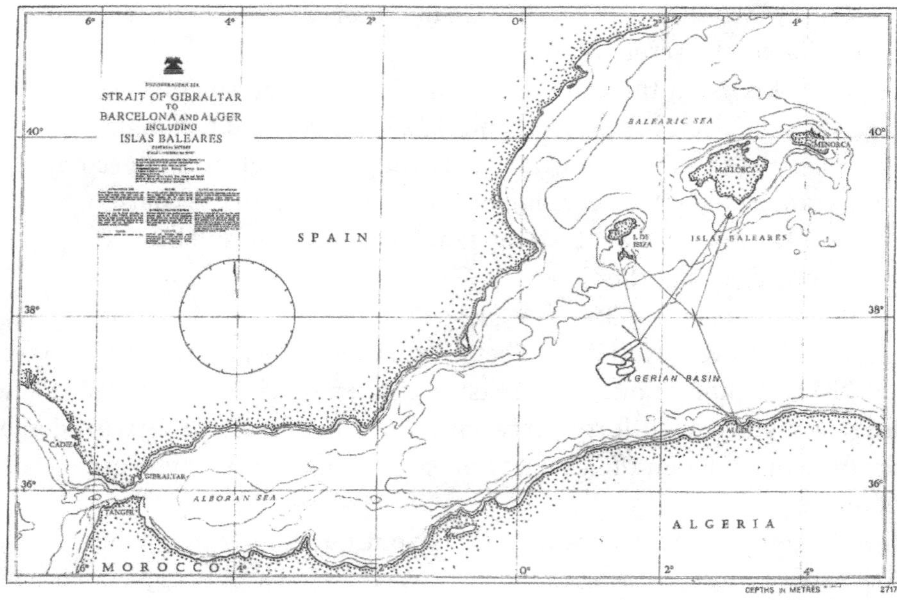

"Very well," Jason directed, "we'll change helmsman every hour. Gunny, you'll relieve Sails at 1600. Handy, you take it at 1700. I'll take it at 1800. Sails, you're at the helm at 1900 while we give you direction and distance for the last leg." He turned to Sails. "You okay for another half-hour?"

"Yes, I am fine."

"Okay, then. Yell out if you need something. We'll be in the salon."

▪ ▪ ▪ ▪ ▪

"dzzzzzit.... dzzzzzzit." The salon/galley worked hard to give them respite from the roll. They took their usual seats. Chief had opened a bottle of Madeira and was getting drunk. He ignored the disgusted faces of the crew. Cookie and Bones joined them at the table. Steward poured a cup of coffee for everyone except Chief.

"So," Cookie opened, "are we gonna get back?"

Jason scanned the crew. "Okay, here's the story. The boat's secure, and everything's working okay. We know our transition point and time. *Hope I'm right.* We have adequate time and should be fine assuming nothing breaks down," he peeked at Chief staring vacantly at the table with one hand on the bottle and one hand on his glass, "and provided the margin for error is wide enough for us to slip through."

Gunny released his cup and turned to Bones. "What do you suppose that margin is? Surely there's some margin. We can't possibly be at an exact spot at an exact time."

Bones crossed a leg and put his left index finger through the handle of his coffee mug. He gestured with his right hand. "I don't know the margin. But I do know Captain Joe would never have done this without a margin appropriate to the conditions he thought likely to exist. His planning is meticulous. I suggest you try your hardest to be precise. I expect it will be good enough. I guess we'll learn the answer at 1933."

Cookie rejected pessimism. "Gentlemen, I propose we eat early. I plan the main course of phyllo-wrapped halibut fillets with a lemon scallion sauce, roasted parmesan pesto potatoes on the side, and an apple crumble with vanilla ice cream for dessert." Cookie turned to the galley.

Jason and the crew gaped at Cookie. *Eat?*

■ ■ ■ ■ ■

1900 hours. Sails manned the helm. Jason, Gunny, and Handy were with him in the pilothouse. Outside was pitch black. Wave crests tumbled and smashed into the pilothouse windows with a shuddering roar. They drove headlong into the oncoming seas. A red night light hung over the chart table. Other light came from the instruments.

Gunny followed Handy's finger on the radar screen at the point where they needed to be. Jason passed orders to Sails. "Starboard five degrees."

"Starboard five degrees, aye," Sails responded.

"Steady as she goes."

"Steady, aye."

"Back off to fifteen-hundred revolutions."

"Fifteen-hundred revolutions, aye."

"Port three degrees."

At 1931.75 hours, a massive wave raised them high.

"Port three degrees, aye. But hard time concentrating—prickly sensation, f□eling di□□y, l□yt-headed, whirling, wo0ʘzy and 000□□□ m□□y 00 b0ʘdɥ 000 is □□ siŋ00kı̣0ng & mϴƱ!Ꭻɑ 0000000□□□□□□□□□□□□.................."

31
BALLARD

February 27 - Seattle

Seattle's weather was irrelevant inside the hangar complex deep within its rock cavity. The Control Room clock, labeled SEATTLE, read 1130. The GREENWICH clock read 1930. The clock marked SHIP read 1902. Both date clocks read February 27. The Sea Day display read THREE.

Alyx no longer needed his Red Bull to get his juices flowing. The return transition was due in thirty minutes. He had lost his toothy grin in the wee hours and felt a drop of sweat on his temple. He tightened the last screw on the replacement ioxin slot jumper at Magnetron fifteen and checked the system analysis display. It turned green. He closed the panel and radioed his crew. "Power up fifteen."

"Whizzzzzzzzz." The Magnetron came alive. All eight ioxin slots continued green. He called Paul Gorken, the Transition Coordinator. "Paul, we're good on all fifteen trons."

"Excellent job, Alyx. Have your crew stand by and stay tuned for our next exciting episode."

Paul clicked off and called Jack Wilson. "Jack, we're 'go' at this end. How are the wave propagation curves?"

Jack shifted his screen to the Wave Propagation Reaction Modulator curves. "The blue and green curves match. We're cool on this end. Where do we stand on power?"

"Give me a minute. I'll get back to you."

▪ ▪ ▪ ▪ ▪

The rain streamed off Pete and Phil, standing useless and poker-faced in their Helly Hansen's. It was clear the gang had positioned a black Suburban with tinted windows to watch THEM. Also, two men, their faces concealed by dark rain gear, stood near the fence observing the action. A similar scene played out at the other two substations.

A crew in stolen Seattle City Light gear was raising several strange apparatuses to the high voltage feeds. They jacked six-foot-long, half-round, thick copper pipes under the high-voltage wires, so they were parallel but did not touch. Large cables ran from the copper half-pipes to an enclosure built on the back of an old M35 duce-and-half. One of them spoke into a handheld radio, eyeing the Suburban. Pete and Phil could not hear them. The Suburban flashed its parking lights.

▪ ▪ ▪ ▪ ▪

Keith Larkin, the power supply manager, heard his phone signal. The caller ID read Rolf. Keith took the call. "You got good news?"

"Yep," Rolf growled, "you're 'go' for power. All systems are ready. Everyone's behaving well."

"Okay, I'll tell Paul." He tapped a button. "Paul, Rolf called. We're 'go' for power."

Paul grinned. "Good. I'll tell Jack." He called Security. "Hey. You boys ready with ambulances and any necessary security action?"

"Don't worry about us. We'll cover our side of the business, and you cover yours."

"Yeah, right," Paul called the dock crew supervisor.

▪ ▪ ▪ ▪ ▪

The dock supervisor took the call on a phone built into the wall near the door inside the dome. "Dock crew."

"You guys ready to receive *Serendipity*?"

He recognized the voice and checked his men. They had their ear protection on and were preparing lines, a dinghy, and rescue equipment. "Yes, we're ready."

▪ ▪ ▪ ▪ ▪

"Okay, good. Stand by for the transition. I'll let Jack know." Paul called Jack. "We're 'go' for power, security, and dock. How are we looking overall?"

■ ■ ■ ■ ■

Jack had not moved from his computer in hours. “We're good. The G-WADs are fully functional. Provided we don't have a gravity wave anomaly in the next few minutes, and the boys are where they gotta be....”

■ ■ ■ ■ ■

The pulsating amber glow of the G-WADs increased their intensity. The low-frequency purr grew into a screaming crescendo. “□□□□□□000000 & r⊙0ЖKing & bΘƱηCXng and—” Sails felt a sudden drop. “Holy shit! We're back!”

Doris gasped and took a step away. *Serendipity* dropped into the hangar pool from six feet in the air with an enormous splash. The roar of a wave, washing over the dock's surface, displaced the shrieking G-WAD. The ship bobbed—a rocking mess—no foremast or launch. A rope stayed the mainmast, and her sides had dents. Still in gear, she rammed into the dock with a metallic screech. The bowsprit ripped off, and the boat careened along the bulkhead.

■ ■ ■ ■ ■

Serendipity's crew slammed to the deck. Jason forced himself up and grabbed the wheel. “Woo-hoo! We did it!” He took her out of gear and shut down everything.

The boat rocked in a violent motion. Waves sloshed back and forth in the pool, breaking against the bulkhead before beginning to subside.

No one spoke. Then the loudspeaker echoed in the dome. “Dock crew secure the boat.” Men jumped aboard with lines and tied her to the wharf.

Sails, Gunny, and Handy lay on the deck where they fell, rocking with the boat—coming to grips with having returned.

Bones, in Joe's cabin, rolled over on the floor and grabbed his handheld. click “Hello, the twenty-first century! We have three wounded men aboard, Joe, Bill, and Masters. We need two ambulances and security. Chief stabbed Joe. Come back?" click

Security awaited the call. click "Security, roger. They're on the way." click

Fifteen security men in gray jumpsuits with automatics in polished brown chest holsters were already on the dock. They stood in formation, three by five near the door. The Security Supervisor spoke into a microphone. His voice boomed, "Onboard *Serendipity.* Leave all guns on the boat and come ashore. No exceptions."

Chief hit hard against his seat, then banged forward into the table. He was half snockered but never let go of his bottle. The announcement confirmed they were back. He sat motionless for a moment. Then he took out his pistol and worked the slide, forgetting it had been ready to fire. He contemplated it. "Shit." He closed the hammer, placed the forty-five on the table, and headed on deck.

Jason removed his pistol, set it on the shelf under the forward window, and stepped off. Sails, Gunny, and Handy got up, did the same with their guns, and filed off. Two medical teams with ambulance cots passed them on their way below.

Cookie stood, wiped his hands, and started the dishwasher. It did not work. He switched the cooking equipment off, wiped his hands on his apron, took it off, and started topside. Steward followed. One EMS team streamed past. The other turned aft into Captain Joe's cabin.

Masters undid his hold-downs, threw his legs over the edge of the bed, and adjusted the sling on his arm. An EMS team came in and loaded Berg onto an ambulance cot. Masters saw Berg was receiving excellent care and followed them aft.

▪ ▪ ▪ ▪ ▪

Serendipity's crew assembled in a group on the dock. Doris saw they looked lost. Prim and authoritative in her pantsuit, she perceived there was confusion over authority. She stepped forward and pointed to the crew. "Gentlemen, stay where you are for a few minutes while I sort this out."

She strode to the EMS teams carrying Joe, his IV attached, and Bill. Joe was unconscious, but Bill had his eyes open, lying listless. Doris pointed to the door. "Harborview. Arrangements are in place to receive them." She took Phillip aside by the arm—he would no longer be referred to as Bones. "What happened?"

"Chief stabbed Joe in the chest. It seems to have been an accident. He claims he meant to threaten, but not stab him."

"Will Joe be okay?"

"Yes, the knife missed everything vital. He'll make a full recovery. Security should arrest Chief."

"No. I'm taking charge now. If no one died, Joe would want everything suppressed. How is Bill, and what happened to Mr. Prichard?"

"Bill had his skull grazed by a bullet and needs attention, but he'll eventually be okay. Masters took a bullet in his arm. It didn't break the bone or hit an artery. He'll need treatment, and his arm will be useless for a few weeks, but he'll be okay too. Sorry, Doris, I gotta go."

She nodded, directed a staff member to place a step stool for her to stand on, stood on it, and turned to address the entire assemblage. "May I have your attention, please?" Everyone turned. "*Serendipity* crew to the locker room. Security will accompany you. You may shave and shower if you wish, and there is new underwear. Please change into your original clothes. Your van crew will return you to your pickup point shortly."

The men filed down the hall.

She nodded to the Security Supervisor. "Collect the weapons and ammo, including the entire weapons locker. Verify none are missing. Then meet me in my office." She turned to the dock crew. "Secure the boat to the wall. Attach shore power and ensure the bilge pumps are operational. Then leave the hangar."

The Security Supervisor pointed to four of his men, then the boat. He followed Doris out the door to her hangar office.

Doris's office had an expensive, dignified air. A lighted John Stobart oil painting hung on a light gray wall over her mahogany credenza. The dark gray carpeted wainscot matched the floor above the mahogany wall base. An incandescent brass lamp cast a warm light on her wooden desk. A monitor on a swing-arm, keyboard, mouse, telephone, and one manila folder were the only things on its polished surface. She took her chair behind it and addressed the Security Supervisor without offering a seat.

"Here's how this will work. You'll have two of your men accompany Masters and Chief separately to my office, where I will perform an exit interview. I'll start with Masters. I want him transported to Swedish Medical ASAP."

. . . . .

The bright locker room still smelled of Lysol. The eight crewmen filed in and sat on the bench opposite their lockers. Everything felt the same. Jason checked the right toe of his shoe for his phone—gone.

"My cell's gone," Jason shouted to no one in particular.

"Yeah, mine too," floated in the air.

The Security Supervisor addressed Masters in front of two security officers. "Mister Masters? We will transport you to the Swedish Medical Center. Please follow me for a brief exit interview, first."

Masters got up, led by the Security Supervisor, followed by two security guards, toward Doris's office, his arm in a sling.

"Mister Masters, come in. Sit down, please." She pointed to a seat. The head of security and one guard followed in, closed the door, and stood in front of it. The other security guard stood outside the door.

"So, Mister Peter Prichard," she turned her face from his dossier, "I'm sorry for your wound. Are you in much pain?"

"Yeah, it hurts like the devil."

"I have an offer for you. We will have you treated at Swedish Medical at our expense. I will deposit an additional five hundred thousand dollars into a Swiss bank account with your name on it. You will say nothing to anyone EVER about this incident or trip. Your wound is not from a gunshot. It's from an accident, okay? Tell any story you want, but note you don't know where we are, who we are, and you have no evidence to reinforce any story you might tell. Remember, you signed a non-disclosure agreement. We are sorry for your wound. Is five hundred large enough money to buy your eternal silence? If so, sign here." She produced a paper for his signature.

Peter looked at her, the sheet, the two guards, then grinned. "Yeah, that ought to do it." After a cursory scan, he signed the document.

Doris pointed to the two security guards. "Please accompany Mister Prichard to the locker room. See him clothed and transported to Swedish ASAP. Give his phone back at the hospital. Do not speak to him." Peter left with the two officers.

Doris then addressed the Security Supervisor. "Bring me, Chief."

Chief came in, followed by two other security officers. He sat and stared at his thumbs.

"Now, Mister Mike Hamilton, I'm told you stabbed the Captain?"

Mike's speech had a hint of a slur. His face was flush, and his eyes watery. "It was an accident. This whole goddamn scene ain't what I figured. If he'd just told me we were on our way back.... All he had to do was tell me."

Doris stared at him.

"What's gonna happen now?" He raised his face.

"Well, I want to avoid any further complications. The doctor told me Joe will recover. That's a lucky break. It means we can make the entire incident disappear, provided you tell no one."

Mike's eyes widened with hope. "I sure ain't gonna say nothin'."

"You understand, if you make any trouble over this, Captain Joe will be," she leaned forward, focused into Mike's eyes, and tapped the desk with her fingernail, "... very unhappy."

Mike understood the threat. "You won't hear nothin' from me. I just want out o' this.... Do I still get my money?"

"Yes. Your original sum plus the 100k bonus Captain Joe promised is already in your account. Once you change clothes, these gentlemen," she pointed to the security men, "will accompany you to SeaTac, return your phone, and give you a first-class ticket home. I suggest you keep your mouth shut. Do you understand?"

"Ah, yeah, I get it."

"No, I mean, do you REALLY understand?" She frowned directly into his eyes.

Mike straightened. "Yes, mam, I understand."

"You're dismissed."

Outside the door, the Security boss peeked in after Mike left.

Doris spoke and tapped keys on her computer, "See that son-of-a-bitch gets on his plane. I will address the remaining crew in the locker room. Let me know when they're ready to go."

▪ ▪ ▪ ▪ ▪

Peter and Mike changed clothes without a word, guarded by a security detail.

Peter nodded to the crew and smiled. "So long, boys." He exited through the door.

Mike avoided eye contact, dressed, and filed out without a word.

The rest of the men stayed on the bench, absorbing the departure of Masters, Chief, and Security. Once they left, it grew quiet, and everyone relaxed.

Jason slapped his knees, stood up, and started undressing. "I don't know about you guys, but a shave and a hot shower sound wonderful right now."

They moved to the sinks and started the shaving process. Jason and Sails shaved next to each other. "Mister Sails, if you ever get to Sitka, I won't be hard to find."

"Mister Decker, if you ever go to England, I will be difficult to find." He turned and grinned at Jason, who returned the smile.

Gunny laughed. "Good luck finding me. If anyone ever bothers to write my obituary, I hope it's not the one on this trip."

Jason, Sails, and Handy laughed.

Cookie and Steward did not react.

"Mister Cook," Jason spoke with a nod to both Cookie and Steward, "Thank you both for the fabulous meals served under difficult circumstances. May your next gig be less adventurous."

After showering, the crew dried with warmed towels, put on new underwear, and dressed. No one exchanged their actual names.

Jason perched on the bench and considered his situation. *Survived, clean, exhausted—and have a chunk of money. How am I gonna explain this to Al?*

Doris came in. "Gentlemen, true to his word, Captain Joe had me deposit the additional 100k in your accounts. I have here," she held envelopes, "first-class plane tickets home. You will ride to SeaTac, or wherever we picked you up, in the same van that brought you. Now, I want to make several relevant facts abundantly clear. We will deny this ever happened. You may think you know where you are, but I assure you, you don't. You have no evidence to support any stories you might tell. And let me remind you of your signed nondisclosure agreement. The money you received came from offshore accounts and is untraceable to us. You may keep the gear issued to you—watches, knives, binoculars, and sunglasses—if you brought them off the boat with you. If you left them on the ship, they're lost."

"Damn," Jason exclaimed. "I loved those Steiners." He still had his watch and knife.

"Well, you now have enough money to buy one. Gentlemen, if you tell anyone about this brief adventure, no one will believe you. You'll fall into the category of people who claim abduction by aliens. So, give your story careful consideration. Here are your tickets." She passed them out. "Your van crew will return your phones and whatever you brought off the boat with you at the airport. You may all go."

▪ ▪ ▪ ▪ ▪

The van ride to SeaTac felt different from the drive coming. It seemed longer in the windowless compartment, and the noises gave no clue to where he was. The door opened at the terminal. He grabbed his bag and got out. Angie handed him his phone, watch, and knife, slammed the door, and got in. They drove away without a word.

Jason put his knife in his bag, checked it through to Sitka, passed through security, and stopped at the Alaska Lounge for a quick bite and drink. Flight sixty-seven did not board until 3:15. With a first-class seat, he could board last. That gave him a chance to sit at the bar and make a phone call.

▪ ▪ ▪ ▪ ▪

Al and Loren sat in Jason's corner at the Backdoor Café. Al's phone rang. The caller ID read: Jason.

"Jesus, Jason, you okay?"

"Yeah, I'm fine. I'm on flight sixty-seven this evening. Can you pick me up?"

"Sure. I figured you would not return for a least a week. What happened?"

"It's a hell of a story you will not believe. I'm exhausted. The last seventeen hours defy description. I wish I could sleep, but I'm so hyped, I don't think I can."

"Just a second. There's someone here who wants to talk to you." He passed his phone to Loren.

Loren grimaced, took it, and put it to her ear. "Hi, Jason."

"Loren? Jesus, it's good to hear your voice. I thought you were in Anchorage with some high-flyin' asshole."

"Yeah, well, he turned out to be a low-flyin' asshole. I returned the day before yesterday. A lot's happened. I'm staying on Al's boat with Eluk."

"Loren, I'm sorry I wasn't more attentive. I have the money I owe you, and I may be able to finance a boat and permit. Then I could fish from Sitka."

"Well, we need to talk. The last three days have been tough."

"Yeah, they sure have. But I need a break. You won't believe what I've been through—I mean, you REALLY won't believe it. I need to sleep for a while. Can we meet tomorrow after I get up?"

"That would be great."

"Okay, see you then."

"All right." She passed the phone to Al, her face blushing.

▪ ▪ ▪ ▪ ▪

Jason clicked off, took a drink, and headed for the plane.

▪ ▪ ▪ ▪ ▪

Joe awoke on a comfortable bed in a softly lit private room he kept reserved at Harborview Medical Center. The pain in his chest had subsided. Phillip was replacing the dressing over his wound. Joe gazed at the ceiling. "Where am I?"

"You're at Harborview. You've sustained a serious knife wound to your chest, but it missed your heart and anything vital. You're fortunate. You lost some blood, but you'll be okay."

"What happened?"

"You turned command over to Mister Decker—ah, Jason. The boys made it to the transition point at the proper time, and we all got home okay. Bill is in the room next door." He pointed. "He'll be okay."

"Who's in charge?"

"Doris took control of everything. The boat's a wreck and tied to the dock. She removed Masters to Swedish Medical. The boat crew disbursed. The G-WAD team was ecstatic. They're probably still drunk, except for Jack. I heard he scored a few peyote buttons. He'll probably resolve the differences between relativity and quantum mechanics, eat two bags of cookies, then forget the solution when he comes down."

Joe grimaced at the ceiling. *Holy shit. Almost got everyone killed—or lost in the eighteenth century. What was I thinking? Okay, THAT was too much thrill.... guess there ARE boundaries to excitement. Mildred was right. If I don't show restraint, it'll kill me.* "Doc, you have my cell-phone?"

"Yes, it's right here."

"Look up Mildred Rosen for me in my Contacts and give me the phone..."

"I don't think you should do anything right now except rest."

"Yeah, well, do it anyway."

"You have reached the office of Mildred Rosen. If you have an emergency, call 911. Otherwise, leave a—"

"Hello, Joe? I was on my way out when I saw your name on caller ID."

Joe's breathing was slow, and his voice low. "Hello, Mildred. I'm lying in a bed at Harborview with a knife wound in my chest. It appears there are limits to thrill-seeking, if exceeded, are counterproductive."

Mildred's eyes twinkled. "Oh, an 'Ah-ha' moment. Interesting. Are you calling to make an appointment?"

32
SHEET'KÁ

February 27 - Sitka
Al was chatting with another fisherman when Jason descended the ramp in Sitka. Al ended his conversation and edged toward Jason at baggage claim, trying to appear casual.

"Jesus, Jason, you look awful."

"Yeah, I suppose I do. Did anyone notice I wasn't here?"

"Sure, but I don't suppose your lawyer knows. He called, but we covered for you." He leaned in and muttered. "You didn't tell me he advised you not to leave town. A lot's happened. I didn't expect you in Sitka for at least two more days. Your trip get cut short?"

"No. The five days advertised was a lie. It was always a three-day trip."

"Where did you go?"

"Ah,... well, we traveled from one spot to another. It's a complicated story—I'll tell you later. What happened while I was gone?"

Al glanced around at the other people waiting to get their bags and spoke under his breath. "Let's wait till we're in the truck."

They tramped out of the terminal into a dark, cold parking lot. Jason climbed into Al's truck and slammed the door. "So, tell me."

Al started his rig and headed for Eliason. "Loren got beat up by Bud, her Anchorage dipshit, right after you spoke to her on the phone three days ago. She returned to Sitka the next day. I'm lettin' her stay on the boat. I got a call from Frank Atherton, your lawyer, trying to reach you. I told him I didn't know where you were. He said he'd try Loren."

"Shit."

"Loren returned to Sitka on the 25th. Yashee picked up her and Eluk. I was sitting with them at the P-Bar when he called. He wanted a copy of your bust sketch. Yashee, Loren, and I went out to your place to get the drawing. I had to break into your desk to find it. I faxed it to your lawyer, saying I had reached you by radio, and you'd told me to send it."

"Jesus, thanks, Al. Did Frank buy it?"

"I imagine so. I've heard nothing. Yesterday, Bud landed in Sitka, looking for her. He asked Rita at the P-Bar where Loren was. Rita played dumb and alerted Loren, who called me."

"Crap. Now I have Rita involved." He cupped his hands to his mouth and blew warm air into his fingers.

"Yeah, you do. I called Sly on the *Styrke* and asked him to keep an eye out for her until I got there. She had your truck, so I figure the guy drove around until he spotted it at Eliason. He found the boat and threatened her." Al leaned toward Jason. "Bad move. Loren screamed. Sly, Eric, and Elias intervened. 'Bout then I showed up with Eluk. Dude drew a gun."

"A pistol? Shit. What happened?"

"Eric ripped it out of his hand and flung it over the side. Then Bud grabbed his phone. Eric snatched it and popped it in the water too. Bud took a swing at Sly and nailed him on his chin." Al leaned in again toward Jason. "'Nother bad choice. Almost pissed Sly off. Sly hit him back—may have busted somethin'. Anyway, we encouraged the guy to take the next flight out. He did."

"Holy shit! Is Loren okay?"

"She has a bruised face where he hit her three days ago, but she'll be all right. Hey, that gal loves you, man. I hope you don't screw it up." Al leaned toward Jason to stress the point.

"Yeah...."

"So, what happened in Seattle?"

"It was a weird scene. I made money, but it wasn't worth it. I can't tell you where we went. There was some serious drama between the Captain and crew. If I meet none of them again, it'll be too soon. I'll tell you what, Al, somehow, 'exigent circumstances and adventurous aspects' just doesn't quite get it. My enzyme feedback loop—or whatever—maxed out. I'm lucky to be here. Did you get your money?"

"Yeah, right on time."

"Look, Al, I've been so keyed up, I couldn't sleep on the plane. I haven't slept in something like twenty hours. Let me have some downtime, and I'll talk to you tomorrow, okay?"

They stopped at Jason's truck. "Yeah, okay. Call me when you get up, and I'll meet you at the P-Bar."

▪ ▪ ▪ ▪ ▪

February 28

Jason parked across from the P-Bar. The rain had turned the snow to slush, and everyone wore their XtraTuf boots. The percussion of passing vehicles splashing slop to the side on Katlian Street drummed away. Jason stomped the slush off his feet and entered.

The lunch crowd chowed down at the bar. Al and Loren sat across from each other in the window booth with the duct-taped vinyl seat.

Jason gasped and reddened at seeing her. A purple bruise covered her left cheek and had turned her eye black. "Jesus, Loren, what'd that asshole do to you?" He gritted his teeth and clenched a fist.

Loren patted the bruise with her hand. "Yeah, he did a number on me." Tears welled in her eyes. "Turns out, he was all foam and no beer." She dabbed a tear with a napkin and looked at Jason.

He slid into the seat next to her. Her pale face contrasted with her dark ponytail and open pea coat. *Love her look and spirit.* He could not help noticing the curves of her breasts inside the tight sweater. "Well, I'm thrilled to see you. I was afraid you'd gone for good."

She managed a warm smile and held his eye until she turned away, trying not to react to his closeness. *Does he feel the electricity too?*

Rita brought the usual lunches and coffee. She placed the food before them and glared at Jason. "This story better be good."

His smile was meek.

She turned and marched away.

He raised his burger and turned to Loren. "What're your plans now?"

"I don't know." She looked vacantly out the window. "Maybe go back to school. I really don't know."

"Okay," Al intervened, "tell us what happened in Seattle. What's with this Ullage Enterprises?"

Jason leaned over and kissed Loren on the cheek opposite the bruise. "Baby, it's great to be near you."

Al persisted, "Yeah, yeah, you can make up later. I want to know what happened."

Jason dreaded this conversation. He faced Al and straightened. "I'm sorry, but I can't reveal anything for several reasons. For one, I'm not comfortable with my role in what transpired." He squirmed in his seat. "Think of a soldier who's seen serious combat and doesn't want to discuss it because it's painful. And, as you know, Al, signing a non-disclosure agreement was part of the deal. What happened didn't break any laws I know of, but it was beyond description."

"Try." Al leaned back and folded his arms. "I led you into this thing, and I feel responsible. We," he pointed to Loren, "went way out on a limb to cover for you with your lawyer. You owe us an explanation."

"Yeah, thanks much for your help with my lawyer." He stared at his coffee. "I'm afraid if I told you where we went and what we did, you'd think I was crazy—on the order of having being abducted by aliens." He turned to one, then the other. "I can say the boat was a fabulous schooner, over a hundred feet long. The Captain was a borderline crazy-genius. Besides the Captain, we had two officers and a crew of six, paired for two four-hour watches a day. We also had a chef, a steward and ate like millionaires. But I must take what we did to my grave." *Can't ever tell them and keep creditability.*

Loren looked skeptical. "Which dock did you leave from?"

He paused, considering how to answer. "I am sorry, but I can't tell you. Somewhere in the Seattle area, but other than that, I just can't tell you...."

Al exchanged a suspicious glance with Loren. "Bullshit." He slid out of his seat, then noticed Jason's wrist. "New watch, huh? A souvenir?"

Jason had forgotten the watch. "Yeah, sort of." He held his wrist out for inspection. "Everyone on the crew got one. It's accurate within five seconds a year and water-resistant to ten atmospheres."

Al examined the blackface, stainless-steel case, and bracelet, then raised his head. "I'll be interested to hear the full story once you get your head out of your ass. In the meantime, after you come up for air, you can help me replace my reduction gear. I made just enough money to pay for a rebuild." He laid a ten on the table and left.

Jason's eyes widened, then gazed out the window. *Shit... have to make this okay with Al somehow.*

He turned to Loren. "Look, I'm sorry. I've been meditating a lot the past few days on your 'excitement and adventure' comment. I recognize I may have an unhealthy tendency toward thrill-seeking, but I'd like to change. I know I haven't paid enough attention to you. If you give me a chance, I'll try to make it up to you."

Loren remained silent and considered him. Her eyes searched his. She found it difficult to restrain a tear and hesitated.

Her expression—*She's considering if I'm worth it or to tell me to fuck off.*

She turned toward him. "What's with you? Why should I believe it will be any different if I go back to you? You're not reliable. This crazy-ass thing you have for excitement and adventure will cause your downfall. A weird deal will come along, and you'll be off again—assuming you're not in jail. You make promises but don't keep them."

Jason appeared dispirited, hesitating.

The smile lines by her eyes crinkled. "Jason, I need more than 'I'm sorry.'"

"Yeah. I understand." He fidgeted. "Please believe my trip to Seattle gave me a unique perspective on 'excitement and adventure.' I've had enough this week to last me a lifetime. From now on, living in Alaska will satisfy those needs.

"And hold on there... you're claiming running off to Anchorage with a guy you barely knew didn't have an element of adventure? Aww c'mon. You like adventure too. It's what brought you to Alaska."

Loren stared him down. "So, okay, but I can't watch the paint dry while you go crabbing for months at a time. We can't be a couple if you're not here."

"You're right. We can't be together if I'm always gone. Look, I just want to regain control of my life." He looked beyond the window. "I'm aware I pursue a certain amount of thrill in my life, but so do you."

He took a pre-filled check from his shirt pocket. "First, here's the money I owe you and a little extra. This trip was an event I prefer to forget, but it made me a good chunk of cash. I'll help you do whatever you want if you permit me. I WILL win my case. When I do, I'll be free to get a fine boat for fishing Southeast. A decent boat provides a good living. If so, I won't be crabbing anymore. Maybe we could take another shot together. You could come fishing with me."

"I don't know. Suddenly you go off on a strange four-day trip. You won't tell us where you went or what you did. Now you have a lot of money, and you're a changed person? This entire thing's a little fishy."

"In my case, *Fishy* is a name fit for a boat."

The fingers of his right hand curled over hers under the table. He gave her those puppy eyes. *Sincere? Seems genuine.*

That's all there was to it. A galvanizing zing ran up her thighs.

"Sweetheart, I need you. Is it too corny to say the steady needle of your moral compass helps keep me on course?"

"Oh, puh-lease...." She giggled. "Gimmie a break. Yeah, that's too corny." *He's sincere!*

She felt his left arm encircle her shoulders—protection from life's storm. His lips brushed her cheek. She closed her eyes, caught her breath, and devoured his scent.

He removed his arm from her shoulder and placed it under her coat, around her back, under her breast. He heard her sudden inhale, leaned over, and kissed her—long and passionate. He pressed his palm against her thigh. "Let's blow off lunch and run out to my truck."

She grasped his jaw in her hands and peered into his eyes. *Damn good deal... no better options.* She whispered, "Okay."

Jason slid out and took her hand.

■ ■ ■ ■ ■

They hurried to the truck with their arms wrapped around each other. Jason climbed in the passenger side. Loren straddled him, her arms around his neck. They kissed while he slipped his hands under her shirt, undid her bra, then lightly defined the base of her breasts with his index finger and thumb—slowly stroking toward her nipples.

She pushed herself up and unbuttoned her fly. He put his hands to his belt, undid his jeans, and shoved them out of the way. He grasped the small of her back and drove far inside her.

She gasped. The pressure against her pelvic bone.... *Nobody else.... Oh... my... God!*

▪ ▪ ▪ ▪ ▪

March 15

Joe's Mercer Island home was grand by any measure, standing out at 14,000 square feet and 11 bathrooms. It contained elaborate gardens, fountains, a movie theater, taproom, wine cellar, billiard parlor, putting green, tennis court, squash court, and a seven-room owner's suite. It proved an effective venue for managing business contacts and attracting women.

He was proud of his dock. The Army Corps of Engineers would not grant a permit to cover any more of Lake Washington, but he wanted his yacht at a berth in front during summer. So, he bought two houses with nice docks, removed them from the lake, used their lake surface permits for his new wharf, then sold the homes.

He focused beyond his pool and dock toward Seattle. The drizzle and gray lake made a monochromatic scene. His wound was healing, but 24/7 medical care nagged. The medical staff, having felt his wrath, stayed in the next room. While resting in his recliner, he instructed Doris, made phone calls, and tapped computer keys.

"Oh, and Doris," Joe spoke and punched keys on his phone for Dock Street Brokers, "keep track of Gunny and send another twenty-five thousand to his finder. He was perfect for the job. I may want him again. Were the bonuses delivered to the hangar crews?"

"Yes. The staff was quite pleased and on vacation through the end of the month. In April, they'll start recalibration for their next assignment."

"Um." Joe glanced at the medical people to be sure they could not overhear. "Just between you and me, this trip was the adventure of a lifetime, but doing something similar again gives me pause. We were lucky to get back, but damn, it was fun!"

Doris saw his eyes glow and the hint of a smile.

"Thrill versus risk, thrill versus risk. I may have reached my upper thrill limit. Then again, maybe not. How's my favorite V.P. doing?"

"Bill's fine. He's at work today."

"Good."

Joe listened to two rings. "Dock Street Brokers. May I help you?"

"Hi, Jamie. My name's Joe Plimsoll. I want to help a friend. You got a minute to talk to me concerning the purchase of a boat and permits?"

"Sure."

"My friend is a skilled Alaska fisherman and wants a boat of his own, but he has a bust hanging over him and can't finance anything. If price were no object, how much would it cost for a setup to provide a good living in Sitka? I imagine his significant other will join him as crew."

"Well, for a good living, he'd need a vessel geared to work in several fisheries. In Sitka, the permits would be power troll, shrimp, and Dungeness crab for area 2C. He'd also want a portion of the halibut and black cod quota. In round numbers, a decent boat runs around 300 thousand. A power troll permit is worth 30, shrimp, another 25. Crab depends on how many pots you run. A 225-pot permit is worth 50, and a 300-pot permit might be worth 100. For halibut and black cod, he'd have to buy a slice of the quota. For the boat I have in mind, you'd want halibut quota worth 60 thousand and black cod, oh, about 30."

"If I wanted to pay the total cost, how would I make it happen?"

"Huh. Lucky guy. Well, you provide earnest money equal to 10% of the cost. Once your friend selects his boat, permits, and quotas, we will bill you for the rest."

"Okay. That adds to 545 thousand. Call it 550 and get the paperwork ready. I will send over a certified check for fifty-five thousand. The recipient is Jason Oliver of Sitka. Did you get that? Write his name down."

"Sure, Mister Plimsoll. I got it, Jason Oliver, from Sitka."

"I'm sure you'll get a call from Mister Oliver. When he does, tell him a benefactor wants to do him a favor. He'll know who it's from, but don't use my name. Say you don't know. The deal is up to him. You'll have contact information for my staff if any issues arise. If he doesn't call by June 30, return the money. Okay?"

"Yeah, that will work."

Joe handed his phone to Doris. "Have my attorney contract through another attorney of their choice. Transfer the money from the Grand Cayman account to the Ullage shell. He'll need to gear up, storage, and startup capital. Figure 100k for gear, 350 for a local warehouse, and 100 for the startup, that's another 550. Also, his legal fees and gift taxes… another 300k. Set aside a million and a half for this project. Find a warehouse in Sitka to store his gear and secure it with earnest money and a purchase option. Then get me his attorney's phone number."

Doris raised her head from her notes. "It appears Mister Oliver made quite an impression."

"Hmm." Joe looked off over the lake. "Yes. I like him. He's a rare individual, well-schooled historically, secular, and energetic. We have similar tendencies. He's more simpatico than anyone I've met in a long time. I want him involved in my plans."

33
DECISIONS

March 18

"Hello. I'm Jamie at Dock Street Brokers. May I help you?"

"Hi, Jamie. My name is Jason Oliver. I'm calling to inquire what options might be available for me to finance the purchase of a boat and power troll permit for area 2C."

"Jason Oliver of Sitka?"

"Yeah, that's right. You know me?"

"Yeah, sort of. I was hoping you'd call. Financing for you is simple: 100% down and no payments. A guy—I'm s'posed to tell you I don't know who—has made the financial arrangements. He'll pay the entire expense for you to purchase a good boat, power troll, shrimp, and Dungeness permits and a decent chunk of halibut and black cod quota."

"... Oh, I see...." Jason paused, raised his eyebrows, and put his fingers to his chin. *Don't want to be beholden to Joe.* "Damn. I don't want to owe this guy. Can't I get financing on my own? I've got a hundred grand."

"Your patron told me you have a bust hanging over you. If that's so, no one will loan you money until it's resolved. You can't fish from jail."

"No, I suppose not. If the charges weren't hanging over me, could I finance with a 100k?"

"It's a definite maybe. You might get a seller to carry the note."

"I see." *Depends on when. Resolved soon—in my favor—okay. If not... shit.*

"I can't see how you can pass on this. I know a lot o' guys who'd kill for such a deal."

"Yeah, well, they don't know Captain Joe. What are the terms of his proposal?"

"They're simple. He has provided earnest money. If you want to take the deal, go to our website and check our boat listings."

"How much can I spend?"

"I told him a good boat was about three-hundred thousand, plus another two-hundred-fifty for permits and quota. Course, a few deals include permits with the boat. You have a credit line of 550."

"Hmm. Wow. Okay. I'll look at boats, consider the situation, and call you."

▪ ▪ ▪ ▪ ▪

2nd Thursday in April - Juneau

Jason stepped from the hall into the courtroom. The high ceiling, beautiful wood, and acoustics were impressive. The Great Seal of the State of Alaska overwhelmed the wall behind the raised Court bench, flanked by the American and Alaskan flags.

Frank, Jason's attorney, noticed Jason come in and turned from talking to a colleague toward Jason. They met at the rail and shook hands. "Good morning, Jason. You didn't tell me you had a guardian angel."

"What do you mean?"

"Two hours ago, a Seattle attorney paid your legal fees."

Jason's eyes widened. *Oh, shit.*

"All rise." The black-robed justices filed in, and Frank returned to his table. Someone banged a gavel. Bam, bam, bam. "The honorable justices of the Supreme Court of the State of Alaska."

The chief justice spoke, taking his chair. "Please be seated. The Alaska Supreme Court is now in session." Thump.

The Chief Justice opened his pen and read the paper before him.

"Good morning. This is the time set aside for oral arguments in the case of the State of Alaska versus Jason Oliver." He looked at the District Attorney. "If you are both ready, Mister Blanchard, you may begin."

The D.A. stood at the podium and faced the court. "Chief Justice, if it pleases the Court, the question for review concerns when a police officer may enter a dwelling to seize evidence without a warrant."

■ ■ ■ ■ ■

Frank strode over to Jason, sitting in the corridor outside the courtroom. "That went okay. Our chances are excellent."

"When will we have a decision?"

"Oh, it'll be several months at least."

"Shit. I don't know why I believed there'd be a decision today. Okay. Thanks, Frank. You did a hell of a job. What's with the legal fees?"

"You're no longer a pro-bono case." He leaned forward with a conspiratorial grin. "Your benefactor has paid all your fees to date and any additional time required. My office loves it. I'm a hero. Thank you very much."

"I know nothing about it. Are there any strings attached?"

"No. We received our total fee plus a retainer. You're all set. Now, if we get a positive decision, you'll skate. I advise you to stay out of harm's way."

"Yeah." *Harm's way seems to follow me.* "Well, let me know of any developments." They shook hands, and Frank left.

Jason remained on the bench, leaning forward, his elbows on his thighs and his phone in his hands. He called Al.

"How'd it go?"

"It seemed okay. The State argued the police don't need a search warrant if evidence of a crime is in plain view in someone's home. When I stepped to the porch to take the fall, they had to cross the threshold without a warrant. They claim the pot was in plain view from the porch—which is a lie. Anyway, they figure Alaska is a special case. Warrants in the bush where there's no magistrate take too long.

"Frank reiterated many of the facts brought out in Superior Court. The police lacked probable cause for a search warrant. The plain view doctrine, defined by the U.S. Supreme Court, requires a prior legal intrusion. There are four exceptions for the police to enter someone's home without a warrant. Either intrusion is incident to a lawful arrest, an officer is in hot pursuit, destruction of evidence is imminent, or the police receive consent for the search. None of these exceptions apply. I will skate. That's the good news."

"Well, that is good news, Jason. What's the bad news?"

"There was no decision today. An eventual decision is months off. I can't string Loren along if I don't make something happen."

"Ooh, bummer. Yeah, her patience is wearing thin. What are you going to do?"

"I don't know. I'll overnight in Juneau and return to Sitka tomorrow."

"Okay. Tomorrow, then." Al hung up.

Jason put on his down vest, Filson jacket, and hat, then headed for the Capital Café in the Baranof Hotel.

. . . . .

Seated with a cup of coffee, he considered his situation. *Not going to keep Loren on tap if she doesn't see a future. If I take the deal with Dock Street, Joe will figure I owe him. Hell, already owe him. Damn. In for a penny, in for a pound.* He pulled out his phone, put on his headset, and made the call.

"Dock Street Brokers. May I help you?"

"Hi. May I speak to Jamie, please?"

"Just a moment."

"Jamie. May I help you?"

"Hi, Jamie. Jason Oliver here. I will take the deal."

END

Appendix A
Southeast Alaska and Sitka

Visions of Alaska rarely center on its southeast panhandle. Most people think of Alaska as either arctic cold or midnight sun. I know Southeast Alaska as the banana belt. Its climate is mild compared to the rest of Alaska. And it rains—a lot. The Alaska Current brings moisture that becomes precipitation when it hits land. Ketchikan averages over twelve feet of rain per year.

The islands of southeast Alaska are the tops of submerged coastal mountains that rise steeply from the floor of the Pacific Ocean. They have irregular, steep coasts and dense evergreen forests. No roads connect the largest towns, Juneau, Ketchikan, and Sitka to each other or the outside world. The entire population of Southeast Alaska is about 75,000. It has a landmass of about 35,000 square miles—about the size of Indiana.

The Tlingit people inhabited Sitka over 10,000 years go. Russia "settled" it in 1799. With the purchase of Alaska in 1867, it joined the United States. During the first half of the nineteenth century, Sitka was the most important port on the West Coast. It sits on the western coast of Baranof Island. Smaller offshore islands protect it from stormy Pacific Ocean waves. It receives about 130 inches of rain and 33 inches of snow per year. On average, the temperature rises above 70 degrees Fahrenheit 5 days and does not get above 32 degrees 10 days a year.

The City and Borough of Sitka contain some 2,800 square miles—approximately twice the size of Rhode Island. The road extends only 14 miles. Its population of around 9,000 is about 25% Native American. The most significant economic sector is fishing and seafood processing.

Appendix B
Beaufort Wind Scale

Force	Wind Speed Mph.	Kts.	Description	Wave Height M	Ft.	Sea looks like
0	<1	<1	Calm	0	0	Flat. Mirror.
1	1 - 3	1 - 3	Light Air	0 - 0.2	0 - 1	Ripples with the appearance of scales form without foam crests.
2	4 - 7	4 - 6	Light Breeze	.2-.5	1 - 2	Small short wavelets; crests have a glassy appearance but do not break.
3	8 - 12	7 - 10	Gentle Breeze	.5 - 1	2 - 3.5	Large wavelets; crests start to break; glassy foam; scattered white horses.
4	13 - 18	11 - 16	Moderate Breeze	1 - 2	3.5 - 6	Small waves becoming longer; fairly frequent white horses.
5	19 - 24	17 - 21	Fresh Breeze	2 - 3	6 - 9	Moderate waves with pronounced long form; many white horses; some spray.
6	25 - 31	22 - 27	Strong Breeze	3 - 4	9 - 13	Large waves form; extensive white foam crests; more spray.
7	32 - 38	28 - 33	High Wind, Near Gale	4 - 5.5	13 - 19	Sea heaps; breaking waves white foam blown in streaks; spindrift begins.
8	39 - 46	34 - 40	Gale, Fresh Gale	5.5 - 7.5	18 - 25	Moderately high waves of greater length; crest edges break into spindrift; foam blown in well-marked streaks.
9	47 - 54	41 - 47	Strong/Severe Gale	7 - 10	23 - 32	High waves; dense streaks of foam; sea begins to roll; spray affects visibility.
10	55 - 63	48 - 55	Storm, Whole Gale	9 - 12.5	29 - 41	Extremely high waves with long overhanging crests; great patches of foam are blown in dense white streaks; the whole surface of the sea takes on a white appearance; rolling of the sea becomes heavy; visibility affected.

BOARDING PASS

THOMAS/TIFFANY

DOE - -

NRSA

GEG3UQ

FLIGHT DL3650 | DATE 15AUG | CLASS Y | ORIGIN SPOKANE | DEPARTS 709P

OPERATED BY SKYWEST DBA DELTA CNX | MAIN | DESTINATION SEATTLE | BRD TIME 629P

SEAT 1D

FIRST

DEPARTURE GATE B8 **SUBJECT TO CHANGE**

BOARDING PASS

THOMAS/TIFFANY

DOE - -

FLIGHT DL3650 | DATE 15AUG

SEAT 1D

FIRST

ORIGIN SPOKANE

DESTINATION SEATTLE

OPERATED BY SKYWEST DBA DELTA CNX

A DELTA CONNECTION CARRIER